Been There, Married That

Also by Gigi Levangie

Seven Deadlies

The After Wife

Queen Takes King

The Starter Wife

Maneater

Rescue Me

Been There, Married That

Gigi Levangie

St. Martin's Press New York

First published in the United States by St. Martin's Press,
an imprint of St. Martin's Publishing Group

BEEN THERE, MARRIED THAT. Copyright © 2020 by Gigi Levangie.
All rights reserved. Printed in the United States of America. For information address the
St. Martin's Publishing Group, 120 Broadway, New York, NY 10271.

www.stmartins.com

The Library of Congress Cataloging-in-Publication Data is available upon request.

ISBN 978-1-250-16681-4 (hardcover)
ISBN 978-1-250-16682-1 (ebook)

Our books may be purchased in bulk for promotional, educational, or business use. Please contact your local bookseller or the Macmillan Corporate and Premium Sales Department at 1-800-221-7945, extension 5442, or by email at MacmillanSpecialMarkets@macmillan.com.

First Edition: February 2020

10 9 8 7 6 5 4 3 2 1

To Christophe, Thomas, and
Patrick—the Original LGE

Been There, Married That

1

Happy(?) Birthday!

A toast!"

Trevor, my husband, tapped his Saint Louis glass with a sterling knife, and the glittery couples chattering around the candlelit table snapped to attention. Everyone paid attention to Trevor. Even Pep, our tween with ADD, ADHD, and recent DOATM (Disgust of All Things Mom), paid attention when her father cleared his throat.

Trevor tapped his glass a few more times, sending out warning bells, then stretched to his six-foot frame. His lean shoulders curved into a question mark, a tennis player's stripped physicality from destroying Dexter with his backhand on Trip's court, Krav Maga with Uli in our home gym, and chewing each bite of food that passed his lips thirty-six times.

Even oatmeal.

He grinned, basking in the attention, then drew his long fingers through his internationally documented hair, thick and black and brushed with foil streaks. (Some smart aleck on Instagram had created @TrevorNashHair. His hair had more followers than I.)

Even if he wasn't an Oscar-winning producer, you couldn't *not* pay attention.

"To my wife, Agnes," Trevor said.

I hate the name, too. Someone's great-grandmother on some side somewhere was an Agnes. *What can you do?*

"Happy forty-eighth! You look amazing, darling!" A buttery blonde with a smoky eye and red lips screamed as she leaned across the table, ruby drops from her wineglass spilling onto the cream tablecloth, her extensions hovering dangerously near the candle's flame. Karyn was the kind of friend who's not a real friend but is more dangerous not to have as a friend. She's the best frenemy a girl could have.

Trevor had handpicked the chilly private room at Le Figaro along with the guest list, and we'd crowded into the brick anteroom, enjoying a full view of the wine cellar. I had requested a small, manageable party. We'd recently celebrated a record exec's wife's fiftieth (before they broke up), and Flo Rida performed live on a damp Bel Air lawn for tons of money. We'd shimmied to Flo Rida's three dance songs in a hell circle of rich people biting their lower lips and awkward twerking.

My ears rang for days afterward.

"I want to toast my wife's incredible . . ." He glanced down at me and smiled. "Work ethic!" Cue a symphony of sterling silver on Saint Louis crystal. I blushed, but not because of my hardy stock. Trevor has saluted my work ethic in every speech since our wedding, as though he's surprised that I, a Hollywood wife, still have a job. I blushed because my fertility is on its last heaving throes, my eggs scrambled and crapping out, waving the white maxi pad. All that's left for me is flushing and sweat. Soon, I will be all dried out, a human tumbleweed, rolling along Sunset Boulevard to guzzle martinis at the Polo Lounge.

I sneaked a napkin between my legs. Sixty-six degrees in the room and my dress felt like I peed myself. What's so hot about hot flashes? Who knew a person could sweat buckets sitting still as a rock, and in so many nooks and crannies? Forehead, ears, neck, cleavage, groin, back of the knees! Who has sweat glands on the backs of their knees? (Me, that's who.)

I'd nabbed an appointment to see Izzy. Of course I had. Everyone in town called him by his first name. *Izzy.* Allegedly, he was a medical doctor. You had to wait six months to see him—and by that time, you'd inject rattlesnake venom, toadstools, gulp Xanax, your kid's Adderall, anything, to get relief. He was the most popular man on the Westside, barring LeBron James sightings at the Brentwood Country Mart.

I raised my glass to the unlined faces aglow with candlelight, padded bank accounts, and wine. Karyn and Michael. Karyn you've met. Ex-assistant (to Michael, during his first marriage), current stylist. Hails from Ogden, Utah, with an acquired British-ish accent. Pleasant and bland Michael boasts verifiable Hollywood lineage guaranteeing him a lifetime parking spot at Paramount; I don't think he's ever had a bad day. Juliette and Jordan. Three kids, two from surrogates. Expecting another. From another surrogate. Jordan's an impish, childlike comedy director who watches too much anime porn on his iPhone; lovely Juliette has a sandwich named after her at Malibu Promises. Henry and Elizabeth. Henry, a jock "super agent," upped his meds because he didn't get the big Sony job and his hard-ons have disappeared. Poof. Sporty Liz, quadracial daughter of a Jamaican-Scottish record company czar and Japanese-German model, has a Ph.D. she doesn't use and is bored with Henry's whining and no-rection. We've been on several vacations with these couples. Hualālai, Las Ventanas, Saint Barts. Oscar Weekend in Beverly Hills.

I felt lucky to be in my marriage, with our familiar problems. Problem. *How to handle Trevor.* I hear the song:

♪ *How Do You Solve a Problem Like Tre-e-vor?* ♪

For a brief, shining moment, no one was on his phone.

"Cheers," I said. *Thank you, muted candlelight. And wine, you, too, don't ever leave me.*

Trevor clinked my glass and dry pecked my cheek. "Happy birthday, champ," he said, squeezing my shoulder as he slid a small box toward me.

"Thank you, honey," I said. "Should I wait?"

"Go ahead, open it," he said, and he trained his fluorescent smile on our friends.

"Now that's an auspicious box," Elizabeth said, her eyes crinkling.

I tugged at the blue ribbon and opened the velvet box.

"Martin Katz?" Karyn asked. "I'd recognize an MK box anywhere!"

"Is it Tiffany?" Juliette said, then turned to Jordan. "Love the name Tiffany! Write that down; that's a good name for our next herby, or himby, or theyby."

I blinked and held out the bracelet.

"Fitbit!" I said, as my upper lip perspired.

"Aggie's been begging me for one," Trevor said. "I train every day with it."

"Me, too, every day," Henry said, perking up. "I hit the gym, 4:30, rain or shine."

Begged? I'd never even asked for one. I couldn't program a banana. I willed myself to smile.

All eyes on me.

I feel you, Tupac.

"I love it!" I said, squeezing the napkin between my thighs.

2

The Last Book Party

March. Post–awards season. Awards season exists only in Holly-wood; four seasons weren't enough for us—we had to invent another. My book launch party in the bowels of the Soho House was starting in twenty minutes. Guests would start arriving in an hour and change.

LA, where you at? Not where the books are.

"Oh mah gah you look amazing we have a problem!"

I was perched like a trained parrot at a makeshift makeup sta-tion, submerged in electro-industrial ambient "music." Basically, music without lyrics or melody or music. A makeup artist with post-election PTSD, magenta hair, and a nose stud grumbled about heavy lids as she glued lashes onto my eyes. In LA, "caterpillar-eye" had reached peak saturation.

"Did you hear we have a major major problem?"

"What's the problem, Marie?" I asked, my eyes shut. I could smell her, my crow-boned, aggressively–tanned book publicist. She smelled like Lemon Pledge and Miller Lite.

I liked her, but I also wanted her to die.

I blinked.

"Don't blink!" the makeup artist shrieked; her lip stud quivered. Too late. My left eye glued shut.

"Your card's not working I tried it like twelve hundred times." Marie didn't do commas or numbers under one hundred.

"Hand me my purse," I said, groping space like a drunk and blind swimmer. "I have a Mastercard. I just don't get miles." *Miles. Dear, sweet miles. My favorite serotonin surge.*

"It's okay it's totally okay it's fine we can wait for Trevor—*what the fuck are you doing?*" Marie was gone, chasing after a waiter-slash-app-developer (copping to just being an actor is *so* 2016) balancing a full tray of glasses. *"Those aren't the bishop cut glasses get the bishop cuts!!"* she yelled.

"So you're Trevor's wifey," the makeup artist said, sucking an Altoid while working a tweezer with her tattooed hand. I've had this conversation a million times. I knew how it went. *Suck suck. Suck. Sucksuck.*

"Yep, that's me," I said, then, "joking," "Try not to blind me. I'm bad enough at dressing myself as it is."

Although, I thought, temporary blindness might be a relief. I find myself handicap-yearning lately. A fender bender that resulted in a broken-but-healable femur . . . *Hello, adjustable hospital bed! Hi, gossipy nurses who sit up with me all night! Come to Mama, simple remote!*

I'd bribe Pep with a new iPhone whatever to sleep over in my hospital room. We'd flip through her baby pictures and sip chicken broth and slurp on applesauce and red Jell-O (never green; one of our salient bonds is a mutual loathing of green Jell-O) and watch *RHOA*—which, let's face it, is the best *RHO*. Maybe she'd like me again.

"Do you have kids?" Makeup Artist bubbled.

I "awakened" from my adjustable hospital bed. I could read minds in LA. It's simple. All anyone cares about is who you're connected to and Waze.

Makeup Artist's Brain: Trevor is superrich and, like, powerful, and he's married to . . . what is she, even? So, like, ordinary. So like my mom.

"We have a daughter," I said. Pep. Peppers. *Pep* is short for *Penelope*. I'm not sure why we named her Penelope. Neither of us is Brit-adjacent. There's a law that all Penelopes are adorable and sweet-natured. Our Penelope, almost as tall as her mother, is adorable and what's the opposite of sweet-natured. Pep is sour. Happened over the last year. I keep a mental tally of the things she hates: school, questions about school, girls at school, boys at school, teachers at school, my worried face when I ask about school, my shoes, my jokes (about school).

Where'd she go, my freckled, gap-toothed sidekick?

"You wrote a book, huh?" she asked as my eyelid snapped open. I felt it rip and didn't scream, because courage. "The mixologist told me Trevor optioned it for a movie. Or podcast? Like. You must feel so cool."

Me: Mixologist? Bartender. Right.

"Hidden under a thick, pasty layer of uncool."

I didn't tell her *option* is Hollywood lingua franca for *Don't quit your day job*. My project had a 0.0001 percent chance of getting made. *Option* means a *Hollywood Reporter* or *Variety* announcement that you paid more to your publicist to run than you deposited in your bank account. At the end of the day (there's night?), an option costs you more than no option.

A better option? Not to option.

Okay, I'm done. I'm out of options. ☺

My eye watered, and a tear ran down my cheek, taking my bronzer with it. Perspiration would take care of the rest. The makeup artist frowned and sucked.

I hate bronzer, I thought. *Bronzer is a lie.*

"There she is, that's my kid, over there." Dad's Boston brogue hijacked the room, piercing the electronic music shield. I opened my eyes—left one stuck. Dad's Old Spice reached me, those slate eyes assessed me, those eyes that *see right through your bullshit, young lady.*

"What happened to your freckles?" Dad said. "You're selling books, not cocktails, kiddo."

"Hi, Daddy." I reached over for a hug. He'd left his beloved Red Sox cap at home, *his* team a bright brushstroke in an otherwise gray, broken childhood that exists only in East Coast towns and Ben Affleck movies. Dad was wearing the only suit he owned and a mock turtleneck he'd bought in the '70s, a splurge in menswear, level three at Sears in Hollywood. It's like he's going to old man's prom. Beside him is a languid, fawn-like woman with a punk haircut, her face angled, a slash of cheekbone. She was familiar, and I couldn't decide if that was a good thing. Or if that were a good thing, if you're a fan of the subjunctive. (I am. *Were* it is.)

"Kid, meet Shu Chen," he said. "You're winking."

"Oh . . . oh!" I said, my eye blinking and watering. "Nice to meet you, Shu."

Dad often had a pretty woman on his arm, but not a "Scream Queen"; anyone who'd seen a '90s horror film revered Shu's shriek. The other girls were Dad's "friends," his "pals"; he mentored them, filling the advice void my sister and I had left behind. *Walk with purpose, run with elbows tight, wear a baseball cap at night when driving, punch from your hips*—all of which boiled down to: *Stay away from men.*

Shu smiled and tilted her small, perfect head on her impossible neck. I wanted to ask her to reenact her scream from *Zombie Sorority.*

"How do you . . ." *Know my dad?*

"Starbucks, kid," my dad said. My dad got more play standing in line at Starbucks with his Red Sox cap on than Liam Hemsworth with his squiggly bits on a plate on Grindr.

"Dad, you're early. No one's going to be here for at least an hour."

"I had to find parking."

Here we go. The parking conversation.

"There *is* valet parking."

"Street parking suits me fine. I circled for twenty minutes, found a spot a few blocks down."

Parking is a charged subject, filled with dangerous familial potholes; the Murphys argue about parking the way some families argue about politics. Two of the three Murphys agree—valet parking is for lazy, rich people. I'm the third.

"Shu speaks five languages," Dad said, studying the room, his gaze like Velcro, sticking and then discarding the bar, the PR wizardess, cocktail waitresses, mixologist—

"Where's your husband?"

Dad doesn't call him *Trevor*. He refuses to say his name after a fight on Thanksgiving maybe five years ago. The topic was cranberry sauce. Whole fruit versus jelly. Trevor's not a fan of texture. (Like there's any argument. Team Whole Fruit.)

"His name is Trevor. He should be here . . ."

Now, right now, and I'm trying not to panic.

"Want to introduce him to Shu. That woman's so talented. Speaks five languages. He should cast her. I'm going to talk to someone about turning down that music."

I watched him walk away, full stride, Dad, the Paul Newman doppelgänger. Fin, my baby sister by eighteen months, had inherited not only his full, wide mouth but those eyes and his swimmer's shoulders and long legs. I'd inherited his sense of direction. And his ability to stay out of prison. Not so much Fin. I wonder how she is.

"Amazing so amazing AdrienBrodyjustgothere!" Marie yelled as I stashed my phone in my midget Judith Leiber purse. We were hemmed in against the bar like cattle by whippets in black suits huddled around Tinder or Grindr (or both), their hungry faces and neat, solemn beards illuminated by iPhones. *Agents.*

A cadre of blondes with coyote grins and blood-soled heels, guzzling cocktails and snapping endless selfies, congregated on velvet couches.

My party was as sex-segregated as a middle school dance.

"Is it stiflingly hot in here?" I said with a wink. "Or is that my life force seeping from my body?"

"Great crowd!" she yelled. "We're soooo lucky because a lot of rapists couldn't come, you know."

"Me Too?" I said, referring to #MeToo, Hollywood's favorite hashtag.

"You, too?" she said, her voice grave. "Me, too."

I gave up and soaked in the drinks menu with my "good" eye:

TRES DEADLIES
• Tres Ochos Tequila with cream of coconut and fresh lime
RAISING THE DEAD(LIES)
• Vanilla SKYY vodka with tangerine liqueur and a chili/sugar rim
DEADLIES ON ARRIVAL
• French champagne with muddled raspberry and a sprig of mint

"Have you heard from Trevor?" Marie asked, her eyes like golf balls in her orange head. I wondered how much of her hair was hers and how much was stolen off a sleeping teenage girl's head in Bangladesh.

"Haven't had a chance to check my phone." I winked.

"You haven't?"

"No." I winked.

"Are you . . . kidding?"

"No." I winked, and she scooted off after an actor I didn't know from a show I'd never heard of. I grabbed a glass of ice and held it to my neck.

Party people were already discussing where to go next—the magical "upstairs" for members or home to watch *Game of Thrones*. Meanwhile, I still couldn't pronounce our clever hors d'oeuvres' names.

"These Wagyu salmon fritter blintzen croutes are lit!" I heard a girl say.

I absentmindedly sipped a tequila concoction, hypnotized by bedazzled Hollywood wives' tales. Topics: schools, nannies, #resistance, Aspen, Cabo, poop tea. One wife was very proud of the fact that she does all her son's homework.

He's at USC.

I wished I could go home and catch a glimpse of Pep while she slept, the only time she's not annoyed with me. (I think. She could be annoyance-dreaming.) My feet felt as if I were walking on knives, but the tequila would render me numb yet wide awake when I started signing books that no one in this room will ever read.

The young bartender with James Dean brows (the boy thought I was talking about a porn star) had stage-whispered, "Tequila's a stimulant. Enjoy."

Like everyone at this party wasn't already on Adderall.

"You wore the Tory," a husky voice said above the *incessanta* electronica. "Excellent." Liz, her eyes as bright and clear as the vodka she can't drink anymore.

"Liz approved. I can go home now." My navy crew neck dress was classic and not too sexy. (Like Tory, herself, except this dress wrinkles.). It was fit for a yacht in Saint-Tropez or the produce section at Bristol Farms.

"Diet Coke?" I asked her. "Perrier?"

"Are you enjoying your launch party?" Liz asked.

"Ugh. LA is rotten with launch parties—restaurants, vodka brands, pop-up stores, jewelry . . . books," I said.

"Bread and circuses and launch parties," Liz replied.

Juliette and Karyn and a slender Asian man squeezed through the agent barricade.

"Devastated!" declared Juliette, tiny Band-Aids adorning her face like ornaments. "I found this flyer in Jordan's Range Rover!" She foraged through her Birkin, which I called her "leather vial," and thrust a crumpled hot yoga flyer at my nose. I winked. Juliette's translucent, unmarred skin was peeling in sheets under a thin film of Aquaphor. Aquaphor is the glue that held her face together. Aquaphor is the lifeblood of the Hollywood wife.

Jordan had recently rediscovered yoga and spirituality; he's temporarily Buddhist. Happily married men do not hot yoga. I took comfort in the fact that Trevor would never hot yoga. I feel temporarily smug. *What a great marriage I have!*

Karyn cooed, "Darling, please. Don't be ridiculous." Mystery Asian, whom she toted everywhere nodded and pursed his pillowy lips in support. I wondered how they felt on her neck.

"My face looks smoother, right?" Juliette said, shining her phone light on the contents of her purse. A sliver of cheek dropped in her drink as she fished a white tablet with ink marks from the well; she swallowed the pill and the drink in one swig, and down went the flake.

"Where's Trevor? Don't tell me he's not here," Karyn said with her cat smile, like she knows what you're hiding in the back of your bathroom drawer.

"Late meeting," I said. "He's blowing up my phone, sorry this, sorry that." Karyn is the Westside AT&T, the friend you lie to unless you want information spread like herpes on a Carnival cruise. Behind her, stacks of books on the signing table beckoned. *I'd better start signing before everyone runs out of filters.*

A woman appeared, wearing my Tory Burch, but in red; I immediately regretted buying the blue.

"I brought Sharpies," Petra said, and I swear I'm not upset about Trevor's house manager wearing *the exact same but better dress*. She smiled, showing off new veneers that I paid for. I felt guilty about my straight-ish teeth, and now hers are objectively better. Petra was cheery in the way only a depressed Slovak can be. When we first hired her, she'd told me her parents died hauling a wagon on an icy mountain road escaping civil unrest, then mentioned her pet mule had survived and she'd sold him to a meat factory for a ticket to America. She'd smiled, her teeth small and gray like the pill bugs I used to poke as a child to watch them roll into a ball.

"Oh, A-nus, could you be any more beautiful?"

"No, I really can't," I said. "You look stunning. The red really flatters your teeth."

We all air-kissed each other. Karyn insisted on four, as in a tiny French town she and Michael visited three years ago.

I pulled Petra aside, and it occurred to me that I liked her perfume, as well. It occurred to me that . . . I wore the same perfume. *Guerlain.*

"Have you heard from Trevor?" I asked. Petra knows Trevor better than I; I jokingly call her my wife, but she's more like Trevor's second wife in his current marriage.

"If you don't mind," Petra said, squinting. "I have a migraine." She re-squinted.

"Oh no," I said. "You should leave right away."

"Are you sure? I could stay and help."

"I can sign on my own," I assured her. When you have "staff," there's very little you wind up doing on your own. I was on course to being unable to wipe my ass in a year.

Liz sidled up next to me and cocked her head toward the ninja assistant as she squint-smiled her way through the agent-wife-B-list crowd.

"When did Petra cut her hair like yours?" Liz asked.

"Did she? I hadn't noticed," I said.

"She's you if you were blown up in a particle machine and pieced back together," Liz said. "The teeth were a mistake. You never buy your assistant teeth."

. . .

The actress we want for the movie adaptation (0.0001 percent chance) appeared at my side, pushing her pouty breasts into my triceps; she's nineteen and has cashmere skin and hair of mink; she's inebriated and smells like the morning after and is all over me.

"I fucked the director," she said. Her "whisper" emerged like a clumsy warble. "He has huge balls!" Her trunk-sized LV bag, the latest version, appears to be carrying *her*. (I know it's the latest because Juliette told me I absolutely needed one.)

She could sleep in it if she wanted and probably has.

My head was spinning from tequila drinks and the crowd and balls. Big balls. The director, a Canadian, lived on one of the Italian Riviera–named streets in my neighborhood with his pleasant wife and wriggly mass of towheaded kids. He was soft-spoken and polite and never failed to wave when I drove by while he tended his roses. Which means to say, I assumed he was gay. No straight men in the business are that polite. ("The business," by the way.)

"Let's play," she said, opening her elephantine purse to reveal its tenant: a neon dildo.

"Oh! I only play tennis," I said. In fact, her dildo's as big as my Babolat. (A cool name for a dildo, btw. Market that.)

A spark of realization like a penlight in the back of my cranium. The actress must know I've been given the superfluous executive producer credit on the movie. Poor child. She thinks I, the writer, have *power*. I tell her Liz's producing the next *Harry Potter* and send her and her Babolat in Liz's direction. Liz is a lapsed lesbian; I'm a good friend.

The buoyant temperature dropped; the Enviro-bullies, a subset of Hollywood wives that doesn't wear makeup or have sex with anyone but Robert Kennedy Jr. (totally kidding!), are out in force, sucking fun out of the room like a green-powered vacuum. They have climate change worry lines and berating-gardeners-for-driving-diesel furrows. The prettiest one—a former daytime soap star and heroin addict whose current drug of choice is paper straws—approaches.

"Honey!" She was clutching my book as she kissed my cheek. I smelled lingering cigarette smoke, a weak spot that softened me for whatever was coming next.

"Did you use recycled paper?" She tapped my book with her nail, right between the eyebrows on my author's photo. I winced.

"I'm not sure," I said and then decided to lie. "I asked them to, of course . . ."

"Ink that doesn't kill Indian babies?"

I saw my agent, Lucas, across the room and waved at him like I'd just fallen overboard into choppy seas. As the Enviro-Bullies descended on the Good-Time Blondes, I scurried away; the GTBs drove Range Rovers and wore dyed-pink fur and turned sprinklers on their fake lawns. I couldn't watch.

I dog-paddled across the room to my human lifeboat, Lucas Kirklow, a tall drink of Hollywood legacy water (movie star mother, playwright father). He was forehead to lip with an ethereal giantess with a blue vein that beat beneath the skin of her albino forehead. She was draped in black, light catching at her neckline, illuminating a crystal wrapped in gold. I'd found the one person who belonged here less than I did. She smelled like incense and the musk of other people's darkest secrets. I was scared but also wanted her to hold me.

Lucas, in his hipster Malcolm X-tra glasses, gave me a hug and a moist peck on the cheek. His rich chocolate curls flopped forward and that crooked smile that made women (me) weak and stupid (also me) were out in full electrifying force.

"Agnes, love the party, so good, you're amazing, are you wearing eyeliner? Perfect! Meet Waverly Brown," Lucas said. The woman gazed down at me from her imaginary throne. "Just signed Waverly to a three-book deal."

"Congratulations," I said. Then bowed.

"Waverly is a cognitive," Lucas said, "You know her work."

I bit my lip. "Cognitive?"

"It's like an . . . intuitive," Lucas said.

"You mean . . . a psychic?" I asked.

Waverly sniffed and looked away.

"Have you had a drink?" I gestured over the bobbing agent heads toward the bar. Any minute now, I'd have to start signing books. Waverly opened her clutch and slipped out a card, handing it to me. Silver with black filigree numbers. A phone number. No name.

"Thank you?"

She leaned in and whispered in my ear, "He's getting his ducks in order."

My eyes moved from Waverly to Lucas, who was laughing at something one of the waitresses with perfect teeth said, his curls bouncing with thoughts (I imagine) of Waverly's commissions and sex. I didn't tug on them like I usually do.

"That's a mixed metaphor, and not to be nitpicky, but isn't it *getting your ducks in a row* and *house in order?*" I asked Ms. Cognitive. I was thirsty and aware that I might be hyperventilating. The room felt smaller and the walls were undulating and I needed to sit down.

"Call me," she said, holding my gaze.

"How do you spell your name, again?"

"E-y."

Me: blank stare.

"Agster!" (No one calls me Agster.) "S-h-e-l-l-e-y."

"Oh my God, Shell-i-e, I mean, Shell-e-y, stop, I know!" Ha ha! I smiled outwardly. Inwardly, I died. Twelve books in, my signing devolved into "Hope you enjoy! XoAggie," twenty books in, I'm at the "Enjoy! XAg" stage.

Party was over in ten minutes, not that I was counting. Next in line, beady eyes framed by belligerent lash extensions in a waxy face. A menopausal party girl for whom the party would have ended a long time ago if it weren't for that handy trust fund.

"Carrie!"

I'm thrilled to remember her name, though. We cheek kissed; I could feel her Aquaphor rub off on me.

"I did a walk-through of your house today!" she said, her teeth phosphorescent. I tried to remember what her grandfather invented (shoelace tips?). She's on Liz's and my Instagram "Hall of Shame" for flip-o-gram moms spending weeks picking out fringe for their Coachella halters. Shooters at Sky Bar at 2:00 a.m. Screwing the Brentwood High football quarterback.

"What?" I winked. Even though Carrie's five Deadlies in, she caught my discomfort like a black widow spider.

"Have you ever thought of taking the fireplace down? I mean, a fireplace in the middle of the kitchen? Who does that?" She snorted, tequila dripping from her nostrils.

I loved my fireplace. It's authentic and original . . . except, it's not *my* fireplace. My name is nowhere on the deed. Indeed.

Wink. Wink.

"Oh my God, I'm so sorry!" She's the opposite of sorry. She's ecstatic, like biting into a warm *pain au chocolat* after hot-stranger-sex ecstatic. "What am I even saying? Of course you knew. How could you not know? That would be so weird, right? And sad. So, so sad. Can you sign this to my nana? She's ninety years old. I think she might like it."

She slid an open book over to me.

With shaky hands, I wrote, *Your granddaughter's a bitch, XOAg.*

No, no, I didn't.

(Okay. Yes, I did.)

3

Uber-Hyphenate

I Ubered home in a blacked-out Suburban, Adele crying on the radio, air-conditioning blowing up my dress, and legroom for my emotional baggage. My calls and texts to Trevor went unanswered. I hoped he wasn't lying in a ditch somewhere, but I also hoped that he was. ☺

Crazy, crazy Agnes. I'd assumed Trevor would materialize during my party, a 5 percent body fat rabbit hopping from a magician's hat, waving my book, dedicated to him, my dear husband. Meanwhile, I was checking my phone like Lil Wayne waiting on a codeine cough syrup delivery. I wasn't even the family OCD. That would belong to Trevor, who could make a miniseries out of a meal and a lifetime out of a T-shirt drawer.

Uber driver Sami was a battery-operated Lebanese comic ("Only open mics in Burbank so far, that's okay, that's okay!") with doe eyes and long lashes and the enthusiasm of a Jack Russell kept in a studio apartment too long. He'd driven Trevor home from his office once and *did I know Trevor and was I married to Trevor and could I get Trevor his screenplay and also his 8 × 10?*

"Of course," I said. "I'd be happy to." Don't be a dream-stomper. You never know. Remember what William Goldman said about Hollywood? *You don't know who William Goldman is?* (Sorry. I'm an antique, I mean *"vintage."*)

Mr. Goldman famously said, *No one knows anything.*

Also applies to politics, the media, and AT&T customer service professionals. I'd send the Lebanese comic's 110-page baby to one of Trevor's three assistants and hope that someone would read the script and throw the kid a bone, give him feedback, a little encouragement. If it sucked, Trevor would never be the wiser. As his wife, I was the official buffer; my job was to protect Trevor from incoming scripts, 8×10s, uncomfortable conversations with "civilians."

We drove west on Sunset, my favorite street in a city I knew like the back of my freckled hand (those aren't age spots, I tell you), winding through wide, palatial streets of Beverly Hills, floating past ivy-covered Bel Air gates, to the edge of the Palisades, twisting up a darkened road into the Riviera. Capri, Amalfi, Umeo . . . sexy, curvy streets with no street lighting, no sidewalks, and no pedestrians, thank you very much. Pedestrians were for south of Sunset.

Unless you were four-legged; coyotes padded in from the parched canyon, hunting for saline swimming pool water and Fluffy.

Our gates were closed. I leaned out the window and punched six numbers in the alarm pad—Trevor 68 Pep 07 Me 75.

I waited for the gate to groan open.

And waited. *La la la.*

"My screenplay, it's about childhood buddies who grow up in Beirut." Sami painted the scene with his elegant hands. "They meet this wizard in the rubble of war. Is he real? Is he not? Are the boys dead? Are they alive? Sort of magical realism, you know what I mean?"

"Sounds more interesting than anything I've seen in a long time," I said. "What about car chases? Any superhero costumes? Hot mutants?"

I punched the code again. Waited. Nada. Coyotes howled deep in the canyon, a scraggly, furry Greek chorus.

"Power outage," I lied.

Trevor didn't do power outages. We owned the most powerful backup generator west of the 405 Freeway. Years ago, Trevor one-upped Brad Grey after hearing the former Paramount chief had the beta version. On an autumn night in the aftermath of a jarring earthquake, Trevor mixed margaritas, and we observed the ink city from our balcony and toasted our industrial-strength generator.

Pep slept in my arms, her strawberry head on my chest.

We were happy. Wasn't that a happy moment? I had to write this down, might need to pitch it later. To my husband.

Sami glanced at me over the front seat, his velvet eyebrows knitted together. "You, ah, sure you live here?"

"Listen," I said, my humiliation antennae finely tuned, a human praying mantis. "Do you want your magical realism read or not?"

He adjusted the rearview mirror.

"I'm sorry . . . look, I'll stay, call my nanny," I said. "She's baby-sitting; she just can't hear the ring."

I hopped out, his screenplay and photograph balanced atop my box of extra books that I'd shove into a closet to be dredged up decades from now, after my death at 102 from boredom. *"Great-great-granny Agnes was a writer?" "I think so." "What's a writer?" "Some silly shit."*

"My phone number's on the title page," Sami said as he pulled out of the driveway. "It's called *Escape from Childhood*. It's a home run for a movie star, an Oscar for sure, I'm telling you. I wouldn't lie."

A warm, dry wind blew. I dropped the box on the driveway and checked my phone. No bars. We lived in a dead zone, I'd told Trevor. I'd have more bars on a raft in the middle of the Indian Ocean.

A bar blinked. *Call Gabriela!*

Straight to voicemail, in English and Spanish. FYI, I speak bad Spanglish; I stumble over slippery conjugated verbs but can throw down insults like a native.

I lost service again.

I walked into the street, surrounded by silent, unblinking mansions. I held my phone aloft, raising it like a flag.

Can you hear me now? Can you hear me now? What about now?

One bar. Now two. That elusive third bar. I called Trevor, smiling, slightly younger Trevor hoisting the Oscar popped up on my screen, a favorite shot of his, taken from *People* magazine.

Voicemail. His assistant—the motherly Brit at the office, not the fresh-faced, trembling assistant with the colitis, and not the third, silent, faceless one I never remember because they're always being replaced.

I walked back to the gate, punched in the family code once again. Sniffed. The temperature was dropping. My stomach rumbled. I'd barely eaten the baffling appetizers. I stared down the wooden gate, now illuminated by stingy moonlight.

"Open sesame!" I yelled. Coyotes howled.

Fuck it. I slipped off my heels.

I grabbed the side of the gate, hitched my foot into the center of the wooden *X*, and pulled myself up, my hips hitting the top. I was no Mary Lou Retton. Don't come calling, Wheaties. Using all my strength and lack of common sense, I flipped over the gate, landing on the other side, dropping my phone during the vault.

Russian judge gives silly Hollywood wife a 5.2.

All those hours spent in Pilates and hot yoga and SoulCycle for the Mom Olympics finally paid off.

I ran down the long driveway that curved into a circle in front of the house. Security lights flickered overhead as I dashed past giant hedges, mechanical sentries alerted to sudden movement.

The home I'd lived in for the last ten years emerged.

I imagined Trevor's Realtor, "Westside's Realtor to the Stars™," Peter Marks. The description on his website, next to an old photo. That Peter, bright-eyed, brown-haired, newly married. Today's Peter, baggy-eyed, gray-haired, divorced. Stars will do that to a person.

Newly remodeled, classic mid-century California ranch–style estate in the famed Palisades Riviera. North of Sunset where the wide, sidewalk-free streets are named for the Italian and French Rivieras. Built in 1942 for a legendary movie star, with many original features. Laid out in geometric design as it integrates seamlessly with the natural topography. Peaceful and restrained. You will feel transformed.

Plans for development into thirty-thousand-square-foot Grecian abode or move in today! Price upon request.

Never, ever request the price.

The kitchen door near our garage was usually unlocked. If anyone with bad intentions got past the gate, his aim was to kill you, and good luck behind a locked door.

Feral eyes lit up my back.

"Gristle!" I yelled to my invisible, mangy audience. "Don't waste your time."

I tried the kitchen door. Locked! What? I didn't have a key, there was no key, not even a hidden one. No one used house keys in this neighborhood. We used assistants, nannies, housekeepers, live-in staff, maybe a code. Anything but a simple key.

I ran across the pebbled (*ouchouchouch*) drive, around the majestic sycamore tree, great overseer of pebbles, planted as a sapling and nurtured by the movie star's wife. I hopped to the antique front door that once graced a French village church. Village church doors were a favorite of our designer, who decorated all the "best" homes on the Westside.

"Poor France," I'd told Trevor, "filled with doorless churches."

The door was locked. I pondered hiking around the back and breaking in when I saw lights coming down the driveway. Trevor was home! Oh no! Maybe he *was* sick? His archrival producer with a closetful of muumuus ran him over? A disgruntled writer tried to poison him? Was there any other kind of writer? (And what is the opposite of disgruntled? *Gruntled?*)

There were a million reasons Trevor didn't show up to my book party. Not one of which was that he didn't want to go. Neither did I, so that's no excuse.

A miniature white SUV with ADA stickers on the side panel slid down the driveway, headlights ablaze; it looked like a dog crate on wheels.

"Mrs. Nash?" An extremely average man with a crown of dusty hair and navy windbreaker with an ADA patch plopped out of the driver's seat. He kept the headlights on. A weapon poked from his waistband. I accessed my depleting memory bank.

Jerry? He'd soared down the driveway last year when the house alarm was screaming and no one could shut it off.

Gerry. Not Jerry. Gerry. A *G* where a *J* should be, which tips my bad mood.

"You're attempting to enter this domicile?" His hand on his Taser holster.

"Gerry, right? Yes, I don't know. You were able to use the code?"

His eyes flicked away, then back. "Factually, yes."

"So it's working again? Do you have a key? I can't seem to get ahold of anyone."

Gerry scratched his chin.

"Gerry? I'm sorry, but could you?" I rubbed my arms. Even the earthquake wind couldn't warm me. "I'm freezing. I'm hungry. My feet hurt. I'm cramping. I'm sweating. I'm irritable. I could sob any minute. Are you familiar with perimenopause, Ger?"

"Perry . . . who?"

"My daughter's inside, please."

"There's no easy way of saying this, Mrs. Nash," Gerry kicked his Skechers at the pebbles.

"Saying what?" I rubbed my arms furiously, as though trying to light a fire with my body. My teeth started chattering.

"Okay, here we go." He sighed. "I'm really sorry, I've been told not to allow you in."

Gerry the security guard looked away, abashed. *I wanted to abash his face in.*

I shook my head. "I don't . . ."

I do. I don't. I did. The three phases of marriage?

Gerry wiped his nose. "It's what they call, in the legal profession, *leveraging.*"

"Leveraging?" I asked.

"I went to law school for a year," Gerry said, "then the meth thing happened . . ."

He trailed off in a haze of meth regret.

"Gerry," I said. "Look at me. My daughter's asleep in this house. I don't know what's going on, but this is not your battle. I climbed over that gate. There's nothing I can't do. I am *that* strong. Now, you can either help me or get out of the way, Gerry. I don't want to have to hurt you."

He scooted like a crab, blocking me from the French church door.

I took a step toward him.

Flash. Buzz. Spark. The smell of barbecuing flesh, like Fraxel but without the Valium. I screamed, then crumpled into the fetal position, my face smacking the ground. Seconds of branding plus electrocution culminating in the most intense pain I've ever felt (and I sat through the first cut of *Gigli*). I spit out pebbles as the sycamore spun above me.

I'd been tased.

"What the fuck, Gerry!" I yanked the barbs out of my arm.

"Whoa!" he said. "Whoa, whoa, whoa! I've never tased anyone before. Here, let me help you. I'm so sorry. That must've felt awful!"

I slapped his hands and pushed my body up, panting like a bulldog.

"I swear to God, Gerry," I gasped, "I'm going to kill you with my bare hands. When I can stand. And the tree stops spinning."

"I was told not to let you in," he said. "I'm so sorry."

"Get away from me!" I said, hands on my knees. "You let me in right now, Gerry, or I'll tell your boss you're smoking meth on the job."

"You saw that?"

"Open the fucking goddamned door, Gerry!" I yelled. I leaned up against the church door, like *Les Misérables* without Anne Hathaway's adorable pixie.

Then I keeled over and threw up, spraying the pebbles with partially digested mystery appetizers.

I stumbled into the living room, past the custom-built, brightly lit trophy case, where the Best Picture Oscar was flanked by Emmys and People's Choice Awards, the ugly stepchild of awards shows. The light never burned out on the trophy case, its gleaming inhabitants polished once a week, then set back on tiny markers, as per photos the staff captured from three different angles. The trophy case would then be locked up, the key itself locked in a small drawer in a cabinet inside Trevor's home office, across from our living quarters.

I last held Oscar the night Trevor won. I was wearing red silk and hadn't eaten solid food in three weeks. I had collarbones, and we were giddy and tearful and hungry. The next morning, Oscar was locked up. I never had a chance to touch him again.

I tiptoed into the kitchen and flicked on the overhead lights. The expansive island greeted me, a thick wooden plank worn at the corners, bearer of a thousand nicks. I loved that island. I'd chopped, minced, and grated on that island. I'd mixed, strained, and whisked on that island. I'd had sex on that island. (Early days.)

Everything looked normal, if normal were a *Martha Stewart Living* centerfold. The Gaggenau refrigerator, La Pavoni espresso machine, La Cornue range.

I couldn't pronounce my appliances, but I could use them.

The dictates of Trevor Nash were everywhere, in the smudgeless steel refrigerator, the spotless crystal glasses, the marble floor slick and reflective as a mirror.

A notepad on the corner of the island. A Montblanc cleaved the words printed at the top. The name of our home. The Capri. After our street. (I'd suggested naming it *Howard* or *Stan*. I lost.) The notepads were strategically placed throughout the house in case Trevor had to jot down an idea, phone number, name, vocabulary word, like a bucket for capturing falling stars. Like the trophies, the notepads couldn't be moved. Trevor would know. He could eyeball a quarter-inch breach. Even the pens were placed precisely, though at a deceptively jaunty angle.

The pads were replaced as soon as they were down to thirty-two sheets.

"I can't use this notepad," Trevor had said. "Look at it!" He'd waved the notepad next to his side of the bed. "It's too thin!"

"Just use it up," I'd said. "No need to waste paper."

He'd thrown the notepad against the wall. "What, we can't afford new notepads now? Are we poor?"

Things that made Trevor feel poor: thinning notepads, burned toast, his gas gauge at a quarter tank.

I made a beeline for Pep's room. Fluffy rug, bubble gum–pink walls that she suddenly wanted painted black (nope). Her bed was empty.

Bear, that wasn't a bear but a large, breed-less stuffed dog, was missing, which told me this wasn't a case of kidnapping as much as nanny-napping. Gabriela had taken her to sleep at her place for the night, I was sure of it. I turned on the light and took a deep breath, Pep's baby-powder-and-peaches scent hanging in the air like strings of candy just out of reach.

I'd call Gabriela from the house phone. Christ. I didn't know her number. I hadn't memorized a phone number in a decade.

"Oh, it's you, Agnes," someone said. "I thought I heard something."

In the mirror, a naked, human salamander curved into the doorway, hands hanging on the door casing above his head, elbows like turrets. Cutting out toast and cream in his coffee, working out every single morning, and using three hours to eat a meal had decreased Trevor's body fat to "science class skeleton" percentage. He looked as much snake as man.

"Trevor, you scared me!" I said, my throat tightening. "I was a human bonfire! Right outside our house!"

"Annie Leibovitz wants to do a shirtless photo shoot. Do you think I'm ready?" Trevor ran his hands through his surfer waves, scrunching and twisting until it pleased him.

"Trevor, pay attention." I showed him the twin marks on my shoulder. "I got tased right outside our front door!"

"I always wondered what that felt like," he said, his expression wandering off. "Was it . . . harrowing?"

Monday's vocabulary word. I'd seen the card on his dresser.

"Is Pep with Gabi?" I asked. "She's with Gabi, right?"

"Yeah, I had Gabi take her for a sleepover," he said. "I thought we'd have dinner together and watch a movie, but she wanted me to stop texting. I need my phone, she knows that. What is wrong with kids?"

"Trevor, why didn't you show up to my book party?"

"Oh yeah, how'd your thing go?" Deflection. Classic Trevor. I had to remember where this fit in *The 48 Laws of Power*, the one book found in every spare bathroom west of the 405.

Conceal Your Intentions?

"Were you sick?"

"No," he said. "Do I look sick?" He checked himself in the mirror, looking for signs of illness. He patted his cheeks, examined the whites of his eyes.

"I had to answer so many questions tonight about you not showing up. It was so embarrassing."

"It's always about you," He shook his fist; his dick wobbled. The dick wobbler, a rare Australian bird only found in the bush. Speaking of bush. *Where was Trevor's bush?*

"Well, it is my book," I said. "Did you . . . are you . . . waxing?"

"That's it. I want to go in another direction—"

"Excuse me?"

"I'm putting this marriage in turnaround."

I felt dizzy. Taser or this conversation?

"You know, like when I had that cartel project I was really in love with but then we couldn't get Guillermo to direct and then I kind of fell out of love and I fired everybody?"

"You're explaining to me what *turnaround* means? You're telling me I'm like a project you don't want anymore?" I said. "Marriage is a partnership!" I knit my fingers together, my wedding ring winking.

"I don't want to marriage anymore," he said, sounding like a toddler. "What can I say? It's not working for me."

Had I become the mother Trevor always hated? Multi-married June Carole Nash's face knifed into my brain. *Junie Nash, I blame you for this. I blame your beautiful narcissistic self. I blame your red lips, the perfect bloom of your pale skin. Your guzzling martinis when Trevor crawled around in dirty diapers. Your sleeping with a married B-movie director, a brief, bumbling union that ended here, right here, in my beautiful daughter's room, with this pile of mother-obsessed damage.*

"I'm not happy," Trevor said. "I want to be happy. I really, really want to be happy." He pounded his thighs with his fists.

"Stupid people are happy, Trevor," I said. "You're not unhappy with me, you just think you are. You're . . . more or less satisfied!"

My gravestone would proudly state: *Here lies Agnes Murphy Nash, more or less satisfied for her entire life.*

"Happy doesn't last, Trevor," I said. "Unhappy? That you can build on!"

"Look, I talked to Geffen and Katzenberg, I had a conference call with Ari. Everyone thinks I need someone who knows how to market Trevor Nash and, you know, take care of my social schedule," he said.

"We're getting divorced by committee?" I asked, stumped. "Trevor, we have our issues, but I cook for you, I take care of our child, with help, okay, yes, I give you a blow job once a week—without help, as far as I know—I try to be interested in your work every single day."

"I shouldn't have to ask," he said. "You should be interested in everything I do."

I'd split my interest quotient with Pep the day she was born.

I sat back while Trevor ran his hands through his hair again.

"Trevor?"

Petra appeared, wearing pajamas. And they looked like . . . my pajamas. My flannel Christmas pajamas. My *favorite* flannel Christmas pajamas. The ones with the dogs. You know.

"Oh, I'm sorry," Petra said, not appearing sorry.

"Petra, what the fuck are you doing here, and why are you wearing my dog pajamas?"

"These are my dog pajamas," she said, hugging her sides. "I buy them three years ago."

"Are you sure? Are you sure those aren't mine? I love those pajamas."

"Why are you so concerned with material things?" Trevor said. "This is very painful for me. I don't think you know how hard it is to break up a marriage."

"Petra, are you sleeping with my husband?"

"You know I can't sleep alone! God!" Trevor yelled as he left the scene of the crime.

"Petra? Petra is my replacement?" I called after him. "The woman you said smelled like mothballs? The woman who creeped you out with her staring? The woman who doesn't make soup the way she used to? All you do is complain about her!"

Petra whimpered.

"I'm not fucking Petra. What do you think I am?" Trevor yelled from the hallway, popping his head back inside Pep's bedroom. "Before you, I slept with models and actresses! Supermodels! An Oscar nominee, almost!"

Petra stifled a cry and turned away. I heard Trevor hop toward the kitchen.

"Petra, I was worried about your migraine. This is like surround sound betrayal, no, like Lucasfilm THX betrayal!"

"I work for Trevor," she said, her eyes moist.

"And you're sleeping with him!"

"On your bed," she said.

"On my bed?" I said. "*On?*"

"Like this," she said and mimicked curling up in a ball. "In case Trevor needs water or sleeping pill or thin pillow."

"It's called companion sleeping, okay?" Trevor yelled from the kitchen. "It's new. My buddy at Google started it. You don't even know anything."

I was staring at Petra. "You know you work for both of us, Petra."

"Trevor signs check."

She had a point.

"Ever hear of feminism, Petra? Of women supporting each other? This is why Hillary lost, you know that, right?"

"Hillary is communist," she sniffed. "Feminism is not paying bills. Trevor pays bills."

"Petra! I need my sleep!" Trevor screeched from the kitchen. "You're still on the clock!"

"Is this why the coffee's gone to shit?" We'd become squalling adult babies, completely dependent on Petra. Lately, her work had become lax. About a month ago, I walked in as Trevor was shaving in his bathroom and showed him a Loro Piana cashmere sweater, which was now the size of a waffle. Petra had thrown it in the wash with Pep's towels.

Petra had joined Equinox, losing her "old country" padding. She had pinwheels in her eyes. I'd wondered if she were popping Adderall or snorting coke. She was watching way too much *#RHOBH*, sneaking it on her iPad in the office. I was hoping she'd find a boyfriend, someone to wine her, dine her, check her meds.

I wasn't talking about Trevor.

On the rowing machines at Orange Theory, Liz had warned me about the Single White Nanny phenomenon. "If it could happen to Gwen Stefani," she'd panted, her triceps rippling. "What makes you think you're so special?"

"I don't cost much, in terms of comparative pricing," I'd said in my defense.

I pushed past Petra, catching a whiff of my favorite perfume.

Trevor was in the kitchen, cutting up an apple. He sliced it eight times, each piece even with the next. He placed them on a plate, exactly a quarter-inch space between each slice. Then rearranged.

"She's not your replacement," Trevor said, slipping a slice of apple in his mouth. I stared at the sharp knife he'd been using perhaps a second too long. "I just have to do what's right for me. That's what Dr. Erskin said."

Dr. Erskin, the resident Hollywood psychiatrist. An actual M.D. (*M.D.* standing for *maximum drugs.*)

"I can't listen to this anymore." I rummaged through a kitchen drawer and grabbed my car keys.

"What are you doing?" He followed me, chewing . . . I counted, an automatic, involuntary response to learned stimulus. I was Pavlov's wife.

What other habits had I picked up in the last twelve years?

#8, #9, #10—

"Leaving," I said.

#12, #13, #14—

"Leaving where?"

#18, #19 . . . #22—

"None of your business!" I said. "You're the one who wants a divorce!"

#32, #33 . . . #36. And, swallow.

"I don't want to fight!" Trevor said, then, "Petra! Stop crying! I need to sleep!"

I drove up the driveway, waited for the gate to open, scooped up my heels and phone and the box of books, balancing Sami's script.

I thought about how much an Uber driver pulls in. And would I make a good Uber driver and . . . no. I talk too much and I'd get crazy nervous about people rating me and I probably would pick up a serial rapist on the first ride.

Which wouldn't make a bad movie.

I had to find my girl.

Inglewood, Inglewood always up to no—As soon as I departed the dead zone, I called Gabriela to let her know I was on my way and raced down the 405 past the airport. I exited right on Inglewood Boulevard and slunk along side streets in the dark until I found Gabriela's house, a neat California craftsman bungalow in a row of bungalows and '70s apartment buildings.

I hiked up the concrete steps to the front door, where Gabriela stood with her arms crossed against her chest, my hideous pink Ugg boots I'd gone insane looking for blinking on her feet.

"Petra *es la diabla,*" she snarled, then bear-hugged me. It seemed rude to mention the Uggs, given the circumstances. Inside her home, a small dog wheeze-barked. Gabriela ushered me into the living room as the wheezer jumped at my shins.

"Shush, *mijo!*" Gabriela said.

The house was darkened, but I discerned Jesus and the Virgin Mary atop her mantel. I had gifted her the Virgin Mary last Christmas and she'd cried, and now my email box was filled with *20% off Jesus!* messages from the Catholic Company. But how could I unsubscribe to Jesus?

"Come in, come in," she said. I liked her cozy, manageable home—so unlike the house I'd just left. I started calculating. How much would it cost to rent? Could Pep attend a neighborhood school, or would I have to bus her to Briarwood, her girls' school on the hill? Should I move out of California altogether? And could I make "downwardly mobile" as chic as feathered eyebrows?

A familiar wave of guilt hit me; I'd never stepped inside Gabriela's home, even though she'd worked in our home for close to a decade. Almost the same time I started working for Trevor.

Wink.

I grabbed my mental surfboard and dove under the wave as I took in my surroundings. Gabriela's home was beyond white-glove reproach. You'd be hard-pressed to find a speck of dust or lint or a stray wheezy dog hair. Gabriela had told me she woke up at 4:30 in the morning to clean her house before making the trek to the dead zone, where she then spent eight hours cleaning up our dust and lint and stray Trevor hair.

Living room, dining room, kitchen . . . each room a few steps away from the next. I assumed the bedrooms were down the hallway, to either side. The house felt warm as a womb, and the faint smell of cornmeal tamales made my stomach rumble. Gabriela had brought out the big guns for Pep's arrival. She didn't make tamales for anything but weddings and funerals and Jesus.

And Pep.

Gabriela's husband, Bernardo, our Mr. Fixit who was great at cleaning windows and not so great at anything requiring a wrench, was curled up under a blanket on the couch, snoring softly. I had always just seen him grinning and nodding and pushing Pep in her swing when she was little.

"Where's Pep?" I asked.

"She's in our bed, missus," Gabriela said. My face warmed with further embarrassment. Pep had gentrified Gabriela's house.

We walked down the hallway where a door was ajar. I peeked inside. Pep was sound asleep, her arms overhead, Bear resting in the nook of her neck. She looked so sweet and docile I almost wished I could set her in amber. *Is that a thing?*

"Does she know about . . . ?"

"No," Gabriela said. "Peppy, she just want to sleep over. Mr. Trevor was using phone. We had party for her. Like when she was little."

"I can smell the tamales," I said. "Thank you so much, Gabriela."

She grabbed my hands and held them to her chest. "I sorry, missus."

"Did you know about Petra?" I asked. "I don't think she's fucking Trevor—sorry, having sex with him. That would be normal; this seems a lot weirder."

"*Diabla*," she said, followed by a string of Spanish expletives. Gabriela was Team Agnes. I mentally high-fived myself. Gabriela was good with Jesus and the Virgin Mary and solid with hexes. She'd fought with our neighbor over a parking spot, and he broke his leg the next day and couldn't drive for six months. That's some strong God shit.

"La Reina, I see her tomorrow," she said. "I tell her what to do. She knows."

Gabriela meant *ask* instead of *tell*, but who cares? I was excited. This was the first good news I'd had since . . . since . . .

I'll get back to you.

La Reina was the Latin community's premier psychic. I'd begged Gabriela to take me to La Reina; I had questions! *Would I ever hit the bestseller list? Would Fin ever straighten out her act? And, most importantly, how do I stop Pep from becoming a #richkidsofInstagram?*

Gabriela had explained, patiently, that La Reina didn't meet with *gringas*. "Who can blame her?" I'd said.

"You stay tonight," Gabriela was saying. "I sleep on floor next to Bernardo."

"Absolutely not," I said. "You're not sleeping on the floor."

"I have futon." I braced myself for the monster of all guilt waves. Now that I raced toward a future as a single mother, I'd try to cozy up to guilt, ply it with Chardonnay (so I could feel more guilt in the morning).

The Circle of Life was nothing without the Circle of Guilt.

"Thank you so much, Gabi."

"Anything for you, missus," Gabriela said, kissing my cheek.

"Gabriela?"

She turned back at the door. I had to know.

"Do you . . . are those my Uggs?" I couldn't help myself. I'd spent an hour looking for them the other morning. I literally thought I was going crazy (I'm definitely going crazy).

"No, missus."

"But . . . I . . . are you sure?"

"You didn't want them no more."

"But I did, I think?"

"No, missus, you didn't," she said with infinite patience.

I examined my faulty memory. "Maybe you're right."

"It's okay, I keep them?"

"Of course, of course," I said. "I'm sorry. I shouldn't have brought that up. I'm being an asshole."

"I love you, Missus Añes," Gabriela said.

"I love you, too, Gabriela," I said as she shut the door. I heard wheezy dog bark on the other side as I curled up next to my daughter and hurtled into sleep.

4

On the Job Failing

The job description of the Hollywood wife: Please read carefully before you sign up. The fine print is not just at the bottom.

Your number one job is to socialize. Socializing is Hollywood's lifeblood, and the social circles are very specific.

A Hollywood wife socializes with other Hollywood wives.

Exceptions: A Hollywood wife may socialize with a hairdresser or makeup artist or stylist or interior decorator. She may even be close with her assistant—so close that the lines are blurred and the assistant winds up living the Hollywood wife life.

Ahem.

Be careful who assists you. She may "assist" you right out of a marriage.

Your closest friends will be other wives of _____ (fill in star, producer, director, or major agent). Writers are only acceptable if they also direct or have won an Oscar.

You will "adopt" wives who are new to the city and whose husbands show great promise, and you will close in on them and become best friends in a matter of hours.

Your pre-wifedom friends will fade as you succumb to shiny, bright new friendships that fill your every waking hour. You "literally have no time." You will SoulCycle, Zumba, or PlyoJam. Tracy Anderson will call you by a nickname and know your "trouble spots." You will live in athleisure. Your kids will go to the same three preschools as the other Hollywood wives' offspring, and you will hate the same teachers and love the same teachers and also share grave concerns about the new security guard or coach. You will hire a nanny for each child, and this year goes to the Filipinos, and a manny when your boys get a little older. Your manny will be hot, but you'll pretend not to notice. You're "crazybusy." When your child calls the nanny "Mommy," you'll fire her but kindly and with two weeks' severance. Because that's what all the mommies say is fair.

You will fret about the environment but Snapchat on the Sony jet to see Britney in Vegas (#lovemylife). You'll campaign for progressive candidates but never (never, ever) send your kids to public school. After the first pregnancy, you'll forget the last time you had sex with your husband, but you'll remember the last time you had sex with your trainer / tennis pro / yogi / politician / environmental activist. A few years in, you'll resent your husband because you're unhappy, and yet you have everything so it's his fault. You have a law degree, an art history degree, a business degree, a life coach degree, but you left your career to be a stay-at-home wife.

Not mother, *wife*.

Hubby needs you more than the kids do. The kids, you hire nannies for. The husbands have assistants, but there're never enough assistants. When the kids are in middle school, you'll leave them with a Black Amex as you dance and suck down shots and wake up with a headache too late to take them to that school with the good name. Because you have to keep up the socializing. If you're not out every night with the same people, how will they know you exist?

Worst Fear:

Wife #1: Where's Brooke?

Wife #2: She's not feeling well.

Wife #1: OMG, I hope it's not happening again.

Wife #3 What do you mean? What happened? She looked healthy the last time I saw her.

Wife #2: Yeah, hello, last week. I hear Brody [her three-year-old] can't spell his name and they're freaking out.

Wife #1: I heard they're moving. Steve's [her husband] in turnaround. Again. I mean, once, okay, but . . .

Wife #4 Hey, guys, sorry I'm late—

Wife #1: Brookie! Hi, beauty!

Trevor's second assistant, Dorette with colitis, who occasionally passed gas so pungent my eyelashes curled, cornered me in the kitchen as I tossed back my third double espresso of the day. (Sleep? What's that?) I was running late to pick up Pep from volleyball practice.

"Are you busy?" she asked, eyes bloodshot, blocking my exit like an anxious traffic cone.

"Crazybusy, nuttybusy, kookybusy," I said, hiking my arms like Usain Bolt because we have so much in common. "Literally running out the door."

"Stop," she said and handed me a printout.

"A blueprint?"

"Exactly. So good! A blueprint of this house."

"Well, thank you? Am I adding a bathroom? We have . . . twelve."

"Trevor told me to come up with a plan," she said. "He doesn't want you guys to risk running into each other." She lowered her voice. "He's in a lot of pain."

She flattened the blueprint out on the kitchen island and clapped a presentation pointer, and a laser shot out.

Pep could wait a few minutes while I enjoyed the laser show.

"Here's the main house," she said, gesturing with the pointer. A bright green dot lit up the main bedroom suite.

"Your room—I mean, your old bedroom—is at the far end."

Coliti-Girl had graduated from Brown. I calculated the cost of her education against this moment. Mental note: Send Pep to trade school. How adorable would she look in a tool belt?

"I know where it is," I said, perhaps a little grouchily.

"Of course," she said. "Sorry. Anyway, there's Trevor's closet and bathroom."

"Yes," I said. "I can see his vocabulary cards from here."

"I forgot the vocabulary cards!" she said, her eyes tearing up. "God, I worked on this all night. I haven't slept in two days."

"It was a joke," I said. "I'll pencil them in." I grabbed a ubiquitous pen and drew in tiny vocabulary cards. Today's word: *Asshole*.

"Thanks. Do you think you'll need help moving your things out of the closet?"

"My clothes?"

"Trevor would be more comfortable if any contact could be avoided. Including things you've worn."

I sighed. "Why don't we just do this on a timer?"

"Right, so you can still use your closet and personal bathroom, but not between the hours of 5:00 a.m. to 10:00 a.m. and 3:00 p.m. on."

"Perfect," I said. "I'll hold my bowel movements."

She looked at me.

"Not with my hands," I said.

"I was wondering," she said. "I'm sorry, Trevor requested that you steer clear of here, here, and here." Green dots danced over the blue-print.

"I need the kitchen," I said.

"How about half the kitchen? Would that work?"

"What happens if I need to step onto the other half? Does a blade come down from the ceiling and chop me in half?"

She started laughing so hard I realized someone must've fantasized about it.

"We'll work that out. Meanwhile, good news, you have full access to Penelope's room, the laundry room, and one-quarter of the deck," she said.

"What about the bar?" I asked, looking at the rooms of our home, every furniture item down to minor accessories penciled in. Trevor had demanded and thought of everything—couches, lamps, telephones, notepads, pens(!) . . . even the trophy case. Even Oscar.

I felt my nostrils flaring.

"Not a problem," she said, "as long as it's before 3:00 p.m."

"I'll move happy hour up to 10:00 a.m.," I said.

"Oh my God, thank you!" she said. "I'll tell Trevor how helpful you are! Maybe he'll let you stay!"

"Oh my God! That would be, like, totally amazing!" I clapped, then grabbed my keys from the counter.

Every Monday, Wednesday, and Friday, Pep had volleyball practice in the school gym that cost donors $40 million—and, like any school gym, it was basically a warehouse with bleachers and colored lines painted on the floor.

As I sneaked into the gym, I'd given Pep the tiniest humanly possible wave, and she'd rolled her eyes at me. *Communication!*

I hid in my favorite spot—the corner at the top of the bleachers, avoiding the Volleyball Mafia at the far end. This group of moms showed up

at the start of every practice, finding new life in each well-placed serve
and death in each missed block. You'd think they were raising a flock
of Misty Mays. Besides, I didn't need to talk to the volleyball moms;
they hijacked my Gmail numerous times a day. *Bring sliced oranges to
the game, brie for the adults. Can we coordinate knee pads, PLEEZE Who's
signed up to bring the red? NO PLASTIC CUPS Missie's private coach is
amazing as you can see Looking into new refs for season Summer volleyball
camp in Maine or Colorado? Petition to get rid of current coach please sign!!!*

There were many petitions; coaches didn't last more than two weeks.

"You can sit up front," I said as Pep jumped into the back seat of my car
with her $250 volleyball duffel bag.

She looked out the window, her freckled nose practically against the
glass, as though rooting for escape. "Don't want to."

"Do you want to listen to anything? Gaga? Ariana? Doesn't Ariana
have a new song out about her ponytail?"

She shook her head.

"Funny podcast? True crime podcast?"

"No," she said. "Just . . . drive please, Mom."

"Rightio," I said. "Yes, ma'am." I steered the car into traffic.

"Are you and Dad getting a divorce?" she asked, still staring out the
window.

My mind went blank. "What made you ask that?"

"What made me ask that is that everyone is talking about it except
my parents."

"How would they know?"

"Everyone's mom knows. Greer, Azalia, Porsche, everybody."

"No, honey," I said. "Right now, we're just . . . giving each other
space. Sometimes people need space from each other."

She sniffed, blinked.

"So . . . if you get divorced, do I get to go to another school?"

"Of course not."

"Stay married, then," she said.

"Out here doing my best," I said. "Wait. You liked school last year. What happened?"

She took a deep breath, then exhaled all her tween angst.

"Mom," she said. "You hate the parents at my school. Why would you think I like the kids?"

"*Hate* is such a strong word."

"You told Auntie Liz they were stuck-up anorexic buttholes with vagina lips. I heard you."

"I meant it as a compliment," I said.

That got a small smile out of her.

"Are we going to be poor?"

"What? No."

"I could live with Gabi."

"No, you couldn't."

"She said I could."

"I'm telling you, you can't."

"Are you saying Gabi's not a good mom?"

So hard to make cogent arguments against a smart tween while driving in LA; I needed to concentrate on swearing and shaking my fist at all the illegal left turns.

"Of course not. Gabi's a great mom; her kids all have actual jobs. I'm saying Gabi's already raised her kids. You're my kid. My only kid. I'm not done raising you. I haven't screwed you up enough yet."

I turned up the air-conditioning. I was riding that hot flash highway again.

"What did you say you and Dad were doing? Giving each other space?"

"Yes," I said. "Sometimes people need a break."

"Well, I'd like space, too," she said. "Could I get a break from you guys?"

I sighed and turned on the stereo. My kid was outsmarting me. Maybe she would be better off with Gabriela. Maybe Gabriela could raise both of us.

Operation Blueprint was working! Trevor and I avoided each other—I hadn't run into him in days, although sometimes I'd walk into a cold, empty room and smell his cologne. I imagined his lawyers or a famous actor or the valet parker at Craig's or maybe just the last person he spoke to convinced him not to lock me out. Meanwhile, I could pretend everything was normal when it was never normal; blueprint life was the latest in a string of un-normal. *Was Trevor still getting his ducks on the road (to misquote a misquoted metaphor)?* It was like living with a *Tyrannosaurus rex*—if he didn't see me move or breathe, I was safe.

I made a drastic mistake. Not compared to marriage. (I kid.)

Before falling asleep, I looked up perimenopause symptoms on my laptop. Do Not. Ever. Do This. One article listed fifty-six symptoms categorized under "Common," "Changes," "Pain," "Other."

Insomnia is common. *Check.* So is weight gain. *Check.* So is depression. *How would I recognize it?* Anxiety. *Check.* Vaginal dryness. Um. Between you and me? *From viscous to sandpaper in minutes.* Under "Changes," body odor. Hair loss. Memory lapses. *Where were we?* "Pain," you say? Migraines, joint pain. Burning tongue. Electric shocks.

Electric shocks!

How to overcome these symptoms?

If dying is out of the question—which it is not (check Gabriela's availability to raise Pep)—then one can reduce stress (*ha ha ha ha*), exercise, take hormones, have a good attitude.

I have a fucking great attitude, damn it.

Okay, I can jog.

After a sleepless night, awakened by unforgiving sunlight, I padded over to the gym (after 8:00 a.m., per blueprint).

Trevor, flouting the bylaws of Operation Blueprint, was attacking his Peloton, panting while yelling into the speakerphone.

"GT's into it?" Gasp. Sputter.

"Dude, he loves this role," an agent said. *Dude* the dead giveaway. "This is his role. That's what he said. He told me personally, okay? Through his assistant."

"Great. What'd he think about the ending?"

"Loved it. Wanted to fuck it he loved it so hard. Word for word."

"He read it himself?"

Trevor didn't read; that's what people were for. He would listen while an assistant read a script out loud, droning on while he lay down on his office couch or conference table, invariably napping through the third act. He read through *osmosis*. (Vocabulary word, October last year.)

"What? No, what?" the agent said with a sharp laugh. "He wants a rewrite."

"Let's get a different writer. I'm sick of this asshole. He wants to get paid for another pass."

The asshole had written the very script that GT was interested in, but *okay*.

"Great," the agent said, "I'll tell GT. He's in town through Easter, then he goes to Malaysia to fuck young boys. I'm fucking with you. Fuck me, terrible joke."

(Yes, it was, dude.)

"Great," Trevor said. "Hey, Idiot Number Three, you get that?"

Trevor's third assistant squeaked.

"Hey, Trev," the agent said, "I'll see you at Easter, dude, right?"

"Of course, dude."

"Love Easter. My favorite holiday after Christmas," said the agent. Who happened to be Jewish. "It's the best, I wouldn't miss it, you're coming, of course you're coming, bring the kids. Hey, how's your son?"

"Good, how're your kids?" Trevor didn't bother correcting him.

"Amazing," the agent said.

This agent didn't have children. He rented them for the annual Easter brunch.

"GT will be there; he adopted a bunch of little shits. I have to send fucking iPhones and fucking skateboards and fucking Xbox controllers to his house every other fucking month."

Trevor laughed like a hyena. "Love you, man!"

"Let's make out!" the agent said and hung up.

Great news. Trevor was busy courting George Treadwell, the Australian with the treacherous smile who'd been *People* magazine's Most Beautiful Man five times—three more than Brad Pitt (in his twenties, thirties, and Botox-filler forties). Our divorce had slipped a couple of notches on his to-do list—thank you, Treacherous Treadwell!

Distracted Trevor was the best Trevor.

I skipped off, kicking at the pebbles on our driveway. The sun, already hot, burst through the generous sycamore.

Today was looking to be a stunner.

Then I remembered plans, my worst enemy, had caught up with me.

Juliette's gender-neutral baby shower at her Benedict Canyon mid-century modern (childproofed so that every toilet, cabinet, and staircase was unusable) was off to a shaky start. Juliette (#HappyMom2B) had been scrapping with her surrogate. A month ago, #HappyMom2B had sent out pink invitations embossed with white ink before recalling them in a text frenzy. The surrogate, paying off Bard student loans by renting out her uterus, had tearfully objected to pink.

"Rent-a-Uterus screamed at Juliette for choosing the baby's gender," Liz relayed the gender kerfuffle. To placate Simone (let's call her), Juliette sent out green invitations embossed with silver.

But now, Simone wanted to choose the baby's name. A genderless name. Plus, she didn't want the baby to be "assigned" a gender until the baby was of age. And even then, the baby could choose another gender at any time. *Pins and needles!*

"I've never allowed a surrogate to choose a name," Juliette said, wearing a garland and tossing back pastel Jell-O shots. Her skin had healed from the chemical peel; she looked like a pretty Granny Smith with lips.

"Seems like a bad precedent, if you're planning on surrogating more ankle biters," I said.

"Gender is a societal structure is what Rent-a-Professor told us," Juliette said. In Hollywood, if you don't know or can't do something (most things), you rent a person who knows and can. Juliette and Jordan rented a UCLA history professor once a month for salons, where producers and actors and directors who couldn't pass an AP history class would tangle over Thomas Jefferson and Sally Hemings and Alexander Hamilton and pesky amendments, then ingest salmon spears.

"Simone says the baby will decide its gender whenever she, he, ze, or shim or they is ready," Juliette said.

My eyebrow shot up. At least, I think it did; I wasn't sure with the Botox.

"So exciting!" Karyn said. "The future is so . . . futurey." Mystery Asian, lugged around like a crocodile Birkin, smiled like a sphinx.

"I'm choosing to be the Rock," I said. "Or Neymar. Both! Alternating weeks."

Everyone knows the baby shower must go on, as money's been paid for the sandwiches from Sweet Lady Jane and the mini-cupcakes from Susie Cakes, the valet and the shower planner / life coach. Not to mention the expense of the actual fetus. Baby Crate Simone's SAT scores fetched her top dollar. Better that than working as a barista, if you're trying to pay off that handy victim arts degree. (We're doomed.)

"Anyway, I'm confused," Juliette said, "but of course I'm incredibly thankful."

"Hashtag blessed," Liz said, with a smirk.

"Hashtag grateful," Karyn said, no smirk.

"Hashtag Trevor wants a divorce," I said.

Everyone stopped mid-pastel Jell-O shot.

"On it," Liz said, breaking the silence and pulling out her phone. "I have a top-ten list of divorce attorneys. What kind do you prefer? Flashy? Low-key?"

"You have lawyers? Plural?" I asked. "But you seem almost happily married."

"So do you. But no sex for six months will do that to a girl," Liz said. "I can't get divorced, though. All the rich lesbian soccer players are taken."

Juliette snorted. "I'd kill to not have to fuck my husband."

"Oh, please. Michael threatens divorce every morning," Karyn said. "And we have the perfect marriage. We hardly see each other!"

"Jordan bought me a vibrator," Juliette said as we dismantled the macaron pyramid.

"Finally, some good news," I said.

"Give it to me," Liz said. "I mean it."

"Without my vibrator collection," Karyn said in her quasi-British accent, "I would've left Michael years ago and sailed home."

"You would've sailed to Utah?" I asked.

"By 'bought,' I mean the box was hidden in the back of his closet. Open," Juliette continued. "The battery was run down."

"Red velvet?" I asked, shoving a macaron in Juliette's face. Deflection by sugar. Then we snapped selfies at jaunty angles with a flotilla of filters. #livingthedream. #girlfriendsrthebestfriends #nofilterneeded.

A dozen more "skinny" Jell-O shots and the wives got down to business: Whose husband (present company excluded) was fucking whom. Whose kid was retarded—sorry, *disabled*—sorry, *special needs*—sorry, *learning differentiated*. Whose kid will be a whore—sorry, in charge of her sexuality. Whose kid will be a sociopath—sorry, running an agency. We all knew, deep inside, our kids were probably growing up to be entitled, overeducated blobs. We were raising hothouse flowers, unequipped to climb a fence or fry an egg or spend five minutes bored. They couldn't learn to throw a ball without a private coach or understand basic math without a tutor punching numbers in the calculator. Lord knows, they couldn't get into college without bribing some official. Hollywood moms had thrown our Lululemon-clad bodies atop any "uncomfortable moment" grenade since baby took his first steps.

"When the revolution comes," I said, "our kids will be food."

Outside, a car alarm bleated. We stopped mid-bite, our heads cocked. In LA, we knew the sound of our car alarms better than the cries of our firstborn.

"Don't worry," Juliette leaned over and whispered in my ear, "even if you get divorced, we'll still be your friends."

Trevor appeared in my bathroom doorway, a towel around his waist, his abs multiplying. There was something on his mind; he'd forgotten hair gel. His naturally wavy, messy hair made him look ten years younger.

Of course, I didn't tell him. *Take that.*

"Did I get my pee window wrong?" I asked from my porcelain throne. Cramps. Phantom period? My boobs hurt. Phantom pregnancy? Would I be birthing a phantom baby?

My appointment with Izzy was still weeks away. "I have to consult the blueprint."

"The what?"

He'd already forgotten.

"I'm getting Easter," he said.

"What are you talking about?"

"I need Pep. For Easter."

"We're going to my dad's for Easter," I said. "She's not a prop."

"Of course she's not a prop; she's a kid, and I need a kid to go to the big Easter party."

"I've already made plans with my dad; you're welcome to come."

Even though my dad hates you and now I hate you.

"Let's ask Pep."

"No!"

"Pep?"

Trevor dodged across the deck to Pep's bedroom. I raced after him to find Pep reclining on her bed, pillows piled high around her, transfixed, staring at her iPhone. The iPhone I told Trevor we couldn't buy her until she was thirteen.

"Honey, do you want to go to Grandpa's for Easter, or do you want to meet Ariana Grande?" Trevor asked.

"Not fair!" I said. Trevor knew Pep was an Arianator. Ariana Grande was one of very few things Pep still cared about. There was her iPhone, Christmas, and Ariana. We'd been to five concerts in two years. I couldn't hear a high-pitched note above all the screaming. (*And that was just me.*)

"No one can compete against Ariana Grande!"

"Are you kidding me, Dad?" She actually put her phone down and looked up. My daughter still had eyes!

"Would I kid?" Trevor squeezed in next to her. "I told her all about you; she's dying to meet you!"

"Mom?" Pep asked, her hands in prayer. I was flattered that she asked me anything. I was flattered that she noticed me standing there.

"Fine," I said, my arms folded across my chest. "I'm not going."

"Petra can go," Trevor said. "She can watch Pep."

"What time do I need to be ready?" I asked.

The queens of Hollywood, the director who looked like an angry pear and her brutally bronzed "thought coach" wife, Turkey Jerky, hijacked every holiday. New Year's Eve, Valentine's Day, Easter, Mother's Day, Father's Day, Fourth of July, and whatever else comes after that. Labor Day?

Even Labor Day.

Trevor and I and two hundred others valet-parked our Teslas and Range Rovers and BMWs and gathered our recalcitrant, photo-op-ready children and hiked past paparazzi hives up the long, stone drive-way (Hollywood's Bataan) to the great lawn on a Malibu cliffside where the Easter Bunny had collapsed from heat exhaustion after hiding hun-dreds of eggs and bags of candy and plastic eggs filled with silver dol-lars for children of privilege, white or otherwise, to find.

Before the festivities, Turkey Jerky read a fiery passage from Audre Lorde to the poker-faced crowd of agents and celebrities and celebrity agents and celebrity agent nannies. The kids were handed two Easter baskets—an empty one, the second filled with Easter swag—a pastel cashmere blanket, a cap emblazoned with the studio's upcoming ani-mated blockbuster title, twenty-dollar bills, and various toys. I hauled the swag-sket around while Pep raced a group of bigger kids to the bot-tom edge of a massive, aggressively pruned hedge.

Pep had made me promise to grab her if I saw Ariana Grande. ("But please, Mom, please don't say anything to her, don't look at her, just come find me, please, Mom.")

Trevor took off to find Treadwell.

My thoughts flicked to my dad milling around his bungalow in Venice and the tiny backyard with the bottlebrush tree that molted, its red spikes blanketing the grass. Before blueprint life, we'd made tentative plans to celebrate Easter at his place (I'd begged Trevor and prom-ised three blow jobs a week—as a joke, of course; I'm not insane); we'd "hunt" for eggs and soggy Peeps, then eat brunch on the warped picnic bench beneath the molting tree.

"Have you checked it out with knucklehead?" my dad had asked.

Our connection had been sketchy. My father owned a flip phone, which I'd given him as a gift in '03. He refused to part with it; for a man who was all over Facebook and day trading, he believed texting marked the end of civilization.

"I worked it all out. Don't worry about it," I'd said, crossing my fingers.

"I'll see you here, Easter Sunday, 0900 sharp," he'd said, then, "Be good."

I'd called my dad to tell him we weren't going to make Easter. Trevor knew a producer who'd been on the lot for fifteen years, missed Mother's Day at the Jerkys' because his actual mother was on her death-bed in Palm Beach. He'd lost his deal. He lived in North Carolina now, teaching at a university. (Leaving Hollywood to teach was considered a notch below leaving Hollywood for prison. There's no coming back from teaching.)

"We have to play the game," Trevor said as we drove to Malibu. "GT's bringing all his adopted kids. Brad's bringing the photogenic ones. Everyone's coming."

My father had brushed it off and told me to tell Pep to have fun with Mariana Grande. And he told me to be good. I promised I would try. Couldn't be that hard. *Could it?*

I backed into the famed playwright turned screenwriter who watched in misery as his kids ran screaming in the grass. Beyond the pool, the ocean glimmered, liquid butterfly wings.

We stood shoulder to shoulder, one big sigh.

"What are you doing here?" I finally asked.

"Networking," he said, lowering his broad head.

Gray stubble covered most of his face. Prickly genius, then.

"Do you know where Ariana is?" I asked, realizing I hadn't seen the Pixie Queen.

"What's that?" he asked.

I grabbed a kale Bellini from a passing tray and gulped it down, then realized I'd lost track of Pep.

Pep wasn't lost, but she was lost. It's not as though she'd wandered down one of the trails into the ocean (I think) or onto PCH (I'm pretty sure). Pep was a smart kid, but not street-smart. None of our kids were—they'd never even learned to cross a street by themselves.

I followed the smell of burning meat into the vast kitchen. Staff members in bleached white uniforms buzzed around, preparing food.

"Anyone here see a girl, red hair, tall for her age, sour expression, her mom's wry sense of humor?" I asked.

"Check the screening room," a woman said. "The girls always end up there."

This house had more hidden rooms than a brothel. I opened a door at the bottom of a long, narrow staircase and was overcome, strangled by the smell of strong, expensive, Malibu weed. I waved at the fumes. The screening room was black, the only light coming from a blond actress screaming in some awful horror film flickering on the big screen.

"Pep?"

I heard giggling.

"Pep? Are you in here?" I tried to focus.

"Pep, are you in here?" a squeaky voice mimicked mine. Know this: My voice is not and has never been squeaky. I'm pretty sure.

"Mom, I'm fine."

I felt along the fabric-covered wall and flicked on the light.

"Mom," Pep said, "we're just hanging out."

Pep was seated in the middle of a group of older kids. Teenagers. Mostly boys with greasy hair and squirrely expressions.

"We're going *now*," I said, gritting my teeth.

"Why?" she asked.

"She doesn't have to go," a boy with a sideways smile said. He looked about fifteen. "Party's just beginning."

"I'm her mother," I said. "I say she has to go."

"Well, this is my house," he said, standing. "I think she should stay."

"You may talk to me that way," I said, "exactly never."

"You can't say that to me," he said, slurring. "Do you know who my moms are?"

"I just did say it. What're you going to do, cry to your mommies?" I said. "Pep. Get up. Now. Before I lose my composure all over this screening room."

Pep rose, slowly, stepped down the side, and slunk past me, glaring at me.

"So uncool," the boy said. His friends murmured approval.

"Well, that's one thing you've gotten right today," I said.

"Pep?" he said.

"Yeah?"

"See you soon," he said. And winked.

I dragged Pep out of the house, down the lawn, up the driveway, all the way to valet parking.

"I never even got to see Ariana!" Pep wailed, tears streaming down her freckled face.

That's when I realized Ariana wasn't there. And I knew Trevor would deny he'd ever told her she was.

Word spread even before the hunt was over. Trevor wouldn't speak to me on the way home. I had done the unthinkable. I had criticized Hollywood progeny. I might as well have pushed my entire family out onto an ice floe in the middle of the climate-warmed Pacific where we'd be eaten by . . . kelp?

The rules when it came to Hollywood offspring: 1. They were "charming," not rude. 2. They were "creative," not too soft and stupid for public school. And, 3. They were "stunning," not "I've seen better features on an elephant seal."

Margaritas: The Glue That Held Our Marriage Together, Sort Of:

Our first date was an accidental lunch; he'd been sitting at my table at Peroni's by mistake and stayed. Our second date, at Rosalinda's, was done by the time we'd reached the bottom of our margaritas. They'd been delivered to us over ice in thick blue glasses with salt on the rim and small straws, and they were the most delicious margaritas I've ever tasted, which is why I've tried to replicate them ever since. Or maybe I was just trying to replicate the feeling of that night.

At some point in the conversation, Trevor stopped bouncing in his seat and kissed me. When I came up for air, I said, "You'd better be good."

Trevor and I tumbled through the entrance of his hotel suite, and he already had my (good) panties off and was giving me head before the door closed. He was the most exciting man I'd ever met, maybe the most exciting I'd ever spoken to.

Then there was his penis, famous in these parts. There'd been a whisper campaign for the best and biggest penis in Hollywood; his was in the top three (Liam N**son and Milton B*rle rounded out the rest). This wasn't my first dick rodeo; I'd experienced a comparison sample. Trevor's wasn't just smoke-and-mirrors huge, like the guys who Nair their pubes to make their dicks look like Louisville Sluggers. Trevor had washboard abs and a big dick, and he ate pussy. And he told funny stories and he laughed at my jokes, and to say he was perhaps a genius was no stretch. Here's the kicker—he was rich and successful and ambitious for more riches and more successes. I was just hoping to make a living writing, maybe own a bookstore someday and a cabin in Carmel;

my plans wouldn't get in the way of his ambitiousness. We shared sym-biotic futures—and *symbiotic* was *the* word that year.

After we fucked, we reclined, sex-hausted, on sheets that were more expensive than anything I owned, including my car. I gazed out the floor-to-ceiling windows overlooking the bay, and I heard him say, "I'm finally dating someone I can introduce to my friends."

I looked back at him and smiled. He looked so happy. So relieved.

I would have given him anything.

5

Marital Purgatory

Civil war had erupted in the dead zone. Pep was still not speaking to me. Her two-word sentences had devolved into hiccups and grunts. It was like living with a freckled pug. She ducked out of every room I entered, she turned her cheek when I said good night, and she refused to say goodbye when I dropped her at school.

"Totally normal," Liz said. "My older one didn't talk to me for three years. It was heaven. Give her time."

"How about a spanking? Can I give her that?" I asked. "Is spanking legal?" And then I thought of all the parents who'd be in prison when I was growing up. Spankings were handed out like participation trophies today.

Meanwhile, a battle had broken out (again) between Petra and the Triplets. The Triplets always blamed Petra for everything—the cracks in our marital (Easter?) egg, Pep's elbow psoriasis, their checks being a day late, drought. The first shot had been fired across the bow of the French doorway the moment Petra stepped through, cardigan buttoned to her chin on a warm, cloudless day, no makeup on her sallow skin, trailed by a cloud of thick perfume. The Triplets had weaved in and out of the living room during Petra's interview, eyes narrowed, whispering in Spanish, crows taking turns surveilling the nest.

"I told you don't trust her," Gabriela, leader of the apron squadron said, her eyes red, eyeliner smudged. "What I tell you?" When Gabi was ticked off, she'd sometimes punish me, her recalcitrant daughter, with angry silences, the evil eye, misplaced toilet paper. Once, I disagreed with her on the best baby carrot brand to feed Pep and I couldn't find toilet paper for a week.

"What happens to us?" Caster demanded, Lola clinging to her side like a wet tissue with eyes.

"Don't worry," I tell her. "Don't worry," I tell them all. The Triplets, Esteban the gardener, the blond kid with the ponytail and lingering pot scent who drops off orchids twice a month, the lesbian dog walker with shaved head and dimples, the part-time handyman who just had a baby. But I am worried. I wonder and hope that everyone here (well, everyone except Petra) will have a job once the marital dust settles. The only person not worried, by the way, is my decorator—a Hollywood divorce typically doubles business.

Playing cards were the latest weapon of mass distraction. Caster breathlessly pulled me aside one afternoon, waving playing cards at my nose. Caster, the Sexy Triplet, all full lips and bright smile and recent boob job, was going places. Mostly to the grocery store with that extra grand a week she was charging.

"*Las cartas*, they were in the light," she said, motioning skyward. "*En la cocina.*"

The kitchen light fixture.

"What were cards doing up there?" I shook my head. "Was someone cheating at poker?" Trevor held a monthly poker game when it was trendy, until all the Russians were deported.

"*Diabla*," she said. "*Verdes ojos!* She cursing you!"

"That's ridiculous," I said. I fingered the cards. Joker, queen, king . . .

"Missus, please," she said, grabbing my hands, her big hazel eyes pleading. I dropped the cards.

"I'll find out what happened," I said.

"Fire her, missus," she said, crossing herself and kissing the tips of her fingers. "Please, I beg you. Please."

I couldn't fire Petra, my Single White Nanny. It was too late. I knew it. Everyone knew it.

As Gabriela packed Trevor for his Farewell (to Me) Tour on a yacht with a Russian billionaire and several supermodel girlfriends, playing cards had multiplied like Kardashian pregnancies, dropped in my boots, shoved in a jeans pocket, tucked under my car visor.

"I have no idea what you're talking about, A-nus," Petra said, flipping her (my) layered haircut as she painstakingly organized Trevor's all black, all thin ties. I was living dangerously, breaching the blueprint, but I was feeling self-righteous.

"If you're trying to curse me, Petra, you're too late; I was cursed at birth," I said. "Also, it's Ag-nes, not A-nus." I flipped my hair back at her.

Soon after, I started to find crucifixes hidden all over the house. Crucifixes everywhere, like a bad vampire movie. Or recent vampire movie. Plaintive Jesus staring up at me from our silver drawer. Beatific Jesus hiding under my pillow. Gloomy Jesus snuggled in my coat pocket.

Hot Jesus stashed behind the toilet.

I cornered Caster as she was taking a break in the poolroom.

"*No sé*. Ask Gabriela." She tossed her hair and sauntered off with Pep's laundry folded in her arms. I tracked down Lola dusting the trophy case, but she ran for cover.

I sequestered Gabriela in the pantry, dwarfed by our stock of canned beans and soup, ketchup, dry pasta, and a nuclear holocaust stockpile of Fiji water. The pantry had a steel-reinforced, triple-bolted door—an agent had been hogtied and robbed inside his house a couple of years ago, and this one door made us feel safe. We could survive on ketchup and Fiji for at least a week while our house was being ransacked.

"Gabriela, what's with the crucifixes all over the house?" I asked. "I almost got stabbed this morning putting my Uggs on."

"*Lo siento*, missus, *no comprendo*," Gabriela fibbed and crossed herself.

"*Comprendes estes*," I said as I opened my hand, revealing the CVS pharmacy crucifix I'd discovered in my underwear drawer next to the scratchy lace bras Trevor had bought over the years that I never wore.

"You fire me, missus?" Gabi asked, her hand on her hip. Like I would *ever*.

"No, Gabi, no, of course not; I'm the one who's fired," I said. "Is this like an exorcism? *Para la casa?* Does this have something to do with the playing cards?"

"La Reina!" she said, grabbing my shoulders with her warm hands and staring me in the eyes. "Fight the black magic, missus! *Ay dios mio!*"

Oh no! *Ay dios mio?* Anytime Gabriela had to call on *"dios,"* trouble was around the corner.

Trevor marched out with Petra scurrying behind him, lugging his Louis Vuitton trunk. I waved goodbye at the kitchen window as Gabriela hummed and polished the counter to an impossible sheen. I watched Petra heave the trunk into the back of a waiting black SUV, drop it, then heave it again, while Gabriela gave a sharp laugh, then polished some more.

"Gabi. What did you pack in his trunk?" I asked.

"Something *muy especial*," she said with a Latina Cheshire cat smile. *"Un poquito maleficio . . ."*

"Gabriela . . ."

"I'll be in the laundry room, missus," she said as she walked away.

I'd forgotten I was hosting our monthly book club / trunk show. Karyn was selling her designer jewelry that no one wanted but everyone would buy. Out of fourteen wives, eleven had canceled.

"They're idiots," Liz said when I called her, gasping from her run up Temescal. "They're afraid they're going to catch divorce."

"Lip filler lemmings," I said. "I'd tell them to jump off a cliff into the Pacific, but we all know silicone floats."

I finished the last chapter of our designated novel (a multigenerational family saga set in the Burmese mountains in the winter of 1806, written by a queer-leaning Bangladeshi paraplegic), set up a cheese-and-cracker spread, wine, glasses, more wine, and a bowl of M&Ms on the deck, and screamed into the canyon, just for fun. I turned on music (Amy Winehouse / Deck). Gray dusk settled over the mansions that sat at the top of the hillsides, where the wealthiest of the Riviera inhabitants lived and pointed at the rest of us suckers.

Amy wasn't going to rehab.

I knocked on Pep's door. No answer.

No, no, no.

"Pep?" I said. "I bear M&Ms."

She opened the door a crack.

"Blue ones," she said.

"I have blue," I said. "May I enter?"

Pep stepped aside and let me in. Books were open on her desk, her backpack at her feet. My tween was so much more organized than I, but I had proof she was my daughter because of her freckles and the space between her front teeth. I relished memories of squirting water into boys' ears in third grade. Pep was almost my height, which was alarming, but as my dad had told me, the Scots Irish on his mother's side were big-boned ladies. According to family legend, they'd lifted a Dodge off their family dog (who lived).

Lucky, lucky Pep. So much to look forward to.

She sat back in her chair, pushing away from her desk until I was sure she'd fall backward and crack her skull.

"Can you help me with math?" she asked.

"Is this a test?" I smiled. "How long have you known me? My math acuity ended in third grade—second for you."

"I was doing long division in second."

"Then kindergarten," I said.

"Mom," she said. She rolled the eraser end of her pencil along her cheek. She paused, and I wanted to fill the space with a hug or just begging her to like me again. I couldn't imagine my dad ever having these thoughts, and maybe I was better off for it. His job was to feed us, make sure we did our homework (with no help, certainly no tutors), and make sure we got enough sleep. That was it.

"Do you think I'm pretty?"

"Pretty? You're beautiful!" I said.

"Mom, seriously," she said. "Do you think I'm pretty?"

"I *know* you're pretty. You're a beautiful, smart, funny girl."

"Like these girls?" she asked, showing me her phone.

"You're on Instagram?"

"Everyone is, Mom. Please, focus," she said. "Do you think I'll ever look like those dance girls?"

I stared at the phone. The dance girls looked like their dance moms, but in miniature. I needed to retire from this world.

"These tiny, filtered fairies?" I asked. "I mean, they're adorable. But you have a different look."

"Will I ever be adorable like them?"

"If you cut off your feet," I said.

"I have a pubic hair," she said.

Screech. Breathe through your nose, Agnes, breathe in through your nose and out your mouth,

"Are you sure?" My baby was barely eleven. *This is terrible,* I thought. *Menopause and puberty in the same house? At the same time?*

What kind of God . . .

"Mo-*om*," she said. "I know what a pubic hair looks like. Do you want to check?"

I shook my head until it almost came off. "No, honey, you're a smart girl. You know your own . . . body hair. I'm so sorry. I just think it's so soon."

"Half the girls in my class have underarm hair," she said. "Two are on their periods. I already looked it up. It doesn't mean I'm going to have my period."

"Oh my God," I said. "I can't . . ." I felt for the chair and sat down.

"Are you okay, Mom? It's just one little curly red hair," she said, and she gave me that sweet gap-toothed smile I hadn't seen in weeks. No wonder Pep was moody; she was hormonal. And add to that the divorce.

I wiped my eyes and sprang up, grabbing Pep and hugging her and resisting the urge to stuff her back into a Babybjörn.

The gate rang.

The air was just starting to chill as Juliette, Liz, and Karyn arrived in a blur of floral scents, evening sunglasses, soft pastels, and, in Liz's case, a tennis skirt, which she wore every day, in case a game ever broke out.

We were missing somebody.

"Where's Mystery Asian?" I asked, my synapses snapping to attention.

"Who?" Karyn asked, busily setting up velvet pads to display her jewelry line on the granite outdoor table.

"What do you mean, 'who'?" I asked. "The guy you bring to every brunch, lunch, and SoulCycle class. The guy you claim not to be screwing, but what else would you do with a limber hetero male with a twelve-pack and thick, hard thighs I hadn't noticed?"

"Oh, Kwan. Yeah. Your divorce," Karyn said. "It's difficult on him. He's so sensitive. He would literally die if Michael and I got divorced."

"Would he?" I asked, my sarcasm dripping onto the redwood deck.

"He'll be fine," Karyn said. "I'll tell him you asked about him."

"I didn't really," I said. "I don't know how I could care less."

"Did anyone read the book?" Liz asked. "I read thirty pages and then went into an Insta-spiral." An Insta-spiral is when you look at a girlfriend (or ex's) Instagram, then someone she tagged, then someone she tagged, and so on.

"I read the book," I said.

"How? How do you do that?" Liz asked.

"Do what?"

"Agnes, you always read the book," Juliette said, lying on a chaise with a sleep mask over her eyes. She appeared to be wearing a nightgown. Underwear? Not sure.

"Because . . . it's a book club," I said. "We're supposed to read the book."

"That's not what we do," Karyn said. "That's not how we operate."

"Take a break from overachieving," Juliette said. "It would help your marriage."

"Let's not all pile on at once," Liz said. "We can't blame Agnes for reading. Even if it's weird."

"Guys. I'm not overachieving anything," I said, taking a gulp of wine. "My life is this close to being rewritten. They're about to recast the lead with a Slavic newcomer."

"Who's going to buy these dazzling earrings? Just in time for the holidays!" Karyn asked, holding up a pair of layered gold hoop-upon-hoop earrings.

"What holidays?"

"Christmas, New Year's," she said, then added, "Rosh Hashanah . . ."

"Karyn, it's April," Liz said.

"I know," Karyn said, "but I spent too much this month on my chaise collection. They're French and important."

I sifted through her collection, peering at a pair of pink diamond studs.

"You've worn these," I said, examining them in my hand. "You've been wearing these for the past six months."

"Correction. Lovingly broken them in," Karyn said.

"We're not going to talk about the book at all," I said, "are we?"

"I didn't even buy it," Juliette said. "Books depress me."

"Enough about the book," Liz said to me. "Who've you hired?"

"What do you mean?"

"Your lawyer," she said. "Your divorce lawyer?"

"I don't have a lawyer," I said.

"You always have a lawyer, darling," Karyn said. "I've had a lawyer since the wedding. I *invited* him to the wedding."

"Trevor hasn't filed," I said.

"Interesting ploy," Liz said.

"We're so cool. This divorce might be the best thing that's ever happened to me," I said.

Welcome, Divorce Dream State, where all matter of uncoupling transpires smoothly as Gwyneth and Chris's silky unraveling.

"Trevor and I will go our separate ways but live blocks from each other and raise our happy, well-adjusted, brilliant child. Just like BenJen but without the phoenix tattoo."

"I wouldn't say no to a River Phoenix tattoo," Liz said.

Juliette pushed herself up and glared at me. I think. Sunglasses and Botox. "Trevor Nash, 2005's hottest bachelor, could've had anyone in this town, including me, and he chose you!" she said, wagging her finger. "Never forget that!"

The Dream State soundtrack scratched in the middle of the Go-Go's "Vacation" . . .

"With friends like you, how could I?" I asked.

"My marriage is hanging on by a string," Juliette said. "You're just throwing yours away."

"But I throw like a girl, so," I said, tossing another pit into the green abyss. I waited for the sound of water splashing. Nothing.

"You have to be proactive. Like me. I'm having my boobs done," Juliette announced. "When your husband is fucking around, that's what you do. You get your boobs done. And your vagina."

"Labia majora?" Liz asked. "Or the minor, insignificant labia?"

"My husband is on his way to Port Yacht-Fucking," I said. "And I'm not getting anything done. Unless you count eyebrows. And my cuticles pushed back. That's as much physical pain as I'm willing to endure for Trevor."

"I can't believe you won't fight for him," Juliette said. "I'm fighting like hell."

"By shoving silicone bags into your body and cutting off pieces of your vagina? That's not fighting; that's self-mutilation!"

"I know," she said, smiling and clapping her hands. "I'm going to look amazing!"

"We haven't had sex in so long, I've self-mutilated my clit," Liz said.

"Maybe Jordan's just screwing the nanny," Juliette said. "I could live with that, I guess. Marita's children are so much better behaved than mine."

"If you stopped calling your three-year-old a cunt, maybe she'd be better behaved," I said.

"God, she knows I'm joking!" Juliette said. "We sleep together in her crib. We couldn't be closer."

My phone started buzzing. I gazed at it through my wine filter and answered.

"Hello, New York City," I said, breathing in the cool evening air, the smell of the trees in the canyon. Trevor's house was nice. I'd miss it.

"How're you holding up?" my publisher growled.

"How or what?" I said. "I'm no longer holding up my husband's ego."

"I heard," he said. "Put the brakes on that. *Vanity Fair* wants to interview you."

"*Vanity Fair* the magazine?" I asked. "Hey, shouldn't you be asleep?"

"I never sleep. It's the book business. If you sleep, you could wake up and it's all gone. Poof."

"What does *Vanity Fair* want with me?"

"They want to send a reporter out to follow you around for a couple of days."

"My marriage is on the rocks," I said.

"So? I haven't spoken to my wife in years. We don't need to tell them," he said. "Their angle is . . . the power Hollywood marriage—screenwriter-slash-novelist married to the big producer. How does it work?"

"Power marriages run on batteries," I said. "If you took away everyone's vibrators, there'd be mass revolution."

The girls gasped.

"You need this article. Times are tough in Bookville. No one's selling like they used to. No one's reading like they used to. Have you ever considered hosting a YouTube channel?"

"Yes! A lifestyle channel," I said. "'Agnes's Spectacular Guide to Failing.' I'll invite people who've failed miserably—our advertisers will be firearms, funeral homes, and pharmaceuticals."

"Are you drunk?" he said. "Because that's not a bad idea."

"I can't do this interview," I said. "You want me to lie to a journalist."

"He'll call you first thing in the morning."

"Who is it?"

"Sid Glitch."

"Sid Glitch? The man who's decimated half of Hollywood?" I asked.

"I'll take that as a yes," he said before hanging up.

Sid Glitch was widely known as *Sid Bitch* (I know, way too easy), a bespectacled viper who used his laptop like a bomb, strafing Hollywood with shrapnel. Whoever said all publicity is a good thing had never been pricked by Sid Glitch's poison pen.

You're never alone living in a ten-thousand-square-foot "house." (I know; it's counterintuitive.) Because *staff.* Staff is everywhere you want to be; one can't fart without applause. No one "needs" a huge home. Wood and plaster and concrete monsters are built to impress "above-the-title" neighbors in construction one-upmanship; war with square footage as arsenal. Meanwhile, no one wins. Not you, not your kids, not the environment. Maybe, okay, maybe the gardener wins. What happens six months after you build a monstrosity to depress your friends? Someone you've never heard of—a Chinese widget manufacturer, say, or a guy who invented a dating app for dogs, starts construction on a fifty-thousand-square-foot home next door, and you're back in the fast lane of the self-loathing highway.

But you, like anyone else with more money than sense, build anyway. Because, like all of us, you have to learn the hard way. Then you hire a team of gardeners, housekeepers, a house manager (unless you want to make concrete tyrant a full-time job), a chef, a florist, a feng shui master. Every day, there are people coming in and going out, and half the time you have no idea who they are.

I binge-watched *Downton Abbey* recently, and I can tell you the tears the sisters cry are real. The housekeepers and gardeners and assistants get to leave to go home. The rest of us are surrounded by invisible trip wires.

6

Vanity Unfair

Lunch (along with Aquaphor) was the lifeblood of this town, especially at the frothy Bel Air Hotel. No one really ate—there were too many new diets and new rules—but it wasn't about the food. Lunch made people feel like they did something, like . . . work. Dinner was my style; dinner took place in dim lighting, after you *finished* a day of work. And lunch exposed all your weaknesses to sunlight—that zit you forgot to cover, your wine-stained teeth, the truth about your disintegrating marriage.

I looked presentable enough. Rolled-up jeans and heels, a Frankie & Eileen blouse and scarf. Nothing bad can happen if you wear a scarf; it's like garlic to vampires. I endured a blow-dry by the Romanian lady who scorched all the best tresses in town. She left my scalp with first-degree burns but could predict with Swiss precision accuracy whose Hollywood marriages were circling the marital drain. She had a nose for imperceptible changes in domestic protocol. If a laconic studio chief husband suddenly greeted her at the door with a rare smile, divorce was lurking around the corner. If a Hollywood wife came home from her hairstylist with bangs, she was having an affair. Either way, divorce was the bun in their marital oven.

"Bangs," she said. "Always bad sign." She crossed herself and spit.

I asked. She didn't have Xanax, but she knew where to get Mexican Quaaludes.

The air smelled like white oleander and Chanel suit jackets and red soles fresh out of the box. I spied Sid from across the restaurant, back stiff and chin up, with white tufted hair, like a dowager's favorite shih tzu. I could see his moleskin from here, out of hibernation, his Montblanc poised to rip *moi* a new one.

"I am not getting a divorce," I said, repeating a mantra. "I am not getting a divorce, I am happily married, maybe a little separated by oceans and perhaps supermodel pussy, perhaps, but still, we're together, never happier . . ."

Sid lowered his vintage Ray-Bans and peered at me as I followed the floating Disney princess hostess to his table. Sid had worn all black, even a snug turtleneck, though the day was warm. (Every day was warm, until one afternoon at 2:00 p.m. in mid-November when Southern California suddenly froze.)

His flipper hand grasped his pen. He appeared not to have a functioning circulatory system. If I were playing Celebrity and had to choose a word to describe Sid, I would choose *tubercular.*

"What size are those jeans?" he asked, pouncing before the impala had a chance to approach the watering hole.

"Same size as yours," I said, sizing him up.

Not so fast, cheetah.

He smiled, his pallid features lighting up. "So what's your eating disorder?" He flicked on his tape recorder. Subtle as a knockout punch.

"Sid, I will eat you under the table."

"Oh, I never eat during lunch interviews. It softens me up." His blue eyes glittered like rhinestones. He looked about as soft as a spike to the forehead.

The waiter appeared at our table. "Ready to order?"

"Is *Vanity Fair* paying?" I asked Sid.

"Of course," he said.

"I'll take one of everything," I said to the waiter and waggled my eyebrows at Sid.

"Let's start with a typical day," Sid said, his eyes flicking toward my french fries. His nose twitched as their aroma reached his nostrils.

"Eat the fries, Sid," I said, pushing the fries toward him.

"I don't want the fries, Agnes," he said. "Start from the beginning."

I shoved three more fries in my mouth.

"Let's see," I said as I chewed. "Born. Lived. Worked. Wrote. Lived some more. Wrote more. Married. Wrote. Gave birth. Wrote."

I was a lifelong creature of habit. Until the moment Trevor declared he wanted to be happy. Now, I felt dangerous. Something had happened to me, something I didn't quite expect. Anything was possible!

I smiled, my face relaxing. *Dangerous* Agnes!

"Sid, why interview me?" I said. "Matthew McConaughey must be doing something pretty magical right now."

"You weren't my first thought," he said, dry as a martini. "When my editor mentioned one of the 'queens of Hollywood,' I was hoping for Corrigan Lewin's wife. I hear she's a former hooker, no?"

"Her hourly rate was so high he had to marry her," I said.

He scribbled in his notebook.

"Why the hell did I bother getting blow-dried?" I asked, taking a sip of iced tea. "You don't want to write this, and I don't want to be write-ed."

Sid leaned back and stared at the white beams above us.

"I've just endured the worst breakup of my life," he said.

"Someone broke up with you?" I asked. "Shocking."

"At this point, all I'm interested in is vitamin D."

"Dick."

"Sunshine. It's cold as a witch's tit in New York," he said, eyeing my fries again. "So. You're married to Trevor Nash," he said, staring at me. "And yet, you seem to have sculpted out your own career, as it were."

I wished I hadn't ordered that bottomless iced tea. I needed to pee *now*.

"It's a survival instinct," I said. "In case I ever needed to escape."

How long could I live on the fight-or-flight response? My adrenaline would run out someday. I'd need more. *Can you buy adrenaline on Amazon Prime?*

My phone buzzed as Sid jotted down more notes. What an honor, to have one's obituary written under the byline of Sid Glitch, Queen of the Takedown.

Trevor's smile flashed on my screen.

"Answer it," Sid said. "I'd love to talk to Trevor."

"He'd love to talk to you!" I dropped the phone on the marble tile, then kicked it away. The buzzing stopped.

"Call him back; maybe it's important," Sid said, staring down his long, thin nose. That nose was good for smelling out weaknesses like a truffle pig. Sid had his nose all up in my fungi. *The least fun guy in my fungi.*

I thought, *How gay, exactly, is Sid?* In LA, sexuality existed on a sliding scale. I clocked Sid at a solid cocksucking eight. Meaning, he'd been in vagina at least once more than birth.

My phone buzzed again. I'm glad I had rethought changing Trevor's ringtone to a dirge.

"Trevor!" I said as I grabbed the phone, mania in my voice. "I'm sitting here with Sid Bi—*Glitch*."

A torrent of sweat, the Nile of nervous perspiration, soaked the back of my shirt.

"Who?" Trevor yelled.

"He's great," I said. "He's asking about you, for the article."

"What?" Trevor asked. *"What article?"*

"Yeah, I'm really pleased," I said. "We're talking about writing, and, you know, that carpool life."

"Sid Glitch from Vanity Fair?*"*

"Silly, I know you're excited," I replied as Sid leaned in. "We talked earlier, remember, about how they wanted to do an article ... about me?"

It sounded ludicrous, even to my ears.

"Jesus Christ, I'm having a stroke! Petra, fucking stop rubbing my fucking shoulders!" Trevor gasped. Back to me. "You want me to have a stroke? Graydon hates me!"

"Did he say Graydon hates him?" Sid asked, raising an eyebrow.

I shook my head and covered the phone. "He said, 'Graydon amazes me,' Sid. So sorry he's gone! You should get your hearing checked, maybe?"

I pushed the fries closer to him.

"Trevor, I'll see you when you get home," I said into the phone. "Be safe!" I hung up. Why did I say that? Why?

"Will you excuse me?" I said to Sid.

"Safe from what?" I heard him say as I hopped toward the bathroom. I called Trevor from the stall.

"Waitwaitwait, so it's like, they're doing one of those ... little paragraph thingies, like a sentence," he said, dialing his crazy down to nine.

"No, it's more like, um ..." I hesitated, anxious to protect his male ego by throwing myself on it, like a live grenade. "It's a, how do you say ... a spread?"

He was breathing, but I could tell his soul had died. "What, you mean, like a page ..."

"Or three ... maybe five, depending."

He swallowed hard. I imagined his Adam's apple bobbing in his long, lean neck. I hoped Pep would have that neck someday (without the apple). Pep had the Murphy neck—less like a swan's and more like a toad's. *It's fine.*

"Trevor?" He seemed to have dropped off.

"I can't . . . well, that's, um." He sighed. "Talk to Jennifer." Jennifer was his VP at the company. His consigliere. Brought home a six-figure income and knew where all the bodies were buried—and had probably buried a few. "She'll tell you what to say and what not to say."

"I prefer to go in cold," I said.

"Are you crazy? Have you not heard of Mark Canton?"

"Who?"

"Exactly!" he said, on the verge of hysteria. "Hey, Idiot Number Three, get Jennifer on the line—now!"

"I don't need Jennifer to tell me what I do in my daily life," I said. "I'm well versed in my routine." I held the phone away from my head as expletives flowed like a spittle waterfall. "Trevor, why did you call me?"

"This ocean is bullshit!"

"The Mediterranean?" I asked.

"You made me go here! This is your fault!"

"What?"

"I was unhappy because of you, so I left and now I'm unhappy again," Trevor said.

"Trevor, you are on a yacht in the middle of the ocean with rich, beautiful people—except for the one," I said. "If you're going to blow up our marriage, fucking enjoy it."

"I can't . . ." He paused.

"You can't what?"

"You know," he said quietly.

"No, I don't," I said. Sid was probably going to send the hostess in to look for me. I'd just tell him I'm bulimic. *Too common?*

"I can't . . ." Trevor lowered his voice. "My dick isn't working."

"Oh!" I said, shocked at this new turn of events. I covered my mouth to keep from laughing. I did a little tap dance. The Trevor I know could get it up in gale-force winds. *Maleficio*. A curse! Why, Gabi, you little minx . . .

"It's your fault!" Trevor said. "I'm stressed out!"

"Maybe it's Petra's fault."

"I'm not fucking Petra," he said.

"You're not fucking anyone, apparently."

"You can't do this interview," he said as I heard the restroom door swing open and the *tippy tap* of expensive heels. "Don't you see? This is all about me. This is all about getting back at me for leaving the party early!" I thought back to that *Vanity Fair* party. South African theme, green, red, and black tablecloths. A wiry African band playing tin instruments. In my mind's eye, I saw Monica Lewinsky dancing with Shiloh Pitt. Or was it Maddox? We'd left at 12:48 a.m.; we'd stayed seven hours.

"I'm wearing him down," I said. "Get to know me before you hate me, right?"

"Trust me," he said, "I know!"

"I hope you get dick scurvy!" I hissed, then hung up and pushed open the stall door into a #daytimedrinker, a straw-haired beaver three deep in gin and tonics, dripping in gold.

"And how is Trevor?" She burped.

"Under the weather," I said. Only Trevor could make a yacht trip on the Mediterranean into an ordeal. *Now that*, I thought, *is a talent*.

"Sorry about your divorce," she said. Never believe an apology within a ten-square-mile radius of Paramount.

"Sorry about your veneers," I said, wiping my hands and tossing the towel in the fancy basket under the sink.

Dr. Izzy's office called just as we were heading to my childhood home. Sid wanted to see the touchstones of my youth. I could show him my first sexual harassment corner (I was maybe nine), the house that had all the gypsies, the apartment with the five-foot bong centerpiece in the living room, the duplex with the Armenian kid who ran over his own grandfather with his brand-new Camaro.

"Can you come now?" Izzy's receptionist was asking. I glanced at Sid, chewing his ragged fingernails like a wild and anemic animal. "We had a last-minute cancellation."

"Change of plans," I said, whipping the car around and swiping sweat off my forehead. Hot flashes felt like a roller coaster diving through a pool of salt water. Not to get too sexy. (Let's not mention the chin hair I found in the bathroom mirror. I don't want to mention the chin hair. Why would I mention chin hair?)

At the end of this "passage," I'd look like a female Danny DeVito, without the career.

Izzy would save me.

"Are you under stress?" Izzy asked. He was adorable, a tiny doll of a man with a thick Israeli accent. He had a medical diploma from Tel Aviv University on the wall, so I guessed he was legit. Did I care at this point? No.

"No more than usual," I said, then started to cry.

He jotted down a note, then pushed a box of Kleenex toward me.

"Are you . . . more emotional? Quicker to anger?"

"Why would you say that?" I snapped.

He jotted. I sniffed.

"Your period has stopped?"

"Not yet; I just bought a sixty-pack of Tampax," I said. "Not to brag."

"Do you want to keep menstruating, even when your period stops? We can do that for you."

"What? No! Is that a thing? I don't want to be eighty years old stuffing a tampon up my—I'm not even sure I'll know where it is. My God,

I'm closer to eighty than twenty. How, how did this happen? I was just in high school, making out with Taylor Minkowski with the neck hair."

He ripped a prescription from his pad and patted me on the hand.

"Dahlink," he said, "I would get that filled right away."

Sid was in the waiting room, along with several elderly women on manufactured periods. Kotex should market a pad just for grandmothers. (Jot this down.)

"I've got to get this filled," I said.

"Now?"

"Now, okay, right now," I said, spitting it out.

Prescription finally filled after intermittent tears to the pretty Pakistani pharmacist who said it might take an hour. I was rubbing estrogen cream onto my butt cheek in the CVS bathroom within fifteen minutes. Meanwhile, Sid had given up on exploring my childhood home and wanted to head straight to the belly of the beast, the dead zone. I'd texted Gabriela to take up the tape Coliti-Girl had laid down, dividing our rooms.

We curved up our empty street, and I could see the driveway was blocked by an Eldorado. I felt the hairs on my neck stiffen.

No, I thought. *Not today. Not tomorrow. Definitely not this week.*

Not this lifetime?

We drove up behind the Eldorado. A slender, golden figure with cornrows in her white girl hair, wearing cutoffs and a tank top, was standing outside the car, talking into the intercom, gesturing, her silver rings throwing the sun's rays. An almond-skinned dude at the butt end of a lit cigarette, wearing worn nylon track pants, black horsetail to his hip, was slumped outside the passenger side. His stance told me he was bored and, probably, because he'd driven from whatever dirt patch hours away with this she-demon, at his very last breath of patience.

"What the devil?" Sid said, giving a low whistle. "Do you know these people?"

"Not for public consumption," I said with a dash of salt.

I hit the horn. Fin whipped around, squinting, her mouth in a kittenish snarl, bearing those straight white teeth. Her skin glowed the color of our favorite glazed doughnuts we'd scarfed as kids, her streamlined body every yoga guru in town coveted but couldn't achieve, not even with fasting and raw food and poop tea.

Prison looked good on her, but so did everything else.

"That's Fin," I said. "My sister."

"You just got interesting," Sid said.

"Sid," I said with a decades-old sigh, "you have no idea."

"For your birthday," Fin said as we stared at the Tiffany clock she'd positioned on our Steinway grand in the drawing room, an expensive piece of furniture with keys that no one played, like the art on our walls no one appreciated. A Warhol, a Richter, an Ed Ruscha. Nice, expensive, neglected objects. *Like Hollywood wives.*

I'd moved Sid, against his myriad and creative objections, into the kitchen and instructed Caster to secure him by plying him with her smile and signature pigs in a blanket. Sid had to be starving after pretending he didn't want to eat and driving around for hours.

"My birthday was months ago," I said.

"Okay, it's a thank-you gift," Fin said. "For bailing me out." She adjusted the clock. I glanced through the picture window at her Native American boyfriend smoking a cigarette by the pool while Pep stood over him, glaring and waving her hand in front of his face. In the Riviera, like all of the Westside, smoking was equivalent to murder, maybe worse. Pep had been fully indoctrinated into the smoking Gestapo.

I'd forgotten, in all the divorce excitement, that Fin had depleted my bank account yet again. I thought about my last conversation with Jake Your Friendly Neighborhood Bail Bondsman (on speed dial).

Fin tapped her ankle monitor. "You like my new jewelry?"

"I forgot all about your shit," I said. "My own shit has taken precedence."

"We're on our way to visit Dad," she said.

"I don't think he's talking to me," I said. "I had to skip Easter this year."

Fin walked over to the trophy case glass. "Hey, can I hold the Oscar?" she said. "Take a picture?"

"It's locked. I don't even know where the key is."

Fin leaned in, slid her finger over the lock. "Hey, bud, hey," she said to Oscar. "They got you all locked up in there, huh?"

"He can't hear you," I said.

"How do you know?"

"How do I know what?" I asked.

"Dad's not talking to you," she said. "If you don't talk to him, how do you know?"

"Don't confuse me," I said. "I'm under a lot of emotional strain."

"Okay, princess," she said, raising her calloused hands in defeat.

"I can't take the clock," I said.

"She fits your big ol' Steinway," she said as she dropped onto the satin piano seat and slowly ran her fingers along the keys. Shocking to hear the room filled with music, as though we'd invited in a live tiger.

"If it's stolen, I could get in a lot of trouble, Fin," I said. "I can't afford trouble."

"Rich people don't get into trouble," she said, closing her eyes as she finished "Für Elise" and leaned into "Stairway to Heaven." Fin would sit for hours at the standup piano our grandmother had given us, working out pieces by ear. No sheets, no teachers we couldn't afford. Just Led Zeppelin and Beethoven, battling it out.

I pictured Sid, who probably had his ear on the swinging door between the kitchen and drawing room.

"Come on. Did you . . . steal it?" I asked, keeping my voice low as I slid next to her; her hips took up barely any space on the piano seat.

"No," she said. Her eyes opened, then closed again, her body swaying with the music.

"Did someone else steal it?"

She rocked back and forth as her fingers danced, her white trash homage to Robert Plant and Jimmy Page and misspent youth.

"Fin," I said. "Finley."

Last stanza. I looked outside. Pep was now engaged in serious conversation with the boyfriend, whose cigarette now hung limp from his mouth, unlit. *Why didn't she talk to me like that? What could they be talking about?*

"An antique shop owner gave it to me in a trade," she said. "I owe you. I pictured it right there, on that spot, last night. I dreamed it."

"Could you maybe dream about not going to prison again?"

"Pep doesn't recognize me," she said matter-of-factly as we watched Pep's expression dissolve into a laugh.

"I'm lucky she recognizes me," I said, batting away the moment. "She barely looks up when I talk to her."

"Can I get some gas money?" Fin asked, taking her long fingers off the keys. "We had enough to get here, but not to get back. Maybe something for Denny's, too."

"You don't have to eat at Denny's," I said. "I have food."

"I like Denny's. When I was inside, I can't tell you how many times I ordered that Rootin' Tootin' breakfast in my head."

"Sausage or bacon?"

"Sausage, c'mon, sis," she said, eyeing me. "So. That reporter dude. How long has he been off the stuff?"

"What, Sid?" I asked, "You guys barely met. Caster's running interference."

"He's a tweaker," Fin said.

I blinked. "No way, no, I don't believe it. He's heartbroken. He just had a major breakup."

"He broke up with Mr. Meth," she said.

I thought about Fin's "entrepreneurial" work in San Bernardino; she'd set up labs in various trailers, each one a boyfriend's domicile. I called her Breaking Badass. She preferred Breaking Bitch.

"Never question the master," Fin said, then dove into Elton John and Bernie Taupin's "Tiny Dancer," and I felt a tug in my chest, primal and urgent.

"How much you need?" I said as I wiped my nose.

"Who've we cast?" I was hitting my stride on the elliptical between breaks every few minutes. Liz and I were planning a girls' night dinner for Sid's benefit. If the tweaker was going to bury me, I wanted to be in full hair and makeup, surrounded by friends and photogenic strangers.

"Juliette, a.k.a. Stripper Tits," Liz said into the speaker. "She's introduced her new breasts at lunch at Citron, in a carpool at Briarwood. Oh, she's having trouble sitting, but she's ready to unleash the new-and-improved vagina in a few days."

"Karyn's coming, not sure about Kwan, apparently still reeling from my marital un-status," I said. "Oh, has Juliette decided her kid's gender yet?"

"The baby appears to be the bearer of what we call a *vagina*, but we'll wait and see."

"Looking forward to the gender reveal party at forty," I said, willing myself to elliptic once more.

"We invited the actress who just released her memoir about her evil stage mother," Liz said.

"The new momoir," I said. "Perfect."

I stepped off to catch my breath. If you exercise three minutes a day, how long before you're in shape? Death?

"I'm not serving alcohol," I said.

"What? Why not?"

"I don't want any glitches from my bitches," I said. "This isn't *Real Housewives.*"

"Well, it ain't real life," Liz said. Right as usual.

Liz grabbed me right before dinner as I toggled between music choices on the home system—*Soul or reggae? Soft classical or soft rock? Sitar or acid?* I chose Adele; Adele's like a white T-shirt—she goes with everything.

"Karyn's. Fucking. Jordan." Liz said in a panic.

"She's fucking inside the circle?" I said. "You never fuck inside the circle!"

"It's the ultimate breach; it's terrible," Liz said. "And also, ew, why? Why Jordan? He looks like . . . a Jordan!"

"How did you find out?"

"She downed a bottle of honesty rosé at home," Liz said. "She blurted it out while we were in the bathroom adjusting her personality."

"Juliette's going to smother her."

"Juliette's out of it . . . she's in love with the 'PercoCo'," Liz sang, misquoting the O.T. Genasis song, "Oh, and apparently, that hot *Vanity Fair* photographer."

I glanced toward the bar. Juliette was hovering over the photographer, one butt pinch away from a sexual assault lawsuit. The doorbell rang, and the rest of our party showed up, including Sid, who sneaked in last, circles under his eyes, wearing head-to-toe black, a human misery tree with a sprinkling of angst.

"Sid," I said, greeting him as Liz fluttered by toward Juliette. "Dressed for my funeral? Let me get you a pomegranate faux-tini." I remembered what Fin said about his possible drug use. Could I use that information somehow?

I shook my head. I'd been in Hollywood too long.

"Missus," Gabriela pulled up behind me, "I need to talk to you. Caster, she not feeling good. She has to go home."

Caster was supposed to be serving.

"What's wrong?"

She pinched her lips together and looked off to the side. "The chef," she said. "They did . . . they, how you say, the thing."

"What thing? Oh!" Luis, our chef, had a web tattooed on his elbow, slicked-back hair, inky bun settled at the nape of his neck. And, oh, what a great nape. He was trouble with a capital whisk. But such good sauces! Caster had already gotten to him, beating out all the women at my dinner party willing to throw their hats (and La Perla panties) in the fling ring.

"They fighting," Gabriela said.

I heard a glass shatter. I closed my eyes in silent prayer.

"Can he still cook?" I asked.

Gabriela nodded. "He very fast."

"Apparently," I said as another glass shattered and Gabriela rushed back into the kitchen. I rubbed my hands together and headed into the war zone.

Caster's wailing during the salad course hit the same pitch as Mariah Carey giving birth, so I decided to let her go for the night—after I rubbed her back and dried her tears and admonished her not to screw anyone else I brought into the household.

"Not Esteban?" she asked, choking through tears as we sat on the Victorian daybed in Pep's room. Esteban, the gardener, wore a cowboy hat and boots, and now I understood why he displayed a swagger unusual in the massive Westside gardening industry.

"Sleeping with men in their twenties is a no-no," I said. "Every friend of mine that's done it regrets the extra gyno appointments and vaccines. Besides, he's young enough to be your—"

"My what?" Her tears dried instantly.

"Nephew?"

Caster was ten years older than she looked. Black don't crack and brown don't frown.

"Just wait, Missus Añes," she hissed. "When you divorce, you'll see."

"I'm going to sleep with Luis the Teenaged Chef?" I asked.

"Don't judge," she said, shaking her finger.

We'd rounded third base into the dessert course. Luis, a fresh bandage over his eye, was torching the crème brûlée, bringing the sugar to a crisp brown. The house smelled like vanilla.

"Never sleep with a Salvadoreña," he muttered. "The hotter they are, the crazier."

"Duly noted," I said. "Don't bleed on the crème brûlée."

He pressed the bandage, checked his fingertips.

"You want me to serve?" Luis asked.

"I'll do it," I said. "Let's get this party over with. I want to get back to my bubble."

One of the girls we invited for decorative purposes (blond, vacuum-packed, perky) described her rehab affair during a Promises Malibu stay-cation with an actor named Christian she could've sworn was Bale but later discovered was the diminutive, less-but-still-talented Christian.

"One of them is a Jewish Christian," Liz pointed out. "I love that."

"How could you not know?" I asked the human décor. I set down the crème brûlée in front of Sid. His knees shook under the table. He hadn't cracked open his moleskin in the last half hour.

"You okay?" I asked, nudging his shoulder.

"Fine," he said, then coughed. He wasn't fine. He was hanging on by a pharmaceutical thread.

"If you need a little 'put-me-down,' check Juliette's purse," I murmured. "The girl with that new vagina smell."

"Put-me-down?"

"Instead of a pick-me-up," I said, then moved on. I placed a dessert in front of the actress. Then Karyn. Finally, Juliette. I glanced at my watch. Fifteen more minutes, max. Fifteen minutes and the trial would be over to make way for new trials. My insides danced in beat to Duffy.

I've pulled it off, I thought. A dinner party and no mention of my upcoming divorce. I was almost safe, sliding into home base.

"You want my crème brûlée?" Juliette asked Karyn.

"No, thanks, love," Karyn said. "I couldn't eat another bite."

"I insist," Juliette said, pushing her dessert across the table in front of Karyn.

Karyn pushed it back. "No, thank you, sweetie."

"Take it," Juliette said, tilting her head and smiling. "You took my Jordan, so why don't you take my dessert, too?"

She picked up the crème brûlée and flung it at Karyn's head. Karyn, with the reflexes of a home-wrecking cat, ducked, the crème brûlée shattering all over Trevor's Warhol on the wall behind her.

"Oh, shit," Liz said, her head in her hands.

"I was so close!" I said, smacking the table.

The crème brûlée slithered down Mr. Warhol's handiwork.

"You're crazy!" Karyn screamed at Juliette, who scrambled across the table and lunged at Karyn with her dessert spoon. Karyn bobbed and weaved.

"Yes, I'm crazy!" Juliette screamed. "You're fucking my husband!"

"Why do you care?" Karyn said, warding off the spoon, the earrings she'd tried to sell me flashing angrily. "All you do is complain about poor Jordan; you should be thanking me!"

Juliette leaped onto Karyn, both of them rolling on the Turkish rug, Karyn girl-punching Juliette's new breasts as Juliette cried out in agony.

"Stop!" Liz said, jumping into the fray.

"Juliette! You're going to lose a stitch!" I said. "Karyn, stop!"

In the corner of my eye, I spied Sid slipping away with Juliette's purse.

The girls rolled around. Screaming, spitting while Otis Redding played, poor Otis. I settled back in my chair, self-soothing through crème brûlée. Luis ran in from the kitchen, took one look, and circled back out. The hot photographer clicked away. Surely, this was excellent use of the Pulitzer he'd won for his Iraq War coverage.

Sid slunk back into the room, stepping over the melee, and sat next to me, plucking my spoon from my hand and finishing off my crème brûlée.

"This little affair cost you a cool million," Sid said, tilting his head at the Warhol. Gabriela ran out and started dabbing at the painting with a wet towel.

"Stop!" Sid screamed, snatching the towel from her hand.

The momoir actress grabbed a chair and huddled next to Sid. "Did I tell you my mother fucked my husband? It's all in my memoir, out yesterday, chapter 3, page 78."

None of us had noticed car lights circling the sycamore, nor the slam of the French church door.

"What is going on?!" I heard someone yell.

Liz had Juliette in a choke hold. Karyn was backed up against the fireplace, fanning herself with a napkin.

I scraped my dessert before looking up. Trevor Nash had materialized at the foot of the table, his mouth agape, his alert hazel eyes slowly comprehending, but the words, the words still unformed . . . maybe I should fetch his vocabulary cards?

"Trevor!" I launched from my seat, knocking my chair backward. "Do you know Sid? Have you two met?"

"My ... my Warhol ... ," Trevor said, choking sounds emerging from his throat. I dragged a chair over.

"Someone grab a water!" I said.

"Tequila," Trevor said, whimpering as I sat him down.

"Tequila!" I yelled, and Sid made a beeline for the bar.

"Now, Trevor," I said, taking him by his square shoulders and looking him in the eye. "I can't explain."

7

Mirage Counseling

W ho wants to start?" Dr. Erskin, who had the appearance of an eel that lived ten thousand feet below sea level, assessed us over his wire-rim glasses.

I was pressed into one end of his sticky leather couch; Trevor was seated at the other end, his knees migrating into the middle cushion.

"I yield the floor," I said.

"Go ahead, you go," Trevor said, pitching the therapy ball to my court.

"You called the session," I said, holding a gritty smile.

Welcome to marriage and family counseling, the last refuge of marriage refugees. Trevor took a deep breath before laying out his listicle of demands, which he read from a folded piece of paper; I imagined Number Three had typed them up.

I thought of all the couples I knew who'd tried marriage counseling . . .

Shelly and Grover: divorced.

"I want sex more often," Trevor said. "This would be good for my cortisol levels. My naturopath says my adrenals are shot."

Terry and Michele: separated for two years.

"I feel like I'm not being heard," Trevor said. "Aggie just doesn't care."

Mark and Liam: divorced.

"Look, maybe I shouldn't have relied so much on the . . . our assistant," Trevor said, "but it's like I was confused, you know? Like, she was more of a wife than my wife; she knows where all my best socks are."

Carrie and Brett: suicide/widowed.

How about all the marriage and family therapists who were divorced, separated, confirmed bachelor/ettes? Or the Beverly Hills shrink who hired hookers to keep her marriage together? *The couple that screws hookers together stays together, amirite?*

"Agnes?" The doctor stared at me, his baby mustache twitching.

In LA, therapy detritus was like nuclear fallout—widespread and everlasting. I shook my head.

"You seem to have an opinion," Dr. Erskin said, who overprescribed all the best actors, directors, and screenwriters in town. More than one Oscar winner owed his overdose to Dr. Erskin.

"Why did you laugh?" Trevor said. "See that, Doc? She doesn't take anything seriously, not even our marriage."

"Did you listen to Trevor?" Dr. Erskin asked, a look of concern on his face.

"You're so punishing," Trevor said.

I was speechless, but I managed to spit out, "If I were punishing, you wouldn't be breathing."

"Do you hear that, Doc?" Trevor said. "She talks ghetto."

"Are you sorry, Trevor, for taking a vacation with your house assistant?" the doctor asked.

"We call her our *majordomo*," Trevor said. *Majordomo* was the latest accessory for every "name" in Hollywood. "And I really just needed her for companion sleeping. So even though I'm totally, 100 percent innocent, I apologize."

"Agnes, do you hear him?"

The AC unit whined. I shivered. I wasn't a perfect person. I certainly wasn't a perfect wife. I was tired all the time. I fantasized about Trevor's (relatively painless) death. I flirted with Luis. I thought about doing jump squats on that popular yoga instructor, the Westside moms' human trampoline.

"Do you hear Trevor?" the doctor was asking. "He said he's sorry."

I cleared my throat. "Yes," I said. I felt like Michael Corleone in *Godfather III. Just when I thought I was out, they pull me back in.* I made an enraged yet despondent Al Pacino face.

"Are you sure you didn't *sleep* with Petra?" I asked.

"I don't screw where I shit," Trevor said. "I was on the yacht in the middle of the ocean and I realized I was still unhappy."

"You were probably seasick," I said. "You know how you get."

"You know me so well," Trevor said. "Anyway, I can be unhappy in my own bed, right, Doc?"

"So you didn't fuck Petra," I said.

"If I'm going to fuck someone, it's going to be above the line, okay? I'm not an animal." (Above the line in film: basically, the movie star. Below the line: basically, everyone else.) Trevor had standards. Bad ones—but still. Standards.

"But you have to admit that you haven't been attracted to me for a while," Trevor said.

I hadn't considered my part in this breakup. Even at 5 percent, it was still glimmering and alive. *He's right,* I thought. Maybe, subconsciously, I was trying to hand him over—*Here, you take him; I'm up to my ears in actual child.*

"She told me you said, 'If you can get him, you can have him.'"

Guilty as charged.

"That doesn't sound like me," I lied.

The doctor raised his untamed brow. Did he never look in the mirror and think, *Trim the hedges?*

"I like that you're talking," Dr. Erskin said. "Agnes, I can see what Trevor wants. Do you want to save your marriage?"

I wasn't sure. I wanted to be sure.

"It's already been at the bottom of the pool for five minutes. I don't think life support can save it."

"Well, I want to try," Trevor said, sliding his hand toward mine, his pinkie touching my pinkie like kids in a darkened movie theater. "What do you say?"

I swiveled toward him and held his gaze, trying to read his unique computer printout.

"I need to pee," he said, jumping up from the couch.

Dr. Erskin and I stared at each other for a few seconds. I heard the door to the bathroom close.

"Is this salvageable, this marriage?" I asked. "Is there any hope of us dancing together at Pep's wedding?"

"There's always hope," he said. "I like your sweater, by the way. Your breasts are the perfect size. Just enough to fill a champagne glass."

He winked. I hoped he didn't mean *champagne flute*, because picture *those* breasts. Trevor sat back down beside me, and I grabbed his hand. I recalled a conversation with Liz, when we were imagining possible future suitors. My list: Idris Elba, Warren Buffett, Obama, if he ever divorced Michelle, which he wouldn't. (Of course he wouldn't. She'd kill him.) That's when Liz said it. And she was right. She was always right.

"The grass isn't always greener," she'd said. "Sometimes it isn't even grass."

I didn't want to admit it to myself, but overnight, I was acting like a female cuckold, a woman scorned. I had a purpose in my life: to catch Trevor in a lie.

It was almost thrilling. Not "Starring Matt Damon as Jason Bourne" thrilling, but snooping on my husband did speed up my heart rate. Until Trevor left me with the cunning (cunting?) Petra, I'd never played the victim card. Now that I held it in my hand (or stuffed it in my

Goyard wallet), I was punching my victim card as though after ten uses I'd get a free macchiato. Better yet, I had a get-out-of-jail-free card in case I ever slipped off the marriage wagon into the arms of a tennis pro or trainer or dazzling Brazilian valet.

Hey, I had my excuse.

Of course, I'd never use it.

(Of *course* not.)

"Why not?" Liz asked. "Everyone cheats in this town."

"I don't want another man inside me," I said over Shawarma and couscous at one of the eight hundred Persian places in Westwood.

As befitting my new title, "woman scorned," I had become that thing I used to loathe. A sneak. Now, I understood why Juliette had been driving us insane with thoughts of egregious Jordan playing the field (the field being her best friend). Would I, too, go off the deep end and land on a plastic surgeon's table with the Rolling Stones playing in the background, my face bloodied to a pulp and my breasts the size of a honeydew?

"Have you guys started having sex again?" Liz asked.

"Yes," I said, properly ashamed.

"It doesn't feel . . . weird?"

"You mean, do I picture him with my former confidante? The woman who helped me raise my child? The woman who helped me raise my husband right out of the house? Even though they apparently weren't screwing?"

"So it's not bothering you at all," she said. "Good."

"He said he didn't sleep with Petra," I said.

"Men never lie," Liz said.

I'd been checking Trevor's phone while he showered, and I'd wake up to check it in the middle of the night while he slept. I sniffed his neck when we hugged, a truffle pig searching for eau de strange pussy. I counted and recounted the number of condoms in his travel bag.

(What were condoms doing in his travel bag?)

I'd swing by his office, marching past the pretty receptionist, down the side hall into his inner sanctum. I'd morphed into one of "those" wives—rich bitches with sour faces. I'd wondered why they looked so unhappy as they'd slide out of their Tesla SUVs in their distressed jeans—the only thing distressed about their lives. What could possibly be so wrong in their spoiled, coddled existence?

Well.

"Trevor and I came to the conclusion that divorce isn't the answer."

"It depends on the question," Liz said. "If the question is, 'Did your husband go on a cruise with a boatload of supermodels?' the answer might be divorce."

I dug into the hummus. Was Trevor sincere? He'd apologized in the therapist's office. He'd been behaving extra nice—almost uncomfortably so. He'd banished Petra from our home and never mentioned her name. Except for the house, the cars, the Triplets, and the credit cards, it almost felt like normal life.

My phone buzzed. Strange number. I looked at Liz.

"When you have kids, you answer," Liz said.

"Agnes Murphy," said a voice that sounded like a warm blanket on a chilly November afternoon.

"Who's this?"

"Gio Metz here," the man said. Gio Metz was a legendary director of the old school. Drugs, sex, rock and roll, and operatic gore. "I just read your latest, *The Deadlies*. I want to talk to you."

I rolled my eyes at Liz.

"Whoever this is, fuck off," I said. into the phone. "Gio Metz does not read trash."

I hung up.

Lucas, my book agent, called as I waited at the valet station. "Did you just hang up on Gio Metz?"

The valet handed me my keys and opened the door. His nameplate said *Tom*, but his smile said *Rodolfo*.

"That wasn't Gio Metz," I said.

"You do realize we don't have any traction on this book. You haven't done any publicity. I don't see you Instagramming or YouTubing or live-tweeting *The Bachelor*."

"Did Philip Roth live-tweet *The Bachelor*?"

"You're comparing yourself to Philip Roth."

"No, maybe, of course not," I said. "I hate *The Bachelor*—women crying over a stranger with horse teeth. Makes my second-gen feminist skin crawl."

"Will you please talk to him?"

"Gio Metz? Are you kidding? Of course."

"You know what? Don't. I'll call him. I'll set up a lunch."

"Fucking superlative," Trevor said (vocab word) when I told him I was planning lunch with Gio Metz. I was surprised. Metz was uncontrollable, a filmmaker who veered from in-your-face classics to catastrophic flops. Trevor emerged from a safer era of filmmaking. Metz's cronies were Scorsese and Coppola. Trevor's era sprouted guys who got really, really mad on Twitter.

"It is?" I was sort of hoping he'd be jealous. "I didn't know you were a fan."

"I'm not; he's insane," he said. "But I want him for *Motor City Hustle*. We'll make it a dinner. A double date."

Trevor had been trying to get a historic Detroit pimp project off the ground. Gio Metz was on the short list of directors. The script was a guaranteed Oscar nomination for the actor, like a syphilitic hooker role for an actress.

"He didn't say anything about a girlfriend," I said. I don't know why I said that. I do know why I said that. Because I thought, *Does Gio Metz have a girlfriend?*

"Metz?" Trevor laughed. "He always has a girlfriend."

I checked my phone. Lucas had called me with a time and place for lunch. I didn't call him back. The meal was already in the Trevor Hollywood machine, to be churned out the other end as something I didn't recognize.

For dinner, Trevor chose the overpriced tapas place with esoteric tequilas where he could get his corner table and favorite chair, facing out. When we arrived, Gio Metz's agent, enthusiastic wearer of gold chain bracelets and fan of convertible tans, was sitting in Trevor's chair. Markie K. appeared to be a few shots in. I'd say he was celebrating, but he celebrated like this every day, dodging DUIs like handball at the Jonathan Club.

Trevor stood at the table, vibrating, until Markie got the message.

"My bad. Keeping it warm for the king!" Markie said, jumping up and almost knocking the table over. Markie, with his bald pate and graying sideburns, still used the nickname his mother called him when he was six.

After everyone had calmed down from the near-tragic seating fiasco, Gio Metz appeared at the hostess stand, wearing his signature beat-up leather jacket and his larger-than-what's-acceptable-in-LA presence. The beard looked fuller, the smile bigger, his eyes brighter than his pictures as he approached the table. All eyes in the restaurant were on him.

Markie had been talking about his divorce; his wife had left him for her private manicurist. "I'm bummed because my cuticles were in good shape for the first time in years."

"Gio! Buddy!" Trevor stood up and hugged Gio from across the table. Markie followed suit.

An hour later, Markie was regaling us all with his near-death story, a burglary in his home, one we'd heard many times from various sources, each time the burglars multiplying and getting more and more violent. In a few months, the burglars would be rabid zombie serial killers.

"They tied me up and shoved me in a closet," Markie said. "I shit my pants. I'm not proud." That part, to his credit, never changed.

"Fantastic." Gio clapped his hands together. "I was awaiting the de-nouement."

"They finally figured out where the rich people live," I said, sipping my drink. "I wonder what took them so long."

Markie and Trevor were on to another favorite topic of conversation—net worth.

"C'mon, he can't be worth that much," Trevor said. "The guy hasn't made a hit in ten years."

"Real estate," Markie said. "He still has that house in Malibu."

"Looks like a Mexican whorehouse," Trevor said.

"You need to leave." Gio leaned over and whispered in my ear; heat radiated off his skin.

"What do you mean?" I looked around the table. Did he want me to leave the restaurant?

"Leave LA," he said. "Get out of the bubble. You'll never write any-thing worth a shit here."

"You seem very certain of this," I said.

"Hollywood killed Dashiell Hammett and F. Scott Fitzgerald. Remember that."

"That's why you left."

"No," he said, "I left because of my fourth wife and a nasty coke habit."

"So, Gio, what do you think?" Trevor was asking.

Gio laughed.

"About the script—did you read the script?" Trevor asked, then turned to Markie. "Did he read the script?"

"It's a shit burger. But I'm interested in the story," Gio said. "I'd have to rewrite it. There's no real danger in it. No blood, no life! Where's the heat?"

Trevor looked stunned, then shook it off. "Fucking my thoughts, ex-actly," he said. "Rewrite it, do it fast. Let's make this stinker."

Gio laughed again. "Wouldn't be the first!"

"Who do you like?"

"Whoever's not a complete moron," Gio said. "Actors don't even have high school diplomas, most of them. But they'll pontificate like scholars after reading one fucking book. Get me one who sells tickets and isn't the worst reprobate in the entire fucking Western Hemisphere and we'll make this turkey sing."

"Sounds good," Trevor said.

"What'd you think of your wife's book, Trevor?" Gio asked.

Trevor blinked as though a spotlight were shining in his eyes.

"I liked it," he said.

"Liked it?" Gio asked. "It was fucking great."

"No, hey," I said. "Not fucking great, I mean, close."

"Yeah, it was good," Trevor said.

Gio leaned forward, his nose hovering near Trevor's face. I held my breath.

"Trevor Nash. You haven't read your wife's book," Gio said, pounding the table.

"I read a review," Trevor said. *The New York Times*—that's almost like reading it."

"It's totally okay," I said, patting Trevor's arm. "Trevor has difficulty focusing."

"You know how hard it is to write a book, a book with pathos and humor and a great fucking ending?" Gio thundered.

"Where would one find such a book?" I asked, trying to defuse the situation.

"What the fuck's with this guy?" Trevor said to Markie, spittle forming on his lower lip. "Is he fucking lecturing me?"

"Of course not!" Markie said. "You don't have to read her book. Gio, come on, he doesn't have to read his wife's book, right, honey?" He looked at me. Honey.

"No. He totally didn't have to," I said, excited and horrified at the same time. "I wouldn't expect it. He's very busy."

"You know what, Metz?" Trevor said. "I don't want you to direct shit for me." He pushed himself away from the table.

"Good!" Gio said. "Because everything you touch is boiled shit."

"You fat-ass has-been!" Trevor said.

"You desiccated shmuck!" Gio said.

"Come on, you're my favorite geniuses!" Markie pleaded. "You two kings work this out; this is nothing." I could see the light in his eyes dim as his commission slipped away . . .

"You'll never work in this town again!" Trevor yelled. "Count on that, you blubbery motherfucker!"

"Ha! I've heard that from smarter people than you," Gio said. "That's exactly what David Fucking Putnam said, and we know where he is today!" Gio pushed himself away from the table, stood, and turned to me.

"It's been a pleasure," he said, and he kissed the back of my hand.

His hand was warm and soft, and I wanted to curl up and take a nap in it.

Then he barged out of the restaurant like a bull in a tapas shop.

"What a fucking complete asshole," Trevor said. "And he got big, didn't he, he really got huge." Everyone was huge compared to Trevor.

"What *did* happen to David Putnam?" Markie asked.

"He's not fat," I said. "He's dense." Trevor shot me his death stare.

"I'll talk to him," Markie said, shaking his head, then, "Hey, what do you think of Antoine Fuqua?"

Trevor lit up, and I tried to forget Gio's words. Maybe I was living in a bubble, and maybe my husband didn't read my books, but I was still more or less satisfied. More or less happy. And isn't that all we can ask?

#livingthedream

I sucked down the rest of the margarita.

8

Nuts

Hey, come see Pep's painting of you." Trevor jostled me awake, backlit by the bleached early-morning sun. I blinked, willing my eyes open. Was I dreaming? *What time . . . ?*

"For Mother's Day," he added.

"Pep is painting again? What time is it?" I rolled over to check my phone. 6:10. Today was a Sunday? Yes. Because (vegan/paleo/gluten-free) buffet dinner and science presentation at the TV legend's house Saturday night. The legendary producer keeps trying to raise the local IQ; he keeps failing. He doesn't know he's failing. Hollywood is obsessed with rubbing up against smart people, but no one cares about his guest speaker heart specialists, Oxford lecturers, and Nobel Prize winners. They care about hearing themselves ask self-important questions like obnoxious fifth graders, then beating the crowd to the valet to *Narcos* binge in their Hastens beds.

"Mother's Day isn't for another couple of weeks," I said.

Pep used to draw all the time. From the first time she could hold a crayon, forget reading and games and nap time. Just stick a pencil in her hand and she'd draw anywhere. On paper, on her walls, her pillowcases. In elementary school, she carried paintbrushes and a little sketchpad everywhere. I don't remember the last time I saw her with a brush, and I hate myself for not asking her, *Why don't you paint anymore?*

"C'mon, she's so excited," he said.

I planted my feet on the floor and smiled.

"This painting had better be really special, like a Mike Kelly or a Ruscha, something we can sell when she goes to college and tuition's a million dollars a year."

"She worked really hard," he said, holding my hand, with a sweetness and eagerness that I'd missed. We padded outside, hand in hand, into the silvery morning, across the grass to the guesthouse where Pep had moved her mini–art studio after "making a mess" on a Tibetan rug (as per the Old Trevor). The sun spiraled out over the horizon. I breathed in the fresh air, minted with ocean and grass, a heady, perfectly Southern Californian scent.

Oh. There it was. Happiness.

"I'll make you the perfect espresso," I said, hugging Trevor's arm, "and your favorite protein pancakes. It's going to be a beautiful day."

Maybe Pep would smile again, maybe she'd go back to being carefree Pep, the girl who laughed all the time, freewheeling with that toothy smile and squinty brown eyes.

Everything is going to be great.

Trevor opened the door to the guesthouse. I smelled a familiar perfume, one I recognized as friendly. I heard breathing. I felt a presence, then several presences. My eyes adjusted to the dimness, backlit by emerging sunlight. I teased out several figures seated on the long couch. A few more on chairs. I smelled coffee. Someone had stopped for coffee before they arrived here at our guesthouse.

Was Trevor having a meeting? Trevor often held meetings in the guesthouse. I glanced back at him, in his jeans, long-sleeved T-shirt. Okay. That makes sense, then, that Trevor would've seen Pep's painting and, you know, gotten all excited and had to, simply had to, wake me up.

"Hi," I said. Trevor was standing behind me, silent. "Is this some sort of meet—"

I dropped a syllable as I started to focus.

"Dad?"

My dad was seated in a chair next to the couch, elbows on his knees, clutching a folded-up newspaper.

"Hi, honey," he said. Dad never called me *honey*. We weren't a honey family. Not *honey*, not *sweetie, sweetheart, sugar, doll*. He called me by my name. Sometimes by my first and last name, if circumstances were dire.

"Juliette?" The perfume.

"Hi, doll," she said. I couldn't see, but I was sure she was wearing a see-through blouse. What was she doing here? Had she been up all night?

"Trevor?" I turned to look at him. "What's going on?" I gripped my heart. "Is something wrong with Pep?"

"No, she's fine; she's asleep," Trevor said, shaking his head and then nodding toward another figure in the room. "You tell her?"

A black man who, I could swear, played a doctor on a TV show leaned out of his comfortable chair and stood. "Agnes, can I call you Aggie?"

"Why?" He was at least six foot five. I strained my neck looking up at him.

"My name is Barnaby," he said, sliding his long arm around my shoulder. He had a deep baritone, a lovely spicy scent but phony displays of affection (my bullshit meter blared *honk, honk, honk*) set me off. I swiped away my eye boogers and ran my fingers through my hair. Yes, I was sure of it, he was an actor. Not famous, but not unfamous. *Law & Order* special guest star famous.

"May I call you Barbie?" I asked.

"I'm here to help you," Barnaby said.

"Barnaby?"

"Yes?"

"You have a pirate's name," I said.

"My father's name, my great-grandfather's name," he said. "It's a slave name."

"Cool, okay," I said

Barnaby cleared his throat. "Why don't you have a seat, Agnes?"

I sank into the couch next to Juliette.

"What the hell is going *on?*" I harsh whispered.

"Everything's fine," Juliette whispered back, her breath smelling of clove cigarettes like a dissolute French painter-prostitute. "Is he married?"

"So, Agnes . . ." Barnaby leaned forward in the velvet chair at the head of the low table and clasped his hands together. A gold band glinted against his macadamia skin. He had the best seat in the room, the power seat; Trevor's seat. I wondered how Trevor felt about it. He appeared diminished next to Barnaby, but then, so would The Rock.

"We're here because we care about you," Barnaby said.

"Oh my God! I've been hoodwinked!" Without so much as a wink.

I glared at Trevor, my mouth hanging open in disbelief. "Trevor, what have you done?"

Trevor opened his mouth to speak, then blew out air. Barnaby chimed in, but his voice didn't sound like a chime; he tromboned in. "Agnes, calm down. We just want to talk to you."

"You know what happens when you tell a woman to calm down, Barnaby?" I asked.

"What?" Barnaby asked.

"Nothing!" I yelled.

"This is only a talk," Trevor said. "With the people who really care about you. That's all."

"Grab your popcorn!" I said. "I'm being interventioned, I mean, intervened. Are you trying to intervention me, intervene me?"

"You're upset," Dr. Obvious Macadamia said.

"I'm the only person in this city who *isn't* an addict!" I said. "Unless this is the opposite of an intervention and you all got together to congratulate me on being so fucking not-addicted. Unaddicted. Nonaddicted."

Fin stumbled through the door.

"Hey, late, that motherfucking carburetor," she said, clomping in.

"I'm being intervened by my drug dealer sister?"

"Woo, so this is morning," Fin said, bounced, ushering in competing scents—tobacco and sweat and horses. Somehow, the odors made her even more alluring; if I smelled like Fin, I'd be as alluring as a rodent. "I had to see this for myself. What'd I miss?"

"Fin!" Dad barked. "Sit! Goddamn it! Sit!"

"Fin is at my intervention? Juliette's here? I guess you didn't check bags," I said. "Should we all wait for John Belushi to show up?"

"That's not fair," Juliette said. "I'm not addicted. I can stop at any time."

"Stop what?" Barnaby asked.

"Take your pick," I said. "What, pray tell, do I need to intervene? Perimenopause? Carbs? Writing? You people don't want me to write anymore? I can't blame you."

Trevor sprang to his feet and thrust a sandwich bag filled with almonds in my face. "What do you call this?" he demanded, shaking the bag. My stomach growled; Pavlov's unconditioned stimulus: roasted almonds in olive oil and sea salt.

"An excellent source of protein?" I asked.

He tossed the bag on the coffee table as though he'd discovered dirty needles in my Bottega.

"You're intervening a healthy snack?" I asked, looking around the room.

"You have lost a lot of weight, Agnes," Juliette said. "It's like you're starving yourself. You were way, way heavier years ago."

Barnaby whistled.

"I was pregnant years ago, Juliette."

"Adderall, Agnes?" Barnaby asked.

"I'm the only mom in LA who's *not* on Adderall!" I said. "They steal it from their kids who really just need to play outside. Right, Juliette?"

"Adderall helps Annabelle focus," Juliette said.

"She's three."

"That's why we split it."

We all looked at her.

"I'll deal with you next," Barnaby promised.

"Aggie, I'm worried about you," Trevor said. "I want you to be healthy. I want you to be healthy for Pep. Think of Pep."

"You're so full of it. This is all a ploy," I said. "This is some Pocket Machiavelli Sun Tzu shit." I had a flash of realization. "You're going to use this for custody!"

"No!" Trevor said. "My God. Can you just listen for once?"

"Agnes," Barnaby said, "I promise this will be painless. You may even enjoy the process. Everyone here loves you very much. We all care about you deeply."

"Okay, cool it, brother," Fin said. "The Murphys don't talk that way."

"Fin, you think I need an intervention?" I asked. "You?"

"Hell no, but Trevor called me; he sounded worried," Fin said. "If anything happened to you, it's just me and Daddio."

"I would never do that to you," I said.

"Hey, now," Dad said. "I used to change your diapers, young lady."

"Who wants to begin?" Barnaby asked.

"I'll start," Dad said. He stood up, put on his reading glasses, pulled out a many-times-folded piece of paper, origami but without the swan. We waited while he unfolded and cleared his throat. A minute passed.

"To my first daughter, Agnes," he finally read. "Don't worry about the weight; for Christ's sake keep some meat on your bones." He folded it back up carefully and sat down.

"That's it?"

"I'm not a doctor," my dad said, shrugging.

I shook my head, speechless. Fin raised her hand.

"Fin, come on," I said. "You? You can't believe this shit."

"Young lady," my dad said. "You're not too old for a spanking."

"Sorry, Dad," I said.

"I need a job," Fin said. "My parole officer's on my back. I figured I could network at your intervention." She studied the participants. "Anyone here looking for a driver? Babysitter?"

"I could use a driver," Juliette said. "I keep running into things."

"So will you go?" Trevor asked.

"Trevor," Barnaby said, cautioning him, "let's not be hasty. This has to be Agnes's decision. Agnes?"

"Where am I to go for my imaginary eating disorder? An imaginary rehab?"

Barnaby slid a brochure across the coffee table. I picked it up and riffled through it. Arizona sunshine, swimming pools, cacti, Jacuzzi, award-winning chef, adobe villas, massage therapy . . .

Fin grabbed it from me. "Shit, this is rehab? I'll go! Hey, you think they have job openings?"

Barnaby and I discussed terms while Trevor sat there like a nervous child.

"So it's like a spa," I said.

"Very much like a spa," he said. "It's a recovery home for people, who, let's say, could use a little vacation from their day-to-day lives. It's a place to go to get rid of everyday toxins—maybe people who have a little too much to drink on the weekends, or their partying has gotten out of hand."

"A spa weekend," I murmured. In my mind, I was already stretched out on a chaise.

"Your husband leased a jet all set to whisk you off. All you need to do is pack."

"A jet? For me?"

Trevor never spent that kind of money on me—not his own money, not unless the studio was paying for it. I wondered what kind of jet he leased. Like, one that would actually fly?

"How long would I have to stay?" I could use a change of scenery, a couple of days away from the dead zone. "I don't want to leave Pep for more than a weekend. That's it. Just two, three nights max."

"Entirely up to you," Barnaby said. "But the longer you're there, the more help you'll receive. And the more help you receive, the better you'll be for Pip."

"Pep," I said.

I took a deep breath. Here I was, a healthy, sober person considering a stint in rehab. As a human being, this sounded insane. But I wasn't a normal human being. I was a writer. And to a writer, it sounded . . . irresistible. What happens when a nonaddict goes to rehab? Why, this story would write itself . . .

"When do I leave?" I asked.

"I wish I were going," Fin said, sitting on a bench in my closet, whipping through the brochure. "Look at that, eggs fucking Benedict. I would've said yes to rehab a long time ago if it looked like this."

"Trevor was on vacation from our marriage," I said. "Maybe I need a little vacation from my marriage."

"No booze, no drugs, no phones." Juliette said. "Honestly, sounds like jail with good mattresses."

"You can have drugs in jail," Fin said.

"Wait. No phones?" I asked. "How do I call Pep?"

"It's only a couple of days," Fin said, looking through my shoes. "Don't worry about her. I got this covered."

"Oh! You can smoke there," Juliette said. "So good. Smoking helped me lose baby weight."

"You used a surrogate," I said. "And I don't smoke."

"Once those meth heads start drying out, you'll start needing a cigarette," Fin said. "Hey, can I have these boots? They'd be great for barrel racing."

"Take 'em," I said.

"Do you want to take a pill before you go?" Juliette asked, shaking a prescription bottle. "For the plane?"

"I'll take what she's not taking," Fin said, grabbing Juliette's bottle and sticking it in her jeans. "I can sell these, top dollar."

"I need those; I just had my labia trimmed."

"And I'm the one going away," I said.

"So what was your drug of choice?" I asked Barnaby as we cruised at thirty thousand feet. "Since you know mine. A delicious, protein-filled snack."

"Crack," Barnaby said. His face went slack, his eyes starry. He smiled dreamily.

I looked out at the checkerboard desert and thought, *Get yourself a man who looks at you the way Barnaby looks at a crack pipe.*

We landed in Tucson after having enjoyed a smooth two-hour ride, a seafood platter, and Barnaby's rehababble. I thought about Dad, who'd tapped my shoulder with his rolled-up newspaper before he chugged off in the old Jeep he'd parked on the street so he wouldn't leak oil on the slate driveway.

"I keep calling you, Dad," I'd said. "If you wanted to see me, we could've just had breakfast."

"The stock market's been real jumpy," he said, patting me again with the *LA Times.* "Be good."

"Where I'm going?" I called after him, before following Barnaby into the black SUV. "I don't have a choice."

On the way to the front office, Barnaby and I walked past the swimming pool, where several body-positive girls in bikinis floated and chirped and sunned themselves on deck chairs.

"Who are they?" I asked. They seemed to be grouped by BMI.

"Eating disorders," Barnaby said. "Anorexia, bulimia . . ."

"Sounds like urban first names—" I stopped myself. "How long have they been here?"

"Eating disorders stay ninety days."

Three months. That's more than enough time to gain thirty, forty pounds.

"My God. They're going from skinny to rehab to gastric bypass."

"Try not to cause problems," Barnaby said.

"I don't cause problems; I write problems," I said, turning to face him. Well, his chest. "What's your hurry, Barnaby? Let me guess— another rich white woman with a anoerexipercoxanax addiction at noon?"

He smirked and pushed me through another set of doors. I smelled *hospital.* I hated the smell of hospitals. Then, cigarettes. Antiseptic mixed with nicotine. I gagged.

"She's not white," he said, "but she is rich. Your white privilege is showing."

"Where?" I said, checking my waistband. "I'd better tuck that shit in."

Barnaby greeted everyone, even the security guards, then hugged me goodbye, and I'm not proud to say I had to be peeled off him.

.   .   .

"Hi, I'm Craig, I'm *DSM-5* eating disordered with obsessive-compulsive and related disorders," said the giant, intense potato. "That's me. Craig."

I had checked in and was sitting on a couch in the great room in front of the nurses' station, which was only great, I guess, in size. The décor was doctor's office with a weird plaid obsession and a couch big enough to seat ten people (or four eating disordered). I was busy filling out forms, which I loved because I loved having all the answers.

Where I lived, my occupation . . .

Next of kin.

Say what now?

Craig pulled up a chair, then turned it around and faced me, his arms crossed across the top. He repeated himself in a cheerful tone. Like one of Santa's lost giant elves. "Craig, eating disordered, obsessive-compulsive, and related."

"That's a mouthful, Craig," I said and shook his outstretched hand. He waited with eager eyes.

"Oh! Oh, me!" I said, my hand to my chest. "Hi, I'm, ah, Agnes. And, ah . . . almonds?"

"Almonds?"

"I'm addicted to almonds. I mean, that's what my husband thinks."

Craig looked bewildered, and did I detect a note of disappointment?

"I guess it could be considered an eating disorder?" I said to give him some *DSM* to cling to.

"Good!" Craig said, clapping his hands together, his pallid face brightening. "So nice meeting you, Agnes." He rose from his chair and flipped it back around, and I'd wondered how many times it took him to master that dance move. "Time for my weigh-in. Dr. Marigold hates when I'm late; I'm just super-friendly."

He walked off, and I got the feeling that all of Craig's friends were locked inside this facility. It was like having a great social life inside a stuck elevator.

. . .

No one was prouder of their "accomplishments" than the good folks at Madre de Tucson. Craig was the first of the rehabee onslaught, hijacking my form time with their precious diagnoses. Rehabees were similar to Harvard grads—anyone who went to Harvard made sure you knew within three minutes. Time it.

"Hi, I'm Layla, *DSM-5* substance use disorder."

"'Use disorder'?" I asked. "So you weren't abusing correctly? Is that double speak? An alternative fact?"

"Opioids. Oxy, mostly," she said, missing my point. "I sold my mom's car and stole my grandmother's jewelry. Her parents died in the Holocaust. Hi."

"Hi, I'm Feldman. My drug of choice is co-ca-een-a. What can I say, I love the co-co. I'm in law school," he said, snorting as he talked. "My bros saved me; Doc said I had, like, I don't know, twenty seconds to live. Crazy times."

"Hey, Norrs." A man with a red tattoo on his cheek that said *To Die Is To Live* sank into the chair.

"Norris?"

"No," Norrs whose mother missed a vowel said. "Why does everyone do that?"

I waited. I knew it was com—

"Alcohol use disorder."

"Why don't they call it *alcohol abuse*?"

"I'm jus' sayin', I don't think so." He paused. "I like the big cans, you seen 'em? Had a bad day. Cops said I held up a liquor store with my finger. I got three kids."

The staccato of this rehab mating ritual without the mating part was familiar, like a Hollywood pitch meeting where no one talked about the pitch . . . *My wife left me for her life coach. I'm training for my eight hundredth triathlon. My kid is interning for Iger.*

It's amazing that anything got done in Hollywood.

"Suzanne," the next girl said, plopping down on the couch next to me. She smelled like baby powder. I hadn't finished filling out my forms. My timing had been completely thrown off. I swallowed my resentment.

Yes, that makes me as crazy as the rest of them.

"Hi, Suzanne," I said. She was a dewy brunette, her thick shiny hair pulled back in a ponytail. She was also gorgeous and didn't seem to know it. Annoying.

"What are you in for? Perfect features?" I assessed her. "Are they locking up supermodels now? Is pretty outlawed?"

"Crack." She looked down at her feet, encased in ballerina slippers.

"Are you sure?" I said. "That can't be right."

"I got married eight months ago," she said. "I live outside Chicago, the suburbs. My husband is a saint. It's me. I'm an addict. Do you know how hard it is to live with an addict?"

"No," I said. "Wait. Yes. More or less." I thought about Fin.

She took a deep breath, her eyes so sad I thought I might burst into tears.

Instead, I set my forms aside and leaned forward.

"How long have you been here?" I asked.

"Six weeks," she said.

"Suzanne," I said. "Do you like being married?"

"What?"

"Are you happy?"

"Of course," she said. "Mitch is the nicest."

"I know. Mitch is the best," I said. "When did you meet?"

"College, my sophomore year," she said. "He was finishing up business school."

"And you? What were you studying?"

"Me?" She asked. "I, ah, wanted to go to med school."

I leaned back. "What happened?"

"We fell in love. Mitch had to move for work," she said. "I never finished my undergraduate work. I have eight more credits."

"A whole eight," I said. "That's like two classes. So you moved, then you got married."

"Yes."

"How many people at your wedding?"

"Two hundred and fifty," she said. "Mitch has a big family. His mother was very involved." I detected bristling. "I don't know why I'm sabotaging such a fantastic life."

"Because maybe it's not so fantastic?" I offered.

"But it is. Everyone tells me how great my life is," she said. "My mom, my sister, even Dr. Marigold here. You know, Mitch drove me out, all the way from Illinois. He prayed for me."

"He's perfect," I said. "Mine didn't even get on the plane."

"I've disappointed everybody."

"Hold on, sister. You've disappointed yourself," I said. "Can I give you some advice? As someone much—ah, a tiny bit—older than you. Although still in fantastic shape, right?"

"Yes?" She seemed unclear; who could blame her?

"Have you talked to the doctor about your day-to-day life?"

"Not really."

"You've been here six weeks. What do you talk about?"

"Drugs," she said.

"So it's like breaking up and talking about your ex 24-7," I said. "How do you do it?"

"I don't know!" She laughed. "That's all anyone talks about. Drugs. Drugs and alcohol and . . . sex." She whispered *sex*.

"How is your sex life?"

"It's good," she said flatly.

"Sounds amazing," I said.

"Well . . . he likes me to take a hot shower for a half hour beforehand. And I can't make noise."

My nostrils flared.

"Yeah, okay, listen to me," I said. "You're getting a divorce."

Her hand covered her mouth as she gasped.

"You are getting a divorce or you're getting ugly, then dying. Are you prepared to get snaggle-toothed, scabby, crack-whore ugly?"

"No, no," she said, shaking her head. "Oh my God, no."

"So bite the bullet and tell Perfect Mitch who has an aversion to female odor you want a divorce," I said. "You're not doing him any favors staying married to him. Next, ask your parents if they'd rather have an ugly, dead daughter or an unmarried, live, beautiful one. Three. Is that three? You finish up college and apply to med school. I'm assuming you were a good student."

She nodded, her eyes lit up. "Three point nine in honors classes."

"Jesus Christ, beautiful and smart. And they say God doesn't give with two hands. You're not a crack addict, Suzanne," I said. "You're a coward. Because it's hard. You can't tell your husband and his family and your family that you don't want to be married anymore. You can't tell them what you want. You've never been able to tell them what you want."

She started to cry. I took her hand.

"Why not become a doctor? Or a nurse? Think of all the lives you can save," I said. "But start with your own."

Suzanne sat back and wiped her tears with the back of her hand.

"Thank you," she said. "How can I repay you?"

"My fee is waived, child," I said. "Go forth and set yourself free."

Suzanne smiled and hopped up from the couch, glancing back at me to wave as she walked away.

Two minutes later, a woman in a white coat with a tight smile and slashes for eyebrows, chic prescription glasses, and YSL ankle boots appeared, standing over me.

"Hi?" I was way behind on my forms.

"I'm Dr. Marigold, the head of patient administration here at Madre de Tucson."

"Oh, I thought you were a super-officious patient," I said.

"Funny," she said as flat as the last executive I pitched to. "I wanted to welcome you here. Everything okay so far?"

"I haven't craved an almond in over an hour," I said, rubbing the inside of my arms like a heroin addict in a movie.

"Well, you and I will be meeting later," she said, clipped. "Before we do, I need you to fill out these tests." She opened a folder, pulling out a sheaf of paper. I looked over the form. Bubbles! I loved filling out bubbles; it was one of my key talents.

"Is this like addict SAT?" I asked.

"These are . . . psychological tests," she said, "to aid us in our diagnoses."

"I'm fucking great at these," I said, grabbing them from her.

"I had a feeling you'd say that."

"You're already diagnosing me," I said. "How'm I doing? I mean, I don't have an addiction. I don't belong here, of course."

"On the contrary," she said. "You fit right in."

She turned on her heel and walked back to the administration offices.

"Beeyotch," I said under my breath.

After lunch in the cafeteria that smelled medicinal, where everyone sat with designated *DSM-5*s, Feldman was waiting for me outside.

"Wassup," I said. "Cocaine use–disordered gentleman."

"Yeah, hey. Suzanne checked out," Feldman said.

"That soon?"

"I hear you're like a psychic," he said. "You read her future."

"Not at all," I said. "Not remotely. I just have strong opinions."

"Tell me my future," he said, grabbing my hand.

"I can tell you what it is if you let go of my hand," I said.

He released my hand. "She kissed me."

"Who did?"

"Suzanne. She kissed me before she left. She said somewhere deep down she'd wanted to make out with me ever since she got here. What do you think it means?"

"It means she's in better shape than I am," I said as we walked to the courtyard outside, where patients gathered to smoke cigarettes and drink coffee and gripe. I wanted to catch some fresh-ish air. Two people with blue hair and piercings were puffing on Salems.

"So, c'mon. Tell me what I'm meant to do in my life," Feldman said. "I'm desperate."

"What do you love doing, Feldman?"

"Besides coke?"

"Skip the drug part."

"Tennis," he said. "I'm a really good tennis player. Wicked backhand. I was top five in my state."

"Do you still play?"

"Not much anymore," he said. "I don't get a lot of chances. I'm either studying or partying."

"Oh, this is too easy," I said, rubbing my hands together. "Quit law school. Tell your parents you're taking a year off. After a year, they'll understand, because you're going to teach tennis to inner-city kids. You'll love it."

His eyes smiled. "How?"

"Head to local middle schools and Boys & Girls Clubs. Find city courts, raise money among your frat bros to fix them up."

"You think I can do that?"

"Easy. But first, do the hard thing. Jump off the bullet train of the future your parents envisioned."

Feldman nodded, nodded, thinking.

"What if I still want to do blow?"

"Stop living off your parents," I said. "Make yourself hungry. Be too poor to do blow. Once you start teaching kids, and you look into their eyes, and they're trusting you and depending on you to show up and change their lives, you won't want to party until sunrise with a bunch of bozos. Trust me."

"Do you think she likes me?"

"Who?"

"Suzanne," he said. "She gave me her number."

"Yeah, I do," I said. "But she's learning to like herself. You do the same."

He gave me a sweet puppy-dog hug, and I patted his back and sent him on his way. I needed some alone time.

My alone time in my room reading an old thriller left behind in the "library" lasted twenty minutes. I heard my name called over the loud-speaker.

"We have to talk," Dr. Marigold said as I walked into her office. An icy smile was stretched across her face. "Since you've arrived, two of our patients have left, citing their little chats with you as a reason."

"Oh, I'm sorry," I said. "Hey, did you get a chance to go over my tests? How'd I do?"

"Do you not want them to heal?" she asked. "What could be your motivation for encouraging these young, vulnerable people to leave?"

I sat up straight.

"I gave them real life advice," I said. "I suggested they change their lives and maybe their habits would follow."

"Stop the talking for now. Maybe start listening."

"Rightio," I said and saluted her. "Am I ready for my diagnosis?"

"Eating disorder," she said. "Were you weighed already? What was it?"

She looked down at her papers.

"One hundred and twenty-seven," I said.

"Yeah, that's not really skinny," she said.

I coughed out a *fuck you*.

She looked up.

"Go on," I said.

"Usually, our eating disorders are obviously anorexic or bulimic," she said. "But you don't throw up after eating."

"Not even during a stomach flu," I said. "My people don't do that. Once it's in, it's in."

"I see a touch of narcissism," she said, glancing up from the test scores. "It says here that when you walk into a room, you feel special."

"I live in LA," I said. "I caught a little narcissism."

"My recommendation, which I'll let the other doctors know," she said, shuffling the test scores back inside a folder, "is that you stay for the full ninety-day treatment period. You could really use our help."

"At what cost?" I asked.

She smiled. "I'll see you at the same time next week. And refrain from diagnosing any other patients. It's dangerous; we're not playing a game here. We take our work very seriously."

"I understand," I said, then shifted out of my chair and got up.

Ah, but you know. I couldn't help myself.

"So . . . what's your success rate?" I asked before I opened the door to let myself out.

"What do you mean?" she asked.

"You must know your recidivism rate," I said. "How many times patients relapse before they finally get clean."

"It's about . . . 27 percent."

"And that's . . . good? Is this like baseball? Like, no one bats five hundred right? So that would make 27 percent incredible."

She sniffed. "It's a very good rate."

"Huh," I said. "I bet I can do better."

Her eyes narrowed into slits.

"I'm sure that's just the narcissism talking," I said.

I shut the door behind me and said a silent prayer for Suzanne and Feldman.

After a fitful night's sleep, I knew I wouldn't last ninety more minutes, much less ninety days. The walls were paper thin and addicts NEVER. STOP. TALKING.

2:00 a.m. 3:00 a.m. 4:00 a.m. . . . no recrimination in their self-examination, no comma in their trauma drama.

My roommate was a Spanish girl with big-screen eyes and a drinking problem. She had limited English to go with my limited Spanglish (no mistake on the administration's part). The only words I understood coming out of her mouth were *hola* and *Listerine*. When I told her I didn't have any Listerine, she lost interest in me.

She was still asleep, curled up and softly breathing, when I headed to the cafeteria for breakfast. Tables were divided based on *DSM*. Eating disorders were digging into groaning stacks of pancakes and plates piled high with bacon and french toast. I grabbed a plate of scrambled eggs and walked quickly past the alcoholics and tweakers to a far, empty table to plot my escape.

A guy with cropped black hair and beefy, tatted forearms sat down across from me, his tray clattering.

"You're new," he said before digging into his bacon and eggs. "What're you in for?"

"They got me for eating disorders," I said with prison swagger.

"Brutal," he grunted.

"And narcissistic personality disorder lite," I added. "But that's bullshit. They just want to keep me here. Because I'm so entertaining. Which confirms my narcissism."

He nodded, chomping his bacon.

"You?" I asked.

"I'm in for intermittent explosive disorder," he said. "Really fucking pisses me off."

I took a breath. Anger management was a new one. No one here seemed angry. They seemed all happy—*too* happy. Tamped, not amped.

"And hypersexual disorder," he said, giving me a meaningful glance. "Sex addiction."

"Check!" I said, jumping up and waving down an imaginary waiter.

I didn't look back. I was at the nurses' station, on the phone with Trevor, within seconds, having dumped my food in the trash as I raced out of the cafeteria.

"I'm not staying," I said to him. "I'm outta here."

"Agnes, you should stay," Trevor said. "Let me call someone. Let me call Barnaby. This is not a good idea."

"Call anyone, call the cops, as far as I care," I said, and then sang, "I'mma leaving on a jet plane. I know I won't be back again."

"Well, I'm not sending a plane."

"I'm grabbing a taxi to the airport," I said. "I'll be home this afternoon." I hung up, raced to my room, packed my clothes, retrieved my brush and phone from the check-in, and headed for the exit. A taxi pulled up five minutes later. I was free.

I stared out the cab window as we buzzed down the highway, wondering how a life in which so little happened could suddenly have so much happening.

My phone buzzed, waking me from my stupor. Unknown number.

"Hello?"

"Agnes." A woman's voice but deep and throaty. It could only be—

"Waverly."

"Your husband has filed."

"Wait—how do you know?"

"I'm a cognitive. It's my job."

I took a beat.

"Thank you?" I said.

"Tell your lawyer you want your case filed under *Anonymous v. Anonymous*," she said. "It's important you keep this private."

"What? My lawyer? What lawyer?"

"I can charge you by the hour or monthly. It's tax deductible. ICM, CAA, the big agencies, the studios, they do monthly. I can't talk about it. Trust me, you're going to need me."

And she hung up.

Southwest gate. Instead of drinking Tito's on ice at the bar (isn't that what rehab escapees do?), I headed for Hudson. Oh, how I love a good Hudson—candy, trash magazines, trail mix with chocolate raisins, and books(!), all within arm's reach of each other. I like the heft, the feel, the smell of books. I feel rich when I buy a book, the same way another woman feels when she buys this season's bag. And books ground me, touchstones that remind me of who I once was—a chunky kid battling allergies, reading books inside the classroom while her schoolmates played tag outside in the dirty air.

My phone buzzed as I pondered an author photo on the back of a bestseller. *Hello, handsome.* I could see dating a fellow author when the divorce smoke cleared. Where's he from? San Francisco and South Beach.

Oh.

"Hello?" I asked.

"Hey, you're alive!" Gio Metz.

"Contrary to popular demand," I said.

"This is fucked up!" he boomed. "You don't do drugs. You don't have the constitution."

"I'm hard-core into the almonds, Metz," I said.

"You have to get away from this nonsense," he said. "If you're looking for a place to land, I'm your guy."

"You specialize in broken toys," I said as I slipped a self-improvement book from the bestseller row. *Why not.* "We all know your marital history."

"Bent, not broken." He laughed. "And, honey, I've read your work. You're definitely bent."

I landed in LA and dragged my overnight bag to the taxi station; Fin was already waiting outside for me, hands on her hips, wearing white-framed YSL sunglasses (mine and yes, they looked better on her). She threw my bag in the back of her truck and drove off without saying a word.

That's the first time I'd cried in a long time.

I didn't like to cry as a rule.

"You look fat when you cry," Fin said.

You can imagine why I don't like to cry.

"Fuck off," I said, crying.

9

D–i–v–o–r–c–e:
Tell Me What It Means to Me

Fin switched between Spanish and English, and I switched between understanding and not.

"Like, *como tu* put up *con este pendejo*—"

My sister, the bilingual ping-pong machine, fidgeted in her seat, tapping the steering wheel, saluting tailgaters with the bird. She talked about job interviews at places that paid "shit wages" and then switched radio stations after three notes. I stared out the window and tried not to think about how she'd suddenly acquired a new truck. Fin had never owned anything with alloyed wheels.

"*Yo rompí con* Tone," she said.

"You what with Tone?"

"You should know Spanish already. Everyone in your damn house speaks Spanish."

"I took three years of high school Spanish, and all I remember is my teacher asking me for cheerleading photos."

"Did he at least ask *en Español*?"

"Which one's Tone?"

"Where've you been? He was my soul mate, you know. The Indian."

"Native American."

"Okay, Native American; he says Indian," she said. "How was your vacation?"

"Rehab."

She snorted. "For a big twenty-four hours."

"I flunked out," I said. "What kind of loser flunks out of rehab?"

"You," she said. "Anyway, I don't think I can trust him. Tone."

"What gave you that idea? His felony record?"

She glanced at me.

"Three arrests in two years isn't bad," Fin said. "And two of those were for protesting, but they got him for looting. He's evolved."

"Would it kill you to date someone who doesn't have a record?"

"You sound like Dad."

"Good, I'm glad," I said. "Even though he sent me away to rich people asylum."

"You married someone who doesn't have a record," Fin said. "Look how good that's working out."

"That's not my fault," I said. "I can't compete against the other woman."

"Petra?" Fin snorted. "Her pussy probably smells like cabbage."

"No," I said. "Hollywood."

"Oh, that bitch," Fin said, nodding. "Have to get the truck back before four."

"What happens at four?"

"Owner comes home," she said as she hung a left onto Wilshire from Sepulveda. "Let's gas it up; that'd be nice for your neighbor, right?"

"My neighbor?" I said. "Fin!"

At the gas station on Sepulveda, the air was hot and dry, and a haze lingered over Los Angeles, familiar yet ominous, like the beginning of a

Wim Wenders movie. I kept sliding my Amex and it wasn't working, and sweat started rolling down the side of my face. I'd forgotten to bring my hormone creams to Tucson.

"What the hell?" I said.

"Try another one," Fin said as she leaned against the truck, holding the gas nozzle.

I slid the Visa through the sensor.

Declined.

I scratched at my neck as my hairs stood on end. Nerves, the suffocating heat, or rehab bed bugs?

"Do you think Trevor canceled my cards?" I asked.

"Don't you have any of your own?" Fin asked.

"No," I said, rummaging through my purse. "Wait. I have a Neiman Marcus card; would that work?"

"When was the last time you filled up your own car?" Fin asked.

I didn't answer. She slapped the side of the truck. "Dang!" she said. "You're pathetic!"

"I'm trying to think!" I said. I didn't need time to think; the Triplets filled up my car once a week. I was surprised when I first moved in, when Caster had taken my car to the gas station to fill it up, then I stopped questioning it. Then I got used to it. Now, I expected it.

"I have some cash," I said, opening my wallet. I handed her forty bucks. Fin snatched it and stepped away to the cashier. "I'm getting licorice, too; I deserve it. You want something?" she asked over her shoulder, her hair tangled and bouncing off her shoulders.

Fin drove into the dead zone and pressed the intercom at the gate. Gabriela answered. Fin told her we'd arrived, said something in Spanish, I heard "Peppy *fue* something," and Fin said, "Cocksucker," then we drove down the long driveway. I thought about the parties we'd thrown there, the golf carts hauling Warren Beatty and Jim Carrey and Jeffrey

Katzenberg, not knowing the valet was twenty-five minutes behind and the biggest names in Hollywood were waiting in frigid canyon weather outside our gate.

Inexplicably, or maybe explicably, the thought made me smile.

"Before you get out," Fin said, turning to me, making her nervous face, her teeth bared like the stray dogs that always found her on the way home from school.

"What?" I closed my eyes. "What now?"

"Pep isn't here," Fin said. I jumped. "Hold on," she said, grabbing my arm. "Steady. She's with her dad. He had Petra pack a bag, and we'll find out where she is; just don't worry or cry or throw anything."

"He can't just take her; he can't take my daughter."

"This is not the Sally Field movie, okay? She's, like, a mile away," Fin said. "He'll get tired of her soon enough. You know that."

"I feel like I'm losing my mind," I said, my hands on my head.

"Honey, anyone would lose their mind in this place," Fin said, gesturing toward the house. "Shit, I feel dumber just hanging out here."

Fin laughed, and like some buried impulse, I found myself laughing as well.

"Where did Trevor take Pep?" I headed to the CNN headquarters of home: the laundry room. I'd called Trevor, but of course, it went straight to voicemail. Proud to say I refrained from guttural swearing.

Caster was crying into Gabriela's arms.

"Missus, Mr. Trevor, he move out, and he want me to go with him," Caster said, her face slick with tears. Lola opened her mouth, but no sound came out. Three pairs of eyes, each pair sadder than the next, gazed at me.

"Why you can't make nice to Mr. Trevor?" Caster asked.

Fin lit a cigarette and handed it to Caster.

"No smoking in the house," I said.

Caster drew on Fin's cigarette, smoke escaping her nostrils; she looked impossibly glamorous, a Latin movie star from the '40s.

"Let me have a puff," I said.

"He packed a bag," Gabriela said. "He told me he didn't want me to do it."

"Well, you did put a hex crystal in his underwear when he went on that cruise," I said. "He went soft on a Russian supermodel."

Fin snorted and high-fived Gabriela.

"He wants me to work for him," Caster said, shaking her head as tears pinwheeled off her face. She took another puff and raised her carefully painted-on eyebrows. "You think Mr. Trevor pay me more?"

Ensue Spanish flurry as the Triplets discussed. What I gathered was that there was sudden interest from the other sisters.

"Where did they go?" I asked.

"He went to the bish," Gabriela said.

"Petra?"

"No, the bish."

"Malibu?"

"Santa Monica," Gabriela said. "He rent, how you say . . ."

Spanish. Spanish. Spanish. Faster Spanish. Flurries, furious flurries.

"Penthouse," Fin said. "On Ocean."

"The Tower of Testosterone?" I asked. "Where all the divorced Hollywood men go to lick their wounds and girlfriends? Pep is going to hate that place!"

"I gotta jump," Fin said, hopping off the dryer. "You need me?"

"More than graham crackers and milk," I said.

"Aw, I miss Li'l Fatty Patty. Remember when you used to eat way too many of those?" Fin said, grabbing my tummy.

"Thanks again for the ride in someone else's truck."

I happened to look down; her ankle monitor was missing.

"Fin, what'd you do?"

"It's right here," she said. She opened a drawer. The ankle monitor was hidden, fully intact. "I took it apart and put it back together. I told you about those computer science courses in prison, right? We had to take apart and build a computer ourselves."

"Does prison make more sense than college?" I asked.

"Maybe. Okay, it was only off for two minutes, but I'm gonna scooch down to San Bernardino after I drop off the truck before my parole officer starts barking. I'll bring her Hot Cheetos; she'll be fine."

Fin gave me a hug, rushed out, then circled back.

"Oh, hey, sis, can I give her this address as my residence? I can't go back to Tone's place. Not after the fire."

"Fire?"

"Don't freak out," Fin said.

I glanced wide-eyed at the Triplets. A new, quiet panic washed over me.

"I'm just using your address until I find a job. Don't be a puss."

She punched me in the shoulder.

"Jesus." I winced.

"Oh, and before I forget . . ." She took a crumpled piece of paper from her jeans pocket and tossed it to me. "I went to Vicente Foods to fill out a job app; I wound up in the deli line—great meatballs—the lady in front of me was talking to her *amiga*, and she was saying her *jefita* had *el primero abogado para* divorce, and I said, 'Hey, *digame* that number, boo.'"

"Stay off those almonds!" Fin added, beating a path to the kitchen door on her Timberlands. I waited until I heard the neighbor's pickup truck rumble to a start before I rubbed my shoulder.

Universal truths in LA: death, taxes . . . and divorce. A Hollywood marriage is 80 percent more likely to fail than civilian marriages. Take a look at *Star* or *People*. Or the bleating folks on camera at TMZ.

No one really knows why, though there are theories.

My theory? It all comes down to this: taking out the trash.

(You could also fault: filling your gas tank.

Or: buying groceries.

And: driving your kids to school.)

The dirty little secret (that you won't ever have to clean up yourself) is that after the thrill of the first few weeks of not performing these mundane tasks, less thrilling tasks take their place. Another luncheon. Shopping. A charity event. Therapy (because you feel strangely unfulfilled even though you have more money than God, certainly more than Bernie [though not as much as Hillary]). A premiere. Another dinner with people you don't care about who don't care about you. You'll even plan "family" trips with these people. Even though the only thing that matters is what you can do for each other (until one of you becomes irrelevant—and irrelevance is always just around the corner, conveniently located next to a liquor store).

Your life becomes more disconnected and less meaningful as the normal daily, monotonous tasks fall away. You're not connected to your food, your transportation, your waste, your own kids.

Nice work if you can get it, you'll say. What's to complain about? Kids? Kids are overrated. The pay sucks.

Who wouldn't trade normalcy for living large in a giant house where no one (except housekeepers and gardeners and assistants and dog trainers and orchid handlers) can hear you scream?

Meanwhile, the spouse making all the money works long, stressful hours, wineglass-thin ego on the firing line, ready to be (publicly, humiliatingly) shattered 24-7.

The spouse who's not bringing in the big bucks thinks, *I'm going to be a different kind of wife (or husband). I'll fill those hours with meaning. I'll be unique. I'll be super-interesting. I'll change the world (if not my underwear— leave that to someone else.) I'll meditate. I'll become a yoga teacher working in prisons. I'll write more.* (And I did. Not more. Just spread out, like a word every twenty minutes.)

When you don't have to worry about rent or heating bills or putting

food on the table, the only person you can blame for that nagging dis-
content is, guess what . . . that clown in the mirror. You.

But in Hollywood, we don't blame ourselves.

So the blame falls on the other. The person lying in bed next to you.

Hi. Have we met?

Suffice it to say (or write), in practice, this theory cuts both ways. The
comedy director married to the scowling news addict who blamed him
for ruining her "photography career." The action star whose makeup
artist wife blamed him for her not becoming the next Laura Mercier.
The vegan whose body burst in a full bloom of eczema after her studio
chief husband stuck to the no-kid clause in their prenup. (They later divorced after she was past her childbearing years; he remarried a young
pastry chef; their Christmas cards include twins. Her Christmas cards
include a rescue cat.)

And so on.

I can only speak for me. Agnes. I could only dance so fast and jump
so high and bob and weave for so long—mid-race, I dropped the baton,
tripped over my feet, and skidded down the marriage track.

Still, there was a time I thought we could beat the odds.

Trevor and I, in the first years of our marriage, would sip our Ivy
margaritas and marvel at all the issues other Hollywood couples had.
They had nothing to talk about. They weren't interested in each other.
She'd let herself go. He'd let himself go. She was on antidepressants and
drinking. He was gambling millions. She was bipolar. He was bi. Their
marriage was bye-bye.

We'd have a dinner date at least once a week, just the two of us.
Other couples would gaze at us from their group tables and ask, "How
did we do it after six, seven, eight years? How?"

This was *my* marriage. This was it. There were none before; there'd
be none after.

Then this chick sneaked up on us. Stealthy beeyotch.

Hollywood.

She wanted everything. Your time. Your attention. Your undying devotion. She played on your fears and dashed your hopes. She'd throw you a bone every once in a while, then steal it back.

Hollywood attracts a certain type of person. Bright but not chemical engineering bright. Charming. Socially adept. High self-regard but low self-esteem. Pleasure-seeking rule-breakers.

Just your basic, everyday sociopath.

"One in twenty-five Americans is a sociopath," Liz told me when we discussed a *HuffPo* article on dating sociopaths. Something about the diagnosis seemed familiar.

"And they're all in my neighborhood," I said.

I left word for Trevor, again. Pep had finally texted me back that she was with her dad and *where did you go, Mom? Dad said you went 2 spa? I kno u hate massages Auntie Fin said you were kidnapped by elves she's funny*

Auntie Fin is hilarious, I texted. *Wasn't exactly a spa we'll talk about it. When ur 30.*

Dad wants me to be an influencer

A what no no no no a what?

he says I need more followers

you don't need more followers no one "needs" followers. You shouldn't even have an IG account. Go to sleep honey, I love you.

Okay but maybe it's a good idea he said medical school is hard

Everything is hard, honey. Everything. I love you.

A second later.

Did you brush your teeth? I asked. *I love you so much!*

I slipped into bed, exhausted. Not enough energy to brush my teeth or smooth on one of my 153 face creams that kept multiplying like guppies on my bathroom counter. Almond rehab seemed so far away and like it happened to some other wife.

I dialed Trevor one more time.

Click. Someone answered. I heard breathing.

"Hello?" I sat up in bed, blinking in the darkness. I could see canyon lights twinkling and Jay Leno's fifty-car garage built into a hillside from our room. "Trevor?"

"Yes."

"You can't just take Pep—"

"Yes, I can. She's my daughter, too. She's mine. And you were supposed to be gone for weeks."

"I don't need rehab; you know that. You have to bring her back."

Pause.

"Okay, but only because I have meetings all day. Can you take her to school? She needs lunch. And pick her up?"

I could see lights on in the Katzenberg mansion, where lights were always on because success doesn't sleep. I could hear samba music coming from Matt Damon's Mediterranean, and I wondered if he were really that happy or just mocking the rest of us.

"Of course," I said. "And she doesn't need to be an influencer, okay? That's a ridiculous term, and it's way too much pressure. Our daughter is actually smart. She can do real things with her life."

"Bob's daughter is an influencer. She's got over a million followers. She's not even cute. Jason's daughter, too. I'm just trying to be helpful so she's not some weird loser with her head stuck in a book."

"Good night, Trevor," I said. "Oh. You canceled my credit cards, right?"

"I don't want to talk about it; you know my rule—no bad conversations after 5:00!"

"Last question, I swear. Just to be clear," I asked. "We are getting divorced?"

Pause.

"I was talking to Kevin Bacon, and he said our marriage sounded shaky."

"Well, then," I said. "Um, I guess I'll see you . . . well, hopefully, we can be civil—"

"Gotta go; Geffen's calling," he said and hung up.

I woke up with a sense of calm, peace, and relief that I hadn't felt in years. I could breathe. It was like a six-foot, 165-pound weight with 4 percent body fat had been lifted off my chest. It didn't matter anymore if I didn't ace my perpetual marriage SATs. I'd never need that virtual number 2 pencil again in my life.

"I guess it's official if Kevin Bacon has weighed in," Liz said as we hiked up the bike trail into the Santa Monica Mountains.

"Trevor can be Trophy Dad," I said. "He can see Pep whenever he wants, take her on exotic vacations. I'll be the boring, reliable oak, making sure she's well fed and doing her homework and chores."

"Trophy Dad," Liz said, rolling it around her mouth. "I think you can sell him on that. Got a nice ring to it."

"Do you know any kids who do chores?" I asked.

"Yes," Liz said. "They're east of the 405."

I stopped and took a breath. "I'm feeling pretty good about all this."

"What does your lawyer say?"

"Oh, I don't have a lawyer yet," I said as we reached the peak of the hiking trail where the vista opened up all the way to the coastline and Nobu Malibu. "I was going to look into it this week, maybe post something on Nextdoor."

Liz grabbed me. "You need a lawyer. Today." She took out her phone and started punching numbers. "Damn it," she said. "The reception here is shit!"

"What's wrong?" I asked, panicked.

"We have to run back," she said as she started running back down the bike trail.

"At least I'll get some cardio in before I go down!" I yelled, but she was already halfway to the bottom.

"You need a land shark," Liz said, scrolling through her phone as she sat at my desk in my favorite chair; I briefly wondered if I could sneak it out before I lost everything. "The meanest thousand-dollar-an-hour son of a bitch you can find. This is your job!"

"I'm a writer, not a divorcer."

"You're fired. Do you think Trevor wouldn't try to have your hands broken if he could? To stop you from working? He wants revenge!"

"Revenge for what?"

"For scaling the wall," she said.

"I can't even scale a fish."

"Have you read the malignant narcissist handbook?"

"The WME directory? I'm not even the one asking for divorce," I said, my throat tightening.

"It doesn't matter. None of it matters," she said. She tapped her phone twice. "Sit down. We're going lawyer shopping."

I started pacing; my phone buzzed.

Briarwood. I answered.

"Mrs. Nash," the head of school said, and I immediately pictured his florid cheeks and beaver hair. "Could you please come down to the school?"

"Pep has never cheated in her life," I said. "She's never needed to."

I was seated next to Pep, slouched in front of Dr. Hanley's desk. Trevor, tapping his long fingers on his chair, was there when I arrived.

"I admitted it," Pep said, blowing a strand of red hair from her eyes. "So when do I get kicked out?"

"Pep has always been a top student," Dr. Hanley said. "She's always gotten straight As. I'm not sure what happened here. And it was so obvious."

"I took out my phone and tapped in questions," she said. "Obviously, I need to be punished. I'd say at least a suspension."

"I think this is because my wife—" Trevor said. "Well, my current wife—"

"We're getting divorced," I explained.

"What?" Pep said. "You said you were just taking a break."

"I am so sorry," I said, grabbing her hand.

"Well, that might explain sudden behavior patterns," Dr. Hanley said.

"What behavior patterns?"

"Pep refuses to participate in PE," he said. "She's been lying down during track. On the track. She claims she's a dolphin. A stranded dolphin. And she can't breathe."

"Oh, well, I love dolphins," I said.

"I don't belong here. The whole thing makes me so tired," Pep said. "Why are you getting divorced?"

"You'll have to ask your mom," Trevor said. Pep and the president eyed me with a flicker of accusation.

"Excuse me?"

"Am I getting kicked out or not?" Pep asked.

"Of course not, dear," the president said. "You'll have to take the test again, obviously. And you'll be on probation."

"Oh," Pep said, her shoulders slumping. "What does it take to get kicked out? Pull the fire alarm? Pinch Mr. Marcucci's butt?"

Mr. Marcucci was the eighty-year-old science teacher with a single-haired comb-over.

"Pep, what's this all about?" I asked.

"My wife just got out of rehab, if you have to know," Trevor said.

"Are you kidding?" I said, and I turned to the president. "Trevor sent me to rehab because I eat almonds! A lot of almonds, but still!"

"Stacy's mom went to rehab," Pep said. "And Manny's mom. And Collette's dad."

"Honey, I don't have a drug problem."

"That's okay, Mom," Pep said. "It's totally fine."

"But I don't—"

Trevor pretended to be drinking out of his thumb.

"A lot of our moms are having Pinot and Perco issues," Dr. Hanley said. "It's an epidemic, frankly. Mrs. Nash, I wish you all the best. I know how hard this journey can be. We're here for you. Think of us as family." He smiled, and I stared at the gap between his front teeth. He stood and shook my hand.

"That's okay," I said. "I already have a family, and they're a pain in the ass."

His face froze. "Pep, head to your next class," he managed. "I expect you to be on your best behavior. No more shenanigans."

Trevor stepped past as Dr. Hanley gave me a parting sad glance. "Mrs. Nash, have you considered therapy?"

I headed to my car in the visitor's parking lot. Briarwood was housed in the old Masonic lodge on Sunset. We snagged a coveted spot for Pep when she was a nameless fetus, which, even then, was late in the game. Trevor, eager to get his zygote into the same school as his peers, had breakfast with a board member and promised his kid a part in a movie.

(Yes, there was diversity at Briarwood; at least 15 percent of the parents of the student body were agents.)

The Holier-Than-Thous, carpool moms wearing Chanel bracelets, Alo tights, and expressionless faces, stood in a perfumed, selfie-ready, judgmental clump, watching as I fumbled with my car keys.

"Agnes Nash?"

A young woman with a bright, open face and a streak of pink in her hair tapped me on the shoulder and smiled. She looked like one of our newer teachers.

"Yes?"

She slapped an envelope against my chest.

"You've been served," she said, all sparkly, and trotted off to her awaiting Honda, the engine still running. Lucky me, the judgmental clump witnessed the whole exchange.

Perfect, I thought, *I'll be starring in an Instagram story.*

I hopped in my car and peeled out onto Sunset before pulling over to a side street. I ripped open the envelope as a gardener wearing a giant leaf blower worked the patch of grass in front of an apartment building.

The first page of the beginning of the end, in black and white. The name of Trevor's attorney at top left. *Ulger Blecks.*

"Sorry you didn't use it, Dickens," I said.

Page upon page with tiny boxes marked with an *X* and Trevor's giant, wriggly signature at the bottom of the last page. Irreconcilable differences. I mean . . .

My phone buzzed.

"Darling," Karyn said. "Are you coming to RAPE?"

"What?"

"RAPE Committee? Did you not get the email? Are you still using your same name?" she said. "We're at Le Pain. The meeting started fifteen minutes ago."

"Oh, I forgot all about RAPE."

"I heard you just got served; so sorry, how awful," she said. "I'm afraid you might be too distracted for RAPE."

My divorce was trending on Hollywood Twitter.

"I've never been too distracted for RAPE," I said

"I'll sign you up for Ancillary RAPE Committee," she said. "It's not as brutal."

. . .

I googled Liz's list of Terrible, Horrible, No-Good, Very Bad Divorce Lawyers. Three were obese, with hollow-point eyes. Two had pitted faces, deep scars from the ravages of teenaged acne, partially hidden with scraggly beards. One appeared to have scurvy.

"Why are they all so . . . appearance-challenged?" I asked. "Am I just being looksist?"

"The job does it to them," Liz said. "Every single one would sell their firstborn to a Chinese skin factory for a deposit. This woman, right here, modeled to get through law school."

She pointed to a photo of a truck with ears.

I punched in my first number.

"Hi, this is Agnes Nash," I said.

"Can you repeat that?"

"Agnes Murphy Nash?" I said. "I'm calling to talk to Magnus Nelson."

"Hold, please," she said.

A second later, she came back on the phone.

"I'm sorry," she said.

"That's okay," I said. "We can talk later."

"Um," she said. "No, that's not what I'm sorry about. Mr. Nelson can't speak to you. He's already spoken to your husband."

Confusion. Sweaty palms. Dread.

"But . . . he's not representing my husband."

"He met with your husband."

"I don't understand," I said.

"I know," she said, sighing. "Mr. Nelson can't meet with you because your husband has already paid him for a meeting. Conflict of interest, 'kay? Have a nice day!"

I made five more calls. It seemed the same receptionist was working at each firm and they'd all expected me to call.

Can't I have a fun divorce? Like in the movies, where perimeno-pausal divorcees dance in nightclubs and meditate on mountaintops and screw housepainters in Italy. Can we fast-forward to the housepainters?

I called Liz. I could hear women cawing in the background over restaurant clatter.

"Trevor cockblocked me," I said. "He took a ten-minute meeting with each lawyer and gave each a nominal check."

"Okay. Don't panic! Do not panic!" Liz said, sounding like someone had lit her hair on fire. "Do you know who he's hired?"

"Ulger Blecks."

Liz whistled. I think it was the first time I'd heard her whistle.

"Find someone. Anyone. Today," she said. "Remember Angela, Lilo's ex? Remember her?"

"I don't think so . . . no?"

"Do you know why? Because she's living in Ontario."

"Canada?"

"Riverside. She gets her water from an old well! Her ex got every-thing—the kids, the house—and she had to pay for it! He had all the money, and she pays him alimony and child support!"

I hung up.

"Gabi!" I yelled, bolting up the stairs. "Gabi!"

10

Family Law 101

Gabriela had saved that crumpled piece of paper Fin had given to me, the one with the lawyer's name. Anne Barrows. Anne, Annie. Sounded friendly and competent. I crossed my fingers.

The receptionist took my name. *So far, so good.*

"Is she available to meet today?"

"Sounds like someone's in a hurry," she said, but her voice had a smile layered on it. "She has an opening at 5:00, after court. She could be a few minutes late."

I called Liz to tell her the good news.

"Never heard of her," she said.

We were to meet at Anne's office in what I figured was an acceptable zip code. I parked and looked for her name on the automated list of offices in the lobby—lots of lawyers and all of them with three names. Anne's had only one.

I walked through the door marked ANNE BARROWS, ESQ. in gold lettering. The office was small and cozy, decorated in warm colors. The receptionist offered me Hershey's Kisses. I was home.

"I'm here to kick ass and take names," I said, popping the chocolate in my mouth and grabbing another.

She smiled and told me Anne would be out in a few.

"Would you like something to drink?" she asked.

I thought about it. "Gasoline."

"You sure?"

"How about bourbon?" I said. "A pint. Neat. I don't know what neat is, but I like the sound of it."

"Perfect," she said. "One Diet Coke coming up."

Anne Barrows, a tall, slender grandmother of many, twirled her fingers through her gray-blond bob, then cracked her neck. She had the thinnest wristwatch gracing her wrist, scant hints of jewelry, no wedding ring. In another life, she'd been a San Marino debutante and Pasadena Rose Bowl Queen, married at twenty-one to her high school sweetheart. That much I'd ferreted out on my phone, sitting in the lobby, too nervous to read *Us Weekly*—"Kylie Minogue's Hidden Heartbreak," "Chris Pratt's Weight Loss Secrets." I couldn't keep up with all the famous Chrises.

Her small desk in her tidy office was surrounded by framed photos of her grandchildren, needlepoint pillows plumped on chairs. One said, *World's Best Grammy*; another: *I Love My Schnauzers*. I spied a brochure for the Peace Corps on her coffee table.

"The Peace Corps? Is that still a thing?" I asked. "Someone joining?"

"Oh, I am," she said. "As soon as I retire."

I cleared my throat. Schnauzer pictures, needlepoint, and the Peace Corps. Did any of this scream "killer attorney"?

"Okay, so you were married almost ten years," Anne said, flicking on a set of red-framed reading glasses and pulling out a yellow legal pad.

"And happy for six," I said. *"Ba dum bum?"*

She gave me a small smile. I liked the way the wrinkles around her eyes fanned out over her cheekbones, a rare sighting in these parts.

"You've brought a copy of your prenup."

I sifted through the giant purse that women in Beverly Hills carried around like grocery bags, then handed the prenup over.

"I haven't looked at it since the wedding."

She took her time reading, glancing at me occasionally. A few soft murmurs. Twisting her mouth. Scratching notes onto the pad. I stared at the clock above her head, watched the second hand *tick tick tick tick-ticktick.*

"Huh, okay," she said finally. "May I ask you a question?"

"Will it hurt?"

She leaned back in her chair. It squeaked, piercing the air, a giggling rebuke. "Why did you sign this?" *Squeak.*

I felt my face burn. "It seemed pretty standard," I said.

"Standard for what?" She smiled. I saw pity and admonishment in her smile lines. I felt like one of her grandchildren (or schnauzers) trekking mud into the kitchen.

"My lawyer said it was a standard agreement."

"Let's see . . ." She peered over her glasses at what I assumed was the signature page. "Corwin C. Brown."

"Yes," I said, picturing a weasel with a tropical tie and chapped lips. "Trevor found him for me. I didn't know anyone."

"How kind," she said dryly. "We have our work cut out for us."

"So you'll take my case?" Beat. "Is that what I call this? A case?"

"Who's opposing counsel?" she asked.

"Ulger Blecks."

She whistled.

"Why is it everyone whistles when they hear his name? Is he a dog?"

"A pit bull that frightens rabies."

"You're scaring me," I said.

"You should be a little scared," she said. "It'll help you be aware of your environment. And aware of what you're signing when you sign a legal document." She waved the prenup, its pages giving off a slight breeze.

"A little scared calls for a lot of wine," I said.

"Wait on that. I need you to bring all your calendars for the last ten years to the office. I want you to go through everything in detail. Every meeting, every conversation you can remember having with your husband that counteracts this prenup."

My knees started shaking.

"Custody of Pep," I said. I cleared my throat. "That's all I want. Our daughter. She's at a vulnerable age. I can see her going either way, influencer or pediatrician."

"What's an influencer?"

"You're so lucky," I said.

"Can you afford to support Pep on your own?"

"Of course," I said.

"In the manner to which she's used to?" Anne clarified.

My heart sank. I calculated how much I'd spent on my dad and Fin and the relatively meager figure left in my accounts. Strange to be living rich and cash poor. But so was half of Bel Air. I knew people driving Rolls-Royces who'd quietly sold off their furniture and lived in twenty thousand square feet of echoes. *Broke broke broke broke broke broke . . .*

Hard to feel sorry for them, but still.

Nope. Still hard.

"I can't afford all those bathrooms. I can't even use all those bathrooms. And housekeepers. And Postmates. Pep's just discovered Postmates. It's like buying a car every month, but instead it's tacos."

Anne stood and smiled. "Keep that sense of humor," she said, holding out her hand. "You're going to need it."

"Of course I'll keep it," I said, shaking her hand. "Unless you think I can sell it."

I was halfway to the elevators when my phone buzzed.

Dad. I answered and stepped into an empty elevator.

"Hello? Daddy?"

Static static static.

"Dad, I'll call you back! I can't hear you; I'm in an elevator—"

His voice popping in and out.

"Son of a bitch . . ."

A man in a pin-striped suit, wearing a Rolex and lugging a bulging briefcase, hopped into the elevator. He smelled like ill-gotten gain. I squeezed into a corner, making plenty of space for him.

"Daddy, what're you talking about? What's going on?"

"You didn't tell me you were getting a divorce—"

"I'm sorry, I didn't want to upset you," I said. "It's no big deal. Lots of people get divorced . . . hello?"

Static static.

"I'll call you back," I said, hanging up.

Pinstripe eyed me with a hint of appraisal. "Who do you have?" He took a card out of his breast pocket.

"Sorry?"

"Who's representing you?"

The card twisted in Pinstripe's fingers. He was wearing his college ring on his pinkie.

"Anne Barrows."

His trimmed eyebrows knitted together. I could practically hear him pulling up a face from his mental roster.

"Who does he have?"

The elevator doors opened.

"Ulger Blecks."

Pinstripe whistled, shoved his card back in his vest pocket, then skipped out.

"What is with the whistling?" I called out as I hustled out of the elevator.

My phone was buzzing again.

"Dad."

"Sitting at Starbucks with Shu minding my own goddamn business. Squirrelly guy tells me you're getting divorced. Son of a bitch, he's lucky I didn't punch his lights out."

My dad still talks about the cauliflower ears he dished out back in Boston as a Golden Gloves champ. Six decades ago.

"Well, I am getting divorced," I said.

"Does this have something to do with Easter?"

"Strangely enough, yes."

"Damn. I told Shu you could get her into a movie," he said. "She's a terrific actress. Very talented. And so smart. She speaks at least four, maybe five, languages."

"Dad," I said. "I have to go."

"Hey," he said. "Don't worry, kiddo, I'm on your side. I'm sticking with you."

My phone buzzed. Another call. A New York number.

"Great. Thanks. Talk to you later, Dad," I said.

"Be good." I'd have to be good, extra good, for the next two to four years or however long a Hollywood divorce takes.

I picked up the new call as I made my way through the lobby.

"I heard the news," Waverly said, sounding dour. I mean, dourer than usual. *Funeral for golden retriever puppies* dour. "Who's his lawyer?"

"Ulger Blecks."

She whistled.

"I can't with the whistling," I said.

"It'll be fine," Waverly said in a tone that said nothing would ever be fine again. "I hope you're in full hair and makeup."

"Never."

"From now on, you don't go out without full hair and makeup. Like I told Demi, appearance is everything."

.   .   .

"I want you to be seen," Waverly said, guiding me through the lobby of the Sofitel in West Hollywood for a swag party for a video game awards show sponsored by a Tokyo-based digital currency. (*Come get us, aliens.*) A swag party is where they give people who already have too much, things they don't need. "You need to socialize, to network, to show everyone you're not just Trevor's wife."

"I'm not Trevor's wife," I said.

"You must play a winning psychological battle," she said. "Michelle, Nicole, Jennifer—they were dining al fresco at the Ivy before the ink was dry on the filings. I did that. That was all me."

Waverly explained the three-point plan that helped her through her own twelve-year divorce. I know it sounds crazy to be taking advice from anyone who drew out a divorce way past the presidential term limit, but I wasn't exactly at my most rational. I wanted to whip through this divorce in a few months and have a peaceful Thanksgiving together like a normal dysfunctional, functional family.

"You need to:

1. Socialize.

2. Strategize.

3. Pulverize."

The biggest piece of advice, however, was one I knew I couldn't master.

"Never let them see you sweat," I repeated.

"Unless you're on a hike. I had Nicole hiking the second the order came down. All me."

"I can hike," I said.

"What's your divorce brand?" Waverly asked as we walked through the lobby, past photographers and Euro-hipsters.

"What do you mean?"

"Are you a Ben-Jen?" she asked. "They go to church together. Sweet. A Gwyneth-Chris—they dine together. Vegan, of course. In my opinion, those two waited too long for public dining; they should've called me before *People* got ahold of the story. How about Angie-Brad; I'm helping them with an *Us* piece. You need a brand."

"How about packaging my divorce as an unconscious uncoupling? Not as photogenic Gwyneth's, of course. But hear me out. I get divorced while on propofol."

We stepped into an elevator with awkward millennial actors I didn't recognize but who seemed terrified of eye contact. Meanwhile, I couldn't pick them out of a lineup with a gluten-free bagel to my head.

"YouTube," Waverly whispered in my ear. "Five million followers."

We hit the penthouse, and the agitated YouTube stars scurried away as our senses were hammered by electronic disco music. Waverly yanked me to the side for one more bon mot.

"Think catastrophically," she said. "Plan accordingly."

"People get divorced every day," I said, swallowing my fear and my gum.

"Splitting up is bigger than getting married. You were married for over a decade; you'll be divorced for life," she said. "We could push an Ava Gardner–Frank Sinatra angle."

We gave our names at the door and were ushered inside. The penthouse was packed with mid-level celebrities, none of whom would ever grace the Oscar stage except, maybe, to sweep it. I could see the top of the Beverly Center from the floor-to-ceiling windows and edges of Cedars Sinai. I thought about the postnatal suite at Cedars where I'd recovered from my emergency C-section; the room had been filled with flowers and gifts. Trevor had ordered truffle linguine from a nearby Italian restaurant, and we sang to our new Pep all night long.

"You are my sunshine, my only sunshine . . ."

Sigh.

Waverly handed me a large shopping bag. "Take these," she said, tossing eye shadow and lipsticks in my bag.

Swag stations were set up, giving away, among other goodies, Samsung phones and hover boards.

"Is this the flammable suite?" I asked.

A Kirsten Dunst look-alike screamed as she ran her hover board into a couch.

Waverly tossed cellulite cream and Moroccan hair gel in my bag.

"Cellulite cream doesn't work," I said. "Unless you eat it and throw up."

She grabbed two hover boards and handed me one.

"I don't want a hover board," I said.

"My son wants two," she said.

"Smile," a photographer I recognized from my event-filled almost-former life called to us. She paused before recording our names into her camera.

"What are you going by now, hon?" she asked me.

"She's going by her name," Waverly said. "Agnes Murphy Nash."

Waverly filled my bag and hers with combustible phones and makeup and nail polish and costume jewelry, and then we left, each of us with a hover board under our arm. We waited outside the elevators as I wrestled with my booty.

The elevator doors opened, and my husband-ish stepped out.

"Trevor?"

"Smile," the photographer said as she snapped photos.

We stood there, me trying to balance my goody bag and the hover board and Trevor trying to balance his smile with transparent irritation.

Petra appeared, holding out a swag bag for Trevor.

"A-nus," Petra said, "what a surprise."

"Lady MacSlavic," I replied. "This is Waver—"

I turned. Waverly, all six feet and hover board and musk, had vanished.

I turned back. Trevor shook his head and strode past me into the suite. Petra followed, then stopped next to me and smiled.

"I'm pregnant," Petra said, then pranced off behind Trevor.

. . .

"She beat the Hollywood land-speed record for nanny pregnancies," I said, waiting with Waverly in a line outside valet parking. "I've been Stefani'ed."

"Gwen Stefani's nanny was never impregnated," Waverly said. "Gwen's lovely, by the way."

"Is she a client?"

"I can't say."

"What's with nannies getting impregnated by their employers? I never hear about Hollywood wives getting knocked up by their gardeners. Where'd you go, by the way?"

"I don't want Trevor to know I'm working for you," Waverly said. "I'm staying in Steven's guesthouse."

"Steven . . . ?" There was only one Steven (allowed) in town.

"Yes, that Steven," she said. "I don't want any problems."

"What are you doing for . . . that Steven?"

"I can't say. You'll read about it in the trades."

I watched scurrying valet parkers pick off smooth, fancy, shiny cars. Centerfold- and World Cup–ready Brazilians had cornered the market on valet parking, and I hoped to be lucky enough to marry one of them someday and have a beautiful child and have my future nanny have a beautiful child by my valet parker husband as well.

"She's lying, by the way," Waverly said as she slipped into the back of an Uber Black. "He'd never impregnate staff."

"Of course she's lying," Liz said. I called her immediately from the car. "I don't need a psychic—"

"Cognitive." Liz was a little miffed that I hadn't been to her psychic yet. She had about five of them lined up for various catastrophes.

"Whatever," Liz said. "—to tell me that. Reminds me of the director's mistress who needed a million-dollar 'faux-bortion.'"

"Those cost as much as raising a kid."

My phone beeped. My lawyer, Anne. Her receptionist was on the line.

"Hi, dear," she said, and I loved her for mothering me. I'm sure all the clients felt the same. "Congrats. You have your first mediation scheduled."

"What do I wear?"

She paused. "Something to make him regret the day he walked out."

I thought for a moment.

"I'll wear a coat of hundred-dollar bills."

Mediation was scheduled at the Blecks Holstein Castle offices on Rodeo in a building decorated Southwestern Gucci style, which is to say it managed to look ugly, dated, *and* expensive. I followed Anne into a conference room where we'd be meeting with a retired judge experienced in mediating divorce. I'd spent the last week combing through calendars for the last eleven years and calculating the amount of time I'd spent with Pep as opposed to Trevor. The percentages were divided as follows: Me, 63 percent; Gabriela and Her Sisters (like *Hannah and Her Sisters* without the white upper-class whinging), 35 percent; Trevor, 2–11 percent, partially by accident. Once we got the custody arrangements out of the way, I'd leave the financials up to the divorce gods. And hope for the best.

Like a roof over my head.

"Primary custody," I said to Anne as we sat alone in that bare conference room. "Those two little words. Repeat after me—"

"Agnes, I know you feel that way," she patted my hand, then pushed back her bangs. "We're going to try our best."

"No trying, only doing," I said. "Right?"

"California is a fifty-fifty custody state," she said. "Unless there are extenuating circumstances . . ."

I felt like I'd been kicked in the stomach. The door swung open, and the skeleton in my high school biology class with gray sideburns popped in and rubbed his bony hands together.

"Hey, so here's how we're going to do this," our mediator said as he jumped into a seat across from us. Spry, this man. "I get a wish list, basically, of everything you'd like in the divorce."

"We have our list ready," Anne said, and she slid a piece of paper over. He donned a pair of reading glasses over his sharp nose. We'd been reasonable. I stay at the house until we sell, or at least three months, while I find a new place. Primary custody of Pep. No alimony.

That was it.

"This is it?" he asked. He sounded disappointed.

"What else did you expect?" I asked. "Am I divorcing wrong?"

"Agnes wants as peaceful a parting as possible," Anne said.

"An alliterative adieu," I said.

"I'm a bit thrown off. I thought you'd want to draw this out," he said, looking at me. "Most women do. It's a form of attention. You walk down the halls of your lawyer's office, everyone's happy to see you, right, honey?"

I heard Anne growl, but this poster child for Viagra had already launched from his seat. He was the type of man who medaled at the Senior Olympics.

"I'll run this by them," he said as he hopped to the door. "You're being unreasonably reasonable!"

"That's me. When I'm not basking in divorce lawyers' attention."

He tilted his head. "I'm pretty sure we can have this wrapped up today."

The door closed.

"Let's get this over with and get away from Bobby Riggs," I said. "You want to have lunch? I'm paying."

She smiled. "You're always paying."

"Touché!"

I gulped my water and contemplated the rest of my afternoon, secure in the dream that my divorce would turn out to be a piece of cake.

The door opened.

Mr. Senior Olympics stepped inside, looking deflated.

"He walked out," he said.

"What do you mean?"

"I read your husband your list," he said. "I said it was reasonable. And that we could wrap this up ASAP. And he . . . walked out."

Of course he did. Any negotiation was a loss. Trevor needed to fight, to punish, to emerge victorious, standing atop the heap of divorce booty holding my blow-dryer aloft.

The dryer he'd manage to wrest from me in the divorce.

(I wish I'd kept a receipt for that blow-dryer.)

"Good luck," Mr. Senior Olympics said, shaking his head as Anne and I gathered our things. "You're going to need it."

"So what do I do now?" I asked. "Besides head to the roof and jump onto the hood of an Arab prince's illegally parked Lamborghini?"

"We wait," she said. "In the meantime, relax. If we have a big battle ahead; you need to be healthy and present for your daughter."

"Sounds like I'm going in for chemo," I said.

"I've had cancer and divorce, and I'd rather have cancer," Anne said.

"Stage one or two?" I asked.

"Stage three with 65 percent curability," she said.

"What does Trevor want?" I asked. "Besides twelve Oscars, ninety-two Emmys, $364 billion, an NBA team, a sixty-thousand-square-foot home, and to be loved and adored by all, even the gardener you don't pay a living wage?"

Anne looked at me, giving me a half smile, her eyes crinkling at the edges. Perfect crinkles, hers.

"He wants to win," she said. "And in my line of work, winning usually means the kids lose."

And then she sighed like she wished she'd signed up with the Peace Corps a year ago.

11

Your Life in Turnaround

I'd fallen asleep watching *The Philadelphia Story* on my iPad. Katharine Hepburn was going through with the wedding to her former husband (yes, I get the underlying meaning). Also, yes, I may have shed a tear or two in memoriam to all our Cary Grants.

Earlier that night, I'd set the alarm after urging Pep to get off her (goddamn) phone and go to sleep.

"It's my phone," Pep had said.

"Do you pay the bills?"

"Do you?" Pep had asked.

Kids are great, and I highly recommend them.

"You're going to go blind," I'd said, recalling my dad's warnings about the blind nuns.

"Perfect," Pep had said, "the less I see, the better."

I'd finally snatched the phone out of her hand, and she'd slammed her bedroom door on me.

"I thought I had two more years before you turned into a monster!" I'd said through the door.

"I hate you!" she'd shouted.

"Good night!" I'd shouted back. Then, "Make sure you put the field trip slip in your bag!"

That was me saying, *I love you; I'm sorry, but I'm the mom, not you.*

I was in a REM sleep coma; Cary Grant may or may not have proposed to me—

The screaming wail of our house alarm shattered the proposal. I bolted straight up. I heard a man curse. I reached down under the bed and brought up the Louisville Slugger.

Holding the bat high, I sneaked down the long hallway filled with pictures of Trevor and celebrities. In the moonlight, Trevor and Eddie flashed iridescent smiles, Trevor and Sylvester scowled, Trevor's and Cruise's chiseled jawlines.

Nerve sweat trailed down my back. Hormone sweat had a thicker viscosity.

"Shut that thing off!" a man in black yelled in the dim light of the kitchen, his back to me.

I pulled back to swing—

Flash! Blindness. The island light flickered on.

Trevor, in a Supreme hoodie, stared at me in utter disbelief. Petra, wearing jeans and one of my old sweatshirts, was recording on her iPhone, hovering protectively over Trevor.

"Trevor, you scared the shit out of me—"

The alarm was still blaring. The phone started to ring. The alarm company, making sure they didn't have to bother to come out.

"You change the alarm code?" Petra asked.

I went to the alarm pad and punched in numbers.

"What are you doing here?" I asked. "Didn't you move out in a huff? Wasn't that you?"

Trevor started walking toward the master. "Ulger told me to move back," he muttered. "I need to sleep in my own bed. That other place smells like seaweed."

"Is that my sweatshirt?" I asked Petra.

She tossed her hair and went after Trevor.

I woke up to find Petra massaging Trevor's shoulders between feeding him bites of gluten-free toast. I swallowed locally sourced bile, retreated, and found the El Salvadoreñas huddled in the laundry room, spitting spicy fire.

"Good morning, ladies!" I clapped.

"I don't work for that *puta*!" Gabriela said as her sisters grumbled.

Lola shoved a tampon in my face. Thankfully unused.

"*Diabla*," Caster said. "She using the tampons—she's not pregnant."

"How did you know—"

"We know everything," Gabriela said. "Caster worked in a house for a year, the girlfriend never had period. Because why? Because she wasn't lady—"

Caster crossed her arms against her manufactured bosom and nodded furiously.

I motioned with my hands. "Calm. Calm-o. *Tranquilo*."

"I know people, Miss Añes," Caster said. "People who take care of people. You want I call them?"

"Thank you so much, Caster. I really appreciate that you would have him killed for me. Fin's already offered. Maybe your people know her people and can get together, you know, have a picnic."

She shrugged. *"De nada."*

"Gabi!" Trevor was calling from the kitchen. "Where are my good socks? I have no good socks! Am I fucking poor?" We heard Petra's footsteps, heading for the laundry room.

"Tranquilo, Gabriela," I said as she clenched her fists. *"Tranquilo."*

.   .   .

I dressed and headed for coffee with a screenwriter and a development exec on the other side of town. Before this divorce business, Trevor had optioned *The Deadlies* for a year with four consecutive option periods. The money was nominal, but hey, we were married. I could trust him. And say what you want about Trevor (and I have), the man knows better than anyone how to get a movie made.

The coffee shop was hidden in a nondescript corner strip mall on a stretch of Carthay Circle, a much-beloved pocket of LA. We have many charming pockets, like the super-expensive travel jacket I once bought Trevor for his birthday that he gave to our handyman after a week.

Carthay Circle was populated by charming old Spanish homes in a city famous for casually tossing out the old to make way for the new— homes, careers, or, you know, *wives.*

The bell at the top of the door trilled as I entered. The air smelled like fair trade, with a sweet, naïve sprinkling of young people believing they could change the world (while lugging around bricks of student loans).

At a corner back table, the writer—pixie cut, fashionable black reading glasses—was sitting across from the executive, one of those bland-as-unsalted-butter male feminists always ready to apologize for nothing they've ever done wrong.

I waved. Their eyes widened. Surprise? Joy? I had aged precipitously? (I made a note to start eating my estrogen cream.)

"Sorry, I'm a few minutes late," I said as I snaked my way to the table. I glanced at their plates. Crumbs. Empty coffee mugs.

"Did I . . . I got the time wrong?" I blinked, conjuring the date and time in my calendar.

"Agnes," the executive popped out of his seat, "I'm so sorry—you didn't get my message?"

The writer stared at the grounds of her empty latte, perhaps reading her fortune.

"What message?"

"It's my fault," he said, his shoulders hunched forward. His voice went soft. "I called you yesterday, Agnes. It went through to voicemail. It was kind of a long . . . detailed message."

"The dead zone," I said. "The reception is shit."

"I sincerely apologize again," he said. "I usually like to deliver bad news in person, but given the circumstances . . ."

The writer excused herself to make a phone call. I watched her weave through chairs, directionless.

"Trevor put the project in turnaround," he said. "We're not moving forward."

"But that's my writer," I said, motioning toward the retreating wordsmith. "I mean, not *my* writer; I don't own her, but I did suggest using her, so, like, possession is nine-tenths of the law, obviously."

"She's wonderful; you have fantastic taste!" he said. "She's working on another project for us now."

"Another project." I sucked in my cheeks. *Bitch, what.*

"Yes, it's actually very exciting; you'd love it. It's based on an idea Trevor had."

"I'll give you the option money back. I'll sell it somewhere else. Fuck it, and fuck you guys."

He drew in his breath.

"What?"

"We've . . . optioned your book for the next four years," he said. "As per our agreement. Your film agent didn't tell you?"

"No," I said, picturing my asshole film agent. He was always sending me photos of himself on beaches, the slopes, Machu Picchu. "No, he didn't. He's on terminal vacation."

"You know," he said, rubbing my arm lightly like he was making snail tracks. "This could work out really well for you. I'm sure in a year or so, you and Trevor will be on super-friendly terms, then, you know, you can see about getting *The Deadlies* back on track with us."

"Trevor's killing my book," I said. "He's going to sit on it until it dies. You know that, right?"

"I'm so sorry you feel that way, Agnes," he said, patting my shoulder. "But four years goes by really fast!"

I wanted to punch him in his complicit ferret face. I'd make him pay. I'd make them all pay.

"You're buying me a latte!" I said, waving my finger in his face. "A latte and a scone!"

I called my film agent from the car. The scone had exploded, a blueberry crumb missile all over my lap.

"They canceled my book!" I brushed aside a few crumbs and ate others hungrily like a hamster caught on tape.

"Your book isn't canceled," he said. "Your meeting was canceled. I should've told you; I was in Aspen. You know how it is."

"No, actually," I said. "I don't."

"Didn't you get my pic? Powder all day err'day, playa!"

"My book," I said. "What do I do about my book?"

"They're re-upping the option already!" he said. "Fucking awesome news!"

"Listen, Trevor and I are getting a divorce. He's killing it."

"Oh yeah," he said. "End of the lift. Sorry. Gotta scoot, playa!"

He hung up.

I headed back home down Olympic, too distracted to take the 10. Today was not the day to have an accident on the freeway.

I felt like calling my dad. He'd slap me out of this funk.

"First-world problems," he'd say. "What the hell happened to my tough girl? Write another book. You can always get a waitressing job."

I thought about calling Fin.

"Rich white people problems," Fin would tell me, then launch into a story of her friend who just lost her leg in a barrel racing accident and couldn't afford a wheelchair, and then I'd wind up spending an hour trying to Western Union money to someone who didn't have a zip code.

Suck it up, buttercup. Suck it all up.

I turned up the stereo. An attorney with the nickname "Baby-facekilla" wants you to hire him. I turn it off.

The only way I'd get sympathy from my family is if I slipped from first-world to third-world problems, but then I'd be taking them with me, too. At least I'd have company.

As I turned up San Vicente from Wilshire, I remembered to call Anne.

"That's so Ulger," she said when she answered. "Of course he told Trevor to move back in. Leverage."

"I'm way too familiar with the term," I said. "What's your advice?"

"Be perfectly pleasant and ignore him."

"Them," I said.

"Who else is there?"

"His assistant, well, our former house assistant," I said. "She's giving him massages at the breakfast table. She's his companion sleeper."

"Companion sleeper?"

"It's a new thing. You didn't see it in the Style section? All these execs and producers are hiring them. You pay someone to sleep with someone but don't have sex," I said. "I think it started in the hip-hop industry?"

"The nerve of Trevor," Anne said. "You almost have to admire it."

"Yeah," I said. "No."

"This changes everything," she said. "This doesn't sound like a healthy environment for an eleven-year-old."

"Not for a forty-year-old, either."

"I'll send off a super-nasty lawyer letter right away," Anne said.

"Send away," I said.

"Aren't you closer to mid-forties?" she asked, a lilt in her voice.

"Just send the letter, Ms. Divorce Attorney," I said and hung up.

By 5:00, Petra was gone, swearing in Slavic (good name for a band) and kicking the pebbles in our driveway. Trevor stood at the kitchen windows watching her kick and spit expletives while I did the Nae Nae behind his back because my Floss wasn't up to standard.

"I can see you, idiot," Trevor said to the window. "In the reflection. I can see you."

I froze.

"I was planning on getting rid of her anyway," he said, whipping around. "She started wanting things—like for me to care that her grandmother died. You and your stupid lawyer did me a favor."

"My lawyer isn't stupid," I said. "She's brilliant, and guess what? She wants to join the Peace Corps!"

That came out wrong.

"Terrifying!" he said, and he took two steps toward me. On those long, quick legs, he covered a lot of tiled terrain. Suddenly, he was all up in my grill, as the kids say, his face red and twisted with rage. I watched spittle form at the corner of his mouth. I noticed a tiny piece of spinach between his teeth—

"You just freed up my time. I'll spend all my excess energy destroying you. I'm never moving out of here, you understand? Never!"

He pushed through the swinging door to the living room so hard it wound up hitting the back of his head. I heard him stumble.

"Are you okay?" I asked.

"Fuck you! *Fuck you!*" he yelled from the other side of the door before he stomped off.

"I don't really care if you're okay!" I yelled back.

A few days later, Trevor was planning an important meeting at the house, so he had Coliti-Girl call to ask (demand) tearfully that I clear out in the morning. Make myself scarce.

Trevor's wrath had spread like an oozing sore.

Meanwhile, I'd taken to crossing off the days on the ASPCA calendar like a prisoner, except that I wasn't a prisoner. I could walk out at any time. Except I couldn't walk out at any time because divorce. And lawyers. And leverage. I was drinking the leverage beverage.

"You cannot leave," Anne said. "Do I need to come down there and lock you in a bathroom?"

"Say one of us happens to can't stand it anymore," I said. "Hypothetically. Like, one of us keeps dreaming of strangling the other one in our sleep." I was straining myself to summon my inner Beyoncé, but she'd given way to my inner Marie Osmond. Trevor, in the meantime, seemed to be enjoying the torture of living with me. More like living *at* me. We'd crossed paths dozens of times, yet he hadn't spoken a word to me since the swinging door incident. He'd once told me his mother had given his father a silent treatment that had lasted years. A legendary silent treatment, one for the books! In my house, growing up, the silent treatment couldn't make it three seconds; we were all about the yelling treatment.

"Your presence in that house is the only power you have," Anne was saying. "Where would you go?"

"I've been looking on Craigslist. Maybe I could find an apartment without a homicidal roommate? Maybe just a kleptomaniac or petty larcenist?"

"You'll lose your daughter. Ulger will call an emergency hearing. I've seen this scenario a million times."

"Trevor doesn't want to raise his own kid; none of these guys do." I thought of all the rich, powerful, divorced men I'd seen over the years at parties and premieres and lunches; they'd never looked so uncomfortable and miserable as when they had to help a kid into a child's seat.

"He doesn't have to. He has staff to raise them."

"Well, that doesn't seem fair," I said.

Anne started laughing—a light, bubbling laugh. Then the bubbles expanded and multiplied, a bubble bath of a laugh. Trevor's assistant was standing behind me, clearing her nervous little throat.

"Gotta go," I said, hanging up as she bubbled on.

"I'm sorry to ask, but do you think you could . . ." Coliti-Girl double-cocked her head toward the door.

"Oh, right. The big bad meeting," I said. "Who's it for? Who's coming?"

"George Treadwell." (She actually mouthed his name.)

"Who?" I teased.

"Don't tell him I told you, please please please."

"Don't worry," I said, but she had already gone, leaving behind an air of panic. I made a call. Fin answered before the second ring. Desperate times call for desperate measures (and backup).

"What's up?" she asked, sounding sleepy.

"I need help," I said.

"Get to a landline," she said, and I was right back to the grounds of my elementary school, staring at the business end of a big girl's fist. Hearing my sister's words as she ran up behind me.

"Fuck with my sister," she'd said, "that's the last time you use that hand!" My baby sister (by eighteen months, but still) had always come to my rescue. *Fists up, hip turned, last punch.*

"Not that kind of help," I said. "How soon can you be here?"

"I'm on my way," Fin said.

"What? How are you getting here?"

"Drone," she said. "What do you care?"

I heard Fin all the way from Sunset. A roaring tidal wave of machinery. A thunder storm of badass. A bracket of Harleys.

(What do you call a group of Harley riders? Is it a *pod*? A *gaggle*? A *flock*? I wish there were a '90s band called a Flock of Harleys.)

Trevor flew into the kitchen as the Harley riders circled round and round the courtyard, a torrent of surround sound.

"What is this shit?!" he demanded, spittle flying from his mouth, his face red and gnarled.

"I can't hear you," I mouthed, sipped my coffee. From an empty cup.

"Bitch!" he screeched.

He raced outside, jumping up and down and waving his arms in front of the motorcyclists, who rode a few more spins for good measure, oblivious to the tall, lean gentleman on the razor's edge of a coronary.

"Muerte," Gabriela said as she stared out the window. *He's going to die.*

The motorcyclists took off up the driveway, leaving a lone passenger in their dust. Fin slipped off her helmet and whipped her hair. There was a duffel bag at her feet.

She picked it up, slung it over her shoulder, and walked past Trevor.

"Hey, Trev," she said. "How's it hanging?"

I greeted her at the kitchen door with a big hug.

"You're not staying here," Trevor said, following Fin into the kitchen on his tiptoes, elevated by rage. "You can't stay here!"

Fin smiled at Trevor, swiped a match on her hand, and lit a cigarette. "Take it easy, Trev," she said. "You're going to give yourself a heart attack."

My Solange had arrived.

The thing about George Treadwell is that he's a totally open, friendly guy who also happens to like motorcycles. He sauntered into the kitchen as Fin and I were sitting on the island taking turns eating from a peanut butter jar. Fin had her nose in the script Sami the Uber driver had given me; she'd swiped it from my office, where I'd left it on the box filled with my extra books. She didn't bother to take one of my books. Not bitter, I.

"Hey," Treadwell said. Trevor must have taken a pee break; his movie star had entered the domain of the untouchables.

"Hi," I said, standing at attention. GT, a dazzling creature, seemed to move under an invisible spotlight. Movie stars are different from you and me (unless you happen to be a movie star); they just are. GT, J.Lo, Eddie Murphy (still), Will Smith, Denzel, Julia Roberts—I've been around them and they're just better than the rest of us. Sorry. (Are you okay?)

"Hey, was that your ride?" Treadwell asked Fin after giving me a nod. I saw what he saw. Fin with her long arms, her pert nose. Dragon tattoo on her shoulder. Boy hips. Full lips. And not into him. Fin was aging like Lauren Hutton (look her up); her fearlessness made her even sexier.

Me? When I looked in the mirror, my eyes looked skittish, my worry lines were having worry babies. *I'm fine*, I'd repeat. *I'm fine I'm fine I'm fine.* (Not fine.)

"Nah," Fin said without looking up. I wondered if she had no idea who George Treadwell was. Was that even possible? I thought about the years she'd spent in weird, out-of-the-way places—jail, the desert, the mountains, no TV sets, no phones. Is it possible?

She eyed the peanut butter spoon in my hand. "Yo, are you done with that?"

I handed it to her. She went back to the script. Treadwell cleared his throat.

"I prefer a Triumph—like, say, '93," she said, finally giving Treadwell a slow once-over. "I like a Harley for weekend rides, you know?"

"Cool," Treadwell said.

"My dream ride," Fin said, "hands down—Ducati M900 Monster."

"I, ah, own a Ducati M900 Monster," Treadwell said. He puffed out his chest, his smile blazing.

"You're fucking with me," Fin said, pushing herself up from the chopping block. "No one. No. One. Owns an M900 Monster."

"You're looking at a man who owns an M900 Monster." He shot us that famous smile again, folded his arms across his chest, eyebrows dancing.

"You listening to this guy?" Fin said to me, gesturing with the spoon. "What're you, trying to get in my jeans?"

Treadwell smiled. "Maybe. You have an extra spoon? I'm starving." Then he laughed like a lunatic.

Fin handed him hers. "Help yourself."

He grabbed the spoon. "What're you reading?"

"Nunya," Fin said, turning a page.

"What?"

Fin smiled. "Nunya."

"Fin!" I said, I reached over and pinched her side.

"It's a story about Nunya that takes place in a land called Nunya. The lead's name is Nunya."

Treadwell smacked the island with his hand. "Where did you come from?"

"Jail," I said.

"Punk," Fin said.

"Let me see the cover, at least," Treadwell said, trying to snatch it from Fin. He wasn't fast enough.

"You like Gabriel García Márquez?" Fin asked. "I read him when I was away."

"You read GGM and you didn't read my books?" I asked.

"Gabriel . . . ," Treadwell said, his eyes searching. "He's a director, right?"

"No," Fin said. "Follow me, here. This script is like his novels, magical realism, but in Beirut in 1984."

"Whoa!" Treadwell said. "Mind blown!"

"Yeah, and there's this wizard guy, you don't know if he's real."

"How old?"

"I don't know, thirties, forties," Fin said.

George hit his chest. "I could play that part."

"What? No," Fin said. "He's Lebanese."

"I've played Italian, Jewish," Treadwell said. "I do all the ethnics!"

Fin narrowed her eyes and sniffed, coldly assessing the biggest movie star in the world.

"She's looking at me like I'm bad meat," Treadwell said, looking to me for reassurance.

"Get me a job on one of your sets and I might consider you," Fin said.

"Acting?" Treadwell asked.

"Fuck no," Fin said. "Stunts."

Trevor appeared at the swinging door, puffing through his nostrils, a bull seeing red, red everywhere.

"Oh my God," he said as he stumbled toward Treadwell.

"Trev, man, your sister-in-law is a beast," Treadwell said, looking over his shoulder. "You know what this girl rides?"

"Come on, stop," Fin said, punching Treadwell in the arm. He wince-grinned.

Trevor looked from Treadwell to Fin and pulled on his hair.

"Fin, right? She's badass," Treadwell said. "Hey, can she do stunts on this pic? Let's set her up."

"Jump out of buildings and shit," Fin said. "That's my jam."

"Trev, you'll give me her info," Treadwell said.

"Great idea. Shall we wrap up?" Trevor asked.

"Sure," Treadwell said. "Hey, nice talking to you." He shot at us with trigger fingers.

Fin "shot" him in return. He clutched at his heart.

Trevor glared back at us as he hustled his next big paycheck through the swinging door.

Fin looked up at me and sniffed. "What's up with that guy George? He's pretty . . . enthusiastic, right? Is that real? Is he rich? He smells like he's never had a bad day. He smells like sunshine."

"Fin," I said. "That was George Treadwell."

She twisted her lips and scrunched her nose. Fin thinking face.

"Nope," she finally said. "Hey, you think he'd really give me a stunt job? I need to find something. Parole's on my back."

"Fin, it's not going to happen. Trevor will never let it happen."

"Oh yeah? We'll see," Fin said, slapping the script. "Now shut up while I finish."

12

Membership Revoked

Fin and I had our feet up on the coffee table that had never supported a cup of coffee in the living room no one had lived in. Over a box of Dunkin' Donuts, Fin decided she was moving in for a "bit."

"What is this 'bit'?" I asked as I licked powdered sugar off my lips.

"A bit," she said. "A while, a spell, until my sister can function on her own," she said as she pushed doughnut holes aside in the box. "You need help. Protection. Where the fuck's the apple fritter? What did you do with the fritter?"

"I frittered it away," I said before I burped.

We stayed up playing "Fin-der" (as she christened Tinder) until she caught smartphone thumb. She topped out at 150 matches.

"The last time I dated, you used a phone to call people," I said. "Now, you order up dick just like pizza."

"It's dick-convenient," Fin said. "Better than Uber. Although, Uber delivers dick, too, depending on the driver."

I'd boiled water for tea because tea made me feel calm and righteous. Wine required less work but also made me feel sad. And didn't Beyoncé sip herb tea, if I'm understanding her husband's lyrics? Anyway, chamomile with mānuka honey, if you're wondering. Meanwhile, I wondered if I would be able to afford mānuka honey after the divorce.

"I'm so not ready for this new dating world," I said. "If only Trevor were a little more—"

"Not Trevor? Un-Trevor? Anything but Trevor?"

"Fin, how do you get guys to swipe right?" I asked, grabbing her phone. "It says on your profile that you're on parole."

Fin shot me her *say what, now?* face, which she employed when I'd inadvertently, or maybe advertently, said something stupid. She popped her cigarette box on the side of her hand and flipped a stick into her mouth.

"Do you not understand the male of the species, bruh?" she asked, the cigarette bouncing on her lower lip. "Dudes love a bad bitch."

I braced against her stack of silver rings as she play-punched me.

"And . . . that's going to leave a bruise," I said, looking at my shoulder.

"I'm signing you up," she said, grabbing my phone.

"Don't do it," I said.

"I'm doing it," she said.

"You can't. You don't have my Facebook password."

She looked at me and laughed. "Sis, I know all your passwords."

"You do not."

"Morley89, Password7, Fin73," she recited. "Peppers."

"Shit," I said, interrupted.

"First dog, sister, birth year, favorite number," she said. "Now who's the smart Murphy sister?" Fin grabbed my arm to give me an Indian rub, which is probably racist as well as painful.

"I'm still smarter," I said, pushing her off and wrapping my arm around her neck. "I've never gone to prison."

"You just never tried," she said. She slapped my knee, wriggled out from under my grasp, and jumped up off the sofa.

"C'mon," she said, pulling my arm from its socket. "Let's go have some fun!"

. . .

I woke up groggy and late with doughnut crumbs sprinkled on my chest to find Fin and Trevor on either side of the kitchen island staring each other down as though on a dusty main street in an old Western (substitution: fully stocked kitchen in the Palisades Riviera). Trevor chewed his precisely cut apple slices slowly while Fin, freshly showered, ripped apart a bagel with her teeth.

"I know what you did," Trevor finally uttered, his voice a low growl. "I know what you both did."

I coughed, ducked my head, and made a beeline for the coffee machine.

"Hey," Fin said to me without losing the staring contest.

"G'morning," I said, grabbing the coffee cup Gabriela gave me for a Mother's Day, emblazoned with a picture of Pep dressed as a bumblebee. Her first Halloween. I'd waited years to dress a baby as a bee; it was worth the wait.

"Tell me what you did!" Trevor yelled, banging his fist on the island.

"Why don't you tell us, Trevor?" Fin said. "Because I'm not sure what you're talking about. Are you, Aggie?"

"You're not welcome here," Trevor said, I'm not sure to whom.

"Morning, Trev," I said. "Are you okay?"

"I don't want a felon around my child!" he said.

"Half your friends would be doing time if I took a look at their taxes," Fin said. "Besides, I have every right to be with my sister in her time of need."

"You have to admit she's right," I said. "The Palisades would be wiped out if anyone bothered to audit entertainment expenses."

"I don't care! This is not your sister's house. She is not allowed to move my things!"

"Can you . . ." Fin's lip started quivering; she was trying to suppress a laugh. "Can you describe what was moved?"

Trevor rapped his knuckles on the island. "My pencils, my pads. All my pads. My mouthwash. My toothbrush. My shoes. My Yeezys. My Prada T-shirts. My camos. My Supreme hoodies! My . . . toiletries." (He means condoms.) "My . . . my . . ."

He gestured with his hands.

"Is it . . . furniture?" Fin asked. "Something heavy. Like, a bed, maybe? Am I warm?" She held his eyes as she moved the island notepad an inch to the side. Trevor's nostrils flared. I could hear his breathing intensify.

"I couldn't sleep!" Trevor finally said. "You're going to pay for this!"

Last night, on a sugar high, we'd moved all his belongings just two inches. Everything we could find. The bed took a while, but we moved that, too. He hadn't even seen the gym yet. We'd moved his stationary bike. The TV screens. Anything he touched, every single day.

Trevor grabbed his backpack.

"Hey, Trev," Fin said, "what does a producer do?"

He stopped, mid-stride, an automatic response to a question he loved to answer. "What do you mean?"

"I mean, you've got this beautiful place up here; it's way too big, but it's secluded. I like that. I'm not too fond of people," Fin said. "So I was just wondering what a producer does. Like, what do you do all day long?"

"He makes movies, Fin," I said. I feared where this was going, even though I had no idea the destination.

"And television," Trevor said. "I've won ten Emmys, fifth most in the history of the Emmys."

"The ones that look like angels. You know what kind of metal they use?" She tapped her rings on the counter.

"Why?"

"Just curious about the melting point," she said, smiling. *Oh, please, I thought. Please, Fin, do not make those Emmys into ankle bracelets.*

Trevor looked confused. "Look. I produced the Oscars, too. I produce everything."

"That's true," I said. "*Variety* is like one big Trevor Nash ad."

"The Oscars? Oh God, I watched like a year ago," Fin said. "Seemed like a lot of bullshit, but what do I know, right?"

"Bullshit?" Trevor said. *"Bullshit?"*

"Fin . . ."

"No offense, Trev. I'm sure your Oscars weren't bullshit," Fin said. "So how do you produce a movie?"

"It's me. All me. I have an idea. I find a writer to write the script. I find a director to direct it. Then I find a movie star. Talent. I'm great at talent. I'm the best at talent."

"Talent loves Trevor," I said. "It's true."

"I'm the best at talent," Trevor repeated.

"Talent is actors?" Fin asked.

"Yes. Yes. Yes," Trevor said. "I've got to go!"

"Shit, I can do that," Fin said.

"Excuse me?" Trevor asked, stopping in his tracks.

"You can't do that, Fin," I said. "Honestly. You can't. It's really hard."

"You fucking can't do that," Trevor said. "There's like three of us in the world who can do it. Three! Spielberg, Bruckheimer at his peak, and me!"

"I don't know. People kinda like me. I'm a good persuader."

Trevor sputtered. "You'd better be gone when I come back! And put everything back where it was! *Now!*"

He slammed his coffee cup on the island, slid the notepad back to its original position, and stormed out.

Fin pivoted toward me, a baffled look on her face. "Geez. How did you ever marry that asshole?" she asked.

"On a ring and a prayer."

"I'm serious," she said.

"He wasn't like that when we got married."

"Of course he was," Fin said, snorting. "You just never saw it. You always came to his defense, always."

"C'mon, that's not true," I said. "He had his issues; everyone does."

"Trevor's too stressed to have dinner with us," she said, her hands on her hips, in a whiny voice that didn't sound like me. *At all. I'm pretty sure.* "Trevor doesn't want me to go to breakfast with dad today; he needs me. Trevor doesn't want the family for Christmas at our house because you flicked ashes in a vase."

I don't sound like that in real life, I swear. Really. No. Do I, though?

"You did flick ashes in a vase," I said, remembering that seminal moment. "A Lalique. It's worth more than that truck you keep stealing."

Fin blinked again at me, her eyes widening.

"Did you just hear yourself?" she asked. "Did you just hear what you said? You're defending him. That man is threatening to take your child from you, and you're still defending him. Trevor can do no wrong!"

"All I'm saying is that I understand where he's coming from," I said. "I've lived with the man a long time. I know how his brain operates."

"You're drinking the Kool-Aid," she said. "You always have. You couldn't wait to get away from us."

"Now, that's not fair—"

"You think you're better than we are."

My eye twitched. *Damn it!*

"See!"

"Wait! No!" I said. "That was an accidental twitch! A totally innocent twitch!"

"See that? Yes, you do," Fin said. "You think you're better than the rest of us!"

"Define the 'rest of us,'" I said. Joking. Kinda.

"You know what?" Fin said. "You're a fake, just like your fake fucking friends in your fake fucking world."

"At least in my world, you don't have to shit in public," I said. "I wouldn't be comparing worlds if I were you, sister."

Fin stared at me, eyebrows pinched together, her face slack-jawed. She pushed herself away from the chopping block. "I'm outta here. Fuck Trevor, and fuck you. You deserve each other. The only people worth a damn in this house are Pep and *tres hermanas.*"

She stomped out of the kitchen in her Timberlands, and I found myself rubbing a water spot on the marble countertop. Water spots made Trevor crazy. Water spots made him feel poor. I grabbed a dry washcloth and rubbed and rubbed the spot. Nothing. I looked around. You could eat eggs off the tile floor, perform an operation on the chopping block. I could stick my head in the oven (don't think I hadn't thought of it) and it'd smell like bleach and lemons.

And yet. That spot was not to be denied.

I heard footsteps and a grunt. Trevor. He'd forgotten something. Trevor tossed his backpack on the chopping block and took a step back as he stared at the spot.

"Gabi!" he yelled. "There's a water spot here on the marble! Gabi!"

I slid out of the kitchen and raced toward the guesthouse to stop Fin. She had to stay. I was beginning to think my sanity depended on it.

I grabbed Fin as she was packing her stupid duffel bag, a mean thing to say about a duffel bag, but it felt like she'd been camping her whole life.

"What are you doing?"

"Leaving," Fin said, her lower lip pushed out, a flash of her baby pictures. The sweetest baby. Except when she bit me.

"I can't stay here and watch you slip away again."

"Me?" I said. "*I'm* slipping away? You're the one who moves just out of reach of your family. And then, you know, the whole prison thing. That gets old."

"You didn't visit me," she said.

"Fin."

"You could've visited me."

"I'm a mom."

"I'm your sister," she said. "What do you think it was like in there? Huh? At a women's correctional facility? You think it was a good time? You think it was easy?"

My face flushed with shame. It's true. Her last stint lasted six months. I didn't visit her once. I had no excuse. Oh, wait. I had an excuse—the "crazybusy" life I was leading. All that craziness, all that busyness, and what did it all add up to? A lot of Instagram photos of my fabulous life. And my amazing friends.

Friends who hadn't called me lately . . .

Mental note: check Insta-envy. *Would middle school never cease? Menopausal adolescents competing with their daughters for estrogen levels and likes.*

#youresopretty

#ugh

"I'm sorry," I said, grabbing her hand. "I can't imagine what it was like. I'm sure it was awful."

"Ah, wasn't that bad." Fin sniffed and rubbed her nose.

"You just said—"

"Oh my God, there was this girl"—she grinned—"we fought each other, you know. We'd pound the shit out of each other, and then we'd braid each other's hair and talk about our boyfriends and her kids and such."

"You just said you hated prison."

"I never said I *hated* prison."

I could hear my teeth grit. Sometimes, talking to Fin was like spitting into a fan.

"Oh, the food?" she said. No one had asked about the food. "The food was terrible. Don't get me wrong. I gained ten pounds." She grabbed her nonexistent waistline. "All that disgusting white bread and cheese." She sighed. "But once you get past the grub, my ride or die are those girls I met inside. We keep in touch, you know. Better than you and your friends, right?"

I leaned against the doorjamb and looked over the balcony at the riding ring below. I could smell lavender wafting over the breeze.

"So you staying or what?" I asked.

Fin looked away like asking her to stay in this beautiful home on a hill was distasteful.

"Pep needs you."

"Pep? Pep barely says hi to me," she said. "I hate to break it to you—these Westside kids are really fucked up. I mean, they are going nowhere, sis. And they can't do time like I did; they're not cut out for it."

"Okay, okay," I said. "*I* need you. I can't trust anyone else. And that is pathetic."

I grabbed her duffel bag, and she pulled it back, and soon we were in our backyard of cement and weeds in a tug-of-war.

"Give it!" I said.

"No!" Fin yelled back.

I yanked it back while she kicked at my feet and we both collapsed, and a towel popped out from the opening.

"You were stealing my towels?"

Fin held the towel up against her cheek and closed her eyes.

"It's so soft," Fin said. "And you have so many of them. It's like a Bed Bath & Beyond in here."

She sank her nose back in the towel.

I had to learn to be more like Fin—not the "borrowing," but to enjoy the little things like fresh towels while I still had them.

The RAPE Luncheon was a big deal, even among the numerous charity events that popped up weekly on the Westside calendar. Even thinking about events made my palms sweat—the details like hair, makeup, how to pose, what to wear, what not to wear, what to say, what not to say. How to talk to human Xanax dispensers. I'm not judging, truly, I'm not (*maybe?*). Instead of showing up, I usually hid behind checks with at least three zeros. It wasn't *them*, I'd told Liz, who could be found under a backyard tent at least once a week. It was *me*.

"You have better programming," I'd told Liz, whose earliest childhood memories were invitation only. "I didn't know what a seating chart was until my thirties."

RAPE stood for *Responsive Allied Patient Empowerment*, which sounded both important and bureaucratic, and somehow I'd landed on the board. Years ago, I'd been cornered by several Hollywood wives at another luncheon and told it was unheard of that someone of my "stature" wasn't on a charity board. At first, I was excited, my emotional precursor to dread.

This would be my first year without my most important event accessory, my wedding ring, entering uncharted waters as a separated woman, the scarlet *D* pinned to my silk dress.

"Please tell me we're sitting together," I'd said to Liz. "I can't sit next to anyone else. In fact, can you make sure no one else shows up?"

"I left a message for Karyn, too," she said. "She's renewing her vows. Did you get the invite?"

"Not yet," I said. "Renewing her vows . . . Michael's gay, right?"

"She's starting a trend."

"She's a dollar short and a gay late," I said. "Half the marriages in this town are gay-to-straight."

The day was hot and dry, the city in a drought that would never end, much like my divorce. The palms lining Benedict bowed in abeyance to the Santa Ana winds as I navigated my way up into the canyon. I turned up a side street where valet parkers were lined up like toy soldiers, their foreheads slick with sweat. I stole a final look at my face in the rearview mirror. The hot winds had dried out my skin to parchment; if it weren't for my mother's Slavic cheekbones and my dad's jawline, I'd look like the skull emoji. I needed to invest in duct tape.

A handsome valet knocked on my window. I slicked on more lip gloss for my breakup debut and rolled down the window.

"How do I look?" I asked the young man.

"Good!" he said, smiling sweetly.

"You say that to all the needy women," I said and handed over my keys.

Liz was nowhere to be seen. I stood in line behind a slew of women with the latest uneven, curled, shoulder-length hairdo. In LA, we birthed, then whipped trends to death, and this was the year of the curly bob. I read up on the hairdresser responsible for the *bobopocalypse*. He charged $600 a cut, not counting color. His waiting time could stretch as long as two hours, longer if Madonna or Rachel McAdams cut the line. He snipped several heads at once, spending no more than ten minutes on each head. Still, Liz convinced me to get outside my unruly head of hair comfort zone. I called to make an appointment; the nasally receptionist asked for my email.

I had to fill out a questionnaire first. And attach a recent headshot.

I had to qualify for this haircut.

No, really.

(But I'm the crazy one.)

I was finally at the front of the line to get my table number.

"Hi," I said to the pink-cheeked intern working the table. "Agnes Murphy . . ."

"Murphy . . . ," she said, her eyes sliding down the guest list.

"Nash," I said. "Look under Nash."

I was wearing a slate-gray cotton dress and chunky heels. A Chanel pillow bag over my shoulder to block social artillery. I felt myself starting to sweat.

"I'm sorry, I don't see it," she said.

"Nash or Murphy, sometimes both," I said. "I'm actually on the invite." *Was I on the invite? I hadn't looked.*

She checked again, her brow furrowing. "Give me a second?" She smiled. The line was growing behind me.

"Oh. My. God," said a woman standing behind me, a wide-brim hat over her pulled face. And that curly bob.

The pink-cheeked intern conferred with a supervisor toting a clipboard. She mumbled into her walkie-talkie, eyeing me as though I were trying to pole vault over the White House fence

"Can we just go?" someone else behind me asked.

"We're going to miss the first speaker," someone else said.

Oh, please, I thought, *they make you wait forever for that first speaker. It's like when people are in such a goddamned hurry to get on a plane. Why?*

"I'm sorry," Pink Cheeks was saying to me. "You're not on our list."

Someone behind me made a razzie sound. I heard giggling. Shushing.

"I'm one of the founding members," I said. "I paid for a ticket."

"We don't have any proof of that," she said. "Are you sure?"

"That I'm a founding member?"

"That your payment went through."

"Of course I'm sure," I said, my face hot. Sweat pooling under my arms.

"I'm sorry," she said. "If you could just . . ." She motioned. Move aside.

The woman with the wide-brim hat smiled at me, her teeth like fangs.

"This is just a big misunderstanding," I said. "I'm going to make a phone call."

"Sure," Pink Cheeks said. "If you could just do it over there."

I walked to the side, hiding my face in my phone, ringing Liz.

She didn't answer. I tried again. Nothing.

I raced to the valet.

"Is everything all right?" the valet parker asked.

"Yes," I said. "I forgot . . ."

My proper place in this world . . . and an Uzi.

"My phone!"

He stared at me, a quizzical look on his smooth face. My phone was in my hand.

I rocketed home to find Coliti-Girl bent over the kitchen island, wielding an automatic tape measure.

"What're you doing?" I asked. She jumped, and the measuring tape recoiled like a snake. *Thwap.*

"Ow!" she said, shaking her hand, then moved the notepad to the left. "Trevor wanted me to move everything back."

She pulled the measuring tape out again, checking the distance between the notepad and the edge of the island.

"He wants everything measured and in its rightful place by the time he comes home from Argentina," she said, with a small stamp of her feet.

"Trevor's in Argentina?"

"Oh my God! Don't tell him I told you, please?"

"Don't worry," I said. "It's my fault; let me help."

She looked like she was about to cry, but then she always looked like her dog had just been run over.

"Sometimes I don't understand him. But at least I don't have to clean up semen!" she said, brightening before bounding down the corridor to the master.

Hollywood sets the low bar for bosses. #dobetter

Liz called and called, but I'd already Epsom salt–bathed the toxic luncheon out of my system. I'd lost my luncheon credentials; my Hollywood wife gate pass had been revoked.

"The welcome mat has been pulled out from under last year's Louboutins," I said as Fin and I sipped a heady Bordeaux under the cloud cover.

"Let's drink to that," Fin said, raising her glass.

"Humiliation?"

"Freedom!" Fin said. "And to Trevor, for leaving town and forgetting the wine cellar key." After targeted snooping, Fin had found the key to the wine cellar (using one of my useless credit cards to open Trevor's office and a nail file to open a desk drawer) and pulled out a bottle of Margaux that'd been waiting patiently to be opened since our wedding.

Maybe too patiently; the color was off, more brown than ruby. Still.

She opened the $1,400 bottle of wine before I could stop her by impaling myself on the corkscrew, but I didn't really want to stop her, now, did I?

"You don't know what it's like," I said. "All those women staring at me, talking shit."

"Of course they were staring," she said. "I haven't seen one of them blink since I've been here. They probably sleep with their eyes open."

Wine flew out of my nose as I snorted.

"See? You know I'm right." She sipped. "This grape is a little flat, yeah? I've had better."

"Your palate's been damaged by too many orange foods," I said. "Doritos, Velveeta . . ."

"Trader Joe's Two Buck Chuck beats this slop."

"Salad dressing," I said.

"Look at you, princess," she said. "Let's have a little wine tasting. You won't be able to tell the difference, I guarantee it."

"Bet."

"Great," she said. "I'll bet you a year's supply of that guesthouse shampoo you got."

"You're on," I said.

"I'll be right back," she said. "We're settling this once and for all."

She grabbed my purse.

"I'll give you money," I said. "You don't need my purse."

"Yeah, I do," she said. "I need your ID."

I just shook my head as she scooted out the door.

Minutes later, I heard a car in the circular driveway. Fin had already returned.

"What else could she possibly need?" I asked Pep, who was watching television in the living room.

"She needs a good man," Pep said.

"Who told you that?"

"Auntie Fin," she said.

Then someone knocked at the front door.

I opened the door to two men in matching gray suits with weary expressions that I'd come to know after years of being on the wrong end of my sister's bad judgment.

"Agnes Murphy?" the older one, white, with a gray mustache to match his suit.

"Yes?"

"I'm Detective Raskoff; this is Detective Gonzalez," he said, regarding the olive-skinned, dark-eyed man beside him. They flashed their all-too-familiar badges, and I wanted to shield my eyes.

I felt my heart beating in my chest. Fin. Had she run over a Botox victim in carpool? Had she shoved a bottle of Two Buck Chuck in her pants and driven off? I flashbacked to all the things she'd shoved in her pants over her long, industrious thieving career. *Raisinets. A plum. Stapler. Snickers. A brush. Slim Jims. Lip gloss. Other pants.*

"What can I do for you?" I asked. And then I thought, *Is it my husband?*

Was it Trevor? A terrible, yet pain-free accident?

"We understand you're in possession of stolen property," Raskoff said. "We'd like to search the premises."

"Stolen *excuse me what?*" I couldn't have heard correctly.

"Stolen property."

"I don't have any stolen property," I said. I felt my face redden. Since I was a kid, I had a knack of looking guilty, especially when I wasn't. In fact, whenever Fin told a fib, I looked guilty. I'd never even seen her blush.

"That's not what we hear," he said.

"Do you have a search warrant?" I crossed my arms. I'd seen the TV shows. I know my rights. I think?

Pep had sneaked up beside me. "Mom?"

"It's nothing, honey," I said, turning to the officers. "So . . . do you have one of those thingies I just mentioned?"

"We don't," he said. "We're just asking for your cooperation."

"Mom, what's going on?" Pep asked, her eyes dancing.

"Nothing, honey," I said. "Go back to your YouTube program."

"No friggin' way! It's boring compared to this," she said.

"Go. Now. Penelope," I said. I never called her *Penelope*; she held up her hands, then skittered away toward the kitchen.

"I haven't stolen anything," I said to Raskoff.

"We're not saying you did," Raskoff said.

"Have you?" Gonzalez asked.

"Missus?" Caster appeared behind me.

"Caster, can you make sure Pep stays in her room while I talk to these gentlemen?" I said. Trevor's fingerprints were all over this. Trevor's fingerprints were all over my unstolen stolen property.

What on earth was in our house that could be stolen proper—

Oh.

Fin's mother effing Tiffany clock.

Goddamn it, he wouldn't.

He would. Of course he would.

"That little shit." I said. *How convenient that he had to skip off to Argentina . . .*

"Mrs. Nash? Are you listening?" Raskoff asked.

"I never should've moved the notepads," I said under my breath as I stepped outside and shut the door behind me.

13

Caveat Sister

M a'am," Detective Raskoff said as Detective Gonzalez's black eyes bored holes in my tipsy defense. *Intimidation game off the chain.* "We'd like to question your sister."

"Who . . . m?"

"Finley Caroline Murphy," he said. "The sister who's on probation."

"Oh," I said. "That sister."

"You have another?"

I wish. "No."

"When is she returning?"

"No idea," I said, channeling *The Wire.* I wasn't about to cooperate with the cops. Not when it came to my sister. They could cuff me, haul me off, tase me (been there, sparked that), and I wouldn't say shit. *Prison rules, bitches! Get to know me!*

Blood is thicker than common sense.

"We heard she's living here," Raskoff said.

"Now where would you've gotten that idea?"

Raskoff snorted. Gonzalez stare-glared. I wondered if he could read minds. I thought, *Fuck you, too, Gonzalez,* and hoped he read that.

"I'm going to leave you with my card," Raskoff said. "I suggest you call this number when your sister returns."

"We'll be back," Gonzalez barked.

"Great, dinner's usually around 6:00," I said. "Don't be late."

They walked back up the driveway to their unmarked sedan, Gonzalez stiff and lumbering, Raskoff quick and officious. My heart pounded like a Rihanna song in a sticky nightclub. I turned to see Caster in the kitchen window, hands clasped, tears in her eyes. She crossed herself multiple times. *At least she isn't overreacting.* Pep was next to her, smiling and giving me thumbs-up and making me think maybe I wasn't her mother; Fin was.

Fin appeared on the deck, Trader Joe's shopping bag swinging in her hand.

"You just missed *21 Jump Street*," I said from my deck chair.

"I know, I talked to Pep. She's all excited," Fin said, laughing. "I spied those jokers creeping around. Why'd you think I took so long?"

I sat back and watched the night descend over the hilltops.

Aren't you pretty, I thought. *I'll miss you, show-offy mountain vista.*

"They're going to be back," I said.

"What'd they want?"

"It's about that fucking clock."

"I didn't steal that clock."

My dubious stare is threadbare. Still, I used it on her.

"Someone gave it to me," she said, pouring a glass. "In trade."

"Translation: 'Someone gave me stolen property in trade for drugs.'"

"You want to try the wine or not?"

I thought about big, splashy Hollywood divorces. Brad and Angelina, Gwyneth and Goop, or whatever his name was. Tom Cruise and

Katie Holmes. Did Katie end up arrested? Did Angelina end up doing time? Of course not. I mean, sure, I'd daydreamed about going to prison—who doesn't? Before the Pep of it all.

Three meals a day.

An hour workout.

Tons of cunnilingus. (Receiving end. Trade for cigarettes and writing tutorials.)

Hours upon hours to read! I'd run through all the classics I pretended to read in high school. Maybe a few biographies.

I'd learn to knit.

I'd learn French!

I'd work in the kitchen, learning new ways to cook with blocks of government cheese! The girls would love me!

"Wine?" Fin handed me a glass.

"What do you think he's going to do next?" I asked. "Where is all this going to end?"

"I don't know," Fin said. "But you didn't see me here, and we didn't have this conversation. I'm going underground."

"Finja," I said. "My ninja."

She rubbed her hands together while I drained the Two Buck Chuck.

Fin was right, of course. Chuck didn't suck. After a glass, you couldn't tell the difference. After a bottle, you couldn't tell the time.

Anne called as I was dropping Pep off at school, crouched like a thief behind my steering wheel.

"Are you sitting down?" she asked.

"I'm driving, so I'd better be sitting."

"Guess what I just received?"

"A gift? From Trevor's lawyer? They want to settle?"

"Ha," she said, then paused.

The pause went on for a while.

"I received his declaration."

"Of independence? He's already independent."

"Is Trevor home?"

"No. Flew to Argentina because Tom Cruise doesn't Skype. Because the government. And aliens."

But not before he had LAPD hounding my sister. Multitasker!

Anne sighed. An alarming, drawn-out sigh.

"Our Founding Fathers couldn't have come up with this if they'd tried," Anne said.

"What's a declaration again?"

"He's telling the court why he wants a divorce."

"Can you give me his top three?"

Why why why.

Why why, skip the lies, skip the lies . . .

(Can't wait 'til Taylor Swift gets married and divorced—I'll sell her these lyrics.)

"You'd better come in," she said. "I freed up my morning."

I scrapped my plans for the day. What plans? Sitting at a desk with my favorite coffee mug and my laptop and tapping keys. I was desperate to get back to my writing schedule, but divorce had other ideas; divorce waits for no woman. I checked my watch, which I'd planned to sell to pay rent. I'd been eyeing everything I owned—*Jimmy Choos? Forty dollars on eBay. Lightly worn Manolos? Sixty dollars? I'm already up a hundred bucks!*

"I can be there in twenty minutes," I said.

"I'll have coffee and flask ready," Anne said and hung up.

I was being followed.

No, I swear!

Me, Agnes Murphy Nash! I was being followed! And why was this exciting?

I smiled in the rearview mirror, where I could plainly see the guy following me.

I called Liz. She didn't answer. Who else would appreciate this new and exciting development?

"What?" Fin.

"I'm being followed by a man driving a gray sedan," I said. "Just like in the movies!"

"You're big-time now," Fin said. "Where does he think you're going?"

I glanced in my rearview mirror. The sedan was one gardening truck and a black Prius back. I'd noticed the guy waiting outside Pep's school, parked at the corner on Sunset. Ray-Bans, too young for his thinning hair. Suit jacket, tie, collared shirt. Dressed like an adult even though he was basically a kid.

He'd slipped into traffic after I passed him at Bundy. A little too quickly and herky-jerky. I'd noticed him because, get this, he'd waited at the stop sign for me to pass.

No one stops at a stop sign in LA.

You *drift*, or *"California stop,"* which is the same thing as not stopping. Or you ignore the sign because the law doesn't pertain to you, Westsider.

The sedan looked blandly familiar yet out of place in the traffic heading east on Sunset, and that's when I realized I'd seen it this morning. In the dead zone.

My hawklike senses picked it up! Maybe I *was* a worthy protagonist in the movie of my life.

"I'm kind of excited," I said, a thrill in my voice. "I shouldn't be excited, right? Am I worth tailing?"

"Does Trevor think you're having an affair?" Fin asked. "Wait, are you fucking someone else?"

"No, of course not," I said, and the camera in my head pitched Gio Metz. "Not that I wouldn't."

"You wouldn't," she said. "Of course you wouldn't. You're too scared. Scaredy-cat!"

"I would, too!" I said. "I'm a big cheater. I cheat constantly. Every day. The only time I haven't cheated is never."

"You won't even cross a street unless there's a crosswalk," she said. "Do it. Go ahead, cheat. I dare you. I double-dare you."

The sedan was one car back. I switched lanes.

"Now's not the time."

It switched lanes.

"Your husband left you," Fin said, "for your house manager."

"*With*," I said. "Not *for*. *For* is the wrong preposition."

"He left you, and you're worried about grammar?"

"How do I lose this guy?" I asked.

"Stop the car and talk to him," she said.

"Oh," I said. "I can do that?"

Fin had the simplest solutions to life's problems except those that would keep her out of prison.

"Those tight-ass detectives came by again. *Las hermanas* pretended not to speak English, then Gonzalez spoke his broken Spanish 'n' they just looked at him like he'd crapped his pants. I love 'em."

"They're going to get you eventually," I said.

"To get me, they'll have to find me," she said. "We didn't have this conversation."

She hung up.

I pulled onto one of those side streets in Beverly Hills above Olympic that makes you want to live there. Today. Wide, tree-lined streets, Spanish homes and duplexes, clean, walkable sidewalks. The sedan pulled around the corner.

I stepped out and stood in the middle of the street, blocking him.

He stopped. I walked over to his driver's-side window and tapped it. He waited a moment. He looked even younger close up. I tapped it again. Finally, he lowered the window. I noted a yellow pad in the seat next to him.

"Hi," I said. "Why are you following me?"

"I'm not."

"You are," I said. I leaned in, folding my arms against the base of the window. "I'm heading to my lawyer's office. I'll be there for about an hour, maybe an hour and a half. Why don't you go eat something? Then you can catch up with me back at the house."

He stared straight ahead. His ears were small, like a child's.

"You probably need to pee," I said. "I promise, I'm not going anywhere except to the lawyer's. I'm sure you have the address."

He took a moment.

"You'll be there how long?" he asked, still staring straight ahead.

"At least until 11:00, maybe 11:30."

"I could use a coffee break."

"There's a Starbucks around the corner," I said, rapping my knuckles on the car door. "See you back at the house."

I sat in Anne's office and read Trevor's declaration, and even though she'd shoved a tissue box in my hand, I couldn't cry. Every part of my body was in shock, even my tear ducts. The beautiful, motherly receptionist came in and put her arm around my shoulders. She smelled like pineapple. I loved her.

"I can't feel my fingers," I whispered.

"Reading about what a horrible mother you are can do that," Anne said, seated at her desk, her hands clasped in front of her.

"You know this is all . . ."

"Lies," she said. "Trust me, I know."

"Why would he . . ."

"Divorce attorneys rip their opponents to shreds. Especially in

Hollywood. Then we meet at our book club, act like everything's fine, and make a deal right before we walk into court."

"No deal," I said. "I can't unread what I've just read."

"You'd be surprised what you're capable of," she said, looking at her calendar. "We have a deposition scheduled for the tenth. In the meantime, you are obligated to respond in two days."

"I'll just write VOID across the whole thing," I asked. "This thing isn't worthy of a response. I won't do it."

"Of course you will," she said, pushing her reading glasses up her nose. "Pep is depending on you."

The sedan was parked on the street when I arrived back in the dead zone. I nodded to the young man, then drove down my driveway. Through my open window, I heard what sounded like a child wailing. I circled the courtyard to find Gabriela crouched on our front doorstep, clutching her sides. Fin was embracing her as she rocked back and forth.

"Shit," I said. "Shitshitshit."

I ran over, tripping across those damned pebbles.

"Gabriela—"

Fin was softly speaking Spanish into Gabriela's ear; she paused to squint at me, the sun catching her eyes. "TMZ is what's wrong. Trevor's declaration—it's all over the internet!"

"Oh no! I'm so sorry!" I said. "We were supposed to fly under the radar! We're *Anonymous v. Anonymous*. I'm Mrs. Anonymous!"

"His lawyers leaked it, and people will pick up anything that's filed in court. I know, I've got friends in the circuit."

"We're on the divorce escalator all the way down to the bowels of divorce hell, aren't we?"

Fin handed me her phone. "Goggly-eyed motherfucker."

I focused on the screen.

HOLLYWOOD KNIGHTS PRODUCER TREVOR NASH FAT-
ASS RACIST NANNIES CORRUPTING MY KID

The headline screamed above an unflattering close-up picture of
Trevor looking like a skinny, wet rat.

*Legendary producer Trevor Nash wants his soon-to-be-ex-wife to fire
their nannies (plural), claiming they're fat slobs and their racist attitudes have
rubbed off on their child. Nash filed the declaration in legal separation docs
this morning claiming, among other things, that their nannies are the worst
possible influences imaginable. According to the docs, the nannies (plural!) are
ill-educated, disrespectful, and use extremely foul language.*

"He's lucky he's in Argentina," Fin said. "I got one more prison term
in me. I'm happy to use it."

I squeezed in next to Gabriela and put my arm around her.

"I'm so sorry, Gabi" I said. "Everyone knows this is all lies. Everyone."

"I'm not fat!" Gabriela said.

"Not at all," I said.

"And racist?" Gabriela asked. "No! I love the blacks."

"He's a *mentiroso*," Fin said.

"Of course you do," I said.

"I don't like Mexicans," Gabriela said.

I coughed, shielded my eyes and read further:

*In addition, Nash claims that his soon-to-be-ex-wife, writer Agnes Mur-
phy Nash, often leaves their daughter alone to party and claims that she hangs
with "undesirables."*

*Ms. Nash apparently just cut short a stint in rehab for an undisclosed eat-
ing disorder.*

Trevor Nash is asking for sole physical custody and no support.

"Have you looked at the comments?" I asked, handing the phone
back to Fin. "I'm not strong enough."

Fin scrolled through and started to smile. She snorted.

"The people have spoken," Fin said. "They think he's an asshole."

"Then I'm in real trouble," I said. "The comments section is all that matters; this is going to make Trevor insane. He wants everyone to like him. He needs everyone to like him."

"Doing a pretty shitty job of it," Fin said.

Gabriela said something in Spanish. I caught *pendejo,* then something about knives, which, you know, fair enough, as Fin explained the comments section.

"I'd better get started on my response," I said, brushing off my slacks and heading into the house. "The most important words I'll ever write and no one is ever going to see it except lawyers."

"And TMZ," Fin added.

"No. It'll never see the light of day," I said. "This is going to be buried deeper than a Mafia hit."

"Why?"

"Because," I said, stepping inside the church door. "I'm going to tell the truth."

14

Beyond a Reasonable Lout

Every time Trevor left town, he'd be replaced by a crew working in the house. Men in jeans and work boots, tool belts slung low around their billowing waists. There was always something broken in a house this size, usually more than one thing. Usually, many things. That light, this faucet, that chair, this psyche.

Just kidding. There's no fixing the psyches in the dead zone.

Meanwhile, whatever was broken was guaranteed to cost as much as a Kia.

"What's that dude working on?" Fin said as she sniffed and narrowed her cat eyes at a man traipsing through the kitchen with paper booties covering his work boots.

"No idea," I said. "Light fixtures? And I think a deck chair is broken."

"Huh," she said, her stare following him as he made his way down the hallway to the master.

"It's nothing," I said.

"Uh-huh," she said, chewing her lip. She got up to assess the white van parked in the driveway.

"Why doesn't the van have any markings?" she asked.

"Fin, I don't speak conspiracy," I said.

"Aggie, you don't speak common sense," she said. "Look around you; you have no idea who's coming in or out of this place—"

Another worker was cutting through the kitchen from the deck. *Cap, belt, tool box, booties.* I guessed electrician?

"Hey, dude," Fin said. "How'd it go." She wasn't asking.

He grunted.

"Okay, I have to get dressed," I said. "I'm meeting Liz for an early dinner. Now that I'm forcibly retired."

"Where?"

"Giorgio's. She's paying."

"Bring me back the Dover sole," she said, staring at the van. "Extra lemon sauce. No capers. Actually, bring me back two."

"Two?" I asked, sarcasm dripping off my tongue. "Is that all? Anything else?"

"Nah, that's good," Fin said. "But he may want dessert."

"Who? Who may want dessert?" I asked, having visions of one of Fin's dealer boyfriends moving in.

"I'm meeting with the writer."

"You're . . . doing what with whom?"

"Sami. The writer."

"The writer for what?"

Fin rolled her eyes. "Where've you been? The guy with the script."

Clang. Screech. Plop. My brain finally computed.

"Uber driver Sami?"

"Yeah," she said. "The script's not bad. Has a lot of potential."

"How many screenplays have you read?"

She thought for a moment. "One."

"You've never read one of mine?"

"No. Was I supposed to?"

"Jesus Christ."

"First," she said, "we gotta loosen up the dialogue. It's too stiff."

"I don't . . . okay."

"Yeah, I told him I'd produce it. And I'd bring Trevor in."

"You lied to him," I said. "You totally lied to him."

"Isn't that what Hollywood producers do?"

Stumped.

"Yes," I said.

"I didn't exactly lie to him," she said. "I gave him hope. That's different. Believing is doing."

"Did you get into Trevor's old Tony Robbins tapes?"

"Hey, don't knock him," she said.

Another worker wearing a white hazmat suit snaked silently through the kitchen.

"Almost done?" Fin said to him.

"Uh, ask my boss," he said.

"Yeah, I'll do that," Fin said as he retreated.

"Don't be rude. They're working on the lights," I said. "We've had electrical problems for a year."

"Sometimes I wonder how you manage to feed yourself," Fin said before grabbing an apple and disappearing after the electrician.

I stepped inside Giorgio's, teetering on car-to-table gold heels that Fin insisted I wear and warmed by the familiar dim lighting and the smell of garlic sautéing in olive oil. The room felt like home, if you lived in a renovated, million-dollar home in Tuscany.

"Right this way, Mrs. Nash," the hostess said as she escorted me to a corner table. We took three steps before the owner, an older Italian man with an air of eternal weariness, took her aside. He glanced at me with sorrowful eyes, then whispered in her ear before heading back into the kitchen.

She turned in the opposite direction, making a beeline for the outside tables. I followed.

The screen door slammed behind us.

"I don't want to be seated outside," I said with a shiver.

"It's nice out here." I could see her breath hanging in the air.

The tables shone wet from the afternoon showers.

"Is it possible to get the table we usually have?" I gestured toward the restaurant. There was no one outside.

"No, I'm sorry."

"No? It's empty. And it's so early."

"No," she said with a warm smile. "Would you care for a wine list?"

"Please."

I wiped the moisture off my chair and took a seat.

"I'm being deposed," Liz said as she sat down, slapping a piece of paper on the table. "What are we doing sitting out here? It's freezing."

"Wait, what? You're being deposed?"

"For your divorce," Liz said. "I was just served. Right here at the valet. I thought I was being mugged!"

My phone was ringing. My book agent. Calling from New York.

"Hey, Lucas," I said.

"I'm fucking being deposed," he said.

"For my divorce?"

"Yes," he said. "What the fuck?"

My TV agent was ringing through. I hadn't talked to him in six months.

"I'll call you back, Lucas," I said. "Hello?"

"Your husband's deposing me," TV agent said.

"Sorry," I said. "Hey, did you ever get feedback on my pilot script?"

"Gotta run," he said. "Conference call."

After my coming-out dinner was hijacked by Trevor depo bombs, I headed home and emailed Anne.

To: Anne Barrows

From: Agnes Murphy Nash

Trevor is deposing everybody. Everyone. With the exception of Bernie Sanders and the Progressive Insurance lady.

Cheers,

Agnes

I'd just finished devouring a three-course meal, including a tiramisu. No one except Giorgio's does a good tiramisu in LA, but, valiantly, I keep sampling others. Despite my gluttonous efforts, my stomach grumbled. My new divorce metabolism was working overtime. I grabbed a questionable hunk of cheese out of the refrigerator, set it on the chopping block with water crackers, then padded downstairs to the wine cellar.

Crackers and cheese could only be digested properly when escorted by a red. What would it be tonight?

I grabbed a Beaujolais. *Beau-jolais!* Pretty and happy! *Would I ever be pretty and happy again? If not, I could drink it!*

The phone rang, jangling my nerves. I focused on the screen. My dad was calling me on the house line. I sighed and answered.

"Hey, kiddo," he said. "I'm being deposed. What the hell?"

"I know," I said. "It's all part of the 'discovery phase.' It's like Discovery Channel without the wild hyenas, unless you count divorce attorneys."

"I'm not intimidated by fancy lawyers," he said.

"I know, Daddy," I said. Of course he was intimidated. My dad owned one suit. One dress shirt. One pair of black patent loafers. He'd lived his entire life pretending not to be intimidated by exactly these people.

"It's going to be okay," I said.

"Get some sleep," he said. "It's late."

"You, too," I said.

"Be good," he said, he always said.

"What if I'm not?" I asked, but he'd already hung up. But I was wondering. *What if . . . what if I'm not good, for once? Will it make a difference?* Being "good" had brought me what, exactly? I decided to take the opposite of my father's advice. I drank two glasses of Beaujolais because now I was into being "bad."

Then I did the exact thing you are never to do during a divorce proceeding.

I emailed the petitioner directly. I emailed Trevor.

To: Trevor Nash
From: Agnes Murphy Nash
Really?
Signed,
Agnes

My phone pinged a moment later.

To: Agnes Murphy Nash
From: Trevor Nash
Really what?

I wrote back immediately.

To: Trevor Nash
From: Agnes Murphy Nash
You're deposing my dad?

My agent.

My manager.

My book agent.

My best friend.

Sent.

To: Agnes Murphy Nash
From: Trevor Nash
It's called divorce. Why, is there someone I'm forgetting?

(Okay, I had to smile.)

To: Trevor Nash
From: Agnes Murphy Nash
Yes. That's my point.
It's like a birthday party, Trev—you can't just invite 90% of the people
you know—you have to invite the other 10%.
Aggie

I was halfway drunk with the halfway bottle, and I was an idiot. Trevor'd thrown me a crumb, a reposte, and I ate it hungrily, trying to satiate my hunger for comfort emails. I'd reacted to the tiniest piece of evidence that my ex wasn't, in fact, a monster. I'd signed off with my nickname(!). As though we were friends(!). And, no, you can't hate me anymore right now than I hate myself.

I took myself to bed.

After dropping Pep off at school, I spent the morning huddled in my office directly beneath Pep's room, jotting notes on Trevor's declaration and listening to the sisters' calming voices weaving in and out.

Trevor and his team of Energizer Battery attorneys had reached into their bag of tricks and had come up with ridiculous accusations based on the flimsiest of evidence. So today, I'd play Divorce Monopoly, respond to each and move my piece (life) forward. I needed to pass Go and collect what was left of my self-esteem.

Trevor was the top hat; I was the Scottish terrier.

August 7, 201-

To: Trevor Nash

From: Agnes Murphy Nash

Oops. Forgot Pep's snack in the car. Please notify the Bad Mom brigade.

XoxoAg

Apparently, years ago, when Pep was in first grade, I had forgotten—well, you can see, carrot sticks and a little bag of organic oatmeal cookies (that tasted like wood chips and sponge).

And more recently: November 8, 201-: Agnes went out to dinner, leaving minor daughter alone at home with ex-convict sister.

I'd gone out to a birthday dinner for Liz from 7:10 to 8:45. I'd made Pep's dinner before I left and had returned to put her to bed.

I cracked my knuckles, cracked my neck, lay on the floor to crack my back. I jogged in place for a couple of minutes. I sang notes *do re mi do re mi do re mi.*

I was ready. The only thing I had going for me was the truth. I'm sure that was enough.

(Hahahahahahahaha . . . ha.)

I flipped open my laptop. Blank page, get ready! You and me, we're against a five-headed monster—the hydra of Trevor and his legal team. I read a Native American proverb, typed on a small slip of paper I'd saved from a trip with Trevor—*"He who writes the words runs the world."*

We'd been vacationing at a five-star spa in Wyoming, and housekeeping would leave behind these slips of paper with Native American sayings, along with the day's temperature and what time hot yoga in the woods started.

I started typing. My fingers landed with a series of thuds. I tried again. Something wrong with the keyboard. I checked the cord, the outlet (as though that would make a difference). Reboot computer, reboot my life. Seventy-nine percent. Plenty of power.

Tap. Thud. Tap. Thud.

My keyboard was jacked up.

"Fin!" I yelled as I ran up the stairs. *"Fin!"*

Fin emerged from dodging the LAPD to check out my laptop. She poked the keyboard, then before I could stop her, snapped off the laptop assembly, exposing a yellowed, gooey substance.

"Glue," she said. "That phony electrician glued your keyboard. Trevor's getting you where it hurts—your laptop"

I screamed and banged my fists on the desk. I flung the pillows off my love seat. I kicked the antique wastebasket. (Then apologized, of course.) Fin stared at me, then her chewed nails, then back at me.

"I can fix this," she said. "You want to use mine?"

"You have a laptop?"

"I can get one," she said.

"What does that mean?"

"You want a laptop or not?" she asked. Then, "New or refurbished?"

I thought for a second. "New."

Fin hooked me up, and by the end of lunch, I was five thousand words in. (Nope, didn't ask where she got the laptop.) The intercom rang; I ignored it. A few seconds later, footsteps and a knock at my office door.

"No one's here!" I said. "Don't bother me for another five thousand words!"

"Missus," Caster said, cracking open the door, her eyes nervous, "the Realtor mister is here."

I'd forgotten our house was for sale. Forgotten? Repressed. I followed Caster upstairs just as the "Westside's Realtor to the Stars™" was pulling up the driveway in his black Range Rover. Peter Marks parked, followed by another black Range Rover with tinted windows and another black Range Rover with tinted windows. I observed the Rover parade from the kitchen. Peter, an affable guy with feathered hair, aviator shades, and boots—like an extra from a Hal Needham movie— conferred with his clients, who'd spilled out of the second Rover. America's Sweetheart and That Weaselly Fuck. (No one emerged from the third Rover. To this day, its occupants are a mystery.)

That Weaselly Fuck, a multi-hyphenate Brit of enormous and unfair talent (and appetites), was a well-known jerk. Sorry. Asshole. Sorry. Cunt of the highest order.

"*Muy guapo,*" Caster said, fluttering her eyelashes.

"*Muy* hamster-like," I said, because he was petite, with a face like a hairless rodent and tiny hands. "She's sweet and has hair like whipped butter, and why is she with him?"

America's Sweetheart was carrying That Weaselly Fuck's progeny in her arms. She'd just given birth to a third girl, and I thought that might spell trouble. I'd met That Weaselly Fuck at a *Vanity Fair* party years ago, then multiple dinner parties, award shows, backyard political soirées—each time I was introduced, a constipated expression would descend on his pinched face and he'd slink away, in the direction of a "name." Most movie stars at least pretend to be polite—it's called *acting.*

I'd heard through the Hollywood grapevine his latest issues pingponged from hookers to Jim Beam to heroin. I didn't want to leave America's Sweetheart alone with him behind these gates. I decided they couldn't buy this house.

"Aggie." Peter greeted me with a big hug. "This is Rudy and Sal," he said. "I'm sure you guys have met."

Rudy, his weak jaw slack and stubbled, gazed at me with hooded eyes. There it was, the familiar constipation.

"Of course," Sally said, blowing her famous blond bangs out of her eyes and reaching out with her free arm for a hug. Her skin glowed luminously, her 1,000-watt smile blinding yet sincere. I wanted her to go into witness protection. "Agnes, how are you?"

She smelled like spring. I oohed and aahed over her baby girl, who brought back all the baby smells and baby sounds and baby feelings and baby regrets that at this rate, I'd never have another.

"Richard Ellsworth designed this house for Henry Blake and his bride," Peter was saying. Blake had been a director of many musicals and consumer of much bourbon; he'd died at forty-eight of cirrhosis. "It was their honeymoon home. There was an extensive remodel in 2005, adding over ten thousand square feet."

Rudy grimaced. "I loathe musicals," he said, his nostrils flaring.

"Every room in the house has a relationship to the outdoors," Peter said. "It's sort of a signature touch."

Sally nodded and flashed her dimples.

"Get rid of the fireplace," Rudy said. "It's too old and smells funky."

The fireplace was original and integral to the design of the house.

"It is old," I said. "But it basically holds up the roof, so . . ."

Rudy narrowed his puffy eyes, then sneered at the roof.

"You don't like fireplaces? There're fireplaces all over this house," I said. "Almost every room. Fireplace, fireplace, fireplace . . ."

"Let's take a look at the master," Peter said before shooting me a withering look.

"Have fun!" I said. "If you need help, I'm right here. Just don't light a cigarette, the whole place could blow—"

I turned and grinned at Caster, Gabriela, and Lola, who'd emerged from various hiding places.

"Good job, *jefita*," Gabriela said, and the girls clapped.

15

The Spiral Slide

Fun exercise: Mapping the downhill slide (not a fun slide, like an inflatable slide or a water slide or a playground slide) of our marriage through emails.

> September 10, 2000, 3:23 p.m.
> To: Agnes Murphy
> From: Trevor Nash
> loveyouloveyouloveyouloveyou
> Margaritas at 5?
> loveyou
> me (T)

Trev and I were kinder to each other in the BlackBerry years. I blame the iPhone. If people can name Facebook as a cause of divorce, I can name Apple.

> September 10, 201-, 3:24 p.m.
> Margaritas, rock salt and a bj?

loveyoumore

Me(A)

How. How did we get from margaritas and blow jobs (great name for a Mexicali band, BTW) to this:

April 4, 201- 4:53 p.m.

From: Trevor Nash

To: Agnes Murphy Nash

What the fuck do you think you're doing I know you put something in my suitcase it smells like dead fucking goldfish

Well.

April 4, 201- 5:38 p.m.

From: Agnes Murphy Nash

To: Trevor Nash

You're*

Cheers,

Agnes

It's hard reading that your kid is fat. Especially when the person saying it is her father. In a legal document. That went public. *Sigh.* I thought back to when Trevor first thought Pep had a weight problem.

Found it.

"She's fatter than Brad Pitt's baby," Trevor had said, hovering over us as I diapered baby Pep. "We're feeding her too much. Tell the Triplets; they're sneaking her bottles."

"Shush, she's perfect," I'd said. "You want her to be babyrexic?"

"No," he'd said. "Of course not. Do you think she should go on a diet?"

I covered her little baby ears. She giggled and looked up at me, de-lighted. "Can we wait at least a year before we fat-shame our baby?" I'd asked.

At 5:35, my response to Trevor's declaration was ready. I'd written ten thousand words in one day. At this pace, I'd have a short novel in five days, a trilogy in a week and a half. I could've written the next *Game of Thrones* or *Harry Potter* (if I, you know, had the talent); instead, I'd created lunchtime entertainment for a bunch of misshapen legal turds (excepting the perfectly shaped Ms. Barrows, of course).

Anger was the best muse I'd ever had; sure, she was ruddy and squat and wore a perpetual scowl, but I could've used that bitch years ago.

Before our crack-up, I'd awakened in the middle of the night in a stupor, sitting in the simple rocking chair my father had given me when Pep was born.

A dream, a shiny gold nugget of truth, winked at my subconscious.

"Agnes, if you stay, you will get cancer," the shiny gold nugget of truth said. "And Trevor will make it all about him."

In my dream, I saw a pale, bony, bedridden me, tubes running through my hairless body, the Triplets scurrying in and out of my room, with tears and hushed voices and endless making the sign of the cross over their bosoms. Dizzying amounts of crossing. A portrait of Hispanic Jesus (appearing suspiciously like Luis Miguel) hanging above my bed.

The dream rolled on, and I was hovering above Trevor at the Grill, lunching with a comely junior agent.

"Why are you upset?" Miss Comely is asking.

"My wife . . ." Trevor was shaking his head. "She has cancer."

"Oh my God," Miss Comely said as she rubbed his muscular arm and cooed in agent-in-training style.

"We haven't been able to fuck in like a month," he said, tears welling in his career-making eyes.

"Poor baby," she said as she grasped his hand (where was his wedding ring?) and slipped it under the table. "Poor, poor Trevor."

16

Deposing Made Simple

I stared at the giant kitty-and-doggy ASPCA calendar, their sad doggy and kitty eyes cajoling me to send more money than last year. Every day, I penciled in another divorce reminder. Penciling stuff in is calendar-keeping at its most atavistic, but that's my jam—atavism.

Divorce wasn't just a job; it was a lifestyle.

I could monetize this divorce, like Waverly suggested. I'd brand my divorce! Write a blog: *The Divorce Whisperer, The Divorce Fairy, The Divorce Coach*. Set up divorce kiosks at school fairs. Give speeches on divorce and resiliency (the current buzzword, having lapped *mindfulness* in March of this year). Coin the Divorce Diet! Start off grassroots and end up worldwide, branding the Business of Divorce. The Skinny Divorce would cost as little a day as a soy latte (with a shot of tequila)!

Fin had been playing hide-and-seek with the LAPDicks while I was #livingthedream. The detectives "visited," dropping at odd hours—early morning, late night, right when I had sat down on one of the fourteen (sixteen?) toilets. I stopped answering the gate intercom. I'd wave at our HDTV screens as they gazed stone-faced at our security cameras.

My theory was they didn't have a warrant, and since Fin hadn't officially violated parole, they couldn't officially take her in for questioning. My theory was based entirely on those same guinea pig instincts that brought me to this point and not any semblance of knowledge of legal procedure.

Still, it sounded almost feasible.

Fin wasn't taking any chances. My personal Cato would surprise me, hiding out in my office closet, sleeping in my car, setting up a tent outside the game room where no one played pool. She'd jump out at me at as I sat down to write, or turned a corner in the guesthouse, or started my car in the morning.

I would be dead of a heart attack before Fin ever got caught.

Petra had sold a picture of me holding the bed bat over my head in the middle of the night.

TREVOR NASH'S EX BATSH-T CRAZY was the headline.

"I love you, but I never thought you two were that interesting," Liz said over the phone. "Not like the Jolie-Pitts or the Pittanistons or the Pittaltrows."

"Brad Pitt has sprayed his seed all over the Hollywood pasture," I said. "He's Johnny Applesemen."

"I can't believe I'm being deposed," she said. "How would I possibly help his case? Saying you were a bad wife and mother?"

"Why would you say that?"

"Exactly," she said. "I wouldn't. Even if it were true."

"What?"

"When's your deposition?" she asked.

"Tomorrow morning," I said.

"Are you ready? Have you been practicing? What does your coach say?"

"What are you talking about? I'm not going for the big leagues of deposing."

"I'll be right over." She sighed.

Liz sat me down in my office with as serious (and bruised) an expression she could muster (given that she'd seen Dr. Braden for a "liquid facelift").

"There are four answers you need to give in a deposition," she said as I stared at her swollen lips.

"Four answers," I repeated.

"The answers are: 'Yes', 'No,' 'I don't remember,' and 'Would you like me to guess?' Your lawyer hasn't told you this?"

"No," I said. "She advised me to be honest."

"She what?" Liz struggled with her alarmed face.

"She *what*?" Fin popped up from behind the couch.

"Jesus Christ! What are you doing here?" I asked my sister.

"I'm not here." Fin disappeared behind the couch again.

"Are you trying to be poor?" Liz asked.

"She can't afford to be poor!" Fin said.

"Shut up, couch!" I said. "I'm trying to be fair and get this over quickly and without bloodshed."

Liz looked at me with an expression close to pity. I wish people would stop doing Botox long enough to get their expressions in order.

"Repeat those four answers back to me," she said.

"'Yes' . . . 'No' . . . 'I don't recall' . . . and 'Would you like me to guess?'"

"Stick to those answers. Do not elaborate. Whatever you do, do not write out loud!"

"I can't use just those answers for an all-day deposition," I said.

"Actually," Fin said, popping up again. "It's sort of expected."

"You can," Liz said, "and you will."

"Drop of mercury in his tennis shoe," Fin said. "No one will ever know."

"Let's take this a bit further," I said in my closet, staring at a row of black pants I'd never worn. What to wear for my debut, er, deposition? I snapped a pair of Theory from 2011. I could sell these pants. That's twenty, thirty bucks right there. "How do you get the mercury?"

Fin slipped into a flocked red velvet Dolce & Gabbana, an old premiere dress. Another definite sell. My premiere days were over. My debt days? Just beginning.

"Break open a thermometer," her eyes flashed. "You've never heard of quiet kills? How dumb are you?"

"Smart enough to avoid murder."

"Silent blow to the back of the head," she said, holding up two fingers. "People slip and fall getting out of the bathtub all the time."

"Trevor doesn't take baths," I'd said.

"Never trust a person who doesn't take baths," Fin said. "Maybe you have to go to prison before you appreciate a good bath."

"For argument's sake, how do you not get mercury on you?" I asked. "If you crack open a thermometer?"

"Is this seriously your first rodeo, sister?" She stared at me.

"How do I break this to you, Fin?" I asked. "No, I've never actually killed another human being."

"So you just quit, you just stop trying, is that it?"

The other morning, she'd awakened me as the sun was rising to tell me a dream in which she'd slipped a desert scorpion into Trevor's bed.

"I have a scorpion at my friend's trailer in the desert—don't ask his name," she'd whispered. "Little shit bit me; my hand swelled so big, almost had to amputate."

"I'm not really comfortable with this kind of talk," I said and rolled over.

"You're not part of the solution, Aggie; that's your problem," Fin said, nudging me. "You gotta be part of the solution."

I picked out a forgotten jersey dress as Fin traded the premiere dress for a pair of lime-green Lululemon tights that I bought and never wore because did I say *lime green*? I'm sorry to report she didn't look like a balloon animal.

"I can get in and out anywhere with these things on," Fin said, turning in the mirror. "Like climbing out of windows and such."

"Does this say, 'I ain't afraid of no attorneys'?" Gray Armani suit I hadn't worn in years. Fin pantomimed vomiting. Detailed and protracted vomiting, and I had to get moving.

"How about this one?" Simple black dress, white collar.

"Save it for the funeral."

"This?" White poplin skirt, ruffle-collared shirt.

She laughed.

I sank to the floor. Fin stepped over me and fanned through my dresses. She picked out a purple skirt-and-blouse pairing, an ecstatic choice for a happy occasion.

"I'm not going to a party," I said.

"Exactly. It'll throw them off. You're heading from deposition to like, I don't know, one of those ladies-who-lunch things. Or a tryst."

"You know 'tryst'?"

"Fuck yeah, I know 'tryst'—why wouldn't I know 'tryst'? I went to the same schools as you! I got straight As!" She pressed the purple dress on me.

"By flirting with the teachers," I said.

"I should've married Mr. Palmetto when he asked me," she said, a pensive look crossing her face.

"Our Spanish teacher."

"He was very sensitive," she said.

"He was sixty years old and three feet tall!"

"I know," she said with a sigh as she grabbed a pair of my high, strappy heels. "Put these on, too."

"Thank you," I said, and, boom, I had to choke back tears. I'd never be able to handle this lawyer day.

"No puddling today," Fin said, play-punching my arm.

"Ow!" I rubbed my arm. "Damn it!"

"Stopped crying, right?"

The front gate buzzed. A moment later, we heard a deep engine growl and the boom of a backfire.

"What the—"

"Oh, good; he's here." Fin ran outside and through the kitchen.

I followed, stepped out into the courtyard, teetering on fuck-me heels, or, in this case, fuck-you heels. *Fuck me? Fuck you!*

"Who?" I yelled over the noise.

"Your driver!" Fin yelled back as a plume of smoke blew from the carburetor. A mountain in a suit jacket emerged from the smoke.

"Girl, this is Edmund," Fin said, beaming. "He's taking you to your depo; he'll wait for you in the lobby."

Edmund extended his hand, which could cover half a continent.

"Edmund, this is so nice of you," I said, shaking his hand, "but I really don't need—"

"You remember him from the motorcyclist team?" Fin cut me off.

Edmund's smile filled up the entire Palisades.

"Edmund, wait here for a sec," Fin said, taking me aside. "I paid him, if you know what I mean. And yes, the hands match the gearshift."

I stole another look at Edmund's hands. He waved, blocking the sun.

"Fin, I can't bring him to a lawyer's office; they'll freak out."

"Are you, like, trying to be dim? They. Will. Freak. Out."

I thought about it for a moment.

"If his asshole lawyers get a load of Edmund," Fin said, "they'll think twice before they rip you a new one, much like the old one."

Fin opened her stringy arms and hugged me. I almost cried. Again.

I took a deep breath and stepped into Edmund's muscle car, the dizzying smell of gas permeating the interior. I'd be high on fumes by the time I arrived. Which, you know, perfect.

Edmund and I squeezed into the elevator at Blecks Holstein . . . Etcetera. Anne was waiting in the lobby, documents in her lap, her hair back in a neat ponytail, briefcase at her feet. She looked so studious, I wanted to give her an A for effort and call it a day.

I introduced Edmund to Anne, and she smiled and shook his hand, not even raising an eyebrow. Edmund sank onto the lobby couch with a *People* magazine (Reba McEntire on the cover), his massive knees almost to his shoulders. Anne and I were led down a long hallway, past landscape and nature photos. Snowcapped mountains, shimmering streams, a moose staring into the camera.

Dead Wife Walking.

The receptionist opened the conference room, asked if we needed anything, then pointed at the twenty water bottles already crowding the table.

"I'd like those rice noodles from Mr. Chow," I said.

"We're fine," Anne said.

A thin, wiry man in jeans and thick, black-rimmed glasses stood across the table, a tiny microphone in his hand.

"Do you mind if I secure this?" he asked.

"Anne?"

"They're filming," she said.

"Is this an audition?" I asked. "I thought I got the part already."

I focused. Cameras were already set up against a blue screen. My divorce had high production value.

"This would make a great Netflix show."

"Not quite," Anne said. "This shouldn't go more than two, three episodes."

"I'm so glad I wore purple," I said. "It's a good color on me. Does this firm provide hair and makeup?"

Anne patted my hand. The sound guy hooked the microphone on my blouse. I fluffed my hair, then fished through my purse to get my lip gloss.

"Do you think they'll give me a copy afterward?" I asked. "Maybe I could use it as a sizzle reel. *Divorced Housewives of the Armpit of the Valley.*"

The door opened with a bang, and the march of heavy feet as several men entered—one gaunt with an electrocuted thatch of silver hair, the next had greased-back hair and nervous eyes, then an older gentleman (using the term very lightly) packed into expensive Italian silk, belly hanging over his Ferragamo belt, who pounded his cane. My eyes met his—shiny, greedy eyes in a walnut shell face. Ulger Blecks, ladies and gentlemen.

"Grimm's fairy tales," I whispered to Anne.

Anne greeted the attorneys, and the men muttered their hellos, maintaining their deliberate seriousness.

"Nuremberg trials or Hollywood divorce?" I asked Anne.

"What's that bouncer doing in your lobby?" Trevor traipsed in, dressed in a suit, no tie, collar open. Not a care in the world.

"Apparently, he entered with Ms. Murphy," Ulger Blecks intoned, staring down at me over his reading glasses. His voice exactly how I'd imagined. *In a world where . . .*

I almost smiled.

"I assume he's an integral part of her entourage," Blecks said. "Perhaps another boyfriend."

"He's my driver," I said. Gasps. "Wait. Not my driver, more like a friend."

The three lawyers of the apocalypse melded their misshapen heads together in an unholy triangle as they murmured.

Anne put her hand on mine, then said, "We're ready to start when you are."

No, I wanted to scream. *No, we're not.*

Blecks squeezed beside the camera setup into the chair opposite mine and raised a wild, unrepentant eyebrow. You could lose your keys in those brows.

"Agnes," Mr. Blecks said in his deepest baritone. I waited for the movie trailer to materialize. "May I call you Agnes?" He smiled, his teeth yellowed and sharpened by years of separating children from their mothers.

"Sure," I said. "Ulger." I smiled. He scowled. Trevor scowled. The room group-scowled except for Anne and the camera operator.

"I'm going to read to you a passage from this book," Blecks said. "Do you recognize this book? Exhibit A?"

He tossed the book on the table, then shoved it toward me with a broad, manicured fingertip as though it was coated in dog shit.

Girl Pimp. Exhibit A was the second book I'd written. I didn't want to seem excited as I recalled Liz's instructions: #yesnoIcantrecallwouldyoulikemetoguess.

"Would you like me to guess?" I asked.

"Excuse me?" His eyes almost popped out of their flesh crates.

"One moment," I said, taking a deep breath. *Remember, Agnes. You look good in purple. It's a solid hair day. You are strong. You are invincible. You are woman . . . even if you feel like a gnat.*

"Agnes?"

"Yes!" I said, my high pitch piercing the room.

Another scowl from Habeas Corpulent.

"I've marked Exhibit A," Blecks said. "Can you please read this passage, Agnes?" I opened the book to a paragraph underlined and tagged with a yellow Post-it. Somewhere in Bleck's vast offices, a newbie lawyer, whose parents had sent him or her to college, then law school at a cost of hundreds of thousands of dollars, had been assigned to comb through my books. And mark inappropriate passages.

Kinda thrilling, I thought, suppressing a smile.

Would my writing pass muster? What is muster? Would it pass ketchup?

I side-glanced Anne, who nodded for me to go ahead.

I cleared my throat and read a passage. I'd repeat it here, but hey, buy the book. Suffice to say, the passage was titillating and a wee vulgar, and the words leaped off the page. Okay. Maybe not leaped. Bounced?

And maybe a wee more than a wee.

"Do you recognize the writing?" Blecks thundered.

I widened my eyes and looked at Anne for an answer. She nodded.

"Yes," I said. "It's been a while, but—"

Wait. Wait! Yes, No, I don't recall, Would you like me to—

"Do you remember writing that?"

"Well, no," I said. "But it's not bad." My description of the lead character, a gold digger with a heart of gold and a diamond-encrusted vagina was, dare I say, spot-on.

"Not bad?" Blecks lunged from his seat, almost getting impaled on a water bottle. "You're proud of this character? This harlot sets up an innocent man to steal his hard-earned money!"

I wrinkled my nose. *Harlot.*

"Well, as a writer, I can't say I'm *not* proud. She's not likeable, but she's a well-defined character on a specific journey."

No, Yes, Was I passing?

"Read the second paragraph, please," Blecks said, smoothing his tie and sat back. "Page 103. Second from the top."

I caught Anne out of the corner of my eye, chewing the inside of her cheek. I turned to page 103.

Oh, I liked this part.

I read and glanced up, smiling.

"How about that passage? Are you proud of your, quote, *descriptive writing*, unquote, there, as well?" He chuckled, then sneered, working his belittlement battery of effects.

"They're not going to teach this at the Idaho Writers Workshop anytime soon," I said. "But I did get a nice write-up in *The Times*."

I read Anne's expression.

I wasn't passing Deposition 101.

"Hold on," I said. "Would you like me to recall?"

"What are you trying to get at, Ulger?" Anne said. "Besides wasting time and our clients' money."

"What am I getting at?" Blecks's face turned purple, adding to his appeal (sarcasm). "What am I getting at?" Spittle appeared at the corner of his mouth. If he had a stroke, I wondered if I would feel anything.

Nah.

"Your client," he spat, "is a man-eater!"

The room went silent. I nibbled my lower lip.

Wait. What? I'm a man-eater! Me!

"That escalated quickly," I said.

"I'm shutting down this deposition!" Anne yelled, which managed to sound melodic.

Go, Anne, it's your birthday.

"You'll be lucky if I don't report your despicable behavior to the licensing board!" she added.

Oh no she din't.

Oh yes, honey, she did.

Anne shoved the table away and grabbed her briefcase. The opposing trio followed suit, scraping their chairs against the floor, grunting and swearing under their breath, warthogs in thousand-dollar loafers.

Trevor stood and ran his hands through his hair. I had barely registered his presence. Trevor, the man, the myth, the reason we'd all been gathered in this unholy union. I'd been focused on surviving the deposition, not the raison d'être.

"So," I said to Trevor, "been to any good depositions lately?"

He shook his head and walked out.

Thwack! Squeak!

   Thwack! Squeak!

"Is it Ativan o'clock yet?" I asked as I slid past the volleyball moms huddled in the front row of the bleachers at the Briarwood Gym.

7:00–10:00 belonged to our beloved caffeine.

10:00–12:00 Adderall—appetite suppressant before lunch.

12:00–3:00 paleo, gluten-free, and Ativan.

(Nap or staring into the abyss—the pamphlets at your dermatologist's office)

4:00–midnight: wine o'clock.

I looked up. A man was seated in my designated corner, wearing that familiar gray rumpled suit and Ray-Bans to camouflage his glower.

"Mother *fudger*," I whispered.

"Take this outside?" Detective Gonzalez asked. It wasn't a question.

"I really don't need this today," I said.

"I'd appreciate it," he said, which meant *now* in cop.

Pep looked up from the court. The volleyball moms had stopped posting and tweeting and backseat coaching to turn and stare.

I smiled and waved at Pep.

Nothing to see here, Pep, nothing at all!

The moms cleared a path as I followed the detective outside.

"You came to my daughter's practice? This is low, even for you," I said as we stood outside the gym, my heart beating outside my chest.

"You're tough to pin down," Gonzalez said. Understatement. "I'm serving you."

"Another serving," I said. "But I'm already full."

"Just sign the doc," Gonzalez said, slipping papers from his suit jacket.

"This is not your finest moment, Gonzalez," I said as I signed. "What, there's a shortage of rapists and murderers in LA?"

"Bring your sister in Monday morning 8:00 a.m.," he said, "or you'll be charged for contempt."

"If you could put me away for contempt, I'll be doing life."

Gonzalez didn't look back as he got into his unmarked sedan and sped off. I pushed my hair out of my face, took a deep breath, and headed back inside, tracked by the eyes and buzzing of the volleyball moms.

Like I'm the first person here who's ever had to bring a family member into a police station for an arrest warrant . . . we've all been there, right?

I slunk to the side of the bleachers and slipped on my sunglasses.

I counted five Birkins, eight Rolexes, and seven Chiclet-sized diamond rings.

Ain't nobody in this gym ever seen the inside of a station, I heard the Fin voice in my head say.

17

Arrested Development

I tried to make small talk with Pep about anything except the elephant in the room—the detective in the bleachers.

"I saw that spike, honey," I said. "Great job! You've really improved!"

"Mom. Was that the cop who came to the house?" Pep asked.

I wanted to always have an honest relationship with my daughter. A relationship built on mutual trust and understanding—

"What man?" I asked.

"That man in the gray suit," she said.

"Oh, that man," I said, guiding the car into Wilshire traffic. "A friend of Auntie Fin's." *Throwing my sister under the bus is like tossing underhand—so easy!*

"A friend."

"Of my sister's." *And . . . the bus just backed up over Fin.*

"Mom, are you going to prison?"

"God, no!" I said. "But I could get a lot of reading done . . ."

"You didn't tell me you went to rehab," Pep pointed out. "Why would you tell me if you're going to prison?"

"I didn't go to rehab for drugs; I went for almonds."

"That's what an addict would say," Pep said and put in her earbuds. For once, I was grateful for the earbuds.

Fin waved us down in the driveway, wearing a big headset and brandishing a device that looked very much like a . . .

"Why is Auntie Fin waving a vibrator?" Pep asked.

"How do you know what a vibrator looks like?"

Pep rolled her eyes.

"I'm serious, Penelope," I said.

"I've got to check the car!" Fin said, popping into my window, then dipping and running the device along the wheelbase.

Pep jumped outside to watch her aunt as Fin moved around the back, tapping her headset before coming around, diving under the front of the car, then emerged, grinning, with a tiny black matchbox.

"I was right!" Fin said. "They got the car!"

Inside the house, the staff was wearing headsets. Even the blond kid who dropped off the orchids. The white noise was deafening.

"Why does it sound like I'm in Hawaii during a Category 4 hurricane?"

"They bugged the whole damn house," Fin said. "I've swept everything, all ten-fucking-thousand square feet—"

She fished something out of her pockets, tiny disks with wires attached, some looked like spiders, others like tiny matchbooks.

"He's gone insane," I said. "This isn't normal—"

"Tell me about it. We've been yanking these things out of the wall, out of cabinets, plants, they got 'em everywhere. Even Pep's room!"

"I have bugs in my room?" Pep asked.

"Here," she said, handing us headsets. "Noise canceling. So you can sleep."

"Fin, we're not wearing noise-canceling headsets to sleep."

"How're you going to sleep with this noise?"

"I'm not worried about being bugged," I said. "I've got nothing to hide."

"Well, look at little Miss Perfect," she said. "That works for you—what about me? I've got several businesses to run."

"Not anymore," I said. "We have to talk."

We hid in my closet as Fin unrolled a spool of duct tape.

"For the cameras," she said, checking the ceiling corners. "Aha! I see you!"

She climbed up a large chest of drawers with the agility of a spider monkey, gave a tiny lens screwed into the corner the finger, then slapped a piece of tape over it.

"It's an infestation," I said in awe.

She jumped to the floor, stuck the roll of duct tape in her pants, and wiped her hands.

"Did Pep hear Gonzalez say he wanted you to bring me in?"

"Kids hear everything they're not supposed to hear," I said, checking the door to make sure Pep didn't have her ear to the door.

"I'm so pissed," Fin said.

"Me, too."

"I had plans this weekend," she said. "Edmund was going to take me to Victorville."

"Victorville," I said.

"Yeah, I like Victorville," she said. "What?"

"Nothing," I said. "Sounds . . . romantic. Sorry I have to drag you to the station on Monday."

She shrugged. "Eh. No big deal."

"They're throwing you in jail, Fin," I said. "Who knows what they'll come up with?"

"The clock isn't stolen," Fin said, fidgeting with a cigarette.

"You're going to need proof," I said.

"I'm working on it," Fin said. "Cool your jets."

"Is getting arrested like shopping for groceries for you?" I asked. "This is serious, Fin. Trevor's tightening the noose, he's circling the wagons, he's—"

"Before you bore me with another cliché," my sister said, "this isn't even as stressful as getting my carburetor fixed."

I fought the urge to strangle her.

"Then why were you avoiding them these last few weeks? Why not just hand yourself over? This has been really stressful!"

"Oh my God, girl." She sighed. "What, you've never heard of the chase?"

"The police weren't wooing you," I said. "They wanted to arrest you. This isn't courtship; you're a fugitive."

"Same diff!" She threw up her hands. We were from different countries—no, planets. On my planet, a subpoena wasn't a flirtation.

"There is one thing," she said, pursing her lips.

"Anything you want," I said.

"I want to look cute when I go in. I need a mani-pedi, maybe some highlights."

I walked out.

"What?" Fin called after me. "Appearance is very important!"

Fin drove to the West LA police station, with me in the passenger seat. Apparently, I made her nervous when I drove. She parked outside the station, crossed her arms over the steering wheel, and looked at me.

"You know what you haven't learned, boo?" she asked. "Life is imperfect. If you can't enjoy the imperfections, you're gonna wait a long time for a laugh."

"Sometimes you're just full of shit," I said.

"Got that right," she said and punched my arm, and then I gave her a big hug and I swear I saw her tear up.

Fin slapped the front desk. "I'm here for my appointment!" The watch commander glanced up and frowned as though we were interrupting her crossword puzzle.

"Sorry," I said, nudging Fin aside. "Hi, I'm Agnes Murphy. We're here to meet Detective Gonzalez."

"Hold on," she said, stuck in frown mode. "Gonzalez!"

Gonzalez appeared, barely acknowledging us except to scratch his nose and point. We followed him back to his desk, where he motioned for us to wait, then opened a drawer and pulled out a pair of handcuffs.

"What the hell," I said. "What are those for?"

"Turn around, please," he said to Fin.

"Hey, wait a minute," I said. "You don't need to cuff her."

"It's procedure," Fin said.

"It's procedure," Gonzalez said.

"Don't sweat it, babe," Fin said.

"You're going to feel pretty stupid when you realize how wrong you all are," I said.

"Let's go," Gonzalez said, avoiding my glare, his hand on Fin's arm to steer her away from me.

"I'll call you later, Celie!" Fin said. "I'll never forget you!" I choked up. *Bitch brought out* The Color Purple.

"I love you Nettie!" I yelled, my eyes wet. I watched as Fin was led outside, her skinny bird wrists cuffed behind her back. Gonzalez tucked her head into the back of his unmarked car. Fin and I caught eyes, and I raised my fist in solidarity.

"What are you doing?" the watch commander asked. I turned around.

"That's my blood," I said. "Fight the power. Fight the man!"

"Gonzalez?" she said, folds across her forehead deepening. "Never seen him smile, but he's okay."

"You know, it's kinda disconcerting watching your sister dragged away in handcuffs," I said.

"I feel you," she said. She held up a little candy dish. "You want a peppermint?"

I did. I did want a peppermint. "Sure," I said and grabbed a tiny, sharp piece of kindness.

A few hours later, Fin called me from the Van Nuys station pay phone. Maybe you've never had the privilege of having an incarcerated relative. Well, too bad for you. Because you learn a few things: when the phone rings and you answer and there's a pause . . .

You know what's coming.

You wait for the operator's voice. She asks if you are . . . you. Then she asks if you accept the call and charges from the facility.

All the while, your super-annoying loved one is yelling, cajoling, pleading in the background for you to answer.

This experience gives you phone phobia. For a long time, I was afraid to answer the phone. Any phone. The phone brought bad news—all related to my sister.

In this home, in the dead zone, we had, at last count, twenty-four phones, which rang at different intervals by milliseconds, creating a symphony, a cacophonous multiplier of my phone phobia.

"Accept!" Fin yelled, fighting through prison clamor.

"Accept," I said.

"Guess what Gonzalez said when we were on the way to Van Nuys?" Fin said, when I was patched through. "He said, and I quote," she said, "'You have a very powerful brother-in-law.'"

"No shit," I said.

"Yes shit. We were at a stoplight, he turned that big head around and looked me in the eye," she said. "Trevor put in a call to the chief of police."

"The chief of police? That low-down star-fucker," I said. Our chief, a roguish transplant from Chicago, had clocked appearances at movie premieres, courtside at the Lakers, Dugout Club at the Dodgers. He counted George Clooney, Magic Johnson, and Russell Crowe among his "pals." He came to our sunny coast a pale, plump newbie; he was now burnt sienna, his blue eyes like crayon planets. Trevor had cast his schoolteacher wife, a frustrated actress on the shadow side of fifty, on a TV show in a recurring role.

"Of course," I said, fighting the urge to throw up.

"The fucking LAPD chief made the call to have me arrested," Fin said. "Like I'm some kind of terrorist. What the hell."

"This is LA," I said. "Everyone wants to be a star, even the police chief."

"Those people are morons. I'll tell you what, though. When I get out of here—"

"Fin."

"I always get mine back," Fin said. "Don't you worry."

Reader? I was worried.

"I've seen a lot of dirty tricks. I've even seen attempted murder, but this is a first," Anne said when I called her to tell her the chief of police of the second-largest city in the United States had ordered my sister arrested over . . .

A clock?

"What's my move?" I asked.

"Post bail, if you can," she said. "We wait it out, see what their move is. I have a feeling that's why Ulger called me this morning."

"What do they want?"

"My guess is they're going to use the arrest"—she paused—"as leverage."

"For me to leave the house?"

"For full custody."

I felt my stomach drop.

"That can't be true!" I said. "Trevor doesn't want full custody."

"No, he doesn't want full custody," she said. "He wants to win."

I didn't want to leave Pep in the dead zone, given that I didn't know how much time we had left together, but I had to be at Book Soup on Sunset by 7:00, which meant I had to leave the house by yesterday.

Sorry. Traffic joke.

Most of the time, at book signings, you'll get a few people marooned in a sea of folding chairs. The nice lady who works behind the counter, her reading glasses attached to a chain around her neck, will grab a chair. Maybe an old suitor will show up, or a girl you knew (vaguely) from high school geometry class.

My dad was waiting outside the bookstore when I arrived, along with Shu, who was dressed like she was heading to a premiere for a vampire movie.

"Honey, you remember Shu?"

"Of course," I said. "Five languages—four and a half more than I speak—"

"I want to bring her by the house afterward," he said.

I thought about her recent shoplifting arrest.

"Sure," I said. "Why not?"

I spied him immediately. He's hard to miss. Every novelist of any repute, ill or otherwise, has a stalker. Mine showed up to every book signing I'd had in LA since my first novel was published—never said a word, never bought a book, never even approached me. He just sat in the middle of the middle row, right in my sightline. Like I could ever miss him. Dressed head to toe in silver, black gloves to his elbows, jet-black, greasy hair falling past his shoulders.

I stopped myself from waving like he was an old friend. Still, his presence felt stabilizing—proof that I was still stalkable. I hadn't yet disappeared.

Stalker stared me down as I began to power through my intro schtick.

I raised my hand.

"Hi, my name is Agnes Murphy," I said. "Nash. For now. And I'm a recovering writer."

That got a few titters. The crowd had turned out to be a respectable size. There were even a few people standing in back, confined by tall book-shelves. I wondered how many would actually buy my book. It didn't help that I encouraged readers to save their money (especially in cities battered by recession) and buy the paperback version or check it out at the library.

A great salesman I am not. I'm a person who wrestled with words.

And often lost.

"Thanks for leaving the comforts of home and Netflix tonight," I said. "There're more people here than I'd expected. I hope you guys didn't get the wrong date. I mean, you do know I'm not reading from *Fifty Shades of Dick?*"

Laughs because they A) liked me, or B) were actually nervous about getting the wrong date.

"I'm reading the acknowledgments first, because my dad is in the audience, and if I read his name, he might get laid tonight."

Laughs. Except for Stalker. The Silver Prince of Darkness glowered.

"So let's get started," I said. "Feel free to check your Facebook or Twitter or swipe right while I read. The fewer people listening, the more I feel at home."

I started reading. Taking a breath between sentences. Reminding myself to slow down.

Slow down, Agnes.

Skipping parts here and there that felt clunky. (Why didn't I read this out loud after writing and rewriting and rewriting and rewriting? Why didn't the editor, you know, edit?)

I'd gone over these passages so many times while writing and rewriting (apparently not editing), my mind started to wander . . .

My sister's in jail. Trevor called the chief of police and had her arrested.

The chief of police. The guy who runs the city.

I kept reading.

Choose your enemies wisely, right? Can't say that I have—

I took a deep breath.

Don't think about the phone calls with Anne.

I shivered. Even though the room suddenly felt hot. Stifling.

Didn't this place have air-conditioning?

I was cold.

Palms sweaty.

Mom's spaghetti.

My breathing felt labored, like Bill O'Reilly making a midnight phone call.

Breathe. Slow down.

Anne had called me back again, minutes later. Trevor had filed for an emergency hearing.

"He's doing it. He's going for full custody."

"No, don't panic."

Why did I have this sister?

"Yes, it happens."

Why me?

"No, it probably won't happen."

What did I do to deserve this?

Oh. Shit. What paragraph am I on?

I skipped through pages. The words wiggling and dancing, dropping off the page. Where were they going?

"But this is divorce court. I don't have a crystal ball."

Come back, words.

I'm going to lose Pep. I'm going to lose my child.

Breathe.

I have so much more to teach her. I'm pretty sure she doesn't know how to use a house key—

Help. Help me—

Or to kick an attacker in the shin, not the nuts—

I'm in a tunnel. All is dark. Wind blows my hair back.

My body relaxed. My breathing steadied.

This is what I imagine the luge felt like. I'm not bad at this, I always thought the luge was my sport—

I blinked. My eyes opened to thirty sets of eyes staring down at me. The back of my head felt sore.

"Ow," I said. Someone was holding my hand.

It felt nice.

Was I in a dream? Am I not the 2020 hope of Luge Nation?

A young face, honey-almond skin, soft hazel eyes bracketed by heavy glasses, a pierced septum; he was talking. (Why did he pierce his beautiful septum?)

"Agnes?" he asked. "Hey, are you okay?"

I chewed my lip.

"Yes?" I said. "Other than my head—"

"The kid's always been a fainter." Dad's voice. His head floating above me. A striking resemblance to Paul Newman. The crystalline-blue eyes that will never be passed down. When he goes, they are gone.

"She'll be all right," he said. "Right, kiddo?"

I blinked. My legs felt clammy. I reached down.

"Was I dreaming?" I asked as someone helped me sit up. I stared down at my jeans. Between my legs, my pants were moist, clammy tentacles unfurling.

"You think you'll be cool to sign?" the Book Soup rep asked.

"What happened?" I whispered, spreading my hands to hide the wet spot.

"Your mouth was opening and closing," he said, pantomiming a hungry guppy. "No sound was coming out. Thought it might be your mic. Then you just totally . . . crumbled. You hit your head. It was amazing!"

Liz's face emerged. Glass of water in her hand. "Have you eaten today?" she asked.

"Just my pride," I said. Then, "Did I pee myself?"

"Your water bottle landed in your lap."

"Oh, thank God," I said. "Are you sure?"

Liz and my dad and the rep pulled me up to standing. I heard applause. My reading was over. I scanned the room.

My stalker had vanished, off to find more suitable prey. Who could blame him?

The line was shrinking as I signed books, and the buyers and I pretended I hadn't collapsed and wet my pants in front of them. With a water bottle. But still.

"I'm fine," I said to Liz. I signed, waving my other hand over my pants to dry them, the water stain retreating so it looked like my bladder merely dribbled.

"Trevor's taking Pep. He had Fin arrested. But everything's fine. I'll get through this. I'm the oak, right?"

"Oaks burn down," she said. "Oaks snap. Be the willow. Bent but unbroken."

"I can't be a willow," I said. "Look at me. Peasant stock."

"Can you make it out to Tracy?" asked a woman with Tootsie Roll bangs and the aggressively lined and glossed smile of a former teen beauty queen.

I paid attention to the proper spelling of *Tracie* as opposed to *Tracy* as opposed to *Tracey*. I felt both lucky to be here and like a dinosaur. Books—*for how much longer?* We can't compete against Candy Crush. Or Pokémon.

Or porn.

"My husband divorced me last year," she said, grabbing my hand. "It's been tough—he left me and the kids—but we're fine. We're going to make it."

Lip stain on her eyetooth. Her hand squeezing mine. My fingers going numb.

"I'm so sorry," I said.

"No," she said, whipping her blond hair. "No, no, no. We're fine." Her lower lip started to shake, and she let me go. "Selfie?"

I smiled, and I wanted to cry.

"How's the dead zone?" the next person in line asked.

I looked up. Gio. The black leather jacket. The wide smile. Those soft eyes.

"On its last breath," I said.

"Sign this and let's grab something to eat," he said.

Our fingertips touched.

I'm not going to say it felt like sex.

(Reader: It felt like sex.)

My dad was in heaven. Gio Metz and Shu (and, incidentally, me, his daughter) eating pasta and clams at Dan Tana's.

Dad was vying for captain of Team Gio; Gio was old-school. Gio ate. Gio drank. Gio listened. Gio laughed hard and loud.

Gio could get Dad into film premieres.

My dad and I argued over who would drive Gio back to his hotel after dinner. I won. I wanted to fill up on Gio's laugh before I headed into the dead zone.

I parked outside his hotel on the Strip.

"Did you hear what happened?" I asked. "At the signing."

"You passed out," he said, his fingers interlaced over his stomach. "I was outside, watching you."

"Great," I said. "I needed a new stalker. I lost mine tonight."

"I married one of my stalkers," Gio said. "Agnes, you don't need someone to push you down. You need someone to catch you."

He formed a net with his fingers together.

"Fall into me. I'll give you a soft landing," he said and patted his belly.

A group of girls, all hair and smiles and giggles, held each other up as they stumbled across Sunset toward the Rainbow.

"I'm no knight in shining armor," Gio continued. "I'm not even sure they make armor in my size."

"How about my knight in rumpled khaki?"

He put his warm hands on my face and drew me in for a kiss.

Afterward, I watched the world's best kisser step into his hotel before checking my phone.

Eighteen missed calls. One hundred and twenty-two Google Alerts.

Dear God, not Google Alerts.

"I'm the oak," I said to myself, taking a deep breath. "No, I'm the willow. Oh, God, which fucking tree am I?"

Oh, internet, you sly dog. Someone had downloaded the video of me fainting, then pissing myself. Except I hadn't pissed myself.

I'm almost positive.

Gabriela was at the house.

"It's okay, missus," she said. "I pee myself at my wedding."

"I didn't—"

"It's okay, missus," she said.

"Thank you," I said.

I sat in my bathroom in front of the tray of a thousand creams. The bathtub yawned. *You gonna come in or you just gonna sit there?* I'd just had the best kiss of my life on what was shaping up to be the worst night.

My phone flashed. More alerts. Morse code for *you're fucked.*

It buzzed. "Are you okay?" Liz asked.

"I'm viral," I said. "I'm sick with TMZ, Perez Hilton, and Bossip fever."

"Black gossip? That's big."

"I'm not unproud of that," I admitted.

"Ignore it all," Liz said. "Tomorrow there'll be a #MeToo #DontForgetMe—"

"#WhatAboutMe," I said.

"Exactly," she said. "They're still diving into the '90s; they haven't even touched the aughts, and the Twitter news cycle is thirty seconds long."

"Thank you," I said. I rubbed my shoulder. Granite.

"Now. Gio."

Gio.

"We kissed," I said.

"Scale of one to ten."

"Broke the scale."

"A real man," she said.

"I don't remember ever being kissed like that. Where has that kiss been?"

"Maybe they don't make kisses like that anymore," Liz mused.

"Maybe kissing is a lost art," I said.

"Maybe it's like one of those ancient languages," Liz said.

"It was like . . . slipping into a warm bath."

"Tongue?"

"The tip," I said. "Gentle yet firm."

"Oh," she said. "Oh . . . my God."

We paused.

"Am I allowed to have sex while fighting for my life?" I asked.

"It's mandatory," Liz said. "Check your divorce manual."

My other line was ringing.

"That's him!" I said.

"Go!"

I switched over to Gio.

"Did you forget something?" I asked.

"My heart?" he asked. "My soul?"

"C'mon."

"My common sense?" he opined.

"Anyone who's ever sat through one of your movies knows you have no common sense."

"I'm falling in love with a woman who's going through a divorce," he said. "I've lost my mind."

"Hashtag fake news," I said.

He laughed. I was getting used to that laugh. No, addicted. *Can you be addicted to a laugh? Is there a Gio's Laugh Anonymous?*

"You have a home alarm, yes?"

"Yes."

"Put it on," he said. "There are people out there who care about your health and safety and brain and smile and warm, soft lips."

Then he hung up.

18

It's My Ex Parte and I'll Cry
If I Want To

Sunglasses were my friend.

As were hoodies.

And baseball caps. (Dodgers, Rams, Raiders, Braves, Sox. Clippers. Lakers. I was a polyamorous fan. A sports polygamist.)

I wore them in tandem for days.

One hot afternoon spent trudging up a wide, dusty trail into the brittle Santa Monica Mountains, dodging Lycra-clad kamikazes on $10,000 bikes, I wore all three.

My piss tape had managed to land on the wings of a Spix's macaw—a slow news day—a rare creature emerging from the chattering classes flying from phone to phone. Meanwhile, nary a syllable had escaped the tweeter in chief's leaden fingertips, nor a befuddled media icon taken down by a thirty-year-old buttocks swipe. No mass shooting, no swordplay with nuclear weapons. CNN wasn't sobbing, Fox wasn't shouting.

The news had become an iceberg, stolid, unmoving.

Nothing had happened.

So I'd become a meme.

Memes.

I had a nickname. Nicknames: *Nappy Novelist. Pisseller. Wet Wipe Wordsmith. Urine Time . . .*

Lucas, my agent, left me a message. I hadn't talked to him in weeks. "Superbabe!" he said. "You've cracked the Amazon Top 100 in pop fiction."

Then he paused.

"Pee makes all things possible," he'd said and giggled. I pictured his curls bouncing uncontrollably.

"Off with the sunglasses," said the security guard, hairline receding under her weave, busty figure lacquered into her uniform. "No sunglasses."

I slipped off my glasses and placed them in a bin that looked like a grimy holdover from a coal mining operation. I slipped off my purse and set it in. I watched as the rubber teeth swallowed and gulped.

I stared ahead at the marble tunnel of the courthouse as I stepped through the x-ray machine.

The guard's eyelashes fluttered, big as dust mops.

"I know you," she said, recognition lighting up her green contacts.

I hooked my glasses onto my ears and slunk sideways to the elevator bank.

Anne was running a few minutes late to the emergency custody hearing, so I sat on a cold, unforgiving bench outside the courtroom watching all the other chickens in their midnight blues and blacks, waiting to be plucked and slaughtered. And the lawyers, the roosters, parading by with their overstuffed briefcases, their puffed-up breasts.

The hallway smelled like sorrow and rage and disappointment and reams and reams of paper. Paper used as bricks, filled with hostile, indigestible words. Paper as health hazard, causing stomachaches and heart palpitations and sleepless nights. A forest of terrifying paper.

We can save the environment; kill the divorce industry.

I placed my hands on my knees. *Steady, stop shaking.*

Buzz.

Text from Lucas. *Top 50! Urine play!* ☺

Meanwhile, I stood out in the crowd like an Easter egg in an oil spill. I had chosen a powder-blue dress suit. I wanted to appear benign and carefree; I looked, in a word, ridiculous.

Trevor and Ulger and the guy with the hair like an abandoned bird's nest had noisily filled a bench down the hall. Ulger's basso voice rode over the orchestra of pain.

Waverly had called last night to tell me not to worry. "Worry is a wasted emotion," she'd said, "like guilt. Or trust. Or happiness."

This is what I was paying for, I'd thought.

"You're missing something," she'd said in her droll, flat pitch. "A piece of information. An object, maybe. A letter? Something that could stop the proceedings cold. In the eighth year of my divorce, I'd discovered he'd had an affair with a manicurist."

"The eighth year," I said. "And it went on—"

"Several more years."

Strategy wasn't my strong suit. (Neither was this powder-blue suit.) In a land where women fake pregnancy (then, oh, here comes the tragic, albeit bloodless miscarriage) to trap a guy into marriage, I couldn't strategize. I knew women who'd seduced their hapless spouses into bed after kicking them out, to move the date of legal separation. To get more money.

I knew a lot of assholes with vaginas, too, apparently.

I needed to find me some of that pesky leverage.

Gabriela had slipped an amethyst crystal the size of a small rock into my purse this morning. "From La Reina," she'd said, kissing the tips of her fingers. "She bring you good luck. Maybe Trevor have *pequeño* heart attack in court." I was pretty sure it was a dollar store crystal, but who was I to question La Reina?

"*Gracias*, Gabi," I'd said. "What time do you think she'll be bringing the luck part? I'd hate to miss it."

Gabriela, who'd escaped a bloody civil war, having spent a childhood shoeless and on the edge of starvation, had looked at me with enormous sadness in her eyes, then had given me a big hug before practically carrying me to the car.

I smelled a pop of gardenias. A swan dressed for a funeral floated down next to me on the bench. Her attorney, scraggly beard, large pores, was wearing a suit that had been dry-cleaned so many times it looked like it could crack. He wasn't one of those high-end roosters with gold initial cuff links, pin-striped suits, and Italian loafers who smelled like their grandchildren's weddings were already paid for.

"He's trying to take the car," the swan was saying, tapping her sensible shoes against the marble. "He wants me to not have a car. Can he do that?"

"It's in his name," the attorney said, bored. I hated him.

"How do I get to work?" she asked, pleading. "How do I get the kids to school?"

A man sank onto the bench on the other side of me, wearing work boots and a pressed denim shirt. He smelled like soap wrapped in an honest day's work. "I'm willing to help her out," he said to the attorney, who looked like a child dressed in his father's suit. The sleeves were too long, pants dusting the floor. "They're my children. But, I mean, she wants the juicer. I'm the only one who ever used that juicer. It was a birthday gift, you know? How is that fair?"

He used a juicer; this threw me.

Baby attorney nodded gravely, pushed his father's glasses up his nose.

"If you would just let me do my job," baby attorney said, his voice barely breaching adolescence, "I advised you not to communicate with her."

"She's the mother of my children," he said. "Geez."

"He wants the kids to change schools," the swan was saying. "He won't even pay for soccer anymore. But he can pay for his new girl-friend's boobs."

Ouch. My head hurt. I handed over a Kleenex (thank you, Gabi!) as her attorney slunk away in his shiny suit to use the water fountain. The man in work boots was busy staring at pictures of his children on his phone and audibly sighing.

"I hope her boobs explode," I said to the swan. "I hope those puppies get knocked out by a soccer ball and explode all over the field."

"What a jerk, right?" she said.

"You're too kind," I said. I elbowed the man. "Did you hear about the guy she was married to? Unbelievable."

"Sorry?" The whites of his gray-blue eyes were scribbled over with red lines. I thought of Pep's old Etch A Sketch.

"He won't even pay for soccer," I said.

"My kids love baseball," the man said, blinking at the swan. "I would die before I'd take them out of baseball."

"Hi, I'm Agnes," I said, putting out my hand. He shook it. Warm, calloused. Capable. "I'm here for my divorce. What's your name?"

"Hank," he said.

"Hank, this is . . ." I looked at the swan.

"Alicia," she said.

"Should we, like, meet here every week?" I asked. "Like a book club, but we read briefs instead?"

Hank smiled. Alicia smiled. Their eyes caught. My heart broke, semisweet.

"*Anonymous v. Anonymous,*" the court bailiff called.

"You guys should compare notes," I said, "see who wins the worst ex award. I would play, but that's unfair; I know I would win. You're both long shots, sorry."

"Nope," Hank said, "mine wins, hands down."

"Oh, wait a minute, Hank," Alicia said, sitting up, her neck curving back. "I think you've got this twisted."

"Anonymous v. Anonymous," the bailiff called out.

"Seems like you guys are already fighting," I said. "An excellent start!"

Anne appeared, tapping my shoulder. "Agnes? We're on."

"Oh, that's me," I said. "I'm Anonymous. Forget I ever told you my name."

I looked back before I walked in the courtroom. Hank had just said something that made Alicia laugh. I smiled and thought about that dollar crystal.

"If it pleases the court," Ulger Blecks said, banging his cane on the floor in front of the judge. "Agnes Murphy has proven herself to be a deficient, negligent, wholly unfit mother."

Blecks was giving the performance of a lifetime or maybe the performance of just that morning. This was my first divorce, so I had nothing to compare it to. After a few more, I could judge more discriminately. But so far, I'd say watch your backs, Russell Crowe and Denzel Washington.

"He's missing 'homicidal,'" I whispered.

"Shhh," Anne said.

"She allows a felon to babysit her only child, sir," Blecks wheezed. "A thief. A drug dealer. A parolee."

"No one's perfect," I whispered.

Blecks turned and trained his raisin eyes on me. I thought of angry Cabbage Patch dolls.

"And just recently, Judge, this woman was filmed collapsing at her own book signing," Blecks said, spittle flying from the black gape above his chin. Ah, shit. I wrinkled my nose. "Ac-ci-dent included. Sir, we'd like to ask the court to commence drug testing on a thrice-weekly basis."

Anne sprang up from the table. "Objection! This is an absolute manipulation, a complete twisting of the facts—"

"My client is only asking what's in the best interests of his daughter," he said. "Sir, he's filing for an ex parte judgment of full custody, effective immediately."

The judge, with the silver-blond hair and checkered skin of a man who grew up surfing and probably hit third point that morning, landed his gaze on Anne.

"Ms. Barrows," he said, "I'm assuming you have something more to add."

"I do, Your Honor," she said. "I have quite a bit to add."

Surreal doesn't begin to describe the experience of being on trial for your child. *What's beyond surreal? Surreal-plus? Surreal-extra?* Custody battles are fought every day, but when you become a parent, you don't anticipate proving yourself worthy to raise your child in front of a judge. Unless you're a professional athlete and you accidentally stick your penis in some strange woman's vagina and here you are.

"Your Honor," Anne said, "this is ridiculous. My client's sister has not violated parole. She is charged with knowingly obtaining stolen property, but I had a chance to look at the police documents. It's my suspicion that she'll be released in the next day or so. Just in time for Ulger and his crew to wrest temporary custody from my client."

"Objection!"

"Overruled," the judge said. "Ms. Barrows, how do you suppose these charges aren't legitimate?"

"I talked to the lieutenant on the case," Anne said. "They don't have a victim, Your Honor. No one's reported the property stolen. This is an allegation based on a supposition. Nothing more. And it was orchestrated by Mr. Anonymous."

The silver surfer–haired judge turned from checkerboard to pink like a gecko changing shades. This new tidbit had thrown him for a loop. I watched him carefully and a little acquisitively. He was attractive and seemingly reasonable. A rarity in Los Angeles. No wedding ring, not even a shadow of one. I wondered if he were single. I wondered if he were gay. I wondered if he were single and gay and open to change?

"Counsel, approach the bench," he said.

Trevor stood up.

"Not you, Mr. Anonymous," the judge said. "Your attorney."

Ulger squeezed Trevor's shoulder, and he fumbled with the chair before sitting down. I peered over and caught Trevor's eye. I wiggled my fingers, giving him a quarter wave. I couldn't help it. We knew each other. We had loved each other—or, at least, I'd loved him and he'd loved that I loved him. A small part of me (that I should probably bury) clung to the familiar. Trevor was no mystery to me. I knew everything there was to know about him. And though he was a genius in his work, he was clunky in the game of life chess.

In one breath, the room brightened with realization.

I wasn't going to be afraid anymore.

Of course he set up my sister—of course he was going for full custody.

He knew there was a chance I might survive.

I'd never be forgiven.

I had to think like he did. I concentrated. *What is Trevor's next move?*

He turned away.

I knew he'd do that! I was already good at this.

I looked ahead, straining to hear the hushed conversation between the stately Anne and the belligerent Ulger, who was making a mini-series of his disapproval, shaking his head, stomping his feet, banging his cane.

"Let's move this into chambers," the judge said. His eyes, the color of the murky Pacific, magnified by his aviator glasses, tracked Trevor and me. "Mr. and Mrs. Anonymous, you both may wait outside."

"Is that us?" Trevor asked Blecks.

. . .

Outside the courtroom, I watched Trevor struggling with his phone for a full ten minutes before I decided to walk over to him.

"There's no Wi-Fi," I said. "No wifey, no Wi-Fi. Get it?"

"What are you talking about?"

"You're not going to get much service," I said. "Try turning the Wi-Fi off; maybe that'll work."

He shot me with that infamous death stare that made development execs cry, then skated away as I slowly turned into an ice sculpture.

Not really. I wasn't scared, remember?

I could see him tap on his phone.

"You're welcome!" I said.

He turned and scowled, then went back to his lover, Siri.

"May I make a suggestion?" I'd sneaked up on him.

"No," he said. "Leave me alone."

"Our divorce has been so much fun, not to mention great for my figure, but can we end this circus?" I said. "Our lawyers meet once a month for book club, and they've probably already arrived at our magic number, the one they'll argue this case up to."

"I'm not going to settle," he said. "I don't settle. Ever."

"You settled when you married me," I said. *Smile?*

"Look how well that turned out," he said.

He had me there. I deflated, expelling all the oxygen I'd held on to that morning.

"So how's everything else going?" I asked. "I like the new trailer on that Hanks film."

"Everything's great," he said. "Never better."

"Terrific," I said.

"Are you dating Gio Metz?" he asked.

I blinked. "What?"

"Are you fucking Gio Metz?"

"No!"

"Are you thinking about fucking him?" He sounded jealous. Maybe I didn't know everything there was to know about him.

"What do you mean?" He could tell I was lying. I'm a terrible liar in addition to being a terrible mother. Someone call Blecks.

"He fucks anything that walks," Trevor said.

I pressed my lips into a straight line.

"What if it swims?" I asked.

Trevor actually gave me a smile.

"Just don't be stupid," he said.

"I try," I said.

"Hey, do you know why everyone's into anal now? What's that about?" He looked baffled. Then I looked baffled. We stood there, baffled together, bonding over the anal craze.

"Anonymous!" the bailiff called out.

"That's us," I said, skirting more anal talk. Was this the brave new world of dating? My sphincter winced as I stepped gingerly, following Trevor into the courtroom.

"We have a court order for parenting classes," I told Dad, who liked to call me every day for divorce and Gio updates. He, like everyone else, was madly in love with Gio. And Dad hadn't even French-kissed him. Not that he wouldn't try.

"You need someone to teach you how to parent?" he said, practically spitting out the words. "That's pathetic."

"It's also the law," I said. "I have to go. If I don't, I could lose Pep."

"Who needs classes for parenting? We didn't have those when you were kids. It's the damn government, turning us all into sheep. Wait 'til AI has its way with us. Don't get me started on GMO."

"Well, maybe I can learn something," I said. "Everything I know about parenting is from you and a quarter of a mom."

"Me?" He sounded shocked. "I was a great father."

"You definitely did your best," I said, "but if you recall, I cried every day, and how many times was Fin called in for beating up boys?"

My father laughed, his proud dad psyche dining out on the memory. "You cried every day because you were a scaredy-cat. Now, your sister, on the other hand—I remember a call I got from an angry mother," he said. "Her son came home with a black eye. The kid was a foot taller and fifty pounds heavier than Fin. He was the class bully. Fin whooped his sorry ass."

Point taken.

"Maybe that's why, Dad," I said, tempering my approach, "Fin doesn't mind going to prison. She learned to settle things with her fists. That doesn't work in the real world."

"Let me tell you something, dearie," Dad said and lowered his voice, which was how I knew he was heated. "The world was a better place when we settled matters with fists rather than lawyers."

I opened my mouth to object and found that I couldn't argue with him. I would've loved to pop Ulger in the mouth, but I feared he would eat it.

The intercom rang.

"I gotta go, Dad," I said.

"Let me know next time you go out with Gio," he said. "Be good!"

I hung up and pressed the line to the gate.

"Hey, Agnes," a man said. "We're here."

I clicked on the TV to see the bank of security cameras and narrowed my eyes at the screen. Peter, "Westside's Realtor to the Stars™" was waving at the front gate.

"I see you're here, Peter," I said. "But why?"

There was a pause. People talking in the background.

"My clients are spending the weekend," he said, his voice sotto voce and *mucho* anxious. I heard grumbling. "Agnes . . . you're supposed to be cleared out."

19

You Can't Go Home Again

When famous people decide to buy something, they often want it for free. That Weaselly Fuck and America's Sweetheart wanted to buy the house. Wait. *No.* They were almost positive, somewhat confident, more or less committed to buying the house, but they needed to spend the long weekend in the place.

"I've never heard of such a thing," I said to Peter, who didn't bat an eye. He couldn't bat an eye. It appeared he'd had his eyes welded—but open—by an iron. Evening had fallen, and I'd holed up with the unblinking Peter in our bar where, if you looked east, and bent over at a ninety-degree angle and shielded your eyes from the blaze of sunset, you could see all the way to O. J.'s Rockingham house.

I refilled Peter's bourbon.

"I'm finding myself saying that a lot these days, Peter," I said. "I've never heard of a man who has his sister-in-law arrested on a bullshit charge. I've never heard of a man who sells a house out from under his family. I've never heard of a man who talks to his wife about all the women demanding anal—"

"You're not in my business, Ag," Peter said. "In this market, you're lucky they're not asking for a month. The bottom dropped out, you know."

"Don't talk to me about dropping bottoms," I said, sipping from my glass. "I can't even find mine anymore."

The famous couple was sequestered in the kitchen with the lamentable fireplace, no doubt recharging our French and German appliances (maybe I could sell them?) with their star power, while simultaneously sucking out all the oxygen in the room. With movie stars, it can all happen at once. Judging from their hushed yet urgent tones, they weren't happy with my presence. Stars don't like civilian-mixing unless it's preapproved; like they've notified paparazzi they'll be skipping out of James Perse at the Brentwood Country Mart between 12:15 and 12:20.

Movie stars could pretend all they wanted—they were actors, after all—even the "grounded" ones who drop their kids at school or pump their own gas (in full hair and makeup) expect special treatment. They're all normal and grounded until the restaurant host seats them at the wrong table.

"I don't have any place to go," I told Peter. "Trevor terminated my credit cards. My Amex was denied at Starbucks, then my Mastercard, then my debit card, which wouldn't work anyway because I forgot the PIN code. I even tried an old Sears card. I have a little money in my checking account, but hotels don't take checks, right?"

"There's a West LA Motel 6," he said. "My mother-in-law stayed there once."

"I can only afford a Motel 0.06," I said. "I'm the poorest rich person I know. Or the richest poor person."

"I'm sorry Trevor didn't tell you," Peter said. I poured another bourbon. Hanging with the rich and famous had aged Peter. I notice he'd dyed his hair that olive color Westside men favored. I was suddenly thirsty for a dirty martini, olives on the side, at the Bel Air bar.

Who was I kidding? I couldn't even spring for a clean martini.

"Pep and I could sleep in the guesthouse. They'd never even notice. We'd be quiet as church mice. As Church of Scientology mice, if that feels more appropriate."

Trevor was cutting off my supply lines from every angle, like Rommel of the Riviera. Trevor had imbibed the war-for-business genre—from Sun Tzu's *The Art of War* to Og Mandino's *The Greatest Salesman in the World*, to the CliffsNotes of Ayn Rand's *Atlas Shrugged* (no one in LA actually read the whole thing). The watery broth of self-help books was *The 48 Laws of Power;* I'd flipped through the book from time to time, laughing alone in Trevor's bathroom.

Conceal Your Intentions . . .

Never Outshine the Master . . .

Crush Your Enemy Totally . . .

Guess who wasn't laughing now? Me. Guess who's laughing? Trevor. Trevor was definitely laughing. While deciding on whether to perform anal. (Perform? I pictured a cape and a wand.) For someone as anal-retentive as he is, I'm sure this posed a stark dilemma.

Peter shook his olive head. I licked my lips. "I'm sorry. That's the deal. Your hus—ex-husband is desperate to sell. So far, these are the only people interested."

"What's wrong with our house?" I felt offended for Trevor's house. Who wouldn't want to live here? Besides me.

"Nothing. It's just not . . . grand." He was staring at the final drop of amber at the bottom of the glass. He brought the glass to his mouth, his weary face disappearing momentarily, as though underwater. He came up for air. "No columns, no marble. It's not a 'statement' house."

"Fourteen bathrooms isn't grand?"

"Fourteen is on the more modest end of the bathroom scale, frankly," he said. "They've been pondering a seventeen-bathroom Cape Cod in Brentwood Park. A nineteen-bathroom modern spaceship doohickey in Bel Air. There are never enough bathrooms."

He expelled the longest sigh on record. Oh, the perils of being

"Westside's Realtor to the Stars™." These folks were a special crew, ambitious to the point of violence. I'd seen Peter's rival, a platinum-skullcapped grandmother, bite her way through a Christmas party crowd to get to Floyd Mayweather when it was rumored he was selling.

"Bathrooms are the new pharmaceutical comas," I said. *Was it only a few years ago everyone in town was bragging about their own personal IVs?*

I checked my phone. "Pete, it's almost seven o'clock. I spent the day in court. Pep's had a long week, I'm exhausted, we haven't packed a thing—"

"There's got to be someone you can stay with," he said. "Friends? Family?"

I'd called Trevor, but he hadn't answered. He was hiding. I could feel him hiding. He was probably hiding in a well-appointed vagina. (Or diamond-encrusted anus? Which sounded like an entrée at a fancy restaurant on Canon, btw.) Trevor hated confrontation when he knew he was wrong.

I thought of calling Anne, but what could she say? Who could she call at this hour? Shouldn't I let her just rest up? Also, I wasn't crazy about making a $300 phone call.

Liz was out of town with her mother this weekend, who'd bribed her with a couple of nights at the Montage. I thought of my other friends. I'd texted Juliette the other day just to check in on her and her re-modeled boobs and her new vagina and revenge-fucking. I hadn't heard anything back. Meanwhile, Karyn had renewed her vows without me. Liz attended, and guess who else had showed up? Trevor.

Liz had filled me in on the menu. *Steak, quail, potatoes au gratin . . .*

I was persona non grata.

"Persona non gratin," I said. "Person without cheese. I prefer persona au gratin, don't you?"

Peter mumbled and shook his glass.

So. I stared into Peter's unblinking, ironed face.

That leaves . . .

I poked a number in my phone. Dad answered on the first ring.

. . .

Saturday began at dawn, with the buzz of skateboards whizzing by on the brick walkway and homeless people fighting, yelling incoherent insults, in the sand. Pep and I had slept on the foldout couch in the living room, but when I woke up, Pep was already banging around the kitchen with Dad.

How much banging did oatmeal require?

A *bang* considerable *bang* amount.

"You guys need any help?" I called out.

"Nope," he called back. "Pep's handling it!"

She came out of the kitchen wielding a wooden spoon.

"What are you making?"

"She's making pancakes," my dad said. "You never bothered teaching this girl to cook? What, do you want her to starve to death someday?"

"Yeah, Mom," Pep said. "I could starve!" She giggled and dove back into the kitchen. *Bang.*

My strapping, blue-eyed, lapsed-Catholic father was the epitome of the Jewish mother. When I'd spent every dime I had on that 750-square-foot house a hundred feet from the beach, it was to get my father out of the apartment he'd lived in, in the heart (or bile duct) of Hollywood, since forever. I wanted him to live closer to his granddaughter.

I was so proud. I'd made enough money on a movie I'd written that was rewritten by hacks with sledgehammer fingers until it became the filmic version of marshmallow fluff to buy a house. But I already had a house, or, rather, Trevor already had a house, so I wanted to buy one for my dad. Isn't that what you do as a child of a questionable-neighborhood apartment-dwelling parent? We'd never lived in a house, my family and me. Now, two, actually, two and a half, counting Pep, would live in a house. This was big for us.

He begrudgingly approved of this little abode. A beach cottage built in the 1920s, someone's weekend home. The place was a dump. I stepped onto faded vomit-colored wall-to-wall carpet, and my ankles were blanketed in fleas. Flea socks. The tenant, a bodybuilder who collected strays and crack pipes, stayed in his room, muttering to himself (and his muscles?) ignoring us carpetbaggers (I'd bag a different carpet, sans fleas). The place smelled like tanning lotion, dog (I hope it was dog) urine, and burning plastic.

I don't even want to get into the Jacuzzi in the backyard. I wouldn't want anyone to get into that Jacuzzi without a hazmat suit.

I didn't care. I loved old houses and saw this shit box's potential. I wrote a check and signed papers and became an adult. I owned my own tiny, flea-infested speck of land.

A few weeks later, my dad told me Nic Cage was selling his house at the end of our street, on the beach.

"It's only four mil," he said.

"Dad, I just spent everything I have," I said.

"Yeah, but it's a bargain," he said. "It's $1,105 per square foot. That's a good investment."

After spending the rest of my option money to fix up the house and decorate, I drove Dad to the beach cottage to "present" my gift, which smelled like fresh paint and no more fleas. He folded his arms and walked around, inspecting the tiny home.

"So," I said. "What do you think of the new carpet?"

He looked at it. Sniffed.

"I like blue," he said.

I had chosen taupe.

Nothing I did/wrote/bought would ever be good enough for Dad. That morning, sitting around the kitchen table with Dad and Pep over pancakes soaked in guilt, I realized I'd married my father.

The pancakes were delicious.

. . .

Dad explained to me and Pep that he needed his place back Saturday night; he had a hot date. Pep high-fived him and went to pack.

"You and Trevor have a lot in common, you notice that?" I asked him when Pep left the room.

"Bite your tongue," he said. "My girlfriends are hotter than anything your ex-husband will get."

"You're competing with my ex-husband over his girlfriends?"

"I'm just saying," my dad said.

When we were kids, Fin and I knew Dad loved us because he loved playing tricks on us, like holding us down and dropping a glob of spit an inch from our noses. Or sticking Oreos in his eyes and chasing us around making zombie noises. Or playing "pull my finger" at the dinner table. We'd explode in fits of laughter. We were his pals, his cohorts in bad taste, not pretty little objects to be protected. We were taught and expected to get the last punch—and we did, good little soldiers. I didn't even own a dress and didn't wear one until elementary graduation, a hand-me-down from a neighbor. It was too tight around my middle. When I sat on the bench during graduation, the zipper split. I'd made straight As and gave my first speech, but Dad was disappointed because now Fin couldn't wear that dress.

"Sonia and I are having dinner at 5:00," he said. "So if you could give us some space around 6:00 . . ."

"What about Shu?" I asked.

"What about her?"

"Aren't you two . . ."

Pep walked in. "I like Shu," Pep said.

"You've never even met her."

"She speaks five languages, Mom," she said.

"I like her too, pumpkin. But she's getting a little serious," he said. "I gotta pump the brakes."

"Do you really want to blow what you have with Shu?" I asked.

"Relax," he said. "Geez, how'd I raise such an uptight kid?" He looked at Pep, who just rolled her eyes and shrugged, like, *Who the fuck knows?*

After I helped Dad wash the dishes in scalding hot water (if your skin wasn't peeling off, the water wasn't hot enough), Pep and I took a stroll down to the beach and filled up on negative ions; I needed enough to last me through the divorce. Gabriela had told me we could stay with her family, so that was an option, but I didn't want Bernardo to end up sleeping on the couch again.

My cell phone, sticky with sunscreen, vibrated. An unknown number.

Gio? If I opened my mouth, I might complain. I hated complainers, even me. Especially me.

"Hello!" he said. Of course I answered. What? As Pep ran down to the water, I told him everything. The awful famous couple. The Realtor's ironed face. My dad's mystery date.

"What happened to Shu?" he asked. "I like them together."

"That's what I said."

"Stay at my place," he said.

"I couldn't ask you to do that," I said. Could I? "You have a place?"

"You didn't ask," he said. "I insist. I won't even be there. I'm never there."

"I thought you only stayed in hotels—"

"I've a house in Santa Monica Canyon," he said. "It's empty. I keep forgetting to sell, and then I stay there occasionally, and I realize I like it and I lose my nerve."

I heard French seep out of a loudspeaker in the background.

"Gio, where are you?"

"Just landed in Paris," he said. "It's the only city left where I can smoke outside a café."

I wanted to be Gio when I grew up. Without the cigarettes. Maybe an occasional cigarette. I thought of how sexy I'd look with one hanging off my lower lip like Brigitte Bardot. Without Brigitte's lips. Or skin. Or eyeliner. Okay, maybe not quite as sexy.

"Gio, thank you. We'll stay," I said. "Just for the weekend. Until the horrible famous people leave."

"I hope they never leave," he said.

I hung up, and a tear fell from my eye. The smallest kindness (this kindness was more plus-sized) reduced me to a human puddle. My new hormones? Or was a kind gesture so rare? In LA, favors were on the barter system. Wealthy Angelenos only bestowed favors if they received a bigger one in exchange. Look at all the private school buildings with famous names—you think they paid for the building? They'd pay off 10 percent, get their name splashed across the top, then leave the school struggling to pay off the balance while they bought Junior into college.

Before Junior went into rehab and the singing/modeling/rapping career. *Naturally.*

Pep and I packed up our things, and I gave my dad a hug and he patted my back.

"I love you, Dad," I said.

"Be good," he said and patted me again. *Good dog.*

My dad was a child of the Depression. His father was an abusive alcoholic, his mother a long-suffering saint. To get to school, he walked miles in the snow in hand-me-down shoes from his older sister. He'd been small for his age, but he was tough. He joined the army at seventeen. He was a gunnery sergeant at nineteen, responsible for men much older.

If his life were an equation, the answer would be: *Not a hugger.*

"Watch Pep's diet," he said, waving his finger at me. "She's getting too much sodium. And keep her away from the GMOs. And for cris-sakes, teach her some life skills."

Translated: *I love you and my granddaughter so much.*

"You know what? Just send her to me every couple of weeks," he said. "We'll start with the basics—cooking, cleaning, balancing a checkbook."

"Thanks, Dad," I said. "And no go on the GMOs in the meantime."

"Keep an eye on the stock market," he said. "Might want to stay in cash."

"That's easy when you have, like, forty bucks to your name," I said. "Call Shu."

As I left, I realized I *hadn't* married my father. I'd married a different species, a rare and exotic bird of a man. The more I tried to figure it out, the more the why slithered away from me. Maybe it wasn't about the why. Maybe it was about the who—who wouldn't have married Trevor? It's like asking who wouldn't have slept with Warren Beatty in the '70s.

No. One.

Pep and I puttered along Ocean, passing sunburned hordes of neon tourists and swarms of green Hulu bikes and terrifying scooters buzzing in and out of traffic, motorized mosquitoes diving for prey.

A typical Saturday drive in these parts is what I'm saying.

We pulled down into Santa Monica Canyon, outside a Spanish home, ivy hugging its walls, hidden behind a peeling dogwood, an old fountain gurgling in cool, shaded grass. The house was built in the 1930s for one of Howard Hughes's favorite buxom starlets. Gio had told me she'd died there, having never left the premises for the last decade of her life. Hearing that, he'd bought it sight unseen.

I molded my hand to the tree and looked up at the sun floating through the leaves.

I couldn't blame the old broad. I'd be buried here, if it were up to me.

"It's a fairy-tale house," Pep said, her eyes wide with wonder as I punched in Gio's security code. Four numbers for the year he lost his virginity, in the middle of the Vietnam War.

"Whose house is it?" Pep asked.

"A family friend," I said. "Daddy knows him."

"Is Daddy coming, too?"

That's the problem with kids—so many questions and so few answers. The alarm beeped a welcome, and I pushed the heavy door and ushered Pep inside.

I could see why Gio hadn't sold. The house was Gio—solid, comfortable, pleasantly spooky. Spirits lived here, happy, dancing, drunk spirits. I slipped off my shoes, the cool Spanish tiles awakening my senses as I padded out to the veranda overlooking the pool, which, to no one's surprise, at least not this reporter, was filled with leaves and green blue with algae. The land that time and *The Hollywood Reporter* forgot. No one would find me here. I felt myself exhale. I took another deep breath and filled my lungs with damp Santa Monica air.

I heard a noise.

A phone? A chime. The doorbell. Shit. Someone had found me. So much for the Witness Protection Program for Hollywood wives.

Whatever happened to Agnes Nash? *She knew too much and said it all!*

"Can I go in the pool?" Pep asked as I headed to the front door.

"It's covered in leaves."

"I know," she said, wistful. "Why can't we have a pool covered in leaves? It's like the trees went swimming."

The chime sprinkled the air.

Standing in front of the old Spanish door was a man in a cap and white apron, an oversized knotted plastic bag cradled in his hands.

"Are you Agnes whose smile lights up the room?" he asked.

"Depends on the size of the room," I said, my smile lighting up the doorway, thinking of the man with the golden-tongued kiss who'd given this guy those specific instructions. "What's this?"

"Chicken soup," he said. "Mr. Metz said to make sure you ate right away."

I raked enough dollar bills from my purse and coat pockets for a tip, which he refused, insisting Gio had taken care of everything. I acquiesced and dashed back inside, tiptoe-dancing on the tile, tore open the bag on the stained kitchen block, flipped off the plastic top, and sank my face into the schmaltz-glazed steam.

Pep had fallen asleep on the deep pink velvet "princess bed," as she dubbed the couch in the living room with thick white marshmallow walls and beamed ceilings. I wondered if the old couch were part of the original house, and if the lady of the house had expired on its cushions; it would be the perfect hammock for a last breath. The pillows were exhausted and smelled sweet with age and old perfume, the wood frame with elegant curlicues worn down by human touch, matching end tables new in the 1930s that had circled through the vagaries of interior design fads. They'd survived and emerged like those women you occasionally see with bold white hair and skin that moves with their expressions.

I was wide awake, engaged with the sun's quieting light playing tricks on the faded Persian rug that was definitely worth $60,000. How do I know this? Because every time Trevor ordered a rug from his decorator, he would yell, "Sixty thousand? It's only a fucking rug! An old fucking rug!"

He had a point.

I wrapped Pep in a cashmere throw I'd found in the master and relaxed into that space that held no husband, no father, no sister (currently held in the Van Nuys Women's Correctional Facility), no one except me and my sleeping child.

Delicious, I thought. *This moment feels delicious.*

I knew a girl, an old buddy, who'd used food adjectives for friends. She's *luscious*. He's *yummy*. I wondered what happened to her. As one circle grew, the other receded into a pinpoint.

I heard a faint beeping.

So faint it could only be heard after the sun went down.

It was coming from an upstairs room.

"And the moment's gone," I said as I rubbed my hands together, then let them fly.

I hiked up the cramped spiral staircase toward the upstairs rooms, the beeping beckoning and mocking. "There's no peace," the beeping said. "What were you thinking?"

I tracked the beeping to an office tucked into the back corner overlooking the yellowing backyard, the pool that was more leaf than water. An enormous personal computer with an oversized screen set on a heavy, stained mahogany desk was plunked in the middle of the room, proclaiming itself the great overseer of beeping sounds. I switched on the light. The sound was coming from inside a drawer at the bottom of the desk.

I opened the drawer. Amid a crunch of papers, old scripts, torn checks, pens, children's scribbles, there was a small alarm clock, forgotten.

Eight-track tapes.

A bundle of envelopes, bound by a rubber band worn by age and stretched to its limit. The envelopes were yellowed at the edges, frayed by time.

Addressed to Gio.

In a variety of handwriting. Wisps of letters, wide, airy loops, others slashes and angry blots, several dotted with spilled wine.

Love letters.

I should not open them, of course I shouldn't. I should've popped the batteries out of the alarm clock and shoved the letters back right away.

I shouldn't have opened them. But I did. Why? Because I'm weak. And nosy. And a writer. And a woman. And a human being.

Dear Gio,

I called and called and called.

Is it really over?

Sarah

Dated January 7, 1982. So. I guess it's over, Sarah?

Gio,

These last few weeks have been magical.

Yours,

Emma G.

I checked the date. Emma G. Emma Gainesville, the English Rose, had starred in one of Gio's '80s gangster films. Forever in your debt, huh? I'll bet.

A pinging sound punctured my infatuation bubble (with its thin veneer of jealousy). Was I jealous? What right would I have to be jealous? Does every woman have that right after one life-changing kiss and a half gallon of home-delivered chicken soup?

I say yes. Agreed?

Chime.

The doorbell. *Chime.*

It was 11:08 already, my phone exclaimed. Who rings a doorbell at 11:08?

I shoved the love letters back in the drawer and raced down the stairway before Pep was awakened.

She was outside, still as a lamppost, her inky hair haloed by the hazy streetlight. The Princess of Darkness, appearing custom-wrapped by minions in black cashmere. The dogwood tree swayed in the wind like a woman cradling a baby, and *what the hell,* I thought. *What the hell was Waverly Brown doing here?*

"I have a client who lives down the street," she said as she strode past me on those eight-foot legs into the foyer, taking a moment to glance at the painting of a Spanish Madonna set above the entry table. "I can't talk about it, but he's at WME and he's in a #MeToo mess. Yes, she's underage, but only by six weeks. It involved cocaine and maybe a half dozen Xanax. I can't talk about it."

I willed myself to blink; I felt as though I must be dreaming.

"Anyway. I saw your car. I was just thinking about you." She closed her eyes and took a deep, throttling breath. "Agnes, we need to talk."

"You know I'm not a negative person," Waverly lied.

"Actually, everything you've said so far has been negative," I said.

"Things are about to get really bad," she said, her hands entangled in her long, beaded necklace. "Terrible, in fact."

"Jesus Christ, Waverly."

"Also, you owe me for last month," she said.

"Yes, yes," I said. "I owe a lot of people. But you know, food."

"Do you know George Treadwell?" Her eyebrows mashed together. "I do. I can't talk about it."

"George Treadwell? I mean, I've met him," I said, thinking about his foray into the kitchen, his brief dip into the Fin show.

"Step carefully. Keep your head low. Postpone any court date."

"My head low," I repeated.

"I keep picking up something," she said. "It doesn't make sense."

"There's not a lot in my life that makes sense," I said. I said pointedly. About her. In this room. Right now.

"I feel like you're connected to George," she said. "He's the key."

"George. Treadwell. The actor," I said. "The one who's acting in Trevor's movie."

"For now," she said. Her eyes darted about the living room before they settled. "Someone died in this room."

"Great," I said. "Anything else?"

"This is not your future," she said, her hand outstretched, her impossible fingers playing a sonata in the still air. "Don't get too attached."

"Fuck off, Waverly."

She flashed a smile, and it was as unnerving as if I'd petted a cobra. "I adore that spunk."

And she was gone. I gazed over at Pep, who was still sound asleep. Thank God. No sense in both of us having nightmares.

Years ago, I used to make chicken soup from scratch for Trevor when he was fighting a cold. I used to cook a lot of things for Trevor. That may be the only reason he married me. His mother had fed him frozen dinners, his ex-wife had ordered pizza after he'd come home from a long day at work. Trevor and I had dined out every night, mostly to Italian restaurants because Italian is the only kind of restaurant that exists in Los Angeles. Even if it's a Chinese restaurant, you'll find pasta on the menu. In a city where there aren't a hell of a lot of Italians, where even the waiters at Italian restaurants are Yugoslavian. (It's got to stop.) Well, I was sick of sticky fifty-dollar pasta disguised by boxed sauce and out-of-season truffles. Angel hair in sheep's clothing, I said. The linguine clams have no clothes, I'd said to Trevor. He just shrugged and chowed down. He didn't know any better. How could he? I had to put my al dente where my mouth was. I started cooking for Trevor, and after a while, we stopped going out to dinner. I made him penne with puttanesca sauce and crispy duck and eggplant parmigiana and spicy shredded beef tacos. I made chocolate chip cookies for his pals at CAA and Disney. I made him chicken soup when he was sick. I'm amazed, looking back, at how long it actually took him to marry me.

Maybe my personality is what held him back.

Nah.

Then Pep was born, and Trevor and I thought we'd won the life lottery. We'd figured it out. We were pals and we were lovers. We laughed at the same jokes and relished catching up at the end of the day. We were good company. We talked to each other more than any other couple in our circle. "This is *my* marriage," I'd say with blazing confidence. "It's not going anywhere." My friends would complain about their husbands, their kids, their pets. (My fair-weather friends, I guess, or, in Hollywood, fair box office friends.)

Meanwhile, Trevor and I would stare into each other's eyes over margaritas, our hearts swelling with gratitude that, over time, instead of diminishing, our love was growing. We had beaten all odds. This Hollywood marriage would have a happy ending instead of a TMZ ending.

How could we be so lucky?

I loved him.

I loved him until I couldn't stand him.

20

Quid Pro Stole

On Monday morning, Pep and I headed back home, well rested and well fed. *(Thank you, Gio, I mused, wherever you are, blackening your lungs in the company of Frenchwomen coiled like parentheses around your bulky shoulders.)* The Riviera's curved roads, buffered by a hedge army, were empty save for the occasional nanny, head cocked, attached to a cell phone, as she pushed her bundled, silver-plated ward in a Bugaboo stroller. Rounding a turn, I almost ran over the miniature Paramount chief huffing and puffing up the hill, his trainer cooing encouragement. I felt sorry for trainers of the Hollywood power players—adult babysitters, paid to lie to their clients about their cardio capacity, their body-fat-to-muscle ratio, their marriages.

I'd heard the conversations firsthand. *"Who's stronger, me or Ari?" "Who's a better runner, me or Jeffrey?" "Have you ever seen Harvey work out?"*

My personal crapshoot, the security code, still worked. I breathed a sigh of relief as the gates creaked open, and I compressed Waverly's dire warning from last night into a tight little cube and swallowed. I glanced at Pep, who was staring out the window.

Our future was in the hands of George Treadwell.

"Happy to be home?" I asked as I circled the driveway.

Pep pursed her lips and looked out the window. I pulled into the garage.

"Are you okay?"

"Mom," she said quietly. "I've been thinking . . ." She looked at me, worried, her eyes moist. "Mom, you have to win. I can't just live with Dad. I need you."

I took a deep breath. "Honey, I can't guarantee."

"Mom, promise me," she said. "Mom, *you're* my home. I love Dad, but he can't, you know, handle things. Like, toast . . ." She looked around, worried. "What if I have my period and you're not there?"

Oh, my heart.

My door swung open—

"Also, can we have a princess couch?" Pep asked.

"You won't fucking believe this," Fin said as she popped her head in the door. "Hi, doll!" She waved at Pep.

"Please don't say the F word in front of Pep," I said.

"I don't fucking mind," Pep said.

"See?" Fin said.

"What are you doing here?" I asked. "You got out already?"

"Prison overcrowding." Fin shrugged. "No one wants me!"

"I want you," Pep said.

"And that's all that matters, Peppers," Fin said. "Agnes, listen, you won't fucking believe this."

"There's not a lot left that I won't believe," I said. "And please stop swearing."

"Come 'ere." Fin grabbed my hand, pulling me through the kitchen past the swinging doors and into the living room.

. . .

Well. There it wasn't.

"Where is the . . . ," I said, tapping the side of my cheek. "I could've sworn there was a . . ."

The Steinway.

Our piano, our great, big, lonely piano, was gone. All that was left were four small divots in the rug.

"They stole it!" Fin said. "Those Hollywood people stole my piano!"

"*My* piano," I said. I walked around the empty space where our Steinway once stood, proud and silent. Mostly silent. But hey, it looked nice, and that's what mattered.

"I'm the only one who ever played it. Clock's missing, too," Fin said, "My Tiffany fucking clock."

"*My* Tiffany fucking clock," I said.

"The fucking clock, too?" Pep shook her head.

"Oh, now it's your Tiffany clock. I was letting you borrow it," Fin said. "Who steals something that's stolen?"

"I thought it wasn't stolen."

"*I* didn't steal it," Fin said.

"What the fuck," Pep said.

"I have to call Peter," I said.

"I already called the police," Fin said. "You can't let criminals get away with this shit."

Fin wasn't bluffing. She'd called the cops on the famous couple, but they weren't available to come to us; I had to drive back down to the West LA station, where Fin had been hauled off in handcuffs.

The circle of (my) life. Meanwhile.

"This is just a big misunderstanding," Peter, "Westside's Realtor to the Stars™" said as we conferred under the backyard oak tree that had more legal protections than an actual human being. Peter's voice was shaky, and he neglected to slip off his mirrored Ray-Bans, so I was talking to my reflection. And my reflection was telling me I was old. This divorce was turning me into a shar-pei.

I thought about the shar-pei down the street that was on antidepressants. Maybe like recognizes like and I could borrow some off him.

"You knew this was going to happen," Fin said. Her arms were planted against her chest, staring him down as she occasionally took a drag off her cigarette and blew smoke rings at his Ray-Bans; it was all very *mise-en-scène*.

Peter cleared his throat, shrinking under her gaze. "Are those prison tattoos?" he squeaked.

"Only the ones burned in with cigarettes," Fin said.

"Look, it's just a misunderstanding, girls."

"Girls? Girls! They misunderstood my fucking clock all the way out of this house," Fin said.

"Listen, Peter, Weasel and America's Sweetheart can't steal a whole piano," I said. "Even though they're famous. And rich. And powerful. Stealing is illegal, even for them!" Pause. "It is, right?" I asked.

"Oh, they didn't think of it as stealing," he said. "They'd be horrified if you thought that. They just wanted to see how your living room looked with more space! Hey, good news—they're this close to making an offer." He pinched his finger to his thumb.

"I'm this close to making a police report," I said, mirroring his gesture.

"And I'm this close to calling that donkey-faced Harvey Levin," Fin said. "Let's TMZ this shit—today!"

"No, no! They'll bring it all back," Peter said, waving his manicured hands. "By the end of the week. I promise."

"What do you mean by *all*?" I asked.

He froze.

"Never mind," he said. "I'm on it."

A couple of days later, I walked in on Caster, Gabriela, and Lola in the laundry room, tittering over cups of instant coffee that they'd nuked in an old microwave.

"Why do you keep using this thing?" I asked about the microwave, its door off its hinge. "The coffee machine is *mucho mejor*."

They started whispering, their heads in a tight circle. I would just have to wait.

"Okay," I said. "What's wrong? I mean, now."

"Missus Aggie," Gabriela said, first out of the chute, first to talk. *"Tenemos una problema."*

The Triplets hovered around me like hummingbirds darting in and out as I rummaged through the empty linen closet that should be called something else now. Random hand towel closet? Dust-collecting closet?

"They took my sheets and towels?" I asked. "All of them?"

"I wasn't here, Missus Aggie," Gabriela said. "Lola, tell her."

Lola rolled off a barrage of soft yet urgent notes. I nodded, my fist holding up my chin.

"So what did she just say?" I asked Caster and Gabriela.

"They took everything," Caster said. "Mr. Wolfman, he very handsome, *pero* you can't let this happen, missus. You can't let people jus' steal from you. What you going to do about it?"

"You didn't tell Fin, did you?" I asked. Fin had threatened to go to their house with a truck and pick up the piano herself.

They shook their heads slowly, beautiful exotic birds watching a tennis match. I headed to the bathroom where I could rearrange my collection of facial creams, and I left a message for Peter.

"Peter, they stole my sheets and towels!" I said. "What kind of monsters do you work for?"

He returned my call immediately.

"They were going to include them in the offer."

I tossed an old Noxzema in the trash.

"Peter, you've been working for these people too long."

Eye cream from 2003. Trash.

"Sorry, of course, okay. I'll get them back—or I can pay you for them?"

I didn't have much money.

Vitamin C serum that hurt like a thousand wasp stings. Trash.

I didn't have any money.

"How much are we talking?" I asked.

Fin drove to Peter's office and picked up a check for twelve grand. Those sheets I was sleeping on, Pratesi, those cost six figures. Sheets. Pillowcases. Six figures. You read that right. Are they worth it? Hells yeah. Those sheets is *noice*. But I'd still rather sleep with cold, hard cash.

I guess Peter didn't flinch when Fin demanded that figure, based on her research.

"He only flinched when I told him I'd worked for the Mexican Mafia," Fin said. "Good times."

Before our next court hearing, Trevor and I had to set a meeting with a child psychologist. "I thought we were going to parenting classes with a bunch of normal inadequate parents like us," I said to Anne. "I was looking forward to delving into social media supervision, sleep times, and swear jars."

"Ulger told me Trevor would feel more comfortable in a private setting," she said. "My stipulation is that you do it together. We want an even playing field."

"A therapist's office is an uneven playing field," I said. "Trevor loves therapy. He's a master at therapy. He goes five days a week!"

Trevor, like the rest of Hollywood, had spent some of the best years of his life on a therapist's couch. The narcissist capital of the world (sorry, D.C. and NYC) loved being listened to, even if they had to pay for it. And the therapists in LA were easily corruptible; most pitched pilots and movies and reality shows on the side.

Trevor hadn't learned anything about himself but that he liked therapy.

"I've never been to therapy," Anne said.

"That's why I like you," I said. "Okay, where do I go?"

"By the way," she said, "I hate to bring this up, but we're going back and forth on the fees. There's a chance you'll have to pay your own."

"Oh no," I said. "What are the fees again?"

I was thinking, I don't know, fifteen, twenty grand at this point. I could sell my jewelry, go on a payment plan.

"We're at $75,000," Anne said. "Not counting this phone call."

"'kay, bye!" I said and hung up.

Legal fees are like ordering a chopped salad at a restaurant. No matter how much you eat, how much you chip away at that bounty of lettuce and cheese and whatnot, there's always more. Always. In high school, they should teach kids just to stay away from lawyers if they want to keep their money. Stay away from the court system. Makes so much more sense than teaching them algebra.

Speaking of chopped salad.

The best chopped salad is at La Scala Presto in Brentwood—order it with turkey, garbanzos, cheese, tomatoes, and an Italian dressing that is just the right amount of piquant. A Hollywood ex-wife I know orders it without turkey, without garbanzos, without cheese, and without dressing.

Her action director husband still divorced her skinny ass, dyed his hair blond, and dates teenagers.

She should've just had the fucking cheese.

I tracked Fin to the side of the house, where she sat with her knees screwed into the dirt, pulling up weeds with Pep in our vegetable garden. I hadn't seen the gardeners in a couple of weeks. I wondered if Esteban had been fired or, maybe, his Mexican wife who lived in Calexico—as opposed to his Mexican wife who lived in Whittier—had snapped. Every once in a while, he came to work with a black eye and a sheepish smile. Anyway, the hillside was going to seed. Vines stretched their limbs, threatening to strangle rosebushes. The fruit trees were losing their budding offspring to birds and vermin and deer.

Pep's arms were glazed with sunscreen, her head covered by one of Fin's myriad minor-league baseball caps that she'd managed to collect from all over the country. There were pieces that were missing from my mental puzzle of Fin's life. A year, here and there in her twenties, early thirties. Many months that I hadn't spoken to her. Days I thought she must be dead, and I'd braced against the news that would arrive at any moment, a rock thrown from the sky at my heart.

Of course, she was always fine; I was the sister losing years of my life worrying.

"You won't believe the numbers," I said, struggling to stay balanced in my sensible heels, the perfect height for a therapy session being about two inches, give or take. "Legal fees. It's insanity."

"Divorce is a rich man's game," Fin said while she clawed at the dirt, her skull rings glinting in the sun.

"Well, that works for Trevor," I said. "How do I look?"

"Old?" Pep said, looking up from her work.

"Maternal," Fin said. "Pep, can you go fetch my pack from the kitchen? You know where it is."

"Please don't smoke," I said.

"All this fresh air," Fin said, "makes me miss that Riverside sludge."

"Give me a hug first," I said to Pep, and she wrapped her arms around me, warm and slippery as eels.

She climbed up the hillside, holding on to her Albuquerque Isotopes cap.

"That's what I was going for," I said. "Maternal. Does my daughter all of a sudden smell like BO?"

"She's growing up," Fin said. "Fast. You know, maybe you and Trevor should just get back together."

I picked my lower jaw up from the dirt. "What did you just . . . we hate each other."

"I know," Fin said, shielding her eyes as she gazed up at me. "You hate Trevor. Trevor hates you. That kind of passion is hard to come by."

She pulled out another carrot and brushed it off. "Me, I don't hate any of my exes."

"Who are you talking to?" I said. "Your hate knows no bounds. Your exes know no bounds, either, which is why you have those restraining orders."

"Nope. I'm annoyed by them. Occasionally, I'd slash a tire and they'd put fists through drywall. That's different."

"I give up."

"I'm just saying, if you knew what's out there, maybe you'd make nice for the next thirty or so years."

I stared at her.

"Fin, I'd stay if I could. I stayed for a long time. I can't anymore. It's not even personal to Trevor. It's the world he inhabits. The world he loves. I don't fit in anymore. I don't think I ever really did."

I crouched down next to her.

"I was at dinner in Malibu, and a director said, straight-faced, 'It's not enough that I succeed, it's that my friends fail.' Everyone laughed."

"Because it's funny," Fin said. "You take this shit too seriously."

"I don't want to raise Pep to be like them," I said. "I want her to be normal."

"Normal? What's normal?" Fin asked. "Me? Dad? The way you and I were raised, to never depend on anyone, never trust anyone, and know that no matter where you go, bad luck will follow you. Everything is stacked against the Murphys! That's how we like it!"

I took a deep breath. The air smelled like ocean and manure; the wind was picking up the neighbors' stables below.

"Normal is a state of mind," I said. "It's like the famous line about porn. I can't describe it, but I know it when I see it."

Beat.

"What kind of idiot can't describe porn?" Fin asked.

"Daddy," the icy blonde with breasts as large and firm as the tires on her (educated guess) ten-year-old white Range Rover said as she swung her bare feet toward Trevor, having slipped off her heels. Her toenails were purple, embellished at the tips with rhinestones. "Daddy, what do you like doing with me?"

Trevor ran his hands through his hair.

"I, uh, like to . . ." He looked at me, sitting on the other end of yet another therapy couch. This one was light gray and too soft and too low. The air conditioner blasted the arctic front down our backs, and the blonde's cold nipples pointed toward the SoulCycle across the street.

"You like to watch your old movies with her," I said, prompting him. I had already run through, in my head, *I like to watch her games, I like to put her to sleep, I like to take her to Rosie's ice-cream shop after school.* None of those worked.

"Yes!" Trevor turned toward the therapist. "She—"

"Talk to me like I'm Pep," she said and winked.

"Is this normal?" Trevor asked me, alarmed.

I sighed. Our Pep didn't use therapy as a personal Match.com. But on the other hand, what better place to get to know someone?

"We need a new therapist," I said to Anne, who'd called me after the session. I'd taken to talking extra fast on legal calls, like Audible 3x. I sounded like a human chipmunk.

"Why? What's wrong with this one?"

"Who, Angelyne?"

"She comes highly recommended."

"I'm getting very mixed signals," I said. "I'm not well versed in child psychology, but should family therapists look like they're auditioning for *Real Housewives of Equinox?*"

"In this town, the answer is yes," Anne said. "I called because I have news."

"I hope it's fake news," I said. "It's the only kind of news I can stomach."

"We lost Morris."

"Who?"

"Our judge. He had a surfing accident."

"I knew it," I said. "Surfing in LA shows poor judgment, pardon the pun. Who surfs in those syphilis-coated waters? Who do we have now?"

"Fezel," she said. She didn't sound happy.

"Is he tough?"

"She," Anne said.

"So that's good, right? A she? Sisterhood and all that, fight the power, fight the man, mansplaining and man-spreading and Manhattans, right?"

"No." Anne sighed. "Adorna Fezel. She's basically our worst nightmare. A childless judge. In fact, I'm not sure she ever was a child."

21

Disorder in the Court

Juliette overdosed on a girls' trip to Cabo, but it wasn't like it was a big deal or anything, as she told it. In terms of overdoses or *over-doing-it doses* (as she called them), this one was mild. Her heart hadn't even stopped.

She'd been floating in the hotel infinity pool and one of the waiters had bought her a few drinks, then offered her a few pills, then offered her his dick, and then a few more pills, and before she knew it, she was helicoptered out to an emergency room somewhere on the Baja Peninsula.

Now, she was happily ensconced in her tidy room at New Hope Malibu. (Promises was booked; a bridal shower in the Colony had taken a wrong turn on the Percocet highway.)

"Guys, I'm starting to trace all my issues to my mom," Juliette said. "I think she overloved me and gave me too much attention, and honestly, it just made me hate myself. Who deserves that much unconditional love?"

"I love Pep unconditionally," I said. "I hope she doesn't hate me so much she has to drug herself."

"She already hates you; all girls hate their moms," Liz said. "It comes and goes like a wave. Are you familiar with the self-loathing wave?"

"I surf the self-loathing pipeline every morning," I said. "I just realized something. My mothering is based on TV shows. All I know about mothering is from Clair Huxtable. I'll never measure up."

"My mom touchstone is Carol Brady," Liz said.

"Morticia Addams," Juliette said, raising her hand.

We had a moment of silence.

"Okay. Enough about your semi-overdose," I said. "My legal bills are mounting. I may have to sell Pep."

"I'll buy her," Liz said, "then you could still see her. I mean, you could cook for us and take her to the movies on occasion."

"You're a perfect co-parent already," I said. "I seriously don't know what I'm going to do if I have to pay for my attorneys."

"Why don't you have your jewelry 'stolen'?" Liz said in air quotes. "My mom has hers stolen when she gets tired of it. I know *the* guy in Beverly Hills."

"Insurance pays top dollar," Juliette said.

"Rich people know things," I said. "I'll have awful famous couple visit the house and leave my jewelry draped over the chopping block."

"Sign over that Venice house to your dad, by the way," Liz said.

"I would, but I worry," I said. "He dates women he's met off the internet."

"Start a GoFundMe page," Juliette said. "I did. Half the people here have GoFundMe pages. They raise money for rehab, get out, and spend the rest on drugs."

"It's like the Krebs cycle for sober living," I said.

"I set mine up for my assault," Juliette said.

"Oh my God. Juliette. Why didn't you tell me? You were assaulted? The hotel in Mexico!"

"Oh no. This guy grabbed my ass at a nightclub," she said. "It was like thirteen years ago."

"Are you out of money, too?" I asked.

"She needs to pay off her plastic surgeon," Liz said.

"Times are tough. I just leased a brown BMW," Juliette said with a shudder. "Anyone who drives a brown car is poor."

I looked up Juliette's GoFundMe page as soon as I got in the car. There was a big picture of Juliette with the tight, shiny skin of a mango, playing with a kitten.

There were updates. A few pictures down, it showed her with a bright red face—the result, she claimed, of a sun allergy. Which looked suspiciously like a CO_2 laser allergy.

She'd raised $15,000.

I scanned other GoFundMe posts—a disabled veteran bordering on homelessness in Seattle, a young family burying a toddler raising money for funeral expenses. Both parties were asking for three grand.

I took out a secret card I only used for dire emergencies—one that Trevor had forgotten but I'd felt too guilty to use. I donated money I didn't have while sitting in my car in the hot Malibu sun. I couldn't pay my own bills, but somewhere in Seattle, a veteran would sleep with a roof over his head, and in Omaha, a toddler would be buried.

Perspective is everything, I told myself.

Except cash. Perspective isn't cash.

Trevor and I were hiking in the Santa Monica Mountains on a hazy, damp morning, and I twisted my ankle running down a hillside. So. There's childbirth pain, then there's sprained ankle pain a mile in on a hike. At least in childbirth, you're handed a baby afterward.

Trevor had picked me up and carried me all the way down the mountain to our car. I'd gazed at him, my heart filled with love. He'd kissed me and set me down gently in the passenger seat.

He'd kept kissing me, and we made out in the car, my ankle throbbing, until the windows fogged up. I remember someone's car alarm going off in the distance. To this day, the right car alarm tugs at my heart.

The car alarm in my dream never stopped. I opened my eyes. I'd slept through my iPhone alarm.

I looked at the time—7:10. I had to be in court by 8:00.

Fin borrowed Esteban's hedge clippers and snipped off ankle monitor #3 (we'd named him Ted) to drive me even though I knew I could drive myself even though I was freaking out and finding it hard to see. Google Maps was telling me I was late. Waze was telling me I'd blown it. That's when you knew you were in trouble. Google Maps was the spinster of traffic directions, sending you the safest, longest way to your destination; Waze was your dissolute, alcoholic cousin, guaranteeing a head-on with a trailer truck on a left turn onto a four-lane highway, but you'd arrive three minutes earlier.

Fin flew down streets and alleyways and I closed my eyes, and when I opened them, she was pushing me out the door in front of the looming courthouse on Figueroa.

"Are you coming in?" I asked.

"I just cut off my ankle monitor, so I should call N'Chelle and head out there."

"Sure," I said.

She looked at me. "I'll go find a parking spot."

Anne had cornered Ulger at their monthly history book club (this month's selection: *Warren G. Harding: The Presidential Diaries*) and forced him to streamline the process by not allowing him his Pappy Van Winkle, straight, until he agreed we'd shoot for *one* court hearing for both custody and support. One. Not eight.

Court was already in session. I sneaked in, searching for a familiar face in a sea of marital despair. The atmosphere was so poisonous I hesitated to inhale.

Sitting on the bench in front of the courtroom, before the great seal of California, was a large woman, her pudgy mitt, encircled with gold bangles, serving as a hammock for her chins as she eyed a lawyer in a suit that should've been buried in the '80s. Adorna Fezel clicked her long, red nails, painted with the blood of children. The lawyer's client sat forward, shoulders hunched.

There are places you'd like to live and not visit and places you'd like to visit but not live. This was neither.

"Your Honor, my client is concerned about his *Star Wars* collectibles. His ex-wife hasn't handed over Princess Leia, despite a court order."

The judge replied, then her heavily lined sapphire eyes flicked my way as I tiptoed toward a row of gold watches and pinkie rings.

"Can I sit with you guys?" I asked Ulger. His young, yet-to-be-disfigured henchmen shook their heads and growled.

"Sit with your attorney," Ulger said, scowling.

"Anne isn't here yet."

"Agnes," Ulger said.

"Ulger," I said, mimicking his baritone. "Okay, okay, I'll be back there if you need me. Nice jacket, by the way. Did you wear that for me?"

Who needs drugs when you have nerves? I squeezed into a seat where I could watch Ulger whisper sweet, expensive nothings to his underlings. He glanced back at me. I winked. Anne, just in time to stand in front of my humiliation train, slid in next to me.

"I'm so sorry," she said. "I was just down the hall, another case."

"Business is booming," I said.

"It's certainly not the dry season," she said. "I have good news for you."

"Good news?" It felt like I hadn't heard that phrase in so long. I repeated it to see how it felt, rolling around my tongue like a caramel. "Good news?"

"The *Penthouse* therapist gave us a favorable report," she said. "The judge can't ignore that. I think you'll be very pleased."

Trevor must've rejected her advances. I almost burst into tears. I grabbed her hand.

"I wasn't worried, but I was worried," she said. "So now, the primary focus will be on finances."

"Great! I don't have any," I said. "This should be a breeze."

I barely had time to compose myself when the bailiff turned from the judge's bench and yelled, *"Anonymous v. Anonymous!"* as though we were in Yankee Stadium, not a claustrophobic courtroom filled with people barely keeping their heads above water. A few folks started shuffling out. "You might want to stay for this," I said as I weaved toward the front of the courtroom to take my seat of shame.

The bailiff eyed Trevor's team as five attorneys, two carrying a large poster board, clambered up to the plaintiff's table in front of the judge. It seemed a strange place to bring artwork.

"How many of them are there?" the bailiff asked. "It's like a circus."

"Complete with clown car," I said and settled in.

I remember what happened in that courtroom like a movie sequence, like something that didn't happen to me but perhaps to Sandra Bullock. Like so:

INT. COURTROOM—MIDMORNING

The air is stifling. Outside, the day promises to be a hot one. The courtroom is filled with people—men in suits, men holding their caps in their hands, shuffling their feet in their seats. Women in black and gray, clutching tissues, their lawyers speaking softly in their ears. The presiding judge is a big lady, a massive judicial structure, her dishwater hair with one curl adorning her forehead like an upside down question mark. Her nails are inches long and painted red. She spends a lot of money, time, and effort on her hair and nails. Our heroine, Agnes, sits next to her lawyer, Anne, in front of the judge. Agnes is wearing a light pink dress with a small bow at the collar, a suit jacket, and modest heels. She looks professional and in charge and the type of person who's not afraid to wear pastels to court. She has a, dare we say, Jennifer Garner / Sandra Bullock mom-next-door quality. She looks quite young for her age (and like a really nice, decent person). Anne, her lawyer, is what you want to grow up to be; she's attractive and commanding and looks like someone who should be on a dollar bill.

On the other side, Trevor sits with Ulger Blecks and a slew of other, smaller-in-stature attorneys. A Russian nesting doll of diminishing attorneys. Or an Attorneys "R" Us store, all sharing the same solemn, dour expressions, even though a couple are so young Agnes could've given birth to them. There are poster boards involved.

The judge clears her throat. The bracelets jingle and jangle. Agnes leans over to Anne.

AGNES: This is the person who's going to be deciding the fate of my child.
ANNE: No. You decide her fate. She settles living arrangements.

Agnes leans back in her chair.

AGNES: Duly noted, counselor.
BAILIFF: *Anonymous v. Anonymous.* Honorable Judge Fezel presiding.

Agnes, Anne, Ulger, and his attorneys all stand, making a lot of noise.

Agnes turns and looks at the courtroom. All eyes are on them. No one's left the room.

She turns back.

BAILIFF: *Anonymous v. Anonymous,* case number 46E.

The bailiff hands the judge a file.

JUDGE FEZEL (shuffling papers, looking down): We'll start with distribution of property. Who'd like to go first?

ANNE: Ulger?

Ulger smiles.

ULGER: I'd love to.

Ulger stands and moves to the front of the table. His minions stand beside him, with their visual aids, which have not been unveiled yet. It's all very dramatic.

ULGER, CONT: Judge Fezel, I'm sure you're aware that the economy has shifted, and even clients like mine have experienced a change in their lifestyles. No longer can Mr. Anonymous fly private, for example, to New York, for a meeting with, say, Denzel Washington, or even to a premiere of his newest movie. The Paramount jet is no more, sold to the Russians. The Sony jet is no more; the Universal jet a memory. Producers are paying for their own tickets and sometimes hotel rooms. Per diems have dwindled. Movies have to come in, Judge Fezel, under budget and on time. The Chinese, who now own half the studios, brutally slash film budgets and studio deals and free coffee. Let me show you some statistics.

JUDGE FEZEL: Please.

ULGER (to his team): Unveil the poster boards.

Ulger's minions drop the black covers from the boards, and Agnes can feel everyone in the rows behind her leaning forward in their seats. At least they're getting a show, if not a Princess Leia action figure. Graphs and columns and numbers saturate the boards.

AGNES (to Anne): I got a C, okay C-, in macroeconomics—what does this mean?

JUDGE FEZEL: Mr. Blecks, I'm anticipating that you'll explain, in a timely manner.

ULGER: Of course, Your Honor. Here (pointing to the first board), you'll see the effect that streaming has had on movies and television, my client's bread and butter.

And here, you'll see the concomitant effect on Mr. Anonymous's income.

(The judge squints above her glasses.)

JUDGE FEZEL: Is that . . . how many zeros is that?

ULGER: It's gone from seven to six.

JUDGE FEZEL: Seven zeros.

ULGER: To six, your honor.

JUDGE FEZEL: Please proceed.

Allow me, First-Person Agnes, to step in here to paraphrase the rest of Ulger Blecks's opening statement. Ulger painted a bleak picture of Mr. Anonymous living just above the poverty line—the poverty line providing enough for five lawyers, a kid in private school, and a penthouse at Testosterone Towers. The judge watched him paint a squalid picture, his voice building, then diminishing as he waxed eloquently about the trials and tribulations of a producer finding himself at the mercy of a revolving door of studio heads and the goddamned economy.

Magic show! The master of ceremonies gestured with his cane, and another poster board was unveiled by a magician's assistant / junior lawyer.

Voilà! A graph of Trevor's past to future projected earnings. It had a sort of modern art feel—lines, squiggles, numbers, letters—that I thought would go well in my future dining room, if I were lucky enough to have one.

Forget HBO, Hulu, Netflix, and Chill. I turned and looked around the courtroom. Every sad, anxious, angry pair of eyes was glued to the bull in a suit banging his cane. I didn't blame them. Mr. Anonymous's life was fascinating to me, and I'd lived it as a guest. More like an accessory. A human being that went with everything. You could pair me with a premiere, a dinner party, a trip on a billionaire's yacht. I went with everything until I had too many opinions and a baby, and then I went with nothing.

Anne rose to speak after Ulger collapsed next to his troops, spent; the poster boards were retired. I wanted to ask him if I could keep it as a souvenir.

Anne rebutted Ulger's claims point by point (*"current savings"*) as I tuned out (*"projected income"*) and stared at my feet. I'd wasted years writing books when I could've been working on a series, going to med school even though I hated blood and chemistry—okay, law school, a trade, a skill, anything else. I'd made just enough money to buy my dad a house and pay my sister's legal bills. That had been sufficient. Had been. Was. *That was then, this is now.* But I hadn't put anything away. I was no different from any other observer in the courtroom, except no one would feel sorry for me. I didn't blame them. I didn't feel sorry for me. I felt ashamed.

I forced myself to watch the judge as she responded to Anne. Nails clicking. Pink lips pursed. Bangles caught in the folds of her wrists.

"Have the parties worked out custody arrangements?" the judge asked as Anne sat down, having performed sans banging and raging and poster boards.

"We are close, Your Honor," Anne said.

"Close," the judge said. "Sounds ominous."

"There's been discussion over primary versus joint custody."

"In 99 percent of the cases in my courtroom," the judge said, "I rule for joint."

"May I approach the bench?" Anne said. "I have a report from the therapist who worked with Mr. and Mrs. Anonymous during parenting classes."

"Please."

Anne stepped forward, handed the judge the file, then returned to her seat. We waited while the judge read over the report. I leaned back in my chair to catch Trevor's eye, as if to say, *What are we doing?*

I crossed my fingers and willed my knees to stop shaking.

"Ms. Anonymous," the judge said, looking up from her bench, "what are your plans for future living arrangements?"

I was caught off guard. I looked at Anne.

"I'm not asking your lawyer; I'm asking you," she said.

I stood up. "I haven't exactly, um . . . I was planning to live in our home with our daughter until . . . my husband, until Trevor—"

"Mr. Anonymous," Ulger said.

"Until Mr. Anonymous sold it."

"Your Honor, may I speak?" Ulger wanted to talk. This wasn't good.

"You may."

"Mr. Anonymous has an offer on the property," he said.

"Is he accepting it?"

"He'll very likely accept it," Ulger said. "It's a short escrow. Thirty days."

I closed my eyes. Trevor had done it. He'd sold our house. I flashed on Pep's room, the colorful tiles in her bathroom. Her view of the hillside.

"Ms. Anonymous," the judge said. "Did you know this would happen?"

"No, I mean, I didn't think it would happen so quickly."

"But you knew the house was for sale."

"Yes."

"And you haven't made other arrangements for you and your daughter."

"Not yet. I mean, I've been looking, but I wasn't sure what my budget would be."

"Where could you move in the next three weeks?"

"That depends," I said. "On what I can pay."

"You don't have any savings?"

"I did," I said. "I had saved up a lot. Then my sister kept getting arrested."

Anne kicked my ankle.

"And I bought a house for my dad. I mean, he didn't ask, but the drive was terrible."

Anne kicked my ankle again.

The judge tilted her head at me, breathing heavily. I was tiring her out. My nonsensical babbling was her cardio that morning.

"Where is your father's house?"

I blanked for a moment. "Venice, by the beach, it's adorable. One of those old beach bungalows from the 1920s. I fixed it up; it looks great."

"Ms. Anonymous. How big is your father's house?"

Anne cut in. "Your Honor, may I ask why you're posing these questions? Whatever size her father's home is, it cannot compare to the house Mrs. Anonymous resides in currently."

The judge gazed at her, eyebrow arched, like an animated villain.

And what happens in every animated Disney movie?

The mom dies.

"Counsel, I'm trying to determine if your client has arranged for adequate living space for her daughter."

"Your Honor, I appreciate that; however, I must object."

"On what basis?"

"I could move in with my dad," I said. "No problem. At least temporarily. Pep loves it there."

"How big is his place?"

"It's a one . . . and a half . . . bedrooms . . . ish."

"So your daughter will sleep on the floor."

"The couch is fine," I said. "It's a foldout. Plenty of room."

"Counsel," she said. "I've reached my decision. The court gives temporary custody of minor child to Mr. Anonymous, subject to a hearing in three weeks when I can learn what Ms. Anonymous's new and adequate living arrangements will be."

I felt my knees buckle.

"Anne?" I turned. "Anne?"

For the first time, Anne looked stunned. I turned back to the judge.

"Wait. No. You can't do that," I said. "You don't understand. She's never been away from me. Except for that one time in rehab."

"Excuse me?"

Why? Why do I have a problem keeping my truth vomit mouth shut?

"Long story," I said.

"Your Honor," Anne said as she gripped my arm. "If I could have a word with my client."

I wasn't done. "Your Honor, please. I'm begging you. I know it doesn't seem like a long time, but Pep's never been away from me. Except overnight for faux rehab. Please."

"I've made my decision. I'll see you back here in three weeks. I'm sure you will have figured out a proper living arrangement."

"No, no. I can't. I can't."

Anne had her hands on my waist. I pushed her away.

"Next case!" The judge lowered her gavel.

"No," I said. "No, this isn't right. I object!"

"Excuse me, Mrs. Anonymous," the judge said.

"Agnes, not now, please," Anne said. "I know it seems unfair, but you can do this."

I stood and pointed at the judge. "You're unfair!" I yelled. "This isn't right!"

"Damn straight," someone piped up from the back. Fin.

"You are out of order!" I yelled. "This isn't right—none of this is right!"

"Hell yeah! Fight the power!" Fin said, her fist in the air. "Get the man!"

The judge banged the gavel until a barrette loosened from her hair and hopped off the bench. The bailiff jumped over the plaintiff's table, chasing me down as I leaped to the other side.

"You're out of order!" I yelled as the bailiff caught me and pulled my hands behind my back. "This is a sham! Your courtroom's a sham! I pay taxes for this!" People rose in spurts, clapping and cheering. Fin was still yelling. The judge was banging her gavel, her hair in her plump red face. And Anne, poor Anne, shaking her head, her hands on the table, holding her up.

The last visual I caught as I was hauled away was Ulger shaking Trevor's hand and patting him on the back, and Trevor's eyes wide as disks, as though a flashlight were shining straight at his face.

22

The Writer Gets a Sentence

I hated being overdressed for the occasion, this occasion being Downtown LA Women's Correctional Facility anteroom. I should've worn flats. "You're going to break a toe," a voice said as I kicked at the door of the tiny, puke-beige room; the door served as a trompe l'oeil of the courtroom, Ulger's bloated face, Trevor's hair, and the judge, her bear paws and those blood-soaked nails.

I kicked and screamed and kicked.

"They can't hear you out there," the man said, "but I'm in here getting a headache."

I turned. The bailiff was hunched in the corner, his mountainous form bogarting the room, chin docked in his baseball mitt hands.

"Sorry," I said. "I need to throw up."

"Sure." He kicked a wastebasket toward me. I bent over and expelled Gabriela's breakfast and the last of my pride.

"Can I . . . I need to wipe my mouth." My hands were cuffed behind me. I couldn't remember when they'd slipped on the cuffs. A wave of embarrassment and nausea gripped my stomach. I threw up again.

"Sure thing," he said. He took a Kleenex out of his pocket. "It's unused. I have allergies."

"Can you undo me?"

"You're not a danger to yourself and others, correct?" he asked. I nodded, and he reached over to unlock the cuffs.

"You're no longer a danger to that door?" he asked, flashing a dimple. I could see why he never smiled in court; that dimple destroyed his credibility. On the other hand, that dimple could easily disarm any criminal.

Like myself.

"I'm a danger to common sense," I said, wiping my mouth with the Kleenex, stained red with the lipstick I'd tried this morning. Maybe I could swallow this soiled ball of snot, vomit, and lipstick and suffocate myself.

"I've seen a lot of people lose it in there," he said. "Emotions run high in that courtroom. It's what I call 'emotionally charged,' that room. Me, personally, I'm never getting divorced."

"I don't know what I'm going to do," I said. "I don't know what to do."

"Easy. You're going to cooperate with the judge," he said. "You're going to find yourself a place. A nice place for you and your daughter."

"I don't know if I can find a nice place."

"Of course you can," he said.

"How can you be sure?" I asked.

"You're white," he said. "You're wearing expensive shoes that you can afford to ruin on that door. You're way ahead of the game."

"I see your point," I said as I slunk to the floor. "That judge. She's horrible."

"She's tough but fair," he said. "You know how I know? Everyone hates her."

I shook my head, swallowing bile.

"Mr. Anonymous loves her, I'm sure. I'm sure he wants to buy her lunch, produce her life story," I said. "How did I ever marry that motherfucker? How? All he cares about is winning. He doesn't give a shit about our child. He doesn't want to raise her. He can't. He has to be raised himself!"

The bailiff leaned back, his eyebrow cocked. His shoes reflected the fluorescent lights hanging from the ceiling.

"You chose him, my dear," he said, weary. I got the feeling he'd had this conversation many times.

"I sure did," I said. "My fucking mistake. For which I'll be paying the rest of my life."

"I know one thing, for sure," he said, leaning forward, his hands on his knees. He looked me in the eye. "Heroes don't marry zeros."

Holy ouch, Batman.

"That hurt," I said. "Hey, maybe we should meet weekly."

A long time passed until the door cracked opened. Anne, her shoulders slumped forward, appeared in the doorway; I finally saw her age, which made me feel guilty, of course. The weariness etched on her face was my handiwork.

"Well, that was interesting," she said. "I got the sentence down."

The expanse of time between Anne's statement and my next question lasted hours. Days. A year.

"What sentence?" Blood rushed in my ear.

"You're sentenced to two days downtown," Anne said as she sat beside me and placed her briefcase at her feet.

"I don't . . . I don't understand."

"Contempt of court," she said.

"It could've been weeks," the bailiff said. "Seen it. Told you she was fair."

My eyes bounced from the bailiff back to Anne. They shared the expression of someone who'd warned the dog not to pee on the living room rug.

"Your bail is set at fifty grand," she said. "Can you post bail?"

"What? That's more than Fin's bail," I said. "And she's an actual felon, according to the California penal code. I'm the good sister! I've never broken a law in my life! I didn't even ditch school!"

"She's been like this the whole time," the bailiff said to Anne.

"Do you have the money?" Anne asked, again.

I thought about the sheets and towels money. Thank you, Pratesi. Half of it was already gone to the Triplets, Pep's school, a bit thrown Anne's way.

"Do you know anyone who could help?" Anne had already heard my answer in my expression.

"Trevor, ha ha ha," I said. "My friend Liz. But I don't want to ask."

Anne pushed a lock of blond-gray hair from her eyes.

"I'm a good mother. I'm not good at a lot of things," I said. "Like games that involve balls . . . and Sudoku. And breaking down doors."

Beat. They waited.

"But I am good at being Pep's mommy. I don't deserve this."

Anne sat down next to me and put her arm around my shoulder. She smelled like vanilla and fresh schnauzer. I wanted to ask if I could move in with her.

"I stayed with my husband for twenty-five years," she said. "I waited until the last boy was out of the house. I drove that boy to college, drove back, packed my bags, and left. All so I could avoid exactly what you're going through."

"I'm not sure that's the helpful parable you want it to be."

"It was a choice."

"Was it worth it?"

"No," she said. "The boys had their mother full-time. But that mom was unhappy. Numb. Closed off. 'Emotionally unavailable' is what my middle child calls it now. I was there, but I wasn't there. I was a ghost mom."

I sniffed and nodded and found myself crying. The bailiff handed me another tissue.

"I sacrificed my happiness for theirs, that's what I told myself. But truthfully, I wasn't there for them. They never saw their mom fully happy."

"Robot mom," I said. "Robo-Mom." I moved my hands around like a robot. "Billy, would you like scrambled eggs?" I asked in robot voice.

"You can be divorced and be the best role model for your kid. Once you get over the guilt and sadness."

"Please tell me you're happy now," I said. "I'm not going to be able to make it through the day unless I think there's something to look forward to."

"I am. I'm really happy now," she said. "Believe it or not, someday, you will be, too. Especially if you adopt a schnauzer."

"English bulldog," the bailiff said.

"I don't want a dog; I want my daughter," I said, rubbing my eyes. "I don't think I'll make it through the weekend."

"You're going to make it. You have to. She's counting on you."

"Don't let Pep down," the bailiff urged. "She needs you."

"We're coming back," Anne said. "This isn't over. The judge said this is temporary. It's a temporary edict. We'll come back, and we'll fight."

I shook my head.

"No, I don't want to fight anymore," I said, staring at my hands, my chipped nails, my empty ring finger. "I'm done."

"Hey," the bailiff said, snapping his fingers. "I know where I've seen you before."

We looked at him.

"That pee-pee video," he said. "Oh, boy, I'm glad you didn't do that in here. Hey, would you sign a book for me? I mean, when you get out?"

"You . . . bought my book?"

"Everybody's buying that damned book," he said.

.   .   .

Fin was right. Jail wasn't so bad. I'd endured more discomfort at catered events. Hijacked in a large venue, watching a cross-eyed late-night talk show host kiss the ass of a guy who fired half the studio before lunch—that was suffering. Jail was like high school with orange uniforms. My cell was cold, my bed was hard. My towel was scratchy, the pillow flat. The sheet wasn't exactly Pratesi.

I felt like I could write here.

I slept like a baby.

The next morning, the warden tapped on the cell bars.

Fin was outside the holding area, wrestling the grin on her face.

"I can't believe it! I had to bail *you* out!" Fin said.

"How did you do it?" I asked, "You don't have any money."

"Anyone can get money," she said. "It's not that hard."

"Translation: I don't want to know," I said.

"No, you don't," she said and punched me in the arm.

Fin ripped down the 10, then up the 405 on the way to the dead zone, which would be gone in less than thirty days. I had to pack.

"Have you heard anything from Pep? What happened yesterday? Is she okay? Who picked her up? Did Trevor come back to the house?"

"Hold up," Fin said, rapping her rings on the steering wheel. "First of all, Pep is fine. I talked to her. I laid it all out. I told her you lost your mind in court but only because you love her so much. I told her to call me anytime, day or night. I'm on call, Auntie at your service, 24-7. I said to view this time like it's a vacation with Daddy. She might turn out to be a Daddy's girl, like us."

"Do not *ever* say that again," I said. "Did Trevor pick her up, or did he have assistant number one, two, or three do the honors?"

"Actually. Trevor," she said. "I made it known that if anything happened to Pep, I'd be up his ass with a hammer."

"That should play well at my next court date."

Fin exited off Sunset.

"Just so you know, Trevor called me fifteen times last night. Pep sneezed and he thought he'd catch a cold, and his movie's falling apart."

"Poor Trevor," I said. "Poor him."

"Yeah, he didn't sound too stable," she said. "I told him not to worry about Pep; it's probably just salamander flu. He'll only have to be quarantined for a week."

"What's the salamander flu?"

"There is no salamander flu."

Houses went by, a blur of white clapboards and ivy. "Waverly told me things were going to get worse for me. How did she know?"

"It's obvious," Fin said. "You're divorcing a powerful guy. They hate that, even if it's their idea. Come on!"

I looked at her. "She said George Treadwell was the key to this divorce. That somehow, he'd make things right."

"The actor dude?"

"Yes. George Treadwell. The actor dude."

"Come on."

"Yeah, I know," I said. "Crazy."

"Should we ask him?"

"Yeah," I said, "let's call him right now."

"'kay." Fin scrolled numbers on the console.

"What . . . what are you doing?"

"Calling George—you want me to call him," she said. "He gave me his number. Y'know, I've been thinking about it, discussed it with Sami. We think he'd be pretty good as the lead, the magic man."

I went mute; I felt my mouth drop open.

"Of course, I'd have to see tape," Fin said.

She'd scrolled down to: *George Actor.*

"Stop!" I jabbed the console, ending the call.

. . .

This whole thing was ludicrous, but it made sense if you knew Fin. Men were drawn to her like flies, this mermaid to Hugo Boss pirates with a bad-girl fetish.

I called Trevor because I couldn't get through on Pep's phone. He grunted, more distracted than usual, and handed the phone over to Pep, who seemed fine and not at all down with salamander flu. Which minced the remainder of my heart.

My phone buzzed.

"I'm home," Gio said. "I just landed. Can I come see you?"

"Now's not a good time," I said.

"What're you doing?"

Well. I was sprawled on the floor of Pep's bedroom, a pile of her clothes on my lap. I'd told myself I was "sorting," but what I was really doing was crying into her old onesies.

"It's important that I not tell you," I said.

"Why?"

"I'll just start crying again," I said as I started to cry. And here, I was so sure I'd met my tear ration.

"Hey, hey," he said. "I'll be right over. Is it so sad?"

"I'm that saddest thing of all," I said. "A childless mother."

"Oh no. I'm functioning on three hours' sleep, but nothing would make me happier than to put a smile on your face," he said.

"You'd have to draw it on," I said, "with permanent marker."

"I'll bring a Comté and a good Bordeaux," he said.

"Okay," I said, sniffing, then hung up.

"Fin!" I yelled.

Fin appeared in the doorway. "You okay?"

"Yes. No," I said. "Fin, I'm about to have grief sex, and I haven't even grief-waxed."

"Get it!" she said, high-fiving me.

.   .   .

Gio arrived, as promised, bearing gifts of a twelve-year-old Comté and an Alsatian goat cheese and several bottles of a velvety Bordeaux. He brought crackers and fig jam and those teeny, tiny gherkins that are so cute you don't want to eat them (but you do), and he set everything up, humming Italian opera as he moved along. All of this was done without a cape.

Fin and I watched, sipping from our wineglasses. She leaned over to me. "He has kind eyes."

"You said that about Trevor."

"I never said that about Trevor," she said.

"You absolutely did," I said as Gio belted out an aria.

"No," she said. "You don't listen to me. I said Trevor had vulnerable eyes. That's different. That's dangerous."

"Thanks for the years-after-the-fact heads-up," I said.

"Kinda think you should've known who you were marrying. But that's just me."

I glared at her over my wineglass.

Gio finished the aria and brought the cheese plate over, setting it between me and my sister. I watched as he ate *con gusto*. I wondered if he fucked *con gusto*.

I drank down the rest of my wine.

Fin went to bed after a phone call from her parole officer asking her what happened to her ankle monitor. She'd told her she'd clipped it and gave her the complicated but truthful reason that her sister lost her mind in divorce court, and after some swearing, the parole officer said okay, come in tomorrow. And then Fin said something that made her laugh, and the parole officer said come in when you can and have a good night.

Gio had listened and clapped at the end.

"I wish you were my agent," he told her. "You'd negotiate rings around these idiots."

"Who's your agent?" Fin asked.

"Fin," I said. "C'mon."

"I need one for Sami," she said.

"Who's Sami?"

"My writer," Fin said. She was already talking like a Hollywood producer; writers were considered property.

"The Uber driver," I said. "Fin, you have to be realistic about the way Hollywood works."

Fin looked at me. "Why?"

"Yeah, why?" Gio asked as well, then turned to Fin. "Are you developing a script?"

"Is that what it's called? Developing? Why do they have to make everything sound so important and complicated? It ain't science," Fin said. "I just want to edge it up before I show it to George."

"Fin, come on," I said.

"George who?" Gio asked.

"That guy who was here, funny accent, he looks like this," Fin said and grinned like a maniac.

"Treadwell?" Gio asked. "I did a movie with him."

"Is he any good?" Fin asked.

"I like him," Gio said. "For a star, he's not a total waste of oxygen."

"I want your notes before I give it to George," Fin said. "If we get George, we get China. If we get China, we shoot in Mexico in two months."

My head was spinning. "Impossible! George Treadwell is doing the movie with Trevor, Fin," I said.

"George told me it didn't work out," Fin said. "Creative differences with the director."

"Neither of them was creative," Gio said.

"You made a deal with George Treadwell," I said.

"Sounds like she did," Gio said.

"He likes the idea," Fin said. "He wants to read the script. He's got an opening in his schedule. I told him, 'Don't get your hopes up, dude; I have to see tape.'"

"George Treadwell agreed to do tape?" Gio asked.

"Yeah," Fin said.

"You're a witch," he said.

"Nah, dude," Fin said. "I'm a producer."

"I'll give it a read," Gio said. "Why not?"

"Tonight?"

"I'll be busy tonight," Gio said, eyeing me.

"Priorities," Fin said.

Gio laughed, and his laugh filled the kitchen and made me think of all the laughter that hadn't existed there before.

I walked Fin out to the guesthouse, holding her hand. She hated walking alone in the dark, even when she was little.

"He's like Santa," Fin said.

"I don't want to fuck Santa."

"I always had a crush on Santa," Fin said. "Who better to take care of you? You don't even have to cook, and he brings you presents. Like cheese and wine."

I kissed her cheek, and as I walked back to the main house, I wondered if Gio would be okay that I hadn't shaved my pussy in a year.

I bet he would.

23

Decent Proposal

Gio was splayed out on one of the deck chairs, staring at the sky. He brought out a pack of Marlboro Lights, lit one, and handed it to me.

"I don't smoke."

"They used to think smoking was good for you," Gio said. "Smoking makes you breathe deeply. Calms you. Helps you think."

"Think of it as nicotine meditation," I said.

I hadn't taken a puff on a cigarette since I was eight years old, in the garage with Fin, who'd stolen one of my mother's. I coughed and threw up and got us both grounded.

I took the cigarette and sat on the edge of the chaise, and Gio pulled me in next to him. We snuggled and smoked and looked out at the night sky. A coyote howled, and a Ferrari driver in the canyon below gunned his engine.

"How many women have you fucked?" I asked.

He jolted and looked at me. "Which decade?"

"Start with the '80s."

"Why not start with the '70s?" he said. "I've never really counted."

"If it goes into triple digits, I'm outta here."

"It's just a number, like age." He laughed.

We took a hit off our cigarettes. I felt incredibly sophisticated and drunk and out of my realm.

"That's why I became a director. Pussy. I should've been a doctor like my father. Not some piece-of-shit director."

"You're not a piece-of-shit director. You're an icon."

"Have you seen my last couple of movies?" he asked. "There are scenes I love, perfect moments; they emerged straight from my big head," he said, tapping his big head. "I'm a cog in the system now. I have to listen to notes. Notes from the d-girls, notes from the studio, notes from whoever owns the studio, the Germans, the Chinese, the Japanese, the French. And they're all scared of their own shadows. There's no joy left."

"We were talking about all your hoochies," I said.

"Right," he said.

"How many did you propose to?"

"Every single one," he said and kissed me.

Fin wasn't awake when Gio and I wandered into the kitchen for coffee in the morning. We were all alone. No housekeepers, no gardeners, no orchid replacement assistants.

I made coffee, and Gio took a seat at the kitchen table and opened *The New York Times*. Everything felt calm. Normal. The flickering of a happy new routine, full of promise. I'd write all day, cook dinner, put Pep to bed; Gio and I would have a drink on the deck in his backyard and stare out at the stars and trace patterns on the leaves in the pool. Then we'd fuck until we slept.

"How do you like it?"

"Black," he said. "Like my soul."

We'd broken the antique Indian headboard above the bed. I'd always dated men who had athletic bodies, skinny bodies, bodies with no excess. I figured that was my type. I figured wrong. Sleeping with Gio was like diving into a warm pool. If that pool were a cunnilingus master.

"They'll find another headboard," he said. "Marry me."

"You've been married."

"Only four times," he said. "Fifth time's the charm."

"Fifth's the time when you know it's you and not marriage."

"I take umbrage to that remark."

"Please don't take my umbrage," I said. "You've already taken a piece of my heart."

"Only a piece?"

"A sliver," I said. "Small enough that I can still function once you leave."

"I'm never leaving. I'm never leaving your side. I'm the opposite of 'You're rubber and I'm glue.'"

"Gio, you left your third wife by sticking a Post-it note on the refrigerator."

"That's unfair. You've never met her. I'm lucky I left with my balls intact. By the way, I have a great relationship with all my ex-wives, even Post-it."

I sat next to him and rubbed his warm head for good luck. Fin was right. He had kind eyes. If eyes were the window to the soul, his soul was a clear blue love bucket.

"You're bad at marrying," I said.

"No, not true, I'm very, very good at marrying," he said. "I'm bad at marriage. But I can change. I want to change."

"One broken headboard does not a relationship make," I said.

"You have to admit, Agnes," he said, squeezing my knee, which sent a lightning bolt up my pussy, and I wanted him between my legs again. Did I want to be on top? Bottom? Sideways? Reverse cowgirl? "It's not a terrible place to start," he said, smiling.

. . .

We were back in our broken bed, breathless and spent. My head rested on Gio's chest, my legs wrapped around his body. I loved his smell, and I'd forgotten how important a lover's scent can be. A man can smell like coconuts and vanilla and cinnamon, and if you don't like any of those smells, you can't live with that man, no matter how kind he is or how smart he is or how much he makes you laugh.

Gio smelled like home. If you lived in a pine forest with a babbling brook in the backyard and wild violets springing up in the grassy yard. So that kind of home.

I breathed in his scent and ran my fingers through his chest hair, untouched and unbothered by the manscaping craze. The world of men as hairless Chihuahuas had passed him by. Gio was a human time warp.

"Come with me to Giorgio's tonight. I'm meeting with an actor, some kid from a vampire show. Kid thinks he's a movie star, everyone's telling me he's a movie star. They're fucking crazy."

"Sure," I said.

"His agent will be there," Gio said. "The kid wants to work with me. I don't know."

"Sure, I'll go," I said, feeling a wave of dizziness, hearing a familiar echo.

"Wear that dress you wore when I first met you," Gio said, "the one with the fringe. So sexy."

A stone dropped in the pond of my stomach, circular ripples of dread growing inside me. Shit. I blinked. "I'm sorry."

"Oh, that's okay," he said. "You look great in anything. I just really like that dress."

"No," I said. "I'm sorry. I can't go."

"Oh?" he asked, looking at me with those clear blue eyes. "Do you have other plans?"

I shook my head, trying to keep my tears inside.

"What's wrong?"

"I can't," I said.

"What do you mean? It's okay; we'll go another time."

"Gio, I don't care about a kid who thinks he's a movie star. I don't care about having dinner with his agent," I said. "Maybe I will again someday. Maybe I'll regret all of this. But I find it impossible to care less at this moment."

"I'm the same as you," he says. "I don't give a shit."

But he did.

"No," I said. "You do. You should and you do. And you deserve someone who cares, as well. Who can be by your side at dinners, at meetings, on the set. Who can give you total attention and support. That ain't me. I can't do it. I just can't."

Gio shook his head and folded up the paper. I'd never look at *The New York Times* again without thinking of his sad face. He stared at his hands.

"So that's it?" he asked, finally looking up at me.

"I know I'll always love you," I said.

"Thank you?"

"You helped me when I needed it most," I said.

"My tongue helped you, you mean," he said.

"Right. Can you leave your tongue?"

Gio touched his tongue. "Just the tip."

"And three fingers," I said. "I'll keep three fingers. You don't need all your fingers to direct."

"Now, you're just being greedy," he said.

I leaned forward and put my forehead on his.

"I'm sad," he said.

"Me, too," I said. "I'm sad and happy and clear and mixed up."

"Agnes. Are you sure you want me to go?"

"No," I said. "I'm not sure. I'm really afraid, to be honest. But I need to be on my own. That's the only thing I know for sure."

A big, fat tear rolled down his cheek. I caught it with my lips.

"Now, who'm I going to marry?" he asked. "I had the tux ready and the flowers all picked out and the ring and everything."

"You didn't have the ring."

"I actually do have a ring, but it's used," he said. "Wife number four threw it at my head." He looked at me with big, sad eyes. "Are we still going to be friends?"

"Always and forever," I said.

"What about sex?"

"Check in with me in a few months," I said, then paused. "One month."

He laughed, filling the house again with his happy noise. I already missed him.

Fin shuffled into the kitchen. I didn't want to look her in the eye.

"You got rid of him, didn't you?" she said.

"Yep."

"Idiot."

"Maybe."

"I liked him," Fin said. "I really liked him. And I don't like anybody."

"Me, too," I said, and then before I knew what was happening, I started sobbing into my sister's shoulder.

"It's going to be okay," Fin said, holding on to me. "We'll get through this. We're survivors."

"I don't know, Fin," I said. "Maybe I just didn't want him to stick around to watch me sink."

"No, no," Fin said. "Remember what Mom sang to us before she took off and we never saw her again?"

"'Itsy Bitsy Spider'?"

"After that."

"I don't remember."

Fin smiled and sang, *"I'm goan' to learn to read and write, I'm goan' to see what there is to see . . ."*

"Unsinkable Molly Brown," I said. "Mom turned out to be the Sinkable Molly Brown, but that's not so catchy."

"They can't kill us, Aggie," Fin said. "They can try, but they can't kill us. Hey, you're going to see Gio before you know it."

"How do you know?"

"I left the script in his car," she said. "And yes, before you ask, his car was locked. It's fine." She checked her watch. "Oh, we're supposed to meet Dad at his house."

"Why?"

"I don't know. It sounded mysterious."

"Oh God, he's got cancer, right? He's dying," I said. "He's dying, I know it."

"What is wrong with you?" Fin asked. "Not everything is a tragedy."

Beat.

"But yeah, that's what I assumed," Fin said.

"That would be just like Dad to steal my divorce thunder," I said, grabbing my keys and walking out the door.

Dad was seated next to Shu on the couch in his living room; I was in his favorite chair, the one he sat in to watch the Bloomberg report. Fin was sitting cross-legged on the floor.

"Shu and I are getting married," he said.

I shook my head. *What?*

"That's fucking great!" Fin jumped up and embraced them both. Shu gazed up at Dad with adoring eyes.

"Since when . . . ?" I couldn't wrap my brain around my dad and Shu—

"We're in love," Dad said. "Shu's on a work visa; she needs a green card. And I need someone to take care of me. We're going to need a bigger place now, too."

"This is so fucking cool," Fin said.

"You girls don't need me anymore," he said. "Fin, I'm proud of you, kiddo. You're really turning your life around."

"Wait. Are you proud of me, too, Dad?" I asked.

"God," Fin said. "It's not always about you."

"Dad," I said. "Why do you need a bigger place?"

Shu grasped my dad's hand and beamed. *Ah, I recognized that glow.*

"Jesus Christ," I said. "I cannot."

"Hey, don't use the Lord's name in vain," Dad the lapsed Catholic said.

"I'm going to be an auntie again!" Fin said. "No, I'm going to be a big sister! Finally!"

"So," my dad said, "Shu and I talked. Do you want your house back, kiddo?"

"My house?" I asked.

"It *is* your house," Dad said. "I was just living here."

I blinked.

"Pep likes it here," he said. "She told me. It'll be good for her to come down off that hill."

"The judge won't approve. It's nothing like the dead zone. I couldn't even fit the orchid guy in here."

"Wait. I'll move my shit out of that extra room, and you can fit a bed in there; there's enough room for a second bedroom," Dad said. "And if it's not too late, I want to say thank you. I should've said it a long time ago. I'm, you know, sorry."

My head was spinning. I'd never heard my father apologize.

"Fin, you're not leaving empty-handed. Here. I'm giving you my Boston Red Sox cap."

"Dad, are you dying?" Fin asked.

"No," he said, "Shu hates the Red Sox. She's more of a Yankees fan."

"You must really love her," I said.

He tightened his hand around his bride-to-be's.

24

Irreconcilable Similarities

Word is Trevor's not well," Waverly said. I heard waves crashing in the background. A seagull cawing. Malibu, no doubt. "I've heard it from a studio chief, a director, and his agent. I can't tell you who they are, but I'm saving their latest Marvel movie—total catastrophe. I can't talk about it."

"What do you mean *not well*? Mr. and Mrs. Anonymous have a court date tomorrow." I'd forgotten to tell Waverly she was fired, but I hadn't sent her money in a while and we hadn't talked, so maybe she already knew I was cognitived out.

"Your ex is having a nervous breakdown," she said. "Call your attorney. The judge will never give him custody. Right now, Trevor can't even take care of himself."

"Trevor hasn't taken care of himself in twenty years," I said. "He doesn't need to."

I'd seen people have nervous breakdowns. When I say *people*, I mean my mom. See how healthy I'm becoming? I'm being truthful here. My mom had a nervous breakdown, and then she left. I remember weeks of her hands shaking when she lit a cigarette, her knees collapsing when she tried to wash dishes, sending them crashing to the floor. I remember tears. I remember her screams. I remember puddles of amber liquid ballooning from a tumbler. We were two little girls and one big man, and we were helpless. Whatever was fighting inside her head was winning.

Murphy Family, 0—Head Goblins, 1.

We never even had a chance to score.

I hung up on Waverly; I didn't want to hear any more.

I called Anne and told her we needed to have a meeting with Trevor and his team. We needed to do this outside the courtroom, outside the office. Someplace safe and warm.

I told her his lawyers would understand and cooperate.

"Hey." Fin barged into my bathroom. "How's Gio's health?"

"What? Why? Why would you be bringing that up now?" I clutched my heart.

"He just texted me. Said the script's not a total piece of shit," Fin said. "That's like high praise coming from him, right? I just want to make sure he can be bonded."

Trevor's team agreed to my suggestion for a meeting and filed a motion to delay the court date.

"I could tell they were eager, even though Ulger tried to cover. His usual bluster wasn't up to snuff," Anne said. "What's going on?"

"We need to talk about Trevor," I said.

"Isn't that a movie?"

"This is the sequel," I said. "Apparently, Trevor's having a bit of a breakdown. Pep's fine, she doesn't seem to notice from what I can tell, but he's just . . . not himself." After I spoke to Waverly, I had everyone's favorite Latina triplets do a little reconnaissance with the ladies working for Trevor in Malibu. AT&T had nothing on the El Salvadoran connection. Gabriela had called me at midnight to confirm—Trevor wasn't sleeping, Trevor was taking sleeping pills and still not sleeping; Trevor was drinking and taking sleeping pills and still not sleeping. Trevor was mumbling to himself, Trevor was rocking back and forth. He could pull himself together long enough to hide it from Pep, who was too young and technologically distracted to understand.

It was worse than I'd imagined.

"I see," Anne said. I didn't fill in all the blanks. She was smart enough and kind enough not to push for details. I would say she'd never make it as a divorce attorney, but she'd been at it for twenty years. Maybe it was her calling. Or her penance. Had she been Stalin in a former life? Not saying and not judging.

"So lifeguard station 21?"

"That's the one, outside the police station and the skateboard park, south of Muscle Beach, north of turban guy on roller skates," I said. "I'll set everything up. They just need to bring their client and sunscreen."

Ulger wouldn't stop squawking about getting sand in his Ferragamos.

"Stay on the blanket, Ulger," I said. I thought it'd been a great idea, meeting here on Venice Beach among the negative ions and soft breezes, the skateboarders and the young families, the German tourists and the local homeless. I'd fished a couple of my dad's old beach blankets out of the cupboard, hauled them down onto the sand, and laid them out. I dragged a cooler full of bottled water and Diet Cokes, because only the unhealthiest divorce lawyers love Diet Coke. I set out legal pads and pens and an assortment of bagels from the Strand, which we could share with the pigeons.

Trevor didn't show. Ulger informed us he had a work emergency that needed taking care of right away, but he was fine with his representation taking the meeting. Anne and I exchanged glances from behind our sunglasses.

"Everyone crisscross applesauce," I said as we all took our places on the blanket and set out to make a deal, serenaded by seagulls badgering us for our bagels.

An hour later, Ulger had slipped off his Ferragamos and his silk socks and rolled up his pants legs, and we couldn't get him out of the water to sign off on the final document for the longest time.

Anne and I watched as he looked for shells, digging in the sand with his cane. I didn't have the heart to tell him there weren't any shells left in Venice Beach. *Unless he's digging for used condoms.*

"Keep digging, Ulger!" I yelled, then took a deep breath of salt air with a hint of grime. *Eau de Venice Beach.*

A few minutes later, I walked Ulger back to his Merlot-colored Bentley.

"Why do you divorce for a living?" I asked as he packed his papers in the trunk, which was already filled with files. "You've already got this hideous car and a couple of houses you don't use. What more do you have to prove? We all know you're an asshole."

And then I punched him, sort of lightly.

On the edge.

He sniffed and looked down, then gazed back at me. "Agnes, I hate my job. I've hated it for thirty-six years. Do you like fly-fishing?"

I stopped to think. "I don't know. Do you have to touch the fly?"

"Miss Agnes," he said, gazing up at me. "I'd like to ask you out sometime."

I mentally fainted, then recovered.

"Now's not a good time, Ulger," I said. (Does never work for you?)

On a Saturday morning at 7:00, a moving truck pulled up in the alley behind my dad's place, and two big dudes rapped on my door and asked me if this was the right address and was I expecting a delivery.

I shook my head, but they insisted, so I followed the Oakland Raiders offensive line to the alley, where Fin, with slicked-back hair, was dancing around in a wet suit.

"Oh, hells yeah!" she said, her shit-eating grin stretched ear to ear.

"What's going on?" I asked. "It's seven in the morning, Fin."

"Wait, wait," Fin said. "Look at this."

The linebackers slid open the back, and the metal clanged against the top of the truck. Inside, blanketed like a baby, was our piano. In all the divorce excitement (excrement?), I'd forgotten about our neglected Steinway.

Sitting beneath the piano, wrapped snuggly, was my Tiffany clock.

I looked at my sister, clear-eyed, her hair stiff from salt water. Fin had taken up and mastered surfing in about a week. Of course she had.

"I paid them a visit," she said.

"You paid who a visit?"

"The weaselly guy and his wife," she said.

"Wait, the famous buyers?" I asked.

"I heard he was an actor; is that true?" she said. "He's all teeth. Anyway, we're good."

I had a bad feeling. A bad Fin feeling. A *Fin-tingling.* "Fin," I said. "What did you do? What did you say to them?"

Fin smiled and punched my arm.

"Fin," I said, rubbing my arm and staring at the piano like a giant pet I had no space for. "Where the hell are we going to put a piano?"

Fin is better with a hammer than I remembered.

"Dad taught me," she said. "Don't you remember? I used to help him around the house."

"I vaguely recall being jealous over a tool belt," I said. I'd brought her some water. She was busy tearing up the garage floor in the back of the house, on the alleyway. She'd found pipes in the wall; someone had lived in that little space years ago, and there'd been a bathroom, a doll-sized kitchen. Fin knew guys who knew guys who knew construction, and she supervised them. Lay down a wood floor, install a toilet, a sink. Wire the place and put up drywall.

When she gets tired, she plays the piano. Which is in the backyard. It's unusual, but somehow it feels right, and we cover the Steinway when she's not in use, but she's in use a lot more than in the dead zone. Fin says the piano's fine for now until we find it a permanent home. I have a feeling that means building her a shed in the backyard.

The neighbors like the music. They come over for margaritas and Led Zeppelin.

Did I tell you that Liz had navigated her Range Rover down Venice's mean streets and proclaimed that my dad's house had great bones and just needed a fresh coat of paint and a bit of interior work? Then she took it upon herself to decorate, tossing paint and carpet and drape samples on my desk in the semi-functional workspace I'd carved out. I paid for materials and labor, but she wouldn't take a dime herself, even though Lucas had finally sold my book to a network I'd never heard of until they optioned my work. There are actually several networks I'd never heard of now. Nothing makes you feel as old as not knowing the difference between PEP and CRNCH and VGOR and, well, you get the drift.

Hey, as long as they're buying, I'm selling.

Lucas called me the other day. "Guess what?"

"No," I said.

"Fair enough," he said. "Your book made the list."

Lately, some of his clients are peeing at their book signings. One made herself throw up halfway through her reading.

"No!" I said.

I'd never be a literary darling; I'd sold enough books to write another. More than most, less than some.

I'd made the list.

Number eight with a bullet.

"What a pisser," I said.

"Oh, about that, I got a call on a deal," Lucas said. "As a spokesperson."

"Me? Someone wants me as a spokesperson?" I was grinning, my cheeks heating up. *Me! What could it be? Skin cream? Hairspray? Shoes?*

"You," Lucas said. "Good news is, it's sixty grand for a year's work of doing next to nothing."

"The perfect job for me!"

"The bad news is . . . ," Lucas said. And paused.

Which is how I became a spokesperson for Pampers Adult Diapers. They're quite comfortable, and I haven't had an accident since.

What?

Like you wouldn't.

I'm a spokesperson, y'all. That's some adult shit. (So to speak.)

Oh, and FYI, if you're interested, there's quite a few schnauzer rescue organizations. I know, because that's where I found Edgar. He's a little older and a little not totally housebroken, and Pep and I are his biggest fans.

I got a call. I recognized but didn't recognize the area code, like a phantom arm; this was a phantom number.

I answered.

"You gotta get me out of here," my ex-husband said.

I flew to Tucson and rented a convertible Mustang because why not. I'd told Trevor I'd land at noon and would be at Madre de Tucson by 12:45 and I'd be waiting outside. As it turns out, a heat wave had gripped Arizona, and I'd been lucky to land. Most flights were grounded.

I rounded the driveway at the rehab entrance, and Trevor was already waiting outside with his little suitcase. He was shaved and his hair was clean and flopped forward in his eyes, and he looked like a little boy patiently waiting for Mom to pick him up from camp. He waved as I pulled in front, jumping up and down.

"Drive!" he yelled as he hopped over the passenger's side. "I have a movie to make! We just closed on George!"

"I heard he was out—"

"Oh, not for that piece of shit, no, different movie. I've got the next *Lawrence of Fucking Arabia*. Fuck you, Harvey!"

"Harvey's already fucked," I said. "Did you run into him?"

"Yeah, he tried to grab my dick," Trevor said. "Degenerate."

"I thought you weren't allowed any outside communication. How do you know you have a movie?"

"My coproducer got me the script. She knows a guy who works here. I guess they used to party together. He sold it to me for twenty bucks."

"Trevor," I said. "Who's your coproducer?"

"Fin, you know that, right?" he said. "It's fast-tracked; we're shooting in Mexico in four weeks! Lightning has struck!"

"Trevor, isn't Gio directing?"

"I love that dude!" Trevor looked at me, raising his sunglasses.

"You hate Gio," I reminded him. "You called him all kinds of names."

"Business isn't personal, Ag," Trevor said. "What did I always tell you? Didn't you learn anything from being with me? Nothing is personal!"

"Except divorce," I said. "Divorce is personal."

We were driving the whole way. Eight hours, with luck. Trevor had screamed at his number-one and number-two assistants, but somehow the airlines weren't cooperating. Maybe the number-three assistant would've made all the difference.

"How fast can you get there?" Trevor asked.

"We'll be in LA by 7:00," I said.

"Make it 6:30 and you have yourself a deal," he said.

"I already have a deal," I said.

"Oh," he said. "That's right." The deal we'd made on the beach held. We'd share custody, but we all know what that meant. C'mon, I'd do the heavy lifting, and Trevor, Trevor would be just what he wanted (after I brought it up): Trophy Dad. He'd be fun and exciting and bigger than life, and Pep had incredible adventures in store for her. Perhaps Trevor would adopt me to go on his more exotic trips. Maybe he'd marry Kate Moss and we could all hang on a beach in Ibiza, even though I was over legal Ibiza age.

"Get me there by 6:15 and I'll pay the rest of your legal bills."

"Buckle your seatbelt," I said as we drove into the Tucson Mountains.

Trevor looked out at the desert.

"Should we get back together?" he asked.

"No."

"Right," he said. "You're right."

Twenty minutes later, he was sound asleep.

Gabriela surprised me the other day by taking me to meet La Reina.

A privilege, she'd said, because as she'd told me numerous times, La Reina never met with white people. I told her I'd try to do my best not to shame her. We drove downtown and stopped in front of a small Spanish house with a tile rooftop off Crenshaw. Inside, Christmas lights were strung across the living room above a red velvet couch in front of a shrine to the Madonna and Baby Jesus. La Reina was younger than I'd imagined, a clairvoyant Selena Gomez. Gabriela held my hand and told me she would interpret. I was excited to see how this could possibly work, and once again, I regretted my poor Spanish. Except as it turns out, La Reina's English was fine. Better than mine. She'd majored in English lit at Berkeley.

"You are healthy and . . . not unhappy?" she asked. I nodded, not unhappily. "Your daughter is healthy and not unhappy." Pep had found her equilibrium for the moment—and her serve. She was killing it on the volleyball court. All the moms hated me and somehow dropped me from the email chain in punishment. Elation!

"Like mother, like daughter," I said. "Will I find love again?"

"Yes. There is a good man. He will come."

"How will I know?"

"There will be a few iffy men first," she said, using the universal hand sign for *iffy*. "Stay off Tinder," she said. "Your sister's wrong about this."

My thoughts ran to Gio. Was he enjoying an espresso and a cigarette and someone's unhappy wife at a table outside Les Deux Magots? Thank God for Gio, whose cameo appearance in my life helped propel me once and for all over the wall . . . or the gate at the dead zone.

"La Reina, did I already let him go?"

"Four marriages?" she asked, her eyebrow raised. "Girlfriend, you're kidding me, right?"

25

Oh, Oh, Mexico

The Chihuahuan Desert, Mexico, hot as balls and the first AD had to tape Fin's ankle after she sprained it in a motorcycle stunt. She's limping around, squabbling with Sami over dialogue, which sounds suspiciously like rom-com foreplay, and I wonder if either knows they're falling in love. Trevor's lounging in his producer's chair, consuming a plate of precisely cut apples delivered on Gucci china by a sparkly new assistant who has no idea what's in store for her. The team is gathered around the shot, our eyes glued to the monitor, hands over our mouths as dust spins through the dry air. Gio paces and hovers, paces and hovers, a general in khaki shorts and Chuck Taylors. And that leather jacket.

Dad's fussing over Shu, who fusses over him in return, spreading sunscreen on his dappled skin. She's landed a role as a mystic. Dad was right. She's a next-level talent.

Trev's on chew number twenty-five.

"You happy, Trevor?" I ask.

"Tell Sid he'd better write something nice about me," Trevor says. "Tell him I need top billing. It can't come from me; talk to him—"

Sid Glitch wanders by, his moleskin hoisted, sweating in his black turtleneck, shorts, and Birkenstocks. His toes are albino and long, the toes of a nocturnal marsupial. He's writing a story on Trevor and George and Sami the Uber driver and Fin and Gio and the Mr. Toad's Wild Ride of How This Movie Got Made.

I pull Sid aside.

"Are you using?" I ask.

"I've been clean for months."

"My sister's not selling you anything?"

"No," he says, and he blushed crimson, a rose atop a white, thorny stem. "We just talk. Your sister, she's a natural storyteller. Incredible woman, really."

I recognize that faraway look. I'd seen it since fourth grade. Fin had bagged another one.

"Sid, aren't you . . ."

"Aren't I what?"

I wanted to break it to him gently. "Sid, you're gay."

"What would make you think that?" he says, adjusting his glasses.

"You check all the gay boxes, my dude."

"I'm from Brooklyn, Agnes," he says as if that explained it before scooting off to Fin's trailer to wait for her, heart in hand.

My phone beeps. Ulger sent me a picture, an oil rendering of a fawn from his cabin overlooking a Montana lake. He's retired and taken up painting. He's not terrible. Still not gonna fuck him, though.

In the distance, George revs his motorcycle (goldenrod version), circles the set slowly, then building, circles again, kicking up a sandstorm, a wall of 380cc sound, then the impossible—the man, the myth, the icon, stands up on his motorcycle.

The script supervisor gasps and flips through her pages. Standing on a motorcycle? No! She jabs at her script, her face a silent scream.

The extras, their faces covered in soot, heads wrapped in bandages, yell and gasp as he flies past—

"*Cut!*" Gio yells. "*Cutcutcut!*"

"Oh my *God*, George, you're a genius!" Trevor hops up and claps wildly, his apple slices sliding off the plate. The assistant catches them and smiles at her boss.

"What the fuck?" Gio yells. "Who the *fuck* told you to do that?"

George grounds the motorcycle, laughing maniacally, then high-fives all the extras. Every single extra. Gio lunges toward George and grabs him around his shoulders, gesturing like Jackson Pollock painting a masterpiece.

A hyena's laugh cuts through the dust, and Trevor's waving his phone like a trophy, high above his head. "George, hey, George! George, look at this, dude! *George!*"

We're all drawn in. We stare at his phone. Shaky TMZ video. Brentwood Country Mart. That Weaselly Fuck walks through the shot when suddenly his baseball cap blows off, revealing his head, his hair patchy as a newborn bird. Following on his heels is Petra, who scoops up the cap while wrangling sweet, normal-looking children. Braces, glasses, socks sliding down legs. Petra's dressed in the same James Perse casual-yet-chic style as America's Sweetheart; she's even stolen her signature bangs.

"Jaysus!" George said. "What the heck happened to him?"

"Who cares? Motherfucker stole my Oscar," Trevor says.

"What?" I ask. *Stolen Oscar?*

Pep is running in the dust and making friends while on school break. We have many school breaks; the more school costs, the less school. Behind her is Caster, whom Trevor is paying a bundle and who already has a few proposals—a cameraman, the second unit director, a local politician.

Fin steps away from the dialogue squabble with Sami and walks over.

"I'm suing that fuck," Trevor is saying.

"Heck yeah, Trev," George says. "Get your Oscar back!"

"Yeah," I say, glancing at Fin. "Get your Oscar back, Trevor."

Fin blinks. I see it, even under her Ray-Bans. She taps her fingers on her director's chair, her rings shooting sparks in the relentless sun.

"He's gonna lose the franchise!" Trevor says. "He's bald as an egg!"

"What happened to his hair?" George asks, fingering his own rhapsodic strands.

"No one knows," Trevor says. "Ari, David, Jeffrey, they all sent him to doctors; they can't figure it out."

"That's weird," Fin says, shifting her sunglasses down to the tip of her nose as she watches the tape. *Rewind. Watch. Rewind.*

"Yes, it is," I say, glaring at her. "Very strange."

"Oh, shit," Fin says and laughs. "Oh, goddamn."

"Looks like he's going through chemo," George says.

Fin laughs, slapping her lean thighs. "Oh, fuck! Oh, fuckity fuck!"

"Trevor." Fin slaps his back, and he almost slips off the chair. "That was meant for you!"

"What do you mean?" he asks, on the edge of horror.

"I put Nair in your shampoo bottle," Fin says. "After you had me arrested. Oldie but a goodie, man; he must've used your shampoo!"

"I would've lost my hair?!" Trevor runs his fingers through his hair. "You're a fucking monster!"

"Guys, let's just stop," I say.

"You deserved it," Fin says. "You put cameras up, you spying bastard! You glued my sister's keyboard!"

"Did you glue her sister's keyboard, Trev?" George asks.

"Pep!" I call out, interrupting. "Let's go for a walk! You and me." I stop and call back to Fin. "Fin! A word with the coproducer?"

Pep and I and Fin trudge toward bottles of water. And doughnuts. And frozen yogurt. And cappuccinos. Craft fucking services. The promised land.

I grab ahold of Fin's arm. "What happened to the Oscar, Fin?"

"What do you mean, what happened to the Oscar?" Fin wipes her nose.

"I mean, what happened to the Oscar? That Weaselly Fuck didn't steal it. He has two of his own."

"All I know is, I hope I get an Oscar someday; that little guy gets top dollar, which comes in handy when your sister's been busted."

"You didn't."

"I told you, you didn't listen," Fin says. "Making money's easy."

I close my eyes. "Tell me you didn't sell Oscar."

"Remember I had a Russian cellmate a few trips back? The hooker-physicist? She taught me a few words. Right now, Oscar is probably sitting pretty on a yacht floating on the Crimean Sea."

She paints a picture with her pianist fingers.

"All the Vlads want to get their hands on an Oscar," Fin says. "If I run into trouble again, I know where I can get two more now."

"No!"

"C'mon! Craft services!" Pep yells, releasing my hand, zigzagging toward the tents.

"Craft services!" Fin yells, chasing after her, dust plumes in her wake.

I stroll after them, brushing dust from my eyes, and readjust my diaper.

Acknowledgments

Immense gratitude to my team for their support (and patience): Jennifer Enderlin at St. Martin's Press, my literary agent, Victoria Sanders, Bernadette Baker, Shari Smiley, Andy Patman, and Stephanie Davis (only for 26(?) years). Thank you to Bardonna Café for your lattes and smiles and theOFFICE in Santa Monica for your silence (and Wade Gasque!). Thank you to Jessie Martinez at the George Michael Salon for sanctuary under the dryer. Thank you to everyone who thinks they appear in this book. Thank you to Josh Sabarra, Mimi James, Stacy Title, and Julie Jaffe for their enduring friendship. Thank you to my mother, Phillipa Brown, and my sisters Suzy, Mimi, and Julie, my brothers-in-law Ron and Marc, my nephews Frankie, Jonathan, and John Henry, my niece, Angelina, and the many members of my extended family. Thank you to Josh Gilbert, with whom I started writing, and whom I miss every day.

Finally, thank you to Glock and Peanut for being the very best dogs and Enrique the leopard gecko for his low-maintenance lifestyle.